Advance Praise for *The Unreal Life of Sergey Nabokov*

"This astounding book will remind the reader not of Nabokov, but of Tolstoy: for the epic sweep across history, of course, but even more for the great Tolstoyan trick of finding the one detail in a bit player—the livid scar on the naked thigh of a Russian peasant, the subversive 'hangman's lock' of hair sported by a kid in Nazi Berlin—that somehow conjures up a whole vanished world of seeing and feeling. Sergey Nabokov is a triumphant invention: eyes and heart wide open through every catastrophe, he emerges as a new kind of hero, an intrepid conquistador of loss."

—Mark Merlis, author of *American Studies* and *Man About Town*

"Always readable and compelling, Paul Russell's *The Unreal Life of Sergey Nabokov* is a brilliant impersonation, literary prestidigitation of a higher order, and in the end, a unique and solidly mature work."

—Felice Picano, author of *True Stories: Portraits From My Past*

"What makes this remarkable novel unforgettable is the exact and vivid portrayal of Sergey Nabokov as he makes his way through an extraordinary time in history. Paul Russell's writing is breathtaking. This book will surely become a classic."

—V. G. Lee, author of *The Comedienne* and *As You Step Outside*

"The historical life of Sergey Nabokov was altogether real and all too short. But there are forms of history that only fiction can suggest, and this subtle novel movingly brings back from the shadows a rich, lost life."

—Michael Wood, author of *The Magician's Doubts: Nabokov and the Risks of Fiction* and *Yeats and Violence*

"*The Unreal Life of Sergey Nabokov* advances the art of biography even as it proves itself the very best of Paul Russell's fine novels. I read half of it not even thinking that Sergey Nabokov was a 'real person,' largely because the intimacy author Russell brings to his subject is the total kind one finds only in art, but then something told me, you're reading two sorts of book at once—a stupendous thrill ride all by itself. History and myth combine to tell the saga, apparently from inside, as we've never experienced it—the splendors and miseries of Tsarist Russia, the picnic of modernism that was the 20s Paris of Cocteau, Stein, and Diaghilev, and the unfolding nightmare of the Third Reich. Our hero lacks his brother's genius, but he is that rare creature, the genuinely brave and sweet man to whom one hates to say goodbye. And now we don't have to."

—Kevin Killian, author of *Shy* and *Arctic Summer*

"It takes an accomplished novelist to bring to glittering life a lost and foreign world. Paul Russell achieves this feat with disarming ease in *The Unreal Life of Sergey Nabokov*, a daring, ambitious, playful, intelligent, and deeply affecting novel. Russell lavishes upon Vladimir Nabokov's unheralded and doomed younger brother Sergey the divine attention, sympathy, and patience we all wish to receive from our creator. While compulsively reading this book, I felt an occasional twinge of envy, and I thought that it must have been as exciting to write as it is to read."

—Valerie Martin, author of *The Confessions of Edward Day*

"The only thing 'unreal' about this novel is the skill it took to write it. Paul Russell exhibits uncanny knowledge of the period and its people. He is an unfailing guide through St. Petersburg, Paris, and Berlin, dope dens, literary salons, drag balls, and war-torn streets. From the height of genius and to the depth of the gutter, Russell extends his precise, penetrating, and panoramic gaze."

—David Bergman, author of *The Violet Hour*

"Paul Russell's sublime novel *The Unreal Life of Sergey Nabokov* is an astonishing work of art. In lucid prose, Russell retells the story of Nabokov's gay brother, allowing us a clear window into an overlooked life and an underwritten aspect of history. This mesmerizing novel not only recreates the shifting, unstable epoch of Europe in the first half of the twentieth century, but reimagines Sergey's persona, his loves, and fate with great authenticity and imagination. It's a heartbreaking novel that everyone should read."

—Alistair McCartney, author of *The End of the World Book*

THE UNREAL LIFE OF *Sergey Nabokov*

By the same author

War Against the Animals

The Coming Storm

Sea of Tranquillity

Boys of Life

The Salt Point

THE UNREAL LIFE OF

Sergey Nabokov

a novel

PAUL RUSSELL

Copyright © 2011 by Paul Russell.

All rights reserved. Except for brief passages quoted in newspaper, magazine, radio, television, or online reviews, no part of this book may be reproduced in any form or by any means, electronic or mechanical, including photocopying, recording, or information storage or retrieval system, without permission in writing from the publisher.

Published in the United States by Cleis Press, Inc.,
2246 Sixth Street, Berkeley CA 94710.

Printed in the United States.
Cover design: Scott Idleman/Blink
Cover photograph: George Marks & Fox Photos/Getty Images
Text design: Frank Wiedemann
First Edition.
10 9 8 7 6 5 4 3 2 1

Trade paper ISBN: 978-1-57344-719-5
E-book ISBN: 978-1-57344-732-4

Library of Congress Cataloging-in-Publication Data

Russell, Paul Elliott.
The unreal life of Sergey Nabokov : a novel / by Paul Russell.
p. cm.
ISBN 978-1-57344-719-5 (pbk. : alk. paper)
1. Nabokov, Sergey, 1900-1945. 2. Gay men--Russia--Fiction. 3. Russia--History--Nicholas II, 1894-1917--Fiction. 4. Nabokov, Vladimir Vladimirovich, 1899-1977--Fiction. 5. Gay men--France--Paris--Fiction. 6. Paris (France)--Intellectual life--20th century--Fiction. I. Title.
PS3568.U7684U57 2011
813'.54--dc23

2011025234

1

BERLIN
NOVEMBER 23, 1943

THE AIR-RAID SIRENS COMMENCED SHORTLY before midnight. From the cellar we heard the cough of the antiaircraft guns on the city's perimeter, the bombers' drone, the rolling thunder of gigantic footsteps. All this we have grown accustomed to, but now the drunken giant strode directly toward us. We felt the building above us shudder, heard the windows blow out in a crystalline shower, smelled the weird bloom of the incendiaries. Then the deafening footsteps receded, the din quieted—only to be overtaken some minutes later by the fire's roar as it spread through the neighborhood. The pressure drop sucked the cellar door from its hinges. We scrambled to shoulder it back into place. With damp cloths we shielded our faces against the smoke. Our ears and temples throbbed. We cried aloud. We prayed.

"All the same," I told Herr Silber this morning, "England is the most civilized country in the world."

My words hung almost legibly in the frigid air of our office. A stunned silence met them. Several nervous faces glanced our way, then returned to their paperwork. Most of my associates in the Eastern Front Editorial Department had managed to show up for work. As Dr. Goebbels reminds us, in the Reich there are no longer any rights, there are only duties.

"Obviously, Herr Nabokov," said my colleague, a little unsteadily, "we're all under a great deal of stress. Perhaps you might consider taking the rest of the day off."

I knew he was trying to be kind. Every one of us in that room understood exactly what had just happened. Feeling dangerously lightheaded, I rose, made a bow. "*Danke sehr*," I said. "I believe I will."

What has been said cannot be unsaid. That is the reality of the Reich. Who should know that better than the staff of the Propaganda Ministry?

Herr Silber made the usual stiff-armed salute. There was no point anymore in returning it, so I did not.

I sensed all eyes following me as I left. In the corridor a poster warned: THE ENEMY SEES YOUR LIGHT! DARKEN IT! Shards of glass littered the front steps. Otherwise the Ministry remained remarkably unscathed, though its neighbors on Wilhelmstrasse were not so lucky. The Chancellery, the Arsenal, the Hotel Budapest—all had been reduced to rubble. I skirted a bomb crater nearly as wide as the street, its cavity already filled with water from a severed main. A burnt-out lorry perched on its lip. Nearby lay a headless mannequin which I chose not to inspect closely. All along my nearly impassable route the air hung thick with masonry dust, a hideous oily ash, an odor of char and kerosene and I scarcely dare think what else. Among incinerated trams and buses wandered unearthly shades. On Kurfürstendamm a stout middle-aged woman in a flimsy nightgown and fur stole approached and threw her arms around me. Gratefully I embraced her, if for no other reason than that we were both still alive.

"What despicable barbarians!" Herr Silber had said to no one in particular in that frigid shell of an office. "Murderers. Jackals. Jews! The British are by far the worst war criminals of all."

Who could blame him? The firestorm had overspread the city from west to east. Charlottenburg, Unter den Linden, Alexanderplatz—all were said to be devastated. Nonetheless, I said what I said—"*Trotz allem, England ist das zivilisierteste Land der Welt.*"

Last week a young lady was arrested from the building next door for black-listening to foreign broadcasts. Only yesterday I witnessed an older gentleman plucked from the tram by the Sicherheitsdienst for mentioning to another passenger what hardly needs mentioning: that the war goes very badly for the Reich. The civilized lads of the RAF will not have devastated this city so fully that the Gestapo cannot find their way to me. Flight is out of the question. Where would I go? The Nansen passport we Russian exiles carry is worthless. Besides, I am a convicted sex criminal under regular surveillance since my release from an Austrian jail last year.

I write this in my shell-shocked lodgings in Ravensberg-erstrasse. The windows are gone, the electricity and water are out, my nerves are badly shredded, and I cannot get the sight of that headless mannequin out of my head. For courage I rely on black market brandy I have been hoarding for a wedding next week. In a recent novel by the incomparable V. Sirin—quite popular in our émigré circles—a condemned man wonders how he can begin writing without knowing how much time remains. What anguish he feels, realizing that yesterday there might perhaps have been enough time—if only he had thought to begin yesterday.

2

ST. PETERSBURG

I WAS BORN IN SAINT PETERSBURG, RUSSIA, on March 12, 1900, the second son of Vladimir Dmitrievich Nabokov and Elena Ivanovna Rukavishnikov. My father was a highly regarded criminal lawyer, newspaper editor, and prominent "Cadet," as the Constitutional-Democrats opposed to the Tsar were known in those days. My mother came from fantastic wealth, and if some of my father's many enemies enviously whispered that his marriage betrayed a certain calculation, I never saw evidence of anything but a sustained and altogether enviable love between them.

My parents' initial attempt at a son having arrived stillborn, their firstborn, Vladimir Vladimirovich, was all the more precious to them. I gather my own debut, a scant eleven months later, was less enthusiastically received. Through the years I have given a good deal of thought to my brother's perspective on this premature interloper in his private paradise, and concluded that part of his antipathy for me has always lain in his suspicion that I might represent a hasty revision on the part of the Creator that somehow reflected badly on him.

As for my undoting parents, they were disappointed, as I was later told by my needlessly honest grandmother Nabokova, to find their second offspring such a pallid reprise of their first. I was an uncommonly listless child: nearsighted, clumsy, inveterately left-handed despite attempts to "cure" me, and cursed with a stutter that only grew worse as I matured.

One of my earliest memories: I must have been four. Russia was at war with Japan, and my mother, brother, and I were ensconced with our English governess, Miss Hunt, in the Hotel Oranien in Wiesbaden, having been sent abroad by my father's worries over the deteriorating political situation at home. About our German winter I remember little save for the young man who operated the hotel lift. Though he must have been no older than fifteen or sixteen, he seemed to me the epitome of manhood, dashingly handsome in his brimless gold cap, crimson blazer, and tight ink-black trousers with a single crisp stripe of gray defining the length of each long leg. Though I do not remember this myself, I am told that I had a habit of fondly clinging to his trouser leg as he worked the lift controls—rather like the little monkey that accompanied the organ grinder the hotel staff were incessantly shooing away from the sidewalk just beyond the hotel's front entrance.

It was during that winter of my innocent infatuation that my brother convinced me to escape from the hotel he for some reason considered more a prison than a palace. I no longer recall what sweets or other reward Volodya promised me, but I remember very well our ride down from the fourth floor, and how the enchanting lift boy seemed to think nothing amiss in allowing two unaccompanied children free egress into the lobby. As Volodya dashed forth I paused, placed my hand on my heart, and bade my bemused idol a desperate "*Adieu, mon ami!*" which I had feverishly rehearsed during our descent. Then I raced to catch up with my charismatic brother, who, winding among the legs of guests, had already managed to escape the clamor of the lobby for the even more clamorous street.

The organ grinder and his bright-eyed monkey leered at us. The avenue was a maze of clattering carriages and electric trams spitting terrifying blue sparks. I had never ventured from the Oranien without my mother or Miss Hunt holding my hand; to this day I marvel that Volodya appeared to know exactly where he was going in the chaos of the street. I struggled to keep up, as he kept looking back at me over his shoulder in an exasperation I knew meant he already regretted having cajoled me to join him.

In no time I realized we were lost. I kept my eyes on Volodya's dark-blue navy jacket. The sky was dull and lifeless, the air chill and heavy, the town a uniform gray. Only my brother was a dancing point of color and energy. How long we wandered I cannot say, but eventually we neared the river, to which Miss Hunt had taken us by carriage several times so that we might stroll the promenade.

At a pier where a steamer lay docked, there was commotion as the last of the passengers boarded. Without a moment's hesitation, Volodya bounded up the gangway, only to be brought up short by a stern-looking man with a great mustache.

"Sir, our parents have already gone on board," Volodya explained in silken English. "They will be terribly alarmed if we fail to join them." Volodya addressed the crowd. "Please, is there an Englishman here who can help a fellow countryman?"

They all stared at this stalwart five-year-old and his cowering brother.

"Why, dear, we're Americans," exclaimed a large lady who

held a little black dog in the crook of her arm. "By all means, board with me, my child."

Thus folded in her protective skirts, we passed onto the boat, whereupon Volodya cried, "Mama, Papa!" and grabbing me by the hand, broke away from our temporary savior. At that moment, a quiver ran from prow to stern, a whistle shrieked, and the boat began to pull away from the pier.

I remember the calm of that leaden river as we left the city, and the houses thinned to fields and vineyards. Whenever in later years, whether in Paris or London or Berlin, I have heard those slowly rising chords that usher in Wagner's river maidens, I am back on that steamer on the Rhine, standing beside my brave, mad, thrilling brother and allowing, at last, tears of terror and homesickness to run down my wind-flushed cheeks.

"What are we to do?" I wailed.

"Everything," he crowed. He spread his arms wide. "Seryosha, we're sailing to America. We'll shoot elephants and ride horses and meet wild Indians. Just think of it."

At the next landing, a policeman stood waiting and scooped us up to a nearby police landau. The lift boy, having had immediate second thoughts about the wisdom of allowing us out on our own, had reported our escape, and hotel staff had traced us to the pier just as our steamer moved beyond the range of their frantic hails.

Back at the hotel, my brother took stoically whatever discipline our mother managed to mete out. Our father, when eventually informed of our adventure, laughed heartily. Everyone seemed to sense that I had been the unwilling partner. The only one to suffer any permanent harm was poor Miss Hunt, who, on account of her negligence in allowing us to slip from our rooms, found herself promptly fired—hardly the first or last of our governesses to be bested by my brother. As for the superb lift boy, I never saw him again. Now that I think of it, I suppose he may have been fired as well.

★ ★ ★

My mother's brother, Vassily Ivanovich Rukavishnikov—known to us as Uncle Ruka—was a delightful exotic. He dressed gaily. One never saw him without a carnation in his lapel, or opal rings adorning his long fingers. He favored spats and high-heeled shoes, which I found tremendously elegant, though his mincing gait provoked cruel imitation by my brother. He was vain and passionate, sallow-skinned, raccoon-eyed, dashingly mustachioed and, like the younger of his two nephews, cursed with a stutter.

We saw him mostly in summer, when he alighted at Rozhestveno, his domain which, with my mother's Vyra and my grandmother Nabokova's Batovo, made up the family estate along the Oredezh River.

In late June, up would go the flag atop his house, announcing his arrival from those wintering haunts in France or Italy or Egypt we knew only from his extravagant stories. The shuttered house would be opened, the front portico's grand columns hastily repainted, the furniture unveiled, the carpets beaten and aired. He brought us gifts, which he bestowed upon us gradually, so that the days of June were a continual revelation of colorful books and puzzles, playing cards, hand-painted lead hussars and uhlans, and once, when I was six, an enchanting little bronze bust of Napoleon that I took to bed with me every night for many weeks, till Volodya's scorn eventually caused me to forgo that comforting practice.

For two happy months our uncle would be in our midst, shedding wonder and light. He possessed a sweet, high tenor voice, and in his spare time—of which, despite his soi-disant career as a diplomat, he seemed to have endless store—he composed barcaroles and bagatelles and *chansons tristes*, which he would sing to us on summer evenings, accompanying himself on the piano. No one else seemed much impressed by his artistry, but how I envied his wistful melodies.

I once convinced him to lend me the score to one of his songs, which he did with some reluctance: "Oh, that," he said with half a laugh. "Well, if you wish." I scurried away with the sacred document, and spent many happy hours rehearsing in secret, imagining his surprised smile when, freed of my stutter (for I do not stutter when I sing), I would one day lovingly offer his gift back to him.

Evenings, after dinner, he would regale us, in French rather than Russian, which he spoke quite badly, with tales of the Pyramids and the Sphinx, whose nose Napoleon's troops had shot away one indolent afternoon, or crocodile-hunting expeditions on the Nile with Hamid, his servant. We sat on the verandah, amid steady oil lamps and flickering candles, while Cairo's smoky bazaars teemed with unimaginable bargains. Among the items Uncle Ruka had brought us were a number of weighty cylinders used to render wax seals with the stamp of the caliph. "And yet,"—here he would look around at us with his raccoon eyes—"amongst all those bargains and beggars, there was still the possibility"—he paused dramatically—"of being deliciously taken advantage of!"

"Basile," my father murmured—in warning.

"But I was never," Uncle Ruka hastily assured us, "never, ever taken advantage of!"

Immediately he was off on another adventure, this time in an aeroplane, a Voisin Hydravion, the latest miracle from those amazing French brothers. Did we know he had crashed on a beach near Bayonne, that he had very nearly been killed? And yet—he kissed two beringed fingers he raised superstitiously to his lips—he had emerged with nary a scratch. The orthodox saints Sergius and Bacchus would remain his blessed protectors to the very end.

In the midst of his gaudy patter—on the word *Bacchus*, for instance—difficulty would seize him, and only after several fraught moments would he finally succeed in surmounting the recalcitrant consonant.

For an adoring nephew's stutter, however, he had no patience. My very presence seemed to annoy him, which only reinforced my desire to make him like me—or at least acknowledge me. Finding him in the library, where he idly leafed through a volume of floral aquarelles, I observed, "Hamid sounds like a most interesting character. What adventures you must have with him."

"A scoundrel," my uncle replied with surprising pique. "Don't trouble yourself about Hamid. An infamous wretch if ever there was one. But now, dear lad, please allow your uncle a moment of peace. Can't you see he's busy reading?"

For having penned an appeal for passive resistance to the Tsar's policies (a document known to history as the Viborg Manifesto) Father and several of his fellow Cadets spent the summer of 1908 confined to prison. The rest of the family confined ourselves to Vyra, my mother's estate, where one sultry afternoon an overloaded calèche brought a fashionable St. Petersburg photographer, his assistant, and a panoply of theatrical-looking camera equipment. Why my mother wished, in Father's absence, to undertake a series of formal portraits of herself and her children I do not know—but Volodya violently objected at the prospect of the two of us being garbed in identical short white trousers and long-sleeved blouses. Our latest governess, Mlle. Miautin, whom we simply called "Mademoiselle," reminded her charge that good boys did not throw fits, while the photographer reassured him that the two of us did not look the least bit alike. In the end Volodya acquiesced, and in the series of formal portraits that followed, our two younger sisters, Olga and Elena, stare solemnly at the camera while my difficult brother casts a smug, devilish smile and I manage a foolish grin.

Just as our patience with the tedious process was nearly

exhausted, we heard the rapid click-click of Uncle Ruka's heels as he crossed through our foyer. "*Ah, Lyova! Mes enfants! Je suis arrivé!*" Immediately assessing the situation, Uncle Ruka persuaded the photographer to undertake yet another round of photographs. From the verandah, where Mademoiselle fed the rest of us cakes and cherry juice, I watched as my uncle posed in the garden, first with his sister, then with his sister and her first-born, whose waist he encircled with a possessive arm. The photograph taken, Volodya squirmed free. "Not so fast," said Uncle Ruka. "I've brought you something I think you'll fancy."

Volodya paused mid-escape. "I was hoping to hunt butterflies," he said. "I've wasted half the day as it is."

Since the previous summer, that mania had consumed my brother's energies. His room was now a trove of pinned and spread specimens, much to Mademoiselle's horror.

"Ah, then butterflies you shall have."

Volodya looked skeptical.

"Come," coaxed our uncle, leading his nephew past us and into the house. I followed as well. Uncle Ruka pointed to an enormous book that lay open on an armchair in the sitting room. Volodya approached dutifully, then burst into a swoon.

"Oh my!" he intoned. "Oh my, oh my." Lifting the tome, he slid onto the chair and began to page through it. "*Die Gross-Schmetterlinge Europas.* What I most wanted in all the world. How did you know?"

"Your uncle's not entirely without wit, now is he?" Gliding onto the chair beside Volodya, he drew an arm around his nephew. "I do believe I've seen one of these." He pointed to an illustration.

"Not very likely," Volodya said. "Unless you've been to Nova Zembla, and even there it's extremely rare."

"Well, perhaps it was a southern cousin," Uncle Ruka stammered. "They do all rather look alike, I fear. Family resemblances can be most confusing!" He laughed gaily, and breathed in the scent of his nephew's hair oil. Briefly his lips grazed the crown of Volodya's head. My brother went rigid. His hazel-green gaze met mine. I turned aside, embarrassed not so much for him as for our poor uncle, who, oblivious to his nephew's disdain, soon dashed from the room, his heels click-clicking across the floor. Volodya remained seated as if nothing had happened, unhurriedly turning the pages of his volume, pointedly unaware of anything else around him, neither his departing uncle nor his younger brother, who remained standing in the doorway as Uncle Ruka, with scarcely an acknowledgement, brushed past him.

The next summer Uncle Ruka was again at Rozhestveno. Three or four days a week he would appear at luncheon. When the meal had finished, and everyone else retired to the verandah for Turkish coffee and cigarettes, he would grab Volodya by the wrist. "Now come, dear lad," I'd hear him say as I lingered on the threshold a moment longer than necessary. "Indulge your poor uncle for a moment. In Italy, boys your age are eager for this game. Mount-the-Stallion, they call it." With a groan, he lifted a squirming Volodya onto his lap. "Oof! You've become so very big lately. And look at those handsome thighs. Is that a bruise? It's yellow as a melon. Does it hurt? Boys with thighs like yours grow up to be magnificent stallion riders. Do you want to be a cavalry officer one day?"

Unperturbed, the servants went on clearing away the dishes. On strong adult thighs, Uncle Ruka heaved his reluctant rider to and fro. To no avail Volodya struggled, his long bare legs flailing as Uncle Ruka pressed his lips to the back of his nephew's neck, murmuring, "There, there. *Très amusant, n'est-ce pas?* Shall I sing for you?"

I slipped soundlessly onto the verandah. A rain shower had gusted through while we lunched; rekindled sunlight sparkled on the dripping lindens and poplars of our park. From the dining room came half-sung, half-panted phrases—"*Un vol de tourterelles...strie le ciel...tendre.*"

At last Father spoke. "Lody, do stop bothering your uncle in there." Almost instantly Volodya appeared, hair mussed, one white sock fallen down around his ankle, coral-pink finger marks on his bare thighs. "Come, sit with us," Father invited, but my brother paid no heed, charging down the steps and into the wildwood of the park without a word. Volodya was a very strange child.

Flushed from his exertions, his white summer suit in disarray, Uncle Ruka appeared as well. "Spirited boy," he said.

"Have coffee, Basile," said Father.

"No, no," my uncle protested. "It's bad for my heart."

"There's nothing wrong with your heart," said Father. "You'll outlive us all."

Our cousin Yuri Rausch von Traubenburg also came to us in the summers. The son of divorced parents, he spent his time shuttling between Warsaw, where his father was military governor, and the dispiriting spas in which his mother, my aunt Nina, sought elusive cures and pleasures. Worldly, scandalously at ease with the servants, untroubled by parental neglect, and four years my senior, he was Volodya's friend, not mine. Still, I was in awe of this handsome, lanky interloper. He and Volodya would disappear into the park for hours to pursue elaborate cowboy-and-Apache fantasies derived in part from the penny dreadfuls they devoured, in part from their own dreadful imaginations.

Only on rare occasions did I participate in their fun, most memorably for a brief spell during the summer of 1910 when they approached me with an intriguing proposition: might I consent to play the damsel in their adventure? Easily coaxed, I draped myself in a shawl, allowed myself to be tied to a tree trunk, was danced around for a while with delirious Indian hoots, then left to languish while their complicated plot played itself out elsewhere. I would glimpse them ranging through the shrubbery, shooting at each other with air rifles. Lashed to my stake, I was forced to entertain the depressing thought that they might have forgotten me, but eventually they returned, no longer captors but liberators, untying me with glee while Yuri, or rather the gallant Maurice the Mustanger, pledged his troth to me, the fair Louise Poindexter. One afternoon, in an excess of identification with his character, he went so far as to kiss me on the lips, much to Volodya's disgust and my own perplexity. After that fascinating episode I was no longer asked to participate in their games.

Thus Yuri Rausch receded from my thoughts till one afternoon in August 1913. My mother and my grandmother Nabokova were having a terrific row. The chief cook had been caught thieving and was to be let go. My grandmother strenuously objected: he had been with the family for more than a decade; his children suffered various ailments; no one in the whole district prepared dishes half so well as he. To escape the hubbub I wandered, book in hand, down to the bank of the Oredezh, that placid stream winding its way through our landscape, the better to dream my way further into the stormy friendship of Copperfield and Steerforth. Now, *their* rows were worth paying attention to!

So lost was I in their world that I did not notice approaching horses. Sequestered in a copse of pea shrubs, I saw that my brother and Yuri were not only riding their steeds bareback, but that they were themselves naked, having shed their garments in order to enjoy the languid afternoon au naturel. Oblivious to my presence, they plunged their mounts into the cooling river. The beasts thrashed about, churning up the water, muddying the stream. Teeth bared, they whinnied and sputtered; their hectic eyes bulged; their nostrils flared. Their flanks shone like velvet. After several explosive minutes the magnificent creatures, urged by their high-spirited riders, clambered up the riverbank, where the two boys dismounted and tethered them. Now it was the humans' turn. The horses watched, tails flicking, as my brother and cousin waded out into the river till the water reached mid-thigh. Volodya's flesh was sun-toasted, Yuri's pale as milk. They splashed on each other the holy water of the Oredezh, they yelped and whooped, each took turns carrying the other on his shoulders. Yuri sang snatches of gypsy songs off-key. It was only my brother and my cousin, but in the afternoon light they seemed agents of some heavenly dispensation.

Too soon the episode was over. I was certain they were not in the least aware of my worshipful presence; nonetheless, I lowered my eyes to my neglected book as a precaution, only to find I could no longer concentrate on the page before me.

Even after they had gone I felt all about me a remnant of electricity, as if a storm had broken out and then abruptly vanished into the somnolent blue of a summer afternoon. I tried to recreate the sensation, just as at the piano I would sometimes repeat a dozen times some passage from Gounod or Tchaikovsky in a futile attempt to catch some evanescent promise contained in the music. Only after a long empty interval did the drowse of a bee in the pea shrubs rouse me from the *tristesse* into which I had unaccountably sunk.

The brief parenthesis of Russian summer: by the first of September autumn is at hand, the birch and alders begin losing their leaves, each day the dark falls earlier, a chill insinuates itself in the air. A calèche would take Yuri and his spartan baggage to the regular train stop at Luga, whence he would return to his father in Poland or his mother somewhere in Bohemia or Moravia or Germany. Meanwhile, in the foyer at Rozhestveno enormous traveling trunks would appear. The Nord Express would be bribed to stop at the little station at

Siverskaya. Blowing us all a farewell kiss, Uncle Ruka would depart to another of his foreign refuges: Villa Tamarindo near Rome; Chateau Perpigna in the south of France; a small, exclusive hotel overlooking the harbor at Alexandria, where Hamid waited patiently for his master's return. And our servants, particularly the younger ones, would breathe a sigh of relief that "Mr. Bumtickle," "Lord Grab-Ass," "Seigneur Sodoma," as they cruelly called him, had finally gone.

3

BERLIN
NOVEMBER 24, 1943

SCARCELY TWENTY-FOUR HOURS HAVE PASSED since I walked out of the Propaganda Ministry. When my landlady, Frau Schlegel, raps on my door to announce that a gentleman has come to see me, my heart freezes. Surely the Gestapo would not send a man unaccompanied to arrest me? As it turns out, they have not. My visitor removes the scarf he has wrapped across his face—a common precaution against the ash and dust in the air—and I see it is Herr Silber from the Ministry. Mutely he presents me with my umbrella, which I left behind in my haste to depart, and as I take it from him he says, "Weather continues, after all, no matter what else may happen."

"You've taken an unnecessary risk in coming here," I tell him, though I feel stupidly grateful. "I'm certain I've been under surveillance for some time. Long before my rash words yesterday."

"Perhaps," he says. "But there's no evidence of it at the moment. I lingered along the block for half an hour before finally knocking on your door. Everything seems quite normal out there." Realizing the absurdity of that remark, he giggles. I share for a moment in his hysterical merriment. I do not know the man well, and he has never paid me a visit in my lodgings, but his presence brings a welcome sense of normality, as if I have only dreamt what I have lately done.

"Still," I say when our grim mirth has subsided, "I can't imagine why you've come. In fact, I can't imagine why the Gestapo haven't yet taken me."

The word makes him visibly nervous—as of course it does us all.

"I know nothing about that, Nabokov. Rest assured I haven't turned you in, but your absence has been noted. And it is highly likely that others heard your unfortunate remarks. Magda in particular."

"I was afraid of that. Magda's a wolf."

"I fear she is," he replies. His candor startles me. Such forthrightness is unheard of these days in the Reich. "To tell the truth, I'm rather surprised you're still here as well. Isn't there anywhere you can go?"

"Not likely. We Russians are stuck. But then, as far as I can see, so are the rest of you. Berlin is a barrel full of fish ready to be shot."

"Then can you really stand by what you said?"

"Surely you haven't come here merely to ask me that?"

He looks about my battered room. Alarming fissures have appeared in the plaster. A layer of ash lies on everything. The light is dim owing to the brown paper with which I have covered the shattered windows. A spirit lamp turned very low burns at my desk, where I have been writing. On a bookshelf next to the desk is half a set of a German children's encyclopedia, the only books in the room, relics I presume of Frau Schlegel's youngest son, who is missing at the front. Once upon a time I was an avid collector of books.

"Perhaps one longs for a bit of truth," Herr Silber says. "It's commonly assumed that only a madman would make such a statement aloud in the heart of the Reich. So yes, I am here to ask if you stand by the madness you've uttered."

I consider him for a moment: mild-eyed, graying, with a neat little mustache. His suit is in shambles. "I don't know you well at all," I say, "but you've always seemed a decent chap. So why should I lie to you at this point? I know it's rather hard to believe, given the atrocities the RAF delivers to us nightly, but yes, I believe what I said. I believe the German atrocities have been far worse. You've seen the reports from the Eastern Front, just as I have. You've read the documents I've translated. You know as well as I what the Führer planned to do once he'd conquered Moscow. If there's a just God, and I believe there is, then I fear the Reich will be made to suffer terribly for its crimes. Is that madness? Then so be it."

"It seems to me we're all being made to suffer. As for God—as far as I can tell He's abandoned His creation without so much as a fare-thee-well."

He pauses, and I think he has fulfilled whatever obscure purpose drew him here. But he speaks again.

"I happen to know you were making inquiries," he says. "Before you left."

Once again my heart freezes. "How do you know that?"

"One does not survive very long in the Ministry without remaining on one's toes. Why do you wish to discover the whereabouts of Flight Sergeant Hugh Bagley?"

"I predict you've a very long career ahead of you," I tell him.

He receives the compliment with a remarkably sad smile.

"Since you seem interested," I continue, "Hugh Bagley's

an old pal of mine from university. By chance I heard one of those monstrous downed-pilot broadcasts we send to England. I recognized his voice at once. He was shot down in July, over Hamburg. He said he'd been wounded but was being attended to. If I remember correctly, he said something very obviously scripted, along the lines of 'Despite the fact that I am a murderer of children, a destroyer of cities, I am being treated well. The German people display a compassion unknown to the British and their Jewish masters.' Perhaps you yourself authored those words. Who knows? In any event, I could tell from his voice that he was extremely frightened. If I'm cross with myself for speaking out, it's for having thereby sabotaged my quest to discover his whereabouts."

"You knew how utterly inadvisable such a course of inquiry was when you undertook it?"

"Absolutely."

"And that didn't deter you?

"No, Herr Silber, it did not. Am I being interrogated?"

"No, no, nothing of the kind." He laughs. "After all, I'm the one putting myself at risk by contacting you. And please call me Felix. I'm just curious. What would you have done with any information that happened to come your way?"

"Frankly, I have no idea at all. I suppose I hadn't even gotten that far in my thinking. But why are you interested?"

He looks at me steadily. "As you say, I too have no idea."

We eye each other. He takes from his breast pocket a single bent cigarette and offers it to me. I accept, light it gratefully from the spirit lamp, take a drag, and then pass it to him. For several minutes we pass that precious bit of solace back and forth between us.

"I offer nothing," he says.

"And I certainly wouldn't ask," I tell him.

"My son died at Dnepropetrovsk, you know."

"I didn't know that. I'm very sorry."

"I used to consider myself a Christian, but no more. You, on the other hand, seem quite devout. I've seen the cross you continue to wear around your neck."

Herr Silber is more observant than I have ever given him credit for.

"This may sound very odd coming from someone like me," he continues, "especially at this particularly difficult moment. But I believe I envy you, Nabokov. How absurd that is! You've nothing left to fear. Your fate's almost certain. You must feel wonderfully free."

"I'd be quite happy to trade places with you at the moment," I confess.

"No, I don't think you would. I won't come here again. If it's possible, meet me in three days in the restaurant at the Hotel Eden. One o'clock. Do you understand what I'm saying?"

"Three days seems a very long time under the circumstances."

"So it is," he replies. "So it is. A very long time for all of us. Heil Hitler, for what it's worth."

I look at him in surprise. He shrugs. "Good luck," he says. "With the cloud cover lifting, they'll hit us hard tonight."

After he has left I am perplexed, then increasingly alarmed. It seems impossible that Herr Silber would have paid me this visit on his own. Clearly, he is a dangerously canny individual. Now that I think of it, how did he find my address? Or more to the point, who might have given it to him? The more I think it through, the more convinced I am that such a cautious man would never have risked seeking me out merely to hear me reaffirm an observation the mere whisper of which is a death sentence.

And yet: do I not witness all the time the most surprising instances of the forbidden? When I accompany Frau Schlegel to the black market, have I not heard women in line pass information back and forth? "So-and-so has been arrested." "The air-raid shelter at Alexanderplatz was hit last night. Many casualties." "An allied force is preparing to storm the Atlantic Wall." All the news unavailable on the surrealistically optimistic Wehrmachtsbericht everyone ritually listens to in the evenings, before the air-raid sirens begin. There is no information to be had, and yet information is everywhere. The only trouble is that it is impossible to say which, if any, is true.

All that I have said about Hugh Bagley is, strictly speaking, true—but as usual there are many truths. True, Hugh was a great friend at Cambridge; he was also for a brief and happy spell my lover, though our love was of the amiable rather than passionate sort, and eventually evolved into a friendship that proved more lasting than I think either of us had expected. I have seen him only once in the years since, though we corresponded regularly until recent events severed all communication between the British Isles and Fortress Europa. In his last letter, which miraculously found its way to me in occupied Paris in the summer of 1940, he informed me he was joining the RAF, and would I say an occasional prayer for him. In fact, I prayed for him more often than he might have imagined, fixing his airborne figure in my imagination not so much as a relic of memory but as a nostalgia for all the many might-have-beens that fill out a life. When I heard his harrowed voice broadcast on the radio, not only did a whole past come flooding back to me, but a host of extinguished futures as well.

I have no real hope of aiding him in his nightmarish circumstances—just as I have no hope of helping the love of my life, whom the Nazis took from me early one morning two years ago, from an all-too-pregnable castle in the Tyrolean Alps. The truth is that both Hugh Bagley and Hermann Thieme are completely beyond my reach.

4

ST. PETERSBURG

MY LOVES HAVE ALWAYS AMBUSHED ME.

That winter of 1915 we were a country at war. My father's reserve unit had been mobilized. Patriotic fervor had renamed St. Petersburg Petrograd. In theaters, before the regular concert could commence, the orchestra played the national anthems of each of the allied nations. Wagner and Beethoven and Brahms disappeared from the repertory. Signs in shop windows requested, comically enough, BITTE KEIN DEUTSCH! The German Embassy, three doors down from our house, had been sacked.

None of that mattered. The clock on the nightstand informed me I had a full hour before Ivan would come to rouse me for school. As I lay abed in the boreal gloom, what had seemed entirely trivial the day before—my schoolmate Oleg Danchenko tossing me a tangerine while saying, offhandedly, "I detest tangerines"—now seemed an inexplicable act of kindness, completely overshadowing the world gone mad around us.

"I detest tangerines," he said.

That was all.

Why had he pitched it my way? And how could I have received it so thoughtlessly, without inquiring what he had meant by the gesture? I had taken the gift and shoved it in the pocket of my overcoat, where it remained even now. Now that I realized its significance, I needed to see it once again, needed to touch it, assure myself I had not dreamt this mysterious exchange. What a clever gesture it had been on his part: a secret sign passing beneath everyone else's clueless gaze.

All this excited my young body as thoroughly as it did my imagination, and as I dressed myself in the Gymnasium's regulation black uniform, a desperate inspiration came to me. I slipped a smashing pair of dove-gray, pearl-buttoned silk spats over my regular shoes. For this breach of rules I knew I would almost certainly be punished, but that morning the donning of those illegal spatterdashes seemed utterly necessary, a way of announcing—but what did I wish to announce?

I hardly dared explore that question as I went downstairs to delicious hot cocoa and buttered bread—and the vile yeast concoction I was forced to drink daily in the latest attempt to cure my stutter. I prayed no one would notice what I was up to, though to be noticed was precisely the point. From Father's study came the familiar sounds of his morning fencing lesson with Monsieur Loustalot. Volodya, as usual, came down late, no doubt having hastily completed homework he'd neglected the night before. Downing his cup of lukewarm cocoa, he ignored me completely. Then Ivan bustled us into our overcoats and we were out the door, climbing into the waiting Benz that would carry us to our respective schools.

That gray morning, as we headed up Morskaya, past the gilt dome of St. Isaac's and onto the Nevsky Prospect, our chauffeur

Volkov weaving our formidable auto in and out of the sleighs that thronged the streets, what did I imagine would happen? Would Oleg be waiting there for me, outside the school, cigarette at his lips, his pals conveniently absent? Now that we had shared that tangerine, would he greet me as a friend and comrade? But a dark little doubt had begun to flicker inside me. Perhaps it had all been some obscure joke at my expense. By the time we turned onto Gagarin Street I was in a state of abjection. But by then it was too late. With a queasy mix of satisfaction and alarm I heard Volodya's voice, just as the car door closed behind me: "Where are your boots? And *spats*? You're wearing *spats*? You're going to get in trouble, Seryosha! What are you thinking?"

Oleg was of course nowhere to be seen, and I realized that my imagination, in placing him so conveniently in front of the school, had overstepped the bounds of memory, for I did not, now that I thought of it, recall that I ever saw him when I arrived in the morning. I began to consider the possibility that days might go by without our encountering each other at all.

That realization threatened everything. Already I was aware that the bright nimbus surrounding yesterday's encounter was beginning to fade; it was essential that we see each other again as soon as possible lest the flame that had so unexpectedly flared between us be allowed to flicker out. I scanned the crowded corridor, finding in turn his friends Lev, and Vassily, and Ilya, but nowhere was there a sign of Oleg.

In my anxiety, I entirely forgot my spats.

The first class of the morning had barely gotten under way before Mirsky, our slope-shouldered history teacher, stopped mid-sentence. "Nabokov," he said. His spectacles glinted coldly. He would later be killed by the Bolsheviks at Melitopol, so I feel ashamed to record here that I never liked him.

"Please come to the front of the class, if you would."

I did as I was told. Whispers rustled through the room.

"Class. Observe. What about Nabokov strikes you this morning?"

"Only this morning, sir?" asked a wag in the back.

"He's dressed his feet like an auntie [*On nariadil svoi nogi kak tyotka*]," said a milk-faced boy named Aleksey.

Tyotka. I knew the word well. The previous year, it had driven me from the Tenishev School, where I had followed in my brother's confident footsteps. I had not yet heard the term spoken openly at the First Gymnasium, but now there it was: *tyotka.*

"That will do," admonished Mirsky, though he seemed rather to relish having *tyotka* out in the open. "We know the regulations, don't we? And don't we know the consequences of flouting them? Nabokov, I might have thought you more sensible than that." With his lecturer's pointer he tapped the offending spats, which now seemed such a pointless provocation. "What do you have to say for yourself? Speak!"

I knew I would only stutter helplessly, so I did not.

His cold eyes grew colder. "Very well, then. Have it as you will. Come along with me."

He led me by the arm down the wide corridor where we boys exercised when it was too cold to play outside. Gonishev, the headmaster, was in his study. He looked up from an atlas he had been examining with a magnifying glass.

I had been brought before him on two or three occasions in the past, minor infractions such as passing notes to a frail Armenian boy whose health now no longer permitted him to attend school.

"Explain yourself," Gonishev commanded.

I said nothing.

"Cat got your tongue, young man?"

"Worse than that," Mirsky told him, pointing to the spats I wore.

"I see." Gonishev nodded to himself. "We had hoped, when you matriculated, that the problems you experienced at Tenishev might be put behind you. I am concerned not so much with the infraction per se as with this inexplicable refusal to deliver a proper explanation. My boy, I understand your impediment. Nay, I sympathize with your impediment. Calm yourself. Speak to me slowly, as you would to your father."

I said nothing.

He shrugged his shoulders and threw his hands in the air. "Very well. I shall suspend you for the period of one week, after which, contingent upon the proper apology, which I shall allow in either oral or written form, you may be readmitted. Is this understood, my boy?"

I had only to nod, which I did.

"I'm truly surprised at you," Mirsky told me as he escorted me back to the classroom to collect my belongings, "but I hope you've proved whatever obscure point you intended to make." Seeing that I was to be banished, the other boys let out a cheer—half catcall, half whoop of reluctant approbation.

The empty corridor I walked down on my way to the exit could hardly have been any emptier than my heart. As I pushed open the heavy door frigid air enveloped me, and there he stood, exactly where I had, in vain, wished him to be an hour earlier.

Lounging against the stone balustrade, Oleg Danchenko nonchalantly smoked his cigarette.

"But you're not in school!" I exclaimed.

He scrutinized me indifferently. "Neither, it would appear, are you."

"I've just been suspended for the week."

"Oh?"

"Yes. For wearing these silly things." I turned my ankle for him to see, wanting to tell him I had done it for him, though I knew how absurd that would sound.

"Well, well. Very fashionable. A bit of the criminal, are we? Turns out, I've been suspended as well. Isn't that extraordinary?"

Oleg put his hand on my shoulder. I still remember the lovely weight of that hand. He looked me in the eye. His were brown with flecks of faded gold. Then he smiled, while in the tender chambers of my heart the just-hatched dragon flexed its lovely, lethal talons.

He offered me his half-consumed cigarette, which I put to my lips as if it were the holiest of sacraments.

"So what are we to do now?" he asked as I passed the cigarette back. "We've only got the day, you know. We'll both be kept in after this. At least I will. But for the moment, since we're to be criminals, let's play our parts well."

We had no plan; rather, some vivid energy gusted us along the streets. Our brisk pace left little opportunity for conversation, but that was just as well. We soldiered through the Summer Gardens sleeping under snow to the quay along the Neva where ice-breaking tugboats sent forth their mournful wails and on the other shore the needlelike spire of Saints Peter and Paul rose into the gray sky. Bone-chilling wind swept across the square in front of the Winter Palace, which a single imperial coach traversed, drawn by a pair of Orloff stallions. ("Magnificent!" Oleg exclaimed.) Farther along, in the Admiralty Gardens, the cries of ice skaters came to us; as we paused to watch them, Oleg draped an arm over my shoulder, his visible breath warm against my cheek, and for a moment I was afraid this all might evaporate into nothing more than a dream the gardens were dreaming under snow.

My spats were soaked through, my toes painfully cold, but not for an instant did I regret a thing.

"I'll say, I'm damned hungry," Oleg announced, turning us away from the skaters, pointing us down the Nevsky Prospect. In a stately and ravishingly warm restaurant he seemed to know quite well, he cajoled the waiter, who seemed to know *him* quite well, into bringing us flutes of champagne.

"To our exile," he toasted. "Life on the lam!"

He had a way of talking that made me suspect he had not grown up in St. Petersburg; he confirmed that his family owned several estates near Dnepropetrovsk. I confessed to hardly knowing where that was. Abbazia, Biarritz, Wiesbaden I knew well, but I had never traveled in Russia much beyond our country estates fifty miles to the south. "Your bread comes from the Ukraine," Oleg told me proudly. "Your bread comes from my father's fields." He missed those fields, but the death from typhus of his mother and sister, two years before, had convinced his father to send him to the capital in order to "acquire luster," as he put it. He lived rather unhappily with his mother's sister's family near the Smolny Convent.

I, in turn, spoke of my father, who, ever since my meeting with Gonishev, had been much on my mind, and whose reaction to the day's events I dreaded. It seemed important to develop a line of thought in which my father would sympathize instinctively with his rebellious son. Thus, as we devoured the delicious pirozhkis the waiter kept delivering to our table, I revealed to Oleg my father's own revolutionary impulses. He had defiantly published certain articles that had dismayed the Tsar. At an imperial banquet he had declined to lift his glass to the despot's health. On being expelled from the court, he had had the cheek to advertise his uniform for sale. After the dissolution of the Duma, he and his fellow Cadets had held illegal meetings, in consequence of which he had been imprisoned for a time.

All the usual words presented all the usual impediments, but Oleg sat patiently, occasionally brushing away with the back of his cuff a succulent crumb that adhered to the corner of his mouth.

When I had finished he asked, "But aren't the Cadets a rather frightfully unpatriotic bunch?"

It had failed to occur to me that confiding too much in this perfect stranger might be foolish.

"My father stands firm against tyranny," I told him, though

tyranny, as is tyranny's wont, resisted my tongue's attempt to name it.

"And *my* father has rather different notions, thank God," Oleg said when finally I'd prevailed. He examined his palm, rubbing a finger across it as if to erase something vexing he saw there. When he looked up, however, he was once again smiling. "What does it matter? We both know everything will go on just as it is, everybody arguing this way and that. Only, I must say, with the war on, it seems rather churlish to criticize the government. I only wish I were older. Then the *Boches* would have to watch out."

I hadn't the heart to convey to him, so shiningly brave did he seem, my father's sense that the war was already going very badly for Russia.

Our grand luncheon at an end, my new friend suggested a movie might suit the remainder of the afternoon. Only a day before, I told myself, this happiness would have been unthinkable.

Of that all-too-brief movie claiming the final stretch of an all-too-brief afternoon, I have no real memory. What I instead remember, even to this day, is Oleg's occasional hearty chuckle at the antics onscreen, the palpable warmth of his body next to mine, its drowsy odor of biscuits and champagne, the steady sound of his breathing. Across his profile I could see the play of light and shadow as the projected beam of the movie was reflected off the screen and back onto him. The orb of his entranced eye was luminous and moist, and I could not help but remember how once, when Volodya had got a speck of cinder in his eye, Uncle Ruka told him that the Egyptians, who were well acquainted with sandstorms, would volunteer the tip of a tongue to remove the offending mote.

Cautiously I slid my arm across the armrest till it touched Oleg's. The slight pressure I exerted was returned. For several exciting minutes we sent furtive tactile signals back and forth.

But what did they mean? Did I dare expand upon my presumption, however slight? Was Oleg conscious of intent, or was it all simply reflexive playfulness on his part, like good-natured jostling in the courtyard?

Soon enough I had my answer. He laid his hand on my thigh. Heavy and opulent, for a long moment it merely rested there, as if its placement were entirely accidental. But then gradually it came to life, massaging my thigh with increasing vigor and expanding, exploratory zeal. In the space of a skipped heartbeat I had reciprocated, and with my inveterate, incurable left hand palpated through cumbersome woolen trousers his own firm loins.

How extraordinary! Nearly thirty years have passed, and I can hardly convey the utter calm beneath the nervous excitement, the sense of having arrived somewhere unexpected yet foreordained. As the cinematic ghosts before us enacted their infinitely repeatable destinies, we two madcap lads stroked and petted and caressed—not so much with sexual urgency as with indolent contentment, more the way one might fondle a cat one cradles than a lover one intends to arouse. It was all, after its fashion, entirely innocent.

"Well," said my companion when the final silver hallucination had faded from the screen. "I must say, life seems a most peculiar thing, don't you think?"

We are always taking leave—of a person, an emotion, a landscape, a way of life. Music and dance, the arts I have loved the most: what are they if not an enhanced enactment of continuous leave-taking, the passing note or the daring leap vanishing before one's eyes but living on in the heart? On the wind-bitten corner of Morskaya and Voznesensky streets, by the bleak little square with its statue of Nikolay I, Steerforth held out his ungloved hand. Copperfield returned the gesture by gratefully sheathing Steerforth's in both of his. Whether Copperfield drew Steerforth into the briefest of embraces or whether Oleg was inclined that way without my urging I cannot say, but the bright tear glistening in his eye when we broke apart could hardly, I think, have been caused by the stinging wind alone.

"For a pair of outlaws we've been brilliant," he observed.

Not trusting myself to speak, I could only nod mutely. Oleg bestowed on me, one last time, that unforgettable smile.

I watched his figure disappear down the darkening street. He did not look back.

Our front door's stained-glass tulip glowed from the light within. As Ustin removed my overcoat, he warned me sotto voce that the household had been in an uproar ever since Volkov had returned midafternoon with Vladimir and no Sergey, and the shocking news that the well-behaved son had been sent down.

Upon seeing me, my mother cried out, "Seryosha, are you ill? Are you starved and frostbitten? Come here, come here."

Father intervened. "Let us go into the study."

"But he must be famished," my mother implored.

"No supper for this one," Father said. "He knows full well what he's been up to."

But did I? As I followed him up the stairs, it occurred to me how deliriously unconscious I had been of any consequences that might come my way. For half a day I had floated free of the world. Now nothing remained but to give an account of myself, which I did freely, omitting little save my enchanting indiscretions as I sat next to Oleg Danchenko in the cinema.

"What a peculiar stunt to have pulled," Father said when I had finished. He toyed with an ivory paper knife he had picked up from his desk. "May I ask if any of this is related to your difficulties at your previous school? I had hoped a change of venue and regimen might act as a curative to those childish foibles. We can't have you endlessly shuffled about from school to school. You must learn to live in the world as it is, however difficult that may be for you."

"I understand," I said, though I must say I did not.

★ ★ ★

I would very much like to report that, upon returning to school two weeks later, my reunion with Oleg went swimmingly, that I loved and was loved, but this was not to be. Several days passed before I saw Oleg again. Perhaps his suspension had lasted longer than mine; perhaps his Ukrainian outspokenness had prevented him from penning an apology as obsequiously effective as mine had been. I never knew. When I did see him at last, he was standing with his friends in the courtyard and smoking a cigarette in an uncanny replay of that fateful moment two weeks before. He did not notice me, engaged as he was in entertaining his pals with some amusing anecdote. As I approached, my heart trembling with joy, I caught his words. What a fright they gave me! Indeed, for a long terrible instant I refused to believe what I heard.

Oleg was stuttering. His exaggerated attempt to fight his way past a consonant's obstacle met with great hilarity all around. Finally, with an explosion of relief, he managed to utter the troublesome word: "T-t-tyranny!"

Then, in a perfectly normal voice, his own, he announced, "And now, this is Nabokov tipsy on champagne and trying to eat a piroshki."

Ilya, whom I always thought a decent sort, had by then noticed my approach and was attempting, by frantic gesticulations, to alert Oleg, who would not be interrupted. Finally, eyes bulging in desperation, Ilya called out, "Sergey ahoy."

Oleg turned to face me.

Affection, sadness, apology, shame, disdain: how I tried to understand what I saw in those treacherous, gold-flecked eyes.

5

"I AM FIERCELY IN LOVE WITH OLEG'S SOUL," Father read aloud in a scornful voice. "*How I love its harmonious proportions, the joy it has in living. My blood throbs, I melt like a schoolgirl, and he knows this and I have become repulsive to him and he does not conceal his disgust. Oh, this is just as fruitless as falling in love with the moon!*"

Father put down the diary. "Remarkably silly stuff, wouldn't you agree?" he said.

It was my brother who had discovered my furtive pages—quite by accident. Having read my inflamed words, he showed the diary to our tutor, who immediately conveyed it to Father.

"I don't suppose it's particularly well written," I admitted.

"Style is hardly the point here, Seryosha. There are sentiments so deplorable that no beautiful words can redeem them. So you fancy yourself in love with this fellow Oleg?"

"I'm writing a novel in the style of Bely. These are notes I was assembling."

Father slammed his fist against the pages lying open on his

desk. "Don't play me for a fool, Seryosha."

"I can be a most convincing liar," I said.

Father pierced me with a disdainful look.

"All right. I intended these words for no one but myself. But even had I never written them, I would have felt the emotions all the same."

Father's look of disdain softened. "I've long known," he said, and now his tone was melancholy, "of an inclination, in both your mother's bloodline and my own, toward this defect. I'd hoped my offspring might escape, but that is apparently not to be."

"I fail to understand the defect to which you refer," I told him stubbornly. That my most cherished emotions might constitute a defect had never occurred to me.

Father cleared his throat, hesitated, and then said, in a pained tone, "I am speaking of your uncle Ruka."

"But there's nothing wrong with Uncle Ruka," I protested.

"Seryosha. Your Uncle Ruka may be charming—indeed, in his way, very charismatic—but I am afraid he is *au fond* a lonely and pitiable soul. His ridiculous conversion to Roman Catholicism represents, I fear, but his latest attempt to expiate the depraved pleasures to which his flesh must occasionally yield. I would not wish anyone to go through life enduring such torment as your uncle has. Or my brother Konstantin, for that matter. To see souls condemned to such a life is almost enough to make one doubt the existence of a benign deity. Were I to allow this tendency to go unchecked in my own son, I would be as criminally negligent in the execution of my love for him as I would were I to ignore in him the life-threatening symptoms of typhus or tuberculosis.

"How does Pushkin so bitterly put it? 'To joke with love is Satan's way.' By no means should you accept this evil jest visited upon you. The human will is capable of mounting a defense against any number of humiliations. To that end I've retained the services of my trusted friend Dr. Bekhetev, who, having availed himself of the latest scientific knowledge, will attempt—nay, let us say *effect*—a cure. I would ask you, as a man of honor, as my dearly beloved son, to accept his help. If not for my sake, then for your dear mother's. In the meantime, I'd prefer to keep these pages in my possession. I hope you'll have no occasion in the future to repeat this error. Do you have any questions?"

"I've none," I told him.

He flipped through my pages one last time before depositing the violated diary in the desk drawer where he also, according to prying Volodya, kept a loaded Browning revolver. Did he realize that in confiscating those paltry confessions he was acting like a man who, upon waking to find his bed on fire, tosses the culprit cigarette out the nearest window? In retrospect, I think we both knew perfectly well the futility of his gesture.

Squeamish readers may wish to skip the following brief passage; I would not include it at all were it not for the voice of Jean Cocteau, the great and wise friend of my Parisian years, whispering in my ear, "You must tell them everything, *mon cher!* You must leave nothing out!"

Dr. Bekhetev was late. Father stood at the study window watching for him in the street below as I anxiously paged through a folio of sumptuous Botticelli reproductions Uncle Ruka had brought back from Florence. After half an hour, Ustin ushered the doctor in.

A florid man with a no-longer-fashionable imperial sprouting from his chin, he began by apologizing. An urgent case had detained him; a young woman suffering the loss of her child had threatened to do herself harm. "Sad, sad," he muttered.

"Begin, please," Father told him without turning from his vigil at the window, as if ordinarily dull Morskaya Street were this afternoon filled with fascinating pageantry it would be a shame to miss.

We sat in leather armchairs facing each other. Dr. Bekhetev asked me a few questions: Had I always hated my mother? When had the onset of my contrary sexual feelings occurred? When the onset of onanism? With what frequency did I practice that vice? Then he surprised me—as I suppose was his purpose—by commanding me to stand and lower my trousers. Flushing scarlet, I looked toward my father—or rather, toward his inexpressive back. What choice had I but to comply? With cold fingers the doctor prodded and assessed my parts. I shrank from his touch. He ordered me to kneel on the old Turkish carpet. "Raise your buttocks," he commanded. "Keep your knees apart. There, like so. Relax. Do not clench."

A probing finger elicited an involuntary moan, as well as shame, outrage—what a nightmare my young life had suddenly become!

"You haven't yet habituated yourself to the vicious practice, I see," mused Dr. Bekhetev. "That bodes well. You may dress now."

When I dared look his way, I saw he was carefully wiping his finger on a white cloth.

The doctor spoke not to me but to my father's back. "His would appear to be a classic case: morbid anxieties concerning the masculine principle combined with a neurotic propensity toward hysterical inversion. This is not unrelated to the spastic coordination neurosis he exhibits in speech. That said, there are a wealth of treatments. I myself have employed several. This particular case, at least as it stands now, warrants neither faradization nor trepanning nor cauterization. I shall prescribe bromide for onanism. A strict diet: no oysters, no berries of any kind, no chocolate. But for the main cure, I think we shall best proceed with hypnosis. Don't fear, Vladimir Dmitrievich. Your son is in very good hands."

★ ★ ★

Of all my respectable family, it was my grandmother Nabokova who seemed unfazed by the news of my "attitude." Perhaps her own amours had accustomed her to human foible. Born Maria Ferdinandovna, Baroness von Korff, she had been married off at fifteen to my grandfather, Dmitri Nikolaevich Nabokov, in order to provide cover for the affair he was having with her mother. Only a handful of her ten offspring could reliably be attributed to that "ape with cold feet," as she called him, who attempted to bed both mother and daughter on alternating nights. Indeed, my father's paternity was in some doubt, and rumor persistently linked my grandmother to no less a figure than Alexander II—"dear Sasha"—whose photograph she kept by her bed and a lock of whose hair reputedly nestled in the gold locket she never removed from around her neck. People said she had never fully recovered from the shock of his assassination.

I had always feared my grandmother's imperious presence, in part because I sensed that she and my mother were on less than easy terms with each other. Summers, when she was ensconced at Batovo and my family across the Oredezh at Vyra, were usually peaceful enough, but her winter visits to our house in St. Petersburg were a source of prolonged domestic tension.

She would keep to her bedchamber for most of the day, lying on her chaise longue, eating sweets and drinking coffee, all the while gossiping fiercely with her maid Khristina, a muzhik who had been given to her as a playmate for her tenth birthday, and who, even after Alexander II freed the serfs, had remained faithfully in attendance.

Dressed in black, Khristina sat erect in a straight-backed chair and worked petit point. My grandmother sized me up with new appreciation. "So he's our little *tyotka*. Well, well. I've raised a couple myself, you know. They're no worse than any of the others—rather nicer, in fact—though when I noticed that one of my older sons had begun to take an unseemly interest in one of his younger brothers, well, I'm afraid I had to draw the line." She laughed mirthlessly. "I told him what I shall tell you, my Seryosha—not that you take any unseemly interest in that sleek cad of a brother you've been saddled with, who's so like his father but without any of the civic virtues. I've never seen a child so ill-mannered, so self-absorbed. And those filthy insects he insists on keeping in the house..."

I had begun to wonder what advice she intended for me when she paused and beckoned for me to lean close. "Remember," she said in a stage whisper, as if her words were not meant for Khristina's chaste ears. "When the sweet itch strikes, as it will—there are always servants."

Khristina neither deigned to glance up from her work nor indicated that she had heard. I longed to tell my grandmother that times had changed: such seignorial license was unthinkable these days, at least in our household.

"You're a Nabokov," she went on. "Nabokovs have always taken what they want. That's why I worry about your father, dear man that he is. When he married for money, did I have qualms? Not at all. I wished for him fabulous wealth to go with fabulous blood. But these days he seldom seems to have his best interests at heart. I fear he's fallen in with a very low crowd of do-gooders, and it will all end badly. Mark my word! But you, young man: I must say I envy you. Never having to worry where your *pipiska* goes. Never having to regret inadvertently filling some girl! Yes, my dear, I envy you."

How I desired Oleg! Never mind that awkward moment I had chanced upon in the courtyard. It could easily be explained away—exuberance, a naturally mocking manner, a desire to keep the true nature of his relations with me private. We had not spoken since I returned to school, but even that could be explained away as shyness, caution, a reluctance to repeat what had been so marvelous an experience. How I loved the straight slope of nose, his pale lips, his auburn hair. How I longed to kiss that thick neck rising from the collar of his black school uniform. How I wished to massage so much more than that muscular thigh.

I made plans. I would accost my secret friend one afternoon after school, a scheme more difficult to devise than it might seem, as Volkov was there every afternoon to ferry me home. He would have to be bribed. And I would have to wait for a day when Volodya was ill and unable to attend school.

My brother's health that winter was particularly robust. But finally there came a mild day in April when he woke with a fever, and I heard our mother say the thrilling words, "I'm afraid you won't be going to school today. It's back to bed for you, Volodyushka."

From our well-stocked cellars I helped myself to a dusty bottle of Tokay; I had already purchased a flask of vodka and a rasher of salted cucumbers with which to quiet Volkov. I surreptitiously stashed my hoard under the seat of the Benz for retrieval later that afternoon.

Usually I managed a glimpse of Oleg at midday as he and his friends kicked the football around the courtyard. My heart quailed when I saw he was not among them. Of course Fate would thwart my plan. In dejection, I turned to go back inside and at that moment, hands in his pockets, and whistling a merry tune, he came through the door. We very nearly collided. He looked at me indifferently. I hesitated. Had it all been delusion on my part?

"I have something very important to tell you," I stuttered. "Can you meet me after school?"

"Must it wait?"

"It's very important."

He looked skeptical. I could tell he was longing to join the noisy throng in the courtyard. Indeed, several voices called his name.

"Very well," he said. "After school. It can't take long. I've things to do." He had already started down the steps.

"Promise you'll wait for me."

"I'll be there," he said.

I could scarcely concentrate on my studies for the remainder of the interminable afternoon, and was twice reprimanded for my inattention.

At last we were released. I sprinted to the waiting Volkov. "I've got a bit of a favor to ask. If you don't mind, I'll get myself home on my own. Here's a little token of appreciation."

When I handed over the vodka and cucumbers he laughed, and I suddenly feared my scheming had come to naught.

"How thoughtful. I do relish a thoughtful boy. Don't be gone too long. We don't want trouble, do we? Neither one of us." Then he bestowed upon me a rather hideous wink.

Scarcely had he and the Benz vanished than I heard Oleg's voice exclaim, "I've always fancied that smart limousine of yours. Too bad you weren't planning to abduct me in it!"

Mutely I held out my offering.

"Ho-ho," he said. "What's this?" He took the bottle, hefted it in his palm. "You're certainly a queer one, Nabokov. I can't make you out at all. What with your stutter, and the odd way you look at me at school. Everyone remarks on it. They find it quite comic. But I shouldn't have said that. I don't want to wound you. I feel quite protective of you, in a way. My God. Where did you get this? 1769." He slid it into his school satchel. "I should sell it and purchase fifty new bottles with the proceeds. Or perhaps I'd better save it for my wedding night."

"You're to do with it as you please," I told him.

"That goes without saying. Whenever I do get around to opening it, I'll be certain to think of you kindly. Really, you're quite the lark, Nabokov. Shall we stroll a bit? Since we're wanderers, you and I. Then I must get myself back to Smolny and the somber aunt."

At least he seemed to feel he owed me something.

The first signs of spring were out in the Summer Gardens, yellow and purple crocuses in the muddy lawns, birdsong in the air. Young couples and soldiers in pairs strolled about, chatting amiably. I was conscious, as we walked among them, of our lapse into silence; the encounter that had begun so promisingly now seemed a duty he felt obliged to fulfill. I longed to bare the wonders of my soul, and for him to do likewise, but had no idea how to bring that about. Instead I said, "Your classes have been going well?"

"Don't be a bore," he told me.

"Then come visit me this summer at Vyra," I stammered. Why had I not thought of that marvelous solution before? He could stay with us for several weeks, as Yuri Rausch sometimes did. We would nap together in the hammock. We would eat honey and butter on toast in the mornings. We would cover the stretches of Vyra and Rozhestveno on our bicycles. When the heat became intolerable we would strip off our clothes and bathe in the Oredezh.

"Can't," he said. "I'll be off to the Ukraine. My father needs me there. After all, I must learn to manage the estates. I must impress all the girls with my citified luster so that my father will deem the expense worthwhile. Besides, you hardly know me."

"But we would come to know each other," I said. "That afternoon at the cinema—"

"Haven't you put that out of your head yet?"

"Why should I? That was without doubt the finest afternoon of my entire life."

He smiled, and stared for several long moments into my eyes. "Take care that you don't become too philosophical, Nabokov," he said at last. "You and I both know many a fine chap has gone wrong by becoming too philosophical. So you enjoy a fellow's touch now and again?"

"Perhaps you'd like to see a movie this very afternoon."

He laughed. "Someone less kind would thrash you for such boldness, you know."

"I should like to be friends," I told him.

"Friends," he said. "I have my own friends; they're a good lot, really. I can't let them down. I shan't see you anymore this term, Nabokov. I don't want you becoming a bad habit of mine. Still I wish, just for once—"

He stopped mid-sentence. Heading our way along the graveled path were two of those friends, Vassily and Ilya. Both had an arm around the other's shoulder and were singing the Marseillaise with exaggerated fervor, raising their knees comically high as they marched and swinging their free arms stiffly.

"I must be on my way. Nice seeing you, Nabokov. And thanks," he added, tapping his satchel. "Thanks very much for the jolly gift."

As his comrades passed, he fell in step with them, taking up the melody, and stomping his boots hard into the gravel underfoot.

6

BERLIN
NOVEMBER 26, 1943

LUFTGEFAHR FÜNFZEHN—THOSE TOO FAMILIAR words. Highest level of danger. Nearly every night, and especially if the skies over Berlin are clear, our building's air-raid warden makes his rounds. Climbing the steep stairs (the elevator has long since ceased to function, and in any event it would be madness to risk being trapped inside it), he pauses at each landing to catch his breath, then moves down the corridor, beating a saucepan, knocking on each door, alerting those within to the aerial storm about to break once again over their heads. Everyone keeps a small satchel packed and ready for the descent into the cellar. I gather my valise of essential belongings, consisting mainly of these pages filled to the very margins with the smallest, most economical script I can manage, and my supply of precious foolscap pinched from the Ministry.

We sit on makeshift cots, some thirty of us, women, children, old men, some Germans, others Russian émigrés like myself who work in various ministries. No one makes any pretense of trying to sleep. Instead we keep up nervous, superficial conversation. Two of my compatriots play a distracted game of chess. There was a time, early on, when the old war veteran in room 11 kept our spirits up by lustily wheezing out on a battered accordion "Ach, du Lieber Augustin," the only tune he seemed to know—till one night Frau Schlegel, speaking by prior arrangement for the rest of us, suggested he might be making matters worse rather than better. He still lugs his accordion to the cellar, but now he sits quietly, and disconsolately whittles a stick away to nothing with his pocketknife.

Of late, Frau Schlegel does not join us. She has discovered that once the air raid begins, the factories shut down. She uses the precious surge in electricity to get her ironing done. And when all the bombs have fallen, and the firestorm has done its worst, there she is, waiting at the top of the stairs with her neat stack of sheets and pillowcases and shirts. The RAF, I am afraid, have not counted on the likes of Frau Schlegel.

7

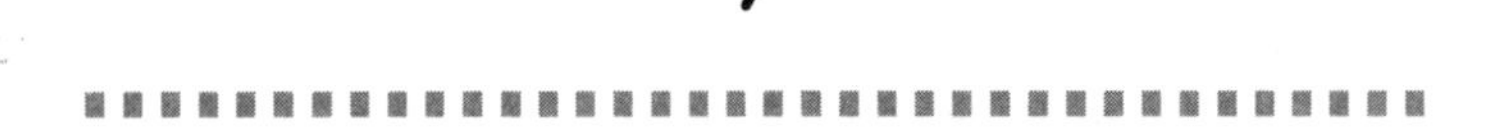

ST. PETERSBURG

TO MY MIND, PUSHKIN BEST SUMS UP THE SEASON: "Lovely summer, how I could cherish you / If heat and dust and gnats and flies were banished."

Our father was away with his regiment; the rest of the family had migrated, as usual, to Vyra. As Uncle Ruka had elected to forgo his customary summer visit, his house at Rozhestveno lay shuttered in its park of romantic lindens and classical nymphs. From time to time I would bicycle out to the estate in order to commune with the melancholy of the place, and to miss my uncle's inspiring presence. It was on one of those forays, as I wheeled up the deserted allée toward the empty house, that I noticed, from afar, two human figures embracing on the portico. Having maneuvered the girl so that her back pressed against one of the pillars, the boy feasted on a bare shoulder that had worked free of her blouse. My first impulse was to call out to them a gentle warning that trespassing on my uncle's property was strictly forbidden, but the instant before the words left me I realized who it was I had inadvertently surprised.

I stopped my bicycle and stared—only for a moment, but it was a moment too long. Volodya broke off his ardors. Shoving his hands into his trouser pockets and turning from her, as she frantically adjusted her blouse and ran a hand through thick, disheveled hair, he called out to me, dispiritedly, "Oh, hello there, Seryosha."

No doubt my brother had chosen Rozhestveno precisely because of its remoteness from prying eyes; nonetheless I felt outraged, as if he'd chosen to violate my uncle's estate on purpose.

At dinner that evening, I could not help but send investigatory glances his way. On his neck a bruise no larger than a thumbprint had appeared—a rosy mark of possession, as if his flesh had been impressed by one of those vizier's seals Uncle Ruka had once brought us from Cairo.

Although I now resolutely avoided Rozhestveno, I stumbled upon the enamored couple with unnerving frequency throughout the rest of that rainy summer. I did not seek them out, at least not consciously—indeed, I would have said I did everything I could to avoid them—but the result was that I found them everywhere. My bicycle's rear tire might burst, and as I attempted to patch it, they would materialize out of nowhere, strolling hand in hand, swinging their arms in unison the way I had seen peasants do. She hummed a popular gypsy ditty and he, though he cared for music not at all, would dreamily repeat the last couple of words from the end of each rhyming line.

Or, as I walked along a deserted road, suddenly, from the brambles, preceded by a spurt of that full-throated feminine laughter I had learned to recognize, the two would emerge, flushed and jolly. Without a word, Volodya offered me a single bilberry from the basket they carried between them, and without a word I accepted. Only then did he announce, "This is my brother, in whom I am well baffled. He's a bit odd, you see." His girl smiled, dimpling, said her name was Valentina, and that she was much pleased to meet me. A bit of Tatar exoticism saved her features from coarseness, but then I have always been fatally indifferent to the physical charms of women, a defect not even the most modern cure could alter.

Then came a thunderbolt from the hazy midsummer skies. Word arrived that Uncle Ruka was on his way. The very next day the Nord Express made an irregular stop at the Siverskaya station and, before the servants had had a chance to fully prepare his room (he was staying with us; Rozhestveno remained closed) my splendid relative was once again in our midst.

I had not seen him since the domestic ruckus my ill-fated diary had kicked up several months before, though I had often longed for his company as one longs, in beleaguered circumstances, for an ally. I did not imagine anyone had written him about my plight; still, I thought our meeting in the flesh might render palpable the invisible bond between us. But in his cream-colored summer suit and customary mouse-gray spats he seemed, as he approached across the sandy drive, curiously diminished. Thanks to Father and Dr. Bekhetev, I no longer saw my uncle as an enchanting individual but as a type (his mincing walk, the gold filigree bracelet on his wrist, the gaudy carnation in his buttonhole). Despite myself, I shuddered. Dr. Bekhetev would have been pleased.

But in the next moment he lofted a magnificent walking stick jauntily over his left shoulder, and that devil-may-care gesture suddenly swelled in me a kind of irrational pride as well as anger that anyone would dare dismiss my uncle as a mere "invert." For if he was merely a cutout, a shadow of a man, what then was I?

We all clamored to know what brought him northward.

"A secret mission," he answered, a glimmer of mischief in his eyes.

We sat in wicker chairs on the verandah. A band of gnats shimmered in the late-afternoon sunbeams. He ate iced cherries from a bowl and sipped cassis and soda.

"Travel no longer agrees with me," he announced in his somewhat formal-sounding French. "I have had a most difficult time of it. Warsaw, where I made the mistake of breaking my journey for a few days, was simply crawling with urchins. Frankly, I'm exhausted. I never wish to see a young face again. Excepting yours, my dear nephews, but then, you're my only family in the world. But how you've changed, Volodya. How sallow and plain you've grown!"

At that he sighed, as he often did.

At supper, my mother insisted that our guest occupy the head of the table, but he demurred, saying, "Lyova, I am but a diplomat. Your husband is a leader. In his absence, it is his son who must head the table." With that graceful gesture he relinquished his position to his elder nephew.

"We see so little of Volodya these days," my mother told her brother. "He's out at all hours, day and night. He's of that age when he's begun taking a greater interest in the local fauna."

"Still chasing butterflies, my dear boy?"

"Nymphs," explained my mother. Volodya stared at the tablecloth, making minute adjustments to the position of his silverware. "But it's unkind to tease. He's in the first flush of love, I think."

Uncle Ruka looked nonplussed. "Charming. Delightful," he stuttered. "May we ask who she is?"

"We may not," said Volodya. "If it's all the same."

Uncle Ruka daintily brushed his lips with his napkin. "Quite. I understand completely. The charm of an escapade is so often in direct proportion to its degree of furtiveness. As I know so well."

And then, looking my way, he winked.

Was it possible? I had no chance to ask him, for immediately after dinner friends of my mother arrived from their nearby estate, and soon they had all settled in for a game of poker that would go very late into the night.

"Something's up," Volodya muttered as the two of us climbed the stairs to our bedrooms. "I don't like the looks of it. I believe he's gotten himself into some kind of trouble, and he's come here to seek Mother's help. I'm certain of it."

"Uncle Ruka? What kind of trouble?" I asked.

Volodya gave me a sidelong look and shook his head, as if to say, *Don't be stupid.*

But I *was* stupid, hopelessly so. I lay awake till long after the sounds of the poker game had subsided and Volodya had slipped out of the house for his nightly rendezvous. Stupidly, I waited for the soft knock at my door, my uncle gliding into the room, seating himself on the edge of my bed, tenderly stroking my knee, telling me, "There, there. No need to be afraid, *mon petit.* I have been told everything; I understand all."

But of course no one came.

The next day our visitor slept till early afternoon. I passed the time in the music room playing, pianissimo, a number of my uncle's songs on the old Becker grand that never wanted to stay in tune. It had been quite a while since I had last rehearsed them, and from time to time my memory failed me. Later, I drew out his walking stick from the hallway stand, admiring the blond shaft flecked with beautiful auburn blemishes and the fantastic knob of smooth coral—evidence of a stylish life of adventure and romance I could scarcely imagine, but that one day, I swore, would be mine as well.

When at last he emerged from his bedchamber, looking more haunted than usual, I asked him how he had slept.

"Well enough," he muttered, "except for the interruptions of some most unheavenly music. Whatever imp commandeered the piano must really learn to play a bit more adroitly before inflicting his soi-disant melodies on others."

With a flick of his head he turned away. Snapping his fingers in a way that invariably distressed my father, who accused him of treating the household staff like slaves, he summoned Aleksey the butler, requesting that he, in turn, summon the young master Vladimir Vladimirovich. He wished to converse with him. When Volodya appeared, looking sleep-deprived, Uncle Ruka took him by the elbow and purred, "Walk with me, my dear. I have news which will amuse you."

Smiling bleakly at my mother and me, he led Volodya away, his arm draped over his shoulder, while my brother did his best to shrink from the affectionate gesture. We could see them taking a turn about the orange sand path by the flowerbeds, and I was certain I could see my brother glancing desolately at the butterflies that fluttered amid the dahlias. Their conversation lasted scarcely five minutes, during which time Uncle Ruka drew my brother so close that his murmuring lips were nearly touching Volodya's crimsoned ear.

When released, Volodya did not flee but remained by his side. He hung his head, stuck his hands in his pockets, kicked at the sand underfoot.

But Uncle Ruka had finished with him. "*L'audience est finie,*" he said briskly. "*Je n'ai plus rien à vous dire.* And now I must be on my way! I have just time to reach the station before the Warsaw train. I needn't be seen off! Tsiganov can drive me. *Au revoir, mes chers!*"

In the aftermath of our uncle's visit, my brother seemed uncharacteristically subdued.

"Volodya," my mother asked at supper. "What on earth was all that about? What did my brother have to tell you that was so important?"

For a long while Volodya did not speak. He toyed with a slice of roast beef on his plate. Then, without looking up, he said in a strange, strangled voice, "He's named me his sole heir. Rozhestveno will one day be mine."

My mother crossed herself. "*Bozhe moy!* Why in Heaven's name would he do such a thing? Basile's only forty-four. He has years to live. Why has he tempted Fate?"

My brother looked miserable. We all knew Fate had nothing to do with it. When a servant brought in coffee, my mother burst into tears. Not even Mademoiselle offering her licorice from the stash she always carried in her capacious handbag could calm her.

8

ALL SUMMER, FROM HIS REMOTE SWISS LAIR, V. I. Lenin—that cowardly German Jew, as Aunt Nadezhda described him—had been urging our Russian armies to lay down their arms and make a separate peace with the Kaiser. Red bunting and Bolshevik rumors began to inflame Petrograd. My father, writing from his regiment, opined to my anxious mother that while such incendiary rhetoric might appeal to urban discontents, in the countryside we should prove perfectly safe. The peasants could be counted on to remain indifferent to the cause of the Internationale.

A series of barn burnings on neighboring estates—mysterious, middle-of-the-night events—had lately begun to raise doubts about his calming appraisal.

"Do be careful," my mother told Volodya one evening after fire had claimed a shed at Batovo. I suspect she wished to forbid his nocturnal prowls altogether, but knew that would be pointless.

Grinning, Volodya pulled from his pocket a set of brass

knuckles. "Let anybody who wants come to terms with these fellows."

My mother frowned. "Does your father know you carry those?"

"He bought them for me last spring at the English shop."

"Really!" she exclaimed. Then, smiling forlornly: "Well, do try to avoid any situation in which you might be tempted to employ them."

Volodya took a swipe at empty air.

After he had left, my mother and I settled down to a jigsaw puzzle that promised, upon completion, to reveal Rubens's *Adoration of the Magi*. How I hated these initial gropings when one scarcely knew where to start. My mother, on the other hand, sorted through the chaos before us with that combination of childish eagerness and adult deliberation that so endeared her to everyone who knew her. I watched her brow furrow, her mouth form a moue. "Your father and brother are too much alike," she said. "Really. They both think they're immortal." She regarded me fondly, then picked up a random puzzle piece. "You're so much more sensible in that respect."

Little did she understand the dangerous things I also carried—not in my pocket but in my heart.

I went to bed early that evening musing on the handsome variety of riches—from girl to brass knuckles to Rozhestveno—Volodya had recently acquired. Sometime around three in the morning, in the midst of a lovely convoluted hallucination in which Oleg had wrapped his arms around me and was about to— But I would never know, for excited cries woke me.

"Come, come, everyone," I heard my mother shout as she hurried down the corridor, rapping on each door.

The disused stable near the bridge where the Warsaw highway crossed the Oredezh was in flames.

Russians love fires. It is one of the stranger aspects of our national psyche, and though I have never quite understood the fascination, I have observed it often enough. Whether in the city or the country, not just peasants but professors and priests and patricians flock to gawk at the sight of a building in flames. My mother was in this respect Russian to the core. All her considerable Western veneer fell away, and what remained was as untamed as those songs we used to hear at the fashionable tzigane restaurants on the islands at the mouth of the Neva.

Still half asleep, I joined my sisters, my four-year-old brother Kirill, and their governess, Mlle. Hofeld, in an old charabanc. Meanwhile Tsiganov, in our red Tornado, drove my mother and her new dachshund. Of course, Volodya was nowhere to be found, and his absence caused much consternation among my sisters.

"I have no idea where he's got to," I told them as our turtling charabanc fell ever farther behind the leporine Tornado. "You'll have to ask Mother." I could see that my words failed to endear me to Mlle. Hofeld, who shared my mother's confidences and was well aware of Volodya's worrisome vagabondage.

The strange hour, my moist dream of Oleg, a certain restiveness combined to enliven me. "Perhaps we'll find our brother's the arsonist. Perhaps we'll catch him red-handed, ha-ha-ha," I said merrily, sending nine-year-old Elena, who adored her eldest brother, into a fit of tears abundant enough to douse the fiercest conflagration.

"That will be enough," warned Mlle. Hofeld.

But I was hardly finished. Under cover of darkness, as the patch of orange in the distance lit our way, I startled myself by clasping my hands to my breast and crooning, "He's in love. The young swain's in love. He burns with love: the fires of the heart light his way, the flambeaux of desire. O lustrous fever in the blood! A hero for our time!" I had made myself very merry indeed, and my stammer was entirely gone. Elena, Olga, Mlle. Hofeld—all stared at me. Even our coachman Zahar turned around in his seat to make sure all was well with his charges. I could see him shaking his head at the foolish young *barin*.

"Are you drunk?" asked Olga. "Please tell us if you are."

"Drunk on love," I wailed, for by now I no longer knew whether I was speaking of Volodya or myself. "Drunker on love than on Slivinka," I whooped. "Drunker than on vodka or champagne or Tokay..."

Our arrival at the scene of the fire brought my spirited performance to an end. By carriage, automobile, bicycle, horseback, and hay wagon quite a festive crowd had shown up. From Batovo just across the river had come Grandmother Nabokova, Khristina, Aunt Nadezhda, and a hodgepodge retinue of servants who formed an absurdly inefficient bucket brigade to ferry water from the river to the by-now-unstoppable flames.

At the margin of the gathering crowd, good-naturedly shoving each other, two muzhik lads caught my attention.

I had seen the pair countless times before, two more anonymous cogs in the vast machinery of our estate. Now firelight transformed them. Was it my imagination? The longer I watched them, as one deftly tripped the other with his leg and both went down in a tumble, the more certain I grew that they kept between them some secret. I had not an iota of evidence save the illogic of desire, but when a slant-eyed old Tatar cuffed one of the boys on the ear and ordered the two of them to join the fire brigade, I suddenly knew that it was none other than they who were responsible for the arson.

From her handbag my mother produced two tumblers and a small bottle of port with which to fortify herself and Mlle. Hofeld. On seeing the bottle, my siblings burst out laughing, much to my mother's confusion.

"What, *mes enfants*?" she kept asking. "What's so funny?" But as they would not tell her, she grew more and more confused.

This left Mlle. Hofeld to cluck, "What a foolish bunch of children! The excitement has caused all of them to completely lose their minds!"

As my mother, grandmother, and aunt nattered away and my siblings milled about, their boredom growing in direct proportion to the flames, which now consumed the shed entirely, I caught sight once again of my two criminals and felt a satisfaction heightened nearly to ecstasy by the simple gesture of one boy putting his arm around the other's neck and whispering something no doubt conspiratorial in his ear.

Had I actually seen them brandish the incriminating torch, I could not have been more astonished. It was mere practice, I saw now, for the greater drama they planned. One day soon, they and their flame-red banners would come for Vyra itself, for Batovo, for Rozhestveno. Our night watchmen, the Tsar's secret police, the scarlet-uniformed Cossacks that patrolled the streets of the capital, the Imperial Guard at Tsarkoe Selo: none could hold the flames at bay. And I was in love with the arsonists!

We rode back in subdued spirits, Kirill and Elena asleep on either side of Mlle. Hofeld, Olga singing under her breath a strange song of her own devising. Ashamed of my antics on the ride out, and chastened by my traitorous emotions at the fire, I gazed at the passing woods. The early light of a Russian summer morning was turning them ashen. Two figures strolled hand in hand; they swung their arms broadly. Volodya had woven his Valentina a garland of lunar flowers; he wore on his face a look of supreme satisfaction.

Olga must have nudged Elena awake, for they both began pointing excitedly, and Volodya acknowledged them with a single gallant wave that roused them to even more hysterical paroxysms of adoration.

A humid afternoon some days after the incident of the burning stable found me guiding my bicycle in lazy figure eights back and forth along a dirt track on the farther reaches of our estate. The object of my scrutiny? Two figures in the middle distance mowing a golden hayfield. Swinging their scythes in long, soul-stirring arcs, my arsonists seemed anything but grim reapers. I longed to ditch my bicycle in the long grass, as Lenin would have our soldiers abandon their rifles in muddy fields, and approach the enemy, arms raised in surrender.

As if prompted by some cue, the two toilers all at once ceased their toil. Flinging aside their tools, they began a bit of horse-play, two colts pawing the ground, butting heads, whinnying with delight. The high grass concealed them whenever they fell wrestling to the ground, but then their shaven heads and naked torsos would bob again into sight. "The peasants are in general quite content with their lot," Aunt Nadezhda was fond of proclaiming, and for the moment that seemed undeniable.

I was beside myself with joy, though the youths' spontaneous eruption of high spirits cooled quickly enough. They stood solemnly facing each other, their uncouth voices a blur; I tried to imagine what tender confessions two criminals alone together in a half-scythed field might share.

Thoughts roiled through me: how the slave Khristina had been given to my grandmother as a playmate; how Uncle Ruka's Egyptian Hamid was a most mischievous but devoted character. Suddenly I wanted my own slave and companion. It was an extraordinarily thoughtless wish, but what use was my family's wealth and power if I were to be so miserable and wanting?

Impetuously abandoning my bicycle, I waded through the waist-high grass.

"Hello," I called out, even though I was expressly forbidden to talk to the peasants who worked our estates. All I wanted, confusedly, was to share in their joy. To make it mine. And if they were the criminals I believed them to be, then so much the better, for I had convinced myself that since those associated with my vice were criminals, insofar as these lads were criminal they must also be receptive to that vice. No brass knuckles for me! They could do with me what they would.

When I emerged from the unscythed portion of the meadow into a circle of sweet-smelling stubble, a confounding sight confronted me. Drawers puddled around their ankles, my criminals, as if obedient to every whim of my fancy, were lazily pleasuring each other!

They started up, alarmed by the scarlet-faced, panting, bespectacled lad who had materialized before them. "Go away!" they hissed, shooing me off. "Go, go, go!"

But I did not move. Up close, my Bolshevik angels appeared unbelievably grimy, their faces smudged, their nails blackened, the reek of their sweat an obscure warning. A livid scar disfigured the older one's creamy thigh.

It quickly dawned on them who I was. The *barin's* son. The young master Sergey Vladimirovich.

"Well, well," I said, adopting all the hauteur I had witnessed in my favorite villains onstage at the Maryinsky. "What have we here?" (Would that I had had a riding crop to tap against a gloved palm.)

That I frightened them excited me. They eyed me with disbelief, miserable amusement, murderous hatred.

"You've not got permission to loaf," I said. "My father doesn't pay idlers. But now that you've begun this droll game, by all means continue."

They hesitated, sullen and cowed.

"Get on with it," I told them, swelling to my role. "Help each other out, comrades. Look lively, there."

It was a tone I had heard Uncle Ruka use on the cringing staff at Rozhestveno, a tone my father rightfully deplored. But for the moment I *was* Uncle Ruka, Seigneur Sodoma. I folded my arms across my chest and observed my victims as coolly as I might observe a mare give birth to a foal in one of our as-yet-unburned stables.

How easily—and justifiably—those two might have wrung my neck. But they did not. Years later, at the Cirque d'Hiver in Paris, I would witness a gaudily dressed young lion tamer wedge open the maw of an ancient lion and slowly, insanely insert his head. With what indescribable forbearance did the long-suffering lion allow his tormentor to make a spectacle of his humiliation. So too my muzhiks shrugged, scowled, then the older one muttered to the younger, "So the little monkey wants an eyeful? We'll give him an eyeful."

And they got on uncomplainingly with the task at hand, as they did with all the labor that dogged their long days. What choice did they have? After all, their grandparents had been slaves of the Nabokovs and Rukavishnikovs, their parents barely better off. Still, I could not get past the suspicion that the clever mice had once more outsmarted the stupid pussens.

They could not fail to observe the excitement their mutual engagement induced in the kind master's depraved son, the brimming cup he could not prevent from spilling.

I have often thought that Russia was lost that very afternoon. Not for an instant do I claim that an incident of no import whatsoever was in any real sense the cause of Russia's downfall. What I am attempting to say is simply this: In the moment I misused my opulent position in the world, I made clear how unworthy I was of it. In a million variations, my actions were being repeated by those of my standing and privilege all over the empire, collectively leading to that inevitable end that none of us wished at the time to foresee.

"I hope you're pleased with your filthy selves," I heard myself say as the muzhiks wiped their milky sap from their fingers. Gamely I sought to rearrange myself inside my flannels and depart the scene with a few remaining shreds of seignorial dignity. Already a dull film of shame was beginning to coat my soul. I had scarcely taken a dozen steps, however, before an inspiration occurred to me; taking from my coin purse a generous assortment of kopeks, I turned and flung them in the direction of my smirking companions. In the dull sunlight the coins did not glitter, nor did either of the recipients of my largesse make a move.

"Ladyboy," the cheekier of the pair called out after me, though his companion, older and more prudent, he of the ugly scar, brusquely shushed him. As I mounted my Enfield Racer—had they ever, would they ever in their poor lives ride such a fine machine?—I could see them scouring among the stubble for every last coin.

In the weeks that followed, crudely etched graffiti linking me to infamous practices began to appear—on tree trunks, bench backs, bridge railings, even in the rainbow-glassed pavilion by the ravine. With my penknife I erased what instances I could, but like the sorcerer's apprentice, I found that my actions that afternoon had generated a cascade impossible to contain. The more I gouged and scraped, the more widely the epithets seemed to proliferate, till a walk in the woods became an accusation at every turn. I had fancied my docile muzhiks illiterate, but thanks to the village school which Uncle Ruka had endowed a few years before, it seemed they could express themselves with brutal effectiveness.

"You appear to be the target of widespread calumny," observed my father, home for a week from his regiment. From behind the gloomy headlines of his newspaper he spoke invisibly.

I offered that I hadn't a clue to what he was talking about.

"Don't pretend you haven't noticed. Everyone else has."

His last remark took me off guard, and I sputtered helplessly.

"What is one to make of it, I wonder?" he went on, lowering the paper to cast me a quizzical look. "Such accusations don't generally materialize out of thin air."

"I have no idea," I lied.

"Will you swear to me that you've not lapsed into vice? Dr.

Bekhetev seems to think you've been doing quite well. Sophie, I believe, is her name?"

A convenient fabrication the physician had easily fallen for.

"I swear," I lied.

Father studied me coolly, as he might a not-very-convincing witness on the stand. "Well, it's a mystery to me," he said at last. "And I have only your word of honor. But without his honor, remember, a man is nothing."

Though for obvious reasons I was ashamed of my actions, I did not altogether regret them. I had learned far more about myself in those ten shameful minutes in a half-scythed meadow than in all my sessions with Dr. Bekhetev put together.

9

BY THE BEGINNING OF 1916 THE STREETS OF Petrograd, which had emptied of young men at the start of the war, were once again thronging with able-bodied fellows. I suppose I knew they were deserters, but I somehow did not comprehend what it meant that there were so many of them. The newspapers, when not censored, offered mystifying accounts of our retreat from Galicia, assuring us, "The heroic and disciplined withdrawal of the Imperial Army has effectively blocked any advance by enemy forces"—desperate euphemisms whose echo I hear daily, some quarter century later, in the crumbling Reich.

Small changes had occurred at school which made my life more bearable: two new boys had entered, Genia Maklakov and Davide Gornotsvetov. Both hailed from the newly minted class of war profiteers; as both were in revolt against their fathers, the source of their recent fortune hardly mattered to me.

A year older than I, Davide Gornotsvetov was tall, slender, with features that were dark and regular. Pleasingly long eyelashes framed his large brown, innocent-looking eyes. He had black, curling hair, and had recently grown his sideburns long—a wonderfully louche touch. A year younger, Genia Maklakov was a slight boy with a sweet smile, short blond hair, and the limpest of handshakes. His gaze was pensive, even dolorous. In his childhood he had been perilously frail, but had since achieved a less precarious foothold in the world due to a physician-ordered regimen of cod liver oil and birch sap. Of the two, Davide was the more extravagant, and I soon began to emulate some of his braver mannerisms by wearing my scarf extra long, parting my hair *à l'anglaise*, wearing too much eau de toilette, and painting my nails with coral lacquer. In a nod to one of several shared proclivities, we dubbed ourselves The Left-Handed Abyssinians, "Abyssinian" being the kind of invention much favored by Davide.

The Stray Dog café, hallowed by the likes of Ahkmatova and Mandelstam, Stanislavsky and Meyerhold, had recently been shut down by the Tsar's police, but other cafés had opened in its place around the city, usually tucked away in dank cellars where the air was thick with the odor of tobacco smoke and overflowed toilets. We became habitués of several, the Red Jingle and the Crystal Petal among them, and would spend hours sipping Turkish coffee (or, in Genia's case, almond milk) and smoking Egyptian cigarettes. We gossiped wickedly about our fellow schoolmates and teachers, whom we scorned, or about the theater, which we adored.

Like our mother, Volodya had no ear for music—he insisted it bored and irritated him; thus from an early age I had regularly accompanied my father to the opera, of which he was a passionate devotee. I cherished the vigorous postmortems we conducted in the carriage ride home from the Maryinsky. I vividly remember a shattering performance of *Die Walküre*, after which he tried to warn me off the suspect allure of Wagner.

Now that his regiment was at the front, however, it was my

new friends who joined me in our subscription box, and it was owing to Davide that I discovered another theatrical pleasure against which my father had long tried to prejudice me. "Ballet isn't art," he was fond of saying. "It's a toy, no better than a Fabergé egg, and we know how tasteless *those* are, despite the Romanovs' enthusiasm for them."

Davide, however, wore the badge of balletomane fervently. Having only contempt for the staid set of subscribers who peopled the boxes and stalls, he preferred the upper standing-room gallery of the Maryinsky, called "paradise" by its habitués. Opera from the subscription box was all very well, but ballet demanded something different. From him I learned rituals. First, there was the business of purchasing a ticket—which, for paradise, could only be done the day of the performance. I had never in my life stood in a box office queue; now I grew accustomed to waiting with a hundred or more bleary-eyed balletomanes on a cold street at dawn, all of us clasping ourselves tightly and stamping our feet to keep warm while around us the city awakened, limbless veterans and child-encumbered gypsy mothers staking out their spots for the day's round of begging, a mounted detachment of the Imperial Guard making its way toward the Winter Palace, shopkeepers sweeping last night's snow from before their doors.

How strange it felt to pass by my family's box on the bel étage and climb the narrowing stairs toward paradise. The chandeliers, unnervingly close at hand, glittered; far below, the audience, perhaps less stylish than before the war, nonetheless filled the hall to capacity. With a sweet ache in my heart I watched the dancers sail across the stage, witnessed the holy simplicity of human gesture highlighted, drawn out, lovingly adored, reluctantly relinquished.

The reigning goddess that season was Tamara Karsavina. At each of her appearances, paradise erupted in cries that seemed, in their prolongation, almost like wounds asking to be healed.

None called out more longingly or for longer than Davide. My father would have been scandalized, but I cheered as well, with all my might. When the curtain closed for the last time, the boxes and stalls slowly emptied, the musicians packed away their instruments, but we in paradise remained in place, still roaring, "*Brava, bravissima, La Karsavina!*"

But there was a final ritual to be enacted, as important as the purchase of a ticket that had begun the day. At the rear of the theater a small crowd would gather at the stage door. Dancers made their way past us to a scattering of applause. Fokine and entourage brushed by and into a waiting landau. Still we waited, and then *she* appeared, looking surprisingly frail. Around her shoulders she had draped an old, many-colored shawl, as if she had left her real self behind on the stage and were now in disguise. No cheer assailed her; rather, as she passed, each man bowed silently in homage. I too made my bow. She smiled sweetly, accepted a sheaf of white roses. She was accustomed to this; it was as much a part of the evening's performance as anything else. Often, after conferring with her driver, she waved him on without her. Then, readjusting her shawl to cover her head, she set out on foot, alone, her small figure slowly receding into the vast emptiness of the moonlit square.

As our étoile in mufti made her leisurely way solo down Kazanskaya Street, we followed at a respectable distance. When La Karsavina paused, we paused. She examined a set of patriotic prints in a shop window, dropped a coin into the outstretched hand of a pensioner. Standing in a circle of light cast by a streetlamp, she studied the clutter of posters on a kiosk—one of which featured herself, in alluring profile.

When she entered the Cathedral of Our Lady of Kazan we entered as well, loitering inconspicuously behind the pink granite columns as she made her way down the dim nave to kneel before the jewel-encrusted icon of the Mother of God, the very same icon by which General Kutuzov had defeated

Napoleon's armies. Lighting a votive candle, she remained for a time motionless, head bowed in veneration and prayer.

My family was religious only in a sentimental sense, attending services at Christmas and Easter, celebrating name days, but otherwise steering clear of the claustrophobic grandeur of Russian Orthodoxy. As a child I would mumble an automatic prayer to Jesus before going to bed; whether that habit, long since atrophied, had been established under the auspices of my mother or one of our many governesses, I can no longer recall. And on my bedroom wall still hung an icon of a stern-looking, emaciated saint, to whom I paid scarcely any notice other than thinking that he looked in need of some medical attention.

To witness the *prima ballerina assoluta* brought to stillness, in absolute submission to one greater than herself, was to understand that this was a self even more real than that brilliant creature who awed us at the Maryinsky. The moment went through my heart, a revelation out of the reach of mere words, but which would, one day, change my life entirely.

At last she rose, and her secret escort scattered into the ample shadows of the deserted cathedral to allow her to pass undisturbed. When she had regained the chill freedom of the outdoors, we regrouped and discreetly followed her through the uneasy city to her brightly lit mansion in Millionaya Street.

One night, our entourage having seen Karsavina safely home, I left my companions to catch their respective trams. Wandering home alone, I noted a figure approaching along the street.

Hands thrust in the pockets of his short jacket, cheeks flushed with the cold, Oleg Danchenko strode toward me. Nearly a year had passed since my mad attempt to woo him with an ancient bottle of Tokay, and my new friends had changed my circumstances for the better—but how my heart leapt at this fortuitous encounter.

"Well, well, well," he said, coming to a halt in front of me. "If it isn't Nabokov. Fancy that. Still wandering the streets as of old. Is that all you know how to do with yourself? What crime are you guilty of this time around?"

Startled though not unpleased by his familiar air, I had difficulty stammering out a response.

Taking me by the arm, he steered me around a corner before I had time even to consider the situation. The night was supernaturally clear; cold moonlight cast vivid shadows. Shoving me against a wall, he pinned me with his arms, thrusting his face inches from mine; I could smell caraway on his hot breath, but I do not think he was drunk. Gratefully I breathed in his scent. I have been afraid many times in my life, but I was not afraid then.

"Do you still want what you used to want?" he whispered. "Answer me, because I know full well what you wanted. I'm no fool, Nabokov. You've had designs on me all along."

Protest was futile, really. We were alone in an alley that backed up to one of the frozen canals. The boulevard beyond was empty. No windows looked down on us. Grabbing my wrist, he guided my hand to the buttons of his trousers. His forwardness took my breath away.

I leaned my head into his shoulder. "Manual release, if you please," he implored—hoarsely, so that I had to wonder whether he was accustomed to speaking to some valet or servant boy that way. "Now, be quick about it. I don't want to be freezing my jewels in this cold."

I complied, my fingertips memorizing that smooth shaft, my fist gripping tightly the imperial wand. When, with requisite swiftness, I had accomplished the asked-for favor, I marveled at the pearly residue clinging to the curve of my forefinger and thumb, how it steamed in the cold air.

Having stuffed his "jewels" back into his trousers, with incongruous courtesy he held out a handkerchief meant to dab that magical trace of him from my flesh—which, reluctantly, I did.

"See?" he observed. "That was jolly, wasn't it? An old Ukrainian pastime. Nothing to it. But one day, Nabokov—mark my word—I'll have you bend over for me. You'd fancy that, wouldn't you? But you'll have to wait for it, you know. You'll have to wait till I'm good and ready. Besides, I see you've gathered together a charming little menagerie of catamites. Have you poked them yet? I'm sure they're dying for a touch of it. Tell them Oleg will oblige. But only when he's good and ready."

I hadn't thought him drunk before, but now I was no longer sure—nor, it seemed, as we stumbled into the street, was the driver of a lone droshky that had just rounded the corner.

"Gentlemen, gentlemen, are you hammered?" called out the muffled-up driver, clearly no stranger to that condition himself.

Oleg clapped me on the shoulder. "Hammered?" he shouted to the driver, to me, to the sham of a city sleeping under moonlight. "More like schoolboy games. Old times' sake, you know." He laughed uproariously, a thigh-pounding guffaw.

I said nothing, and the droshky left us. It occurred to me that, in strictly clinical terms, I had lapsed badly. I had betrayed my father, Dr. Bekhetev, myself. Where was the note of triumph I had felt only minutes before? I saw Oleg quite clearly as he was—a bully and tormentor, a creature entirely unworthy of my esteem. Then he smiled at me, and my certainty melted but for a moment.

"I must go," I told him, adding, "My parents will worry."

"Till we meet again," he said. Without a word, angry now, I turned and walked away from him. I noted with disappointment that he did not call out, or make a move to follow me. Indeed, he seemed willing to relinquish his prey without a trace of regret.

But I was mistaken. Without warning came a blow to the back of my head, an Apache whoop as he knocked my cap askew and dashed past me. The force of his assault caused me to stumble; I fell face forward onto the wooden pavement blocks and cried out in pain. He doubled back and stood over me, panting merrily, as I struggled to sit up.

I was reluctant to take his outstretched hand. "No hard feelings," he urged. Against my better judgment I allowed him to pull me to my feet.

"You're hurt," he said, reaching out to touch my cheekbone.

I told him it was nothing.

"I didn't mean to hurt you," he said.

It was nothing, I repeated.

"I'll see you to your door, then," he offered, and I did not decline; despite the throbbing in my cheek I was grateful that he linked his arm in mine. When he left me at my front door, he kissed my forehead. The expression on his face was wondrous.

"I love a touch of blood" was the last thing he said to me.

10

WHAT A SIGHT WE MUST HAVE BEEN, WE LEFT-Handed Abyssinians parading three abreast down the Nevsky Prospect on one of those mild blue afternoons when the ice in the Neva was splitting asunder with the explosive spring thaw and the gauzy light out over the Bay of Finland made beauty of distance. The smart click of our three walking sticks on the wooden pavements, our elegant spats, our carefully lacquered fingernails, the crimson carnation each of us wore in his buttonhole reminded the world that we too had thawed from our long winter.

People would stop and stare; sometimes a half-sober droshky driver would whistle provocatively, or some of the street boys engaged in poaching water-logged timber from a canal would shout obscenities. We did not mind, any more than if we had played the part of some villainous character in an opera by Donizetti or Rossini. Occasionally we would meet my brother coming from the opposite direction with his Valentina on his arm, the two of them looking elegant and miserable, their lips stung from kisses snatched in the far reaches of public parks or the unfrequented rooms of minor museums, their eyes languorous and melancholy, and somehow I knew that what had blossomed the previous summer had not survived the long, cold winter. I did not pity him, though I wondered, as he gave me and my gay companions the skeptical once-over, whether he, misguidedly, pitied me.

Perhaps inevitably there came the day when I confessed to Davide that I was in love with him. I believe I mumbled something like, "You matter rather dreadfully to me, you know."

We had been lingering, just the two of us, in Peto's, the English store on the Nevsky Prospect, though we were too old for most of its offerings. For weeks I had dared myself to say those words which, now that I had said them, astonished me by their boldness.

He had been handling a rice-paper and balsa-wood model of an aquatic biplane, not unlike the Voisin Hydravion Uncle Ruka had once crashed in. His response was tart and to the point: "Don't be ridiculous."

"But why may I not say it, or at least believe it?" I asked him, cheeks aflame.

"If you do, *moy dushka*, then you are dreadfully deluded. Please, in the future refrain from such macabre admissions. They ruin the otherwise agreeable mood."

I asked him if he thought the present mood agreeable.

"Oh, absolutely. But let's not sully it with anything so untoward as, well, let's just call them the baser impulses. It's so much pleasanter not to, don't you agree? Besides, it would be nice to have *one* friend with whom one hasn't squandered everything."

I told him I hadn't anything base in mind at all.

"Exactly," he said. "Will you buy me this aeroplane? I do fancy it."

"What would you do with it?"

"I'd look at it and think of you," he told me.

I hazarded the observation that he could look at me anytime he wanted.

"One day you'll no longer know me," he said, guiding the plane in loops and barrel rolls. "You'll drop me as if I were contagious."

"Why would I ever do that?"

He looked at me with the saddest expression I had ever seen on anyone's face. "There's much about me you don't know."

"Then tell me."

"Ah, yes. But that's the point. There's much I don't want you to know."

The aeroplane's pointless flight was beginning to annoy me, so I grabbed his wrist and maneuvered a landing on the countertop, whereupon I informed him that he was acting very peculiarly toward someone who had just expressed a frank and simple affection for him.

That made him laugh. He peered at me from under half-closed eyelids. "Imagine," he said, "a pas de deux featuring two ballerinas. How tragic and ridiculous. And when one of the ballerinas has dark secrets she wishes no one to know, well, let's leave it at that."

I told him he maddened me. What dark secrets was he concealing? Why did he talk like that? "It's all very well to adopt a glamorous pose," I told him.

"You're right," he said. "I don't need this aeroplane after all. What was I thinking? When my ruin comes, as it must, I shan't be allowed aeroplanes or anything else by which to remember all that I loved."

I told him I found his words mysterious, even dreadful.

"That's what I am. A woman of dreadful mystery."

I reminded him he was no woman. He sighed and declared that, no, he was very much a man.

As we emerged from Peto's, he took my arm. "What a close

call that was," he said. "But my spirits are now very high—appallingly, inexplicably, ravishingly high. Thank you, darling. Thank you."

That night I dreamt I was called before God. The setting aped, more or less, the Cathedral of Our Lady of Kazan, and God Himself resembled, more or less, Fokine as I had glimpsed him at the rear door of the Maryinsky, though instead of the choreographer's fur coat and astrakhan cap, He wore the regimental uniform of my father. I had difficulty understanding His speech—His accent was a bit garbled, rather like Old Church Slavonic—but I gathered He wished to apologize. "When I made you," He confessed, "I had run out of souls, and so, you see, I filled you with something that resembled a soul but that was not, alas, a real soul. Only a very clever facsimile. I cannot tell you how sorry I am to have to report this, but there is nothing to be done. All your deepest emotions may seem real to you, but they are nonetheless counterfeit. I regret My mistake, Seryosha, but even God cannot undo His mistakes."

Too soon, summer arrived. Never before had I felt so wrenched from my cosmopolitan habits for the sake of desolate rural pleasures. Davide and Genia remained in town, though they bemoaned the capital's aestival listlessness almost as much as I did the countryside's. We all longed for September and the resumption of the theater season.

Yuri Rausch's arrival at Vyra in late July provided the summer's only diversion. I had not seen my cousin in two years. The lanky, gray-eyed boy had filled out into a robust young man. A little mustache accented his upper lip. The smart uniform of an officer's training academy sheathed him becomingly.

Forgotten entirely was that impulsive kiss Maurice the Mustanger had bestowed on Louise Poindexter. A new seriousness informed us. As he and I and Volodya sat on the verandah late into the night, long after Mother and her friends had retired from their poker game and Father and Dr. Bekhetev had smoked their last cigar, Yuri spoke of the war effort, the Tsar's bravery at the front, the danger posed by Rasputin's influence on the Tsarina. We were sixteen, seventeen, nineteen—no longer the children we had been.

Volodya remained indifferent. "What do those ridiculous puppets matter? Here's the real news of the day," he said, proceeding to recite to us a poem he had composed, an accomplished, slightly chilly imitation of Blok.

"That's beautiful, Volodyushka," Yuri told him. "But you know poetry's beyond a simple soldier like me. These days I know only duty, fearlessness, honor."

How unaccountable that Yuri and my brother could be friends! And yet they shared an affinity I could only envy. When I thought of Davide and Genia, they all at once seemed grotesquely insubstantial compared to this young man of the wider world.

I cheered myself up by mentally enumerating the qualities Yuri and I shared. We were both squeamish about insects. We both loved music, though Yuri's love was limited to tzigane melodies and martial flourishes. We were both indifferent chess players. All that distinguished us from Volodya. If those two were as different as night and day, weren't we as similar as dusk and dawn? Why should not Yuri and Sergey be friends, rather than Yuri and Volodya?

His ongoing talk quelled my idle thoughts. "Duty, fearlessness, honor, those three abide, but of those honor is the greatest. Without honor one does not live, one merely exists."

"Some might say the same about love," Volodya observed.

"No." Yuri was adamant. "Honor above all else. Honor above all in loyalty to the Tsar, to Holy Mother Russia, to the Russian Orthodox Church and its seven blessed *mysteria*."

"Please." Volodya popped a cherry into his mouth. "You're

speaking platitudes. I, on the other hand, only wish to live in the details. When I write a poem, I don't write about Love with a capital L; no, I attempt to describe the very particular love I feel for a very particular girl, or for a landscape, or a memory—whatever it is I'm writing about. I strive to do so with the same precision with which a lepidopterist might describe a hitherto unknown butterfly he has nabbed on the wing in some obscure Kazakh or New England meadow. Not just any butterfly, mind you; one particular butterfly."

"But what about classification?" asked Yuri. "Aren't there species, not just individuals? Besides, there's so much in our lives that's simply indescribable. Wouldn't you agree?"

"Nothing's indescribable. To hold that the world's indescribable—well, there lies futility, despair, defeat, all those things I refuse to have anything to do with. The universe is most certainly describable—its designer would have it no other way. And I think it's our duty to engage that intricate task of description—but then we're intricate creatures ourselves, don't you think? Or at least some of us are. I don't mean the common idiot in the street, the man who thinks that giving bread to everyone and flying red banners and turning the factories over to the workers and that sort of rot will solve anything. I mean those of us blessed with the ability to puzzle out the puzzle, so to speak: those of us grateful for that gift, and honor-bound—here's your true honor, Yuri—to make use of it."

"That's very well put," Yuri conceded. "I agree with all you've said. And yet, we who defend with our swords and bayonets your ability to puzzle out the puzzle in peace, aren't we to be valued as well? The Tsar may be of no interest to you whatsoever, but it's his Empire that allows you the freedom to nab your butterflies and compose your poems and solve your infernal chess problems, and, I daresay, fall in love with that particular girl. I fear all that will go by the wayside should Bolshevik instability ever prevail."

"The poet travels lightly," returned Volodya. "He'll always manage to go on doing what he does."

How grown up we sounded, as we ate cherries, sipped tea from the samovar whose magical warmth the servants kept renewing. What did *they* think of our talk? Did they think anything, or only long for bed? Where were my muzhiks from the scythed field of last summer? Had they been sent off to war? Were they giving each other miserable comfort in a gore-splattered trench somewhere? Were they lying dead and unburied in some muddy field? Or were they among the throngs of deserters who filled Petrograd, and on whom the Bolsheviks were said to prey? It grieved me not to know such simple, human things about the world I lived in. The puzzle had far too many pieces; whenever I attempted to focus my thoughts on the whole, it dispersed before my eyes.

Yuri turned to me. "And what do *you* believe, O silent one?"

In the light of the spirit lamp his gray eyes met my own and held there—as if, after long hiatus, he had mysteriously elected to kiss me once more on the lips.

"I don't know," I confessed. "I only know what I value. Friendship and beauty. I value those far more than honor itself. The love of a friend for a f—" I stalled humiliatingly on that final "friend."

Yuri laughed. "Sorry," he said. "That was rude of me. One mustn't make fun of someone's impediment."

"The sound of an argument running aground," murmured Volodya. "Seryosha's usually silent for a reason."

My stutter had once again made comical the most serious of moments. Nonetheless I forged on, much to my brother's eye-rolling impatience.

"There's fearlessness of all sorts in the world," I said. "Soldiers have it, and explorers, and poets, no doubt, but especially lovers. There. That's what I believe. I'd die for my friend."

"Who's this friend?" Yuri asked—whether tenderly or mockingly I could not tell. "And is he a friend or a lover? You seem to confuse the two terms, which in my book are quite distinct."

"I've not yet met him," I said, ignoring for the moment his quibble, which really seemed beside the point, but all the while, to my surprise, sustaining his gaze. How lustrous his eyes were, how grave and thoughtful his expression.

Volodya stirred restlessly. "I think we've had enough of this philosophizing. I'm exhausted. In fact, I think it's time for bed. Yurasha, are you coming? Or do you wish to indulge further my brother's maunderings?"

Yuri continued to look at me for a very long moment; then, disappointingly, he said, "Sure, Volodya. I'm coming. Good-night, Sergey Vladimirovich."

Two days later Yuri left for Warsaw. That same afternoon, Mother received via telegram the news that her brother Vassily Ivanovich Rukavishnikov, my beloved and unattainable Uncle Ruka, had died of heart failure at the Clinique Ste.-Maude near Paris.

"You were fond of him, I know," she said, caressing my hair. "Rest assured, he's finally at peace."

I found Volodya out by the swings, pushing our sister Elena in aggressive arcs. Soaring, she squealed with delight. His brow was furrowed. He ignored my arrival.

"Do you know what this means?" I asked him.

"I suppose it means I'm free," he said, giving the swing a rough shove.

"I don't understand," I said. "Free from what?"

But he only bit his lip, and shook his head, and looked away, and would not answer even when I repeated my innocuous question.

11

BERLIN, NOVEMBER 27, 1943

AS I HAVE GROWN WEARY OF FRAU SCHLEGEL'S turnip soups and margarined radishes, bless her black-marketeer's heart, I find myself looking forward to my lunch with Felix Silber. Though I am filled with irresolvable questions about his motives, and am half expecting that he has laid some sort of trap (but why go to all that trouble?), I am at the same time hungry for this bit of honest human contact. Perhaps he is as well. Perhaps it is all as simple as that.

But then, just as I have half convinced myself that is the case, I remember with a shudder the prankster-executioner from V. Sirin's *Invitation to a Beheading*, that novel which has so unnervingly predicted my present predicament. I must confess that I wonder, from time to time, whether I have somehow unwittingly fallen into one of Sirin's narratives, just as the poor chess master falls into an abyss of chess squares at the end of *Luzhin's Defense*. Was I being warned all those times I sensed an uncanny echo of my own shadow life in his novels? Have I turned out to be what V. Sirin, aka V. Nabokov, despises most—the Careless Reader?

In any event, I dress in dark if threadbare flannels and a crimson bowtie. My shoes have been repaired till there is nothing left to repair, but I can do little about that unfortunate situation. I reinforce the practically nonexistent soles with several pages torn at random from one of the encyclopedia volumes in my room (Dementia, Demon, Demosthenes).

Few trams run any longer, and those that do are windowless and terribly cold. I prefer walking, anyway. Thanks to the battalions of Russian and Italian POWs, the streets are cleared remarkably quickly, and there is a kind of melancholy grandeur to the ruins of this once beautiful city.

The Propaganda Ministry has been busy in my absence. From fire-scorched walls have sprouted a new crop of posters to inspire us, red-and-black placards urging, TO VICTORY WITH OUR LEADER! But other messages are more practical, such as the one that reminds us, RESCUE CREWS HAVE LISTENING DEVICES! Or another, white skull and crossbones on a black field: ATTENTION PLUNDERERS: THE PUNISHMENT IS DEATH!

One sees, as well, more personal pleas chalked in German, in Russian, in Polish, in French: "Reinhart family: I am staying at Elsie's." "Vasla: contact Frieda in Potsdam." "Where are you, my angel? I've looked everywhere. I'm sick with worry. Franz." And on the sole remaining wall of a devastated house: "Everyone here survived."

There is an odor of gas and decay everywhere.

When I get to Budapesterstrasse my heart sinks: as far as I can see along the block there are nothing but gutted buildings, or in some instances merely piles of rubble. But I press on, and to my surprise I find the Hotel Eden standing virtually intact and open for business, though there are few customers in the restaurant and all the windows are shattered. Heavy drapes do not entirely keep out the cold. Bundled, Felix is waiting for me at a table set for two in the far corner.

"You've chosen a rather public place for a private meeting," I note.

"I've always found it best to hide in plain sight."

"Look," I tell him, "before we venture any further I wish to know: how did you discover my address?"

"Oh," he says, "It's quite simple. I followed you home that day. Quite frankly, I was concerned about your mental state. I was afraid you might do away with yourself. I trailed you till I saw you enter your building. I thought of knocking, but then I lost my nerve."

"And then you regained your nerve two days later."

"Yes," he says—quite carefully, as if it matters that we both understand this—"Two days later I regained my nerve."

There is something a bit maddening about him, I decide, and am about to excuse myself when our waiter arrives, a crisp linen towel folded over his forearm. He bows quite formally. In a city where few young men are left, he is a very beautiful young man, sixteen or seventeen. A daring lock of hair hanging down over one eye identifies him as a "swing boy," that much-reviled and mostly eradicated reproach to the stern norms of the Reich. I always used to imagine that in a bombed-out city there must be fantastical license. What my fantasy never took into account was that only the aged and the infirm, the women and children would be left, that young healthy attractive men would all be either dead or away at the front.

"Since I happen to know what's available and what's not, I'll take the liberty of ordering for both of us," Felix says, not bothering to glance at the miracle of our waiter. "Lobster," he says briskly. "Champagne. I trust that will suit you? It's one of this war's smaller ironies, don't you think, that beer and sausage are in such scant supply while occupied France continues to provide us with her unrationed luxuries."

Our food arrives quickly, on elegant plates, and I could easily be back in Michaud's in Paris, or Coutant's in St. Petersburg, were it not for the ghastly odor that seeps even into the restaurant at the Hotel Eden. We both eat with conspicuous appetite. My years of fastidious vegetarianism are yet another casualty of war. That this meal will be expensive I have no doubt; I am by no means well-off, but my time will run out long before my reichsmarks do.

"My house was destroyed two nights ago," Felix remarks, as if mentioning a recent birthday.

"My God," I tell him. "Is everyone…"

He waves his hand dismissively. "I appreciate your concern. My wife and daughter are perfectly safe, staying with her parents in Dresden, which I am told presents no military or industrial targets whatsoever for the RAF. So on that score I rest easy. As for my house…" He shrugs. "I had a simple life. I cherished a modest collection of Meissenware which I had put together over the years. I had recently purchased a very fine Biedermeier escritoire. Given the magnitude of the ruin about us, I shouldn't even think twice about those meager material losses, but I do. I somehow think it my duty to grieve them. Every night that passes takes with it something else of our heritage. What will be left, I wonder? Whoever wins this war will have won it at such cost…. Well, that thought leads me farther into darkness than I wish to proceed. Have some more champagne. It would be a pity to go undrunk today only to be pulverized by a bomb tonight. So here, to our Führer's health." Halfheartedly he raises his glass. "Long may his wisdom guide us." Then he leans forward and says, sotto voce, "Have you heard the latest clever jingle to make the rounds?

'No butter with our eats

Our pants have no seats

Not even paper in the loo
Yet, Führer—we follow you!'"

For a moment I think he has gone utterly mad. Does he consider himself to have some immunity from treasonous utterances? Is he a *Volksschädling*, one of those doubt sowers we are warned against by the very Propaganda Ministry that employs us? All I know is that it is a strange relief to be having this conversation. No one in the apartment building speaks with honesty or intimacy. We are essentially a group of strangers thrown together nightly in a cellar while the world burns around us.

The bill, when it comes, is indeed expensive. We share it, another test he passes easily enough.

Later we walk along the Spree. All the bridges are out, though makeshift ferries ply the befouled waters. Berliners are about in droves, some obviously sporting their finest clothes in a spectral parody of a Sunday afternoon stroll. On an improbably surviving park bench, an elderly couple kisses with unembarrassed urgency. Only a month ago the sight would have been grotesque; now it stirs the heart.

"Did you hear they hit the Zoo? Many of the animals were killed outright, but some escaped. A tiger was found dead in the ruins of the Café Josty on Kurfürstendamm. Apparently he ate one too many Black Forest cakes. And it's said that crocodiles have been seen in the Spree. Personally I doubt it, but who knows?"

We gaze in silence at the debris-clogged waters. Several bodies, hideously mangled, are caught against a pier. I wonder if the crocodiles are dining as well today as we managed to do.

"I have nothing to report, unfortunately, about your friend," Felix says, "though I have been in contact with a colleague in Hamburg whose ability to negotiate the most Byzantine bureaucratic labyrinths is legendary. We shall see what he can discover. Tell me more, if you would, about this Hugh Bagley."

Once again I am wary. What exactly am I being asked to confide? Still, I tell him, "We knew each other at Christ's College, Cambridge. He was an amusing sort, very bright, from a distinguished family down in Somerset. For whatever reason, we've remained in touch through the years. I've met his wife, his children—all very charming in that English sort of way. He was always an enthusiastic amateur pilot. He wrote me at the beginning of the war to say he'd joined the RAF. That was the last I heard from him. It was a great shock to hear his voice on the radio."

"I'm told those broadcasts are quite effective in attracting a British audience who might not otherwise endure the risible rants of Lord Haw Haw, or the pathetic stylings of Charlie and His Swing Orchestra. Have you heard 'Winston Churchill's Lament'?" To the tune of "Stormy Weather" he begins to croon softly, *"Since my ships and German planes came together, I'm beaten all the time.* As if that's going to convince the British to surrender! I've never been to England. It would have been lovely to go there one day."

I want to ask him, apropos of Charlie and His Swing Orchestra, if he noticed that our waiter was a "swing boy," but I do not. Still, it's rather hard to believe anything is lost on Herr Silber. So I ask instead, "Is it true that swing hasn't yet been banned in Occupied France or the Scandinavian countries?"

He chuckles. "I suspect the Reich couldn't afford to stamp out the revolt *that* would provoke."

12

ST. PETERSBURG

"BUT HOW DO YOU KNOW GRAND DUKE NICOLAY?" Genia asked in amazement.

Davide tossed a lock of hair out of his eye. "I'd thought you were done with underestimating my cleverness, dear fellow. If you both swear yourselves to absolute secrecy, I can guarantee the Abyssinians an invitation to the most stupendous fancy-dress ball infernal Petrograd has ever witnessed."

As Davide was our leader, absolute secrecy it was.

"Then prepare to be astonished," Davide told us.

It was the Grand Duke's conceit that boys of a certain age should appear at the event as *demoiselles d'honneur.* To this end Davide took Genia and me to visit one of his more mysterious older friends, a once famous but now reclusive actor to whom he referred only as Majesté. We spent several giddy afternoons in the old actor's cramped rooms in Theatre Street, as he rummaged through boxes of ancient costumes, fitting us each according to his considerable whimsy. He was bald and fat, with twinkling blue eyes and a mobile smile. A fire roared in the hearth. In his stained yellow-and-black kimono he padded barefoot about the room, humming mildly, holding between pursed lips an array of pins with which he made adjustments to our dress. On occasion he would break his silence with a stageworthy outburst:

"Now I ask you, what is our Petersburg but a poor stage set, a splendid illusion of grandeur? Tsar Peter and his sublime troupe of architects, foreigners all, merely duped us. The rest of the world looks on and laughs, but what can they expect of us? We're phantoms in a cleverly managed pantomime of Empire. That mad muzhik Rasputin, who's hypnotized the Tsarina, who in turn has hypnotized her docile husband—what's all that but the fantastical stuff of mystical farce playing itself out against the barbaric backdrop of the Slavic soul?"

Then he would return to his task of garbing us in illusion. So taken was I by our preparations that I decided to offer my own contribution. One evening, when my mother was out with her poker circle, I crept into her bedroom and borrowed, from the safe, a very smart diamond choker whose brilliant fire I had admired as a child. In retrospect I shudder at the foolishness of this caper, but at the time I wished a touch of the real about me as I undertook my subterfuge.

Finally the illustrious night arrived. I donned a green tulle gown with an enormous corsage of hothouse gardenias. Heavy cabuchons hung from my ears, and around my neck I affixed my mother's looted jewels. Grandly bewigged Genia wore a gown of lavender satin and black lace. Davide was fitted in crimson silk embroidered in gold; an aigrette of ostrich feathers nodded above his head. I have never felt quite so sublimely ridiculous, though I must admit I found the sight of my fellow Abyssinians curiously thrilling, as if their costume at once degraded and elevated them. But then, I have always adored men in uniform.

"But what will *you* wear?" good Genia asked Majesté once we three had been fitted out.

"My darlings! You can hardly expect an aged crone like me to mar such a lovely event. No, I shall remain here and knit shadows. Now go forth and shine bravely, and think of nothing but love."

At these words, the Grand Duke's own chauffeur rang for us at the door. As the sleek Torpedo ferried us toward the palace in Moika Street, Davide explained that the fête was in honor of a young Finnish sailor. "I believe his name is Eska. He's apparently quite a beauty. The Grand Duke heard about him from Grand Duke Dmitri Pavlovich, who had him from Prince Yussupov. Hence tonight's gala. I suppose we'll have ample opportunity to observe for ourselves what all the fuss is about. Grand Duke Nicolay may not be the brightest light in the imperial family—they do, after all, call him Uncle Bimbo—but he's said to exhibit remarkably good taste in his young companions. And who knows? Should the Finnish beauty disappoint, well, my Abyssinians,"—he giggled excitedly—"I've been told we should be prepared for anything."

The doorman relieved us of our accoutrements—sable cloaks, muffs, toques: Majesté had not let us venture into the cold world unprotected.

In the first salon, beneath a Venetian chandelier, a lavish spread of refreshments had been laid out. Save for two or three bored-looking waiters, the room was empty. Beyond, however, gaily dressed gentlemen could be seen dancing with uniformed soldiers and sailors. The furniture had been pushed back against the walls; in one corner, a small string ensemble performed a sentimental waltz. Here and there among the dancers bobbed other rouged youths in ball gowns or gypsy garb, some so adept at their disguise that only the jut of an Adam's apple gave them away.

As if much-practiced in such things, Davide began almost immediately to flirt with a gallant-looking officer of the Imperial Guard, who soon rewarded him by caressing his cheek and asking for a dance. "*Bonne chance, mes Abyssines!*" Davide mouthed as he and his officer disappeared into the throng of dancers gliding across the polished floor.

Genia and I were not left on our own for long.

"Unchaperoned?" came a rich baritone. I felt a hand on my bare shoulder. To my astonishment I recognized our interlocutor as Yuri Yurev, the renowned actor whose stirring performances I had so often admired on the stage of the Alexandrinsky. Raven-haired and noble-browed, the very picture of virility, he was, if anything, even more charismatic at close quarters. His dark eyes fixed us with enthusiasm. "Or perhaps I should say—unshepherded?" he continued merrily. "Such lovely lambs. And bleating alone in the wilderness! But what have we here?" He feigned surprise. "Lads in lambs' clothing! Please give my compliments to your inspired couturier."

"A gentleman in Theatre Street," Genia told him. "We know him only by the curious name of Majesté."

"Ah," Yurev roared. "Of course! An old and very dear friend of mine: my unforgettable mentor, in fact, at the Imperial Theatre Academy many years ago. A superb character actor in his day, so effortlessly adaptable. I suppose even actors eventually settle for one role or another, but Majesté has trumped us all and keeps sailing ever further into new personae. Indeed, I believe she has convinced herself this winter she is the force behind the Chrysanthemum Throne. One hardly knows where she will eventually end up. Perhaps as a sphinx, an ocean liner, perhaps a mountain peak of great renown.

"In any event, she has done marvels with you two peacocks. Truly, I can't tell whose plumage I prefer. You're quite the lovely one there," he said, grazing Genia's pale cheek with his fingertips.

That we were there for the taking seemed without question. He caressed our bare arms, our bared necks. "Why, you're blushing," he told me. "You've turned crimson, while your friend here has the most exquisite pallor. What does it all mean?"

Thinking to defend Genia (O vanity!), I began to explain that my friend had not been well, that he had ventured out only reluctantly—but my unerring stutter soon left me in the lurch.

Yurev frowned. "No need to exert yourself. I can see you're the high-strung type. Perhaps some punch might make you more fit for human society. As for you, frail one"—he paused masterfully, addressing Genia—"have you never wished to be swept off your feet?"

Genia's usually listless eyes glistened; his nose quivered like a rabbit's. That was all the answer the famous actor needed. He bowed deeply and offered his hand. Gentle, unwell Genia looked at me—his expression apologetic, pitying, triumphant. A polonaise replaced the waltz, and the improbably minted pair soon joined the couples stampeding up and down the floor.

Both my fellow Abyssinians thus plucked from my side, I stood alone. Despite my blush and stutter, I felt neither anxious nor bereft. All my life I had enjoyed acting. This, I told myself, was no different. In the end, laughing breathlessly—how silly we had been! How giddy! How gay!—we would remove our costumes and return once again to our ordinary selves. But while it lasted, what a divine time we would have.

Wandering back to the room where refreshments beckoned, I downed three or four flutes of champagne in quick succession, and soon felt a welcome sense of elation. The only other occupant of the room was a sallow, perfectly bald little man wearing a bright blue sash. He stood at the table, avidly eating quail eggs from a green bowl.

"Well, you're awfully young to be caught up in all this, don't you think?" He spoke without interrupting his solitary feast. "But I suppose you haven't much of a choice, have you? No, you're inexorably drawn to your spirit brothers in there. And why shouldn't you be? Why shouldn't you expect that here you will find warmth, comradeship, sympathy, solidarity, all those things that have thus far eluded you in your accursed young life. I don't wish to dispel fond illusions, they're the scrumptious food of youth, but I shall tell you this one thing, lest you grow bitter before your time: among those lisping creatures in there, those giggling half-men, so fatally shallow, so incapable of any kind of seriousness, you will not find a single genuine soul. Despite their refined charms, their perfect manners and sugary endearments, their plight has made them cruel, vain, deathly cold. They spend all their solitary hours plotting and conniving. They're as untrustworthy as Jews. But alas, it's no doubt too late to warn you away. It's always been too late for such a creature as you—or me, for that matter, or any of us poor souls lost in this hell." He smacked his lips and popped another quail egg into his mouth.

I left him without a word and reentered the room where my cruel spirit brothers were dancing. As Davide and his officer wafted past to the graceful strains of a minuet my friend sent me a look of icy amusement. I averted my eyes.

In the last of that series of spacious rooms, seated on a gold and crimson sofa, the evening's sacrificial guest held court. I could see at once that the Finnish sailor was indeed very beautiful: blue-eyed, with blond stubble fuzzing his close-shaved head. And what fine cheekbones, what a fetchingly upturned nose. He was already quite drunk, his eyelids half shut, and every now and again he halfheartedly brushed aside the large paw that crept over his thigh. Soon enough he yielded, and allowed that hairy mitt to remain, which, since it belonged to Grand Duke Nicolay, was just as well. No longer young, aristocratically unhandsome, drunk as a peasant, the Grand Duke slowly slid his palm farther up the young man's inner thigh till it at last attained its goal.

All the while, a disheveled, heavyset man, also quite drunk, accompanied himself on the piano as he sang, or rather drawled, "Lads and lasses may be alike, but lads like me like lads like me."

It excited me to observe the Finnish sailor so clearly fallen into depraved hands. He seemed a likable, ordinary young man, a very far cry from the primped and teased likes of us, and I considered how the disillusioned man's comments in the refreshment salon strangely heightened the pleasure I took in the sailor's fall.

Feeling someone touch the small of my back, I turned, half expecting to be embarrassed by the appearance of a merely terrestrial acquaintance in this unabashedly lunar world.

"What's a young beauty like you doing unescorted at a debauch such as this?" the stranger asked me in French.

He was a gentleman in his forties, trim and correct in appearance, with a precisely managed goatee and, behind steel-rimmed spectacles, rather piercing eyes.

I attempted a witty answer, but my stutter arrested the sentence midstride.

"Oh!" said the stranger, unpleasantly startled. I could feel myself once again blushing.

Only after an interminable struggle did I manage to utter, "I seem to have lost my way."

Now the stranger seemed charmed, as I had wished him to be. If only my charm were not barricaded by such thorns!

"Do you have a name?" he asked.

"Sergey Vladimirovich," I told him.

"No, no," he cried. "That won't do. I mean, do you have an *enchanted* name, a *nom de bal*, as it were?"

I must have appeared perplexed.

He appraised me keenly. "You're very new to all this, aren't you?"

I admitted I had never been to such a ball.

"The very first time! There's nothing grander than one's very first time. Any beginning is to be cherished, but such a magnificent beginning as this—oh my! I hadn't thought to come out tonight, but as I was feeling rather bored, staring into the fire and seeing nothing there but phantoms, I ordered up my sleigh and driver, and now I must say I'm most glad I did. I shall call you 'Svetlana'—my Shining One."

I wondered politely what I should call him in return.

"Monsieur Tartuffe will do nicely," he said with a bow. Having never before curtsied, I did my laughable best.

The Finnish sailor, I could see, had succumbed to circumstance as well. He was messily attempting to sip champagne from a flute the Grand Duke held to his lips; the spillage darkened the front of his white frock. He barked with laughter. Caressing his shoulder, the Grand Duke leaned in to whisper a few words.

I allowed M. Tartuffe to lead me by the hand into the dancing salon. I had danced often enough with young ladies my age, leading as they followed, but I had of course never danced the lady's part. I did my best to follow his lead; indeed, I found it shamingly easy as we revolved across the floor to the sweet lilt of a Glazunov waltz.

I must confess that I thought my newfound M. Tartuffe not the least bit attractive, though I found his masculine attentions comforting.

Near us, Genia's cheek pressed to the famous actor's chest while Yurev swayed, head thrown back, eyes closed, in a state of exaltation. And from time to time, amid the throng, Davide and his officer would sail into view.

When the musicians took a break, everyone followed them into the refreshment salon. Finding myself separated from my dancing partner, I held back, flushed and pleasurably out of breath, hoping perhaps that he might vanish into the crowd, or that I might happily vanish into thin air. I had had my moment:

a man had chosen me; a man had held me. Nonetheless, the sight of the musician's instruments, lying abandoned on their chairs, filled me with melancholy. Then M. Tartuffe was once again at my side, having brought me a bit of caviar on toast, which he insisted on depositing on my tongue, as a priest does the host.

More music. More dancing. At last it was time to leave. Grand Duke Nicolay having disappeared upstairs with his Finnish prize, the rest of us were left to carry away whatever we had won as well.

When he brought me my cloak, toque, and muff, the doorman, seeing M. Tartuffe at my side, peered gravely into my face. I was on the verge of telling M. Tartuffe, whose name rather irked me, that I wished to remain with the friends with whom I had arrived—but at that moment Yurev came over, grinning like a bear deep in honey and saying merrily, "So, my dainty, I see you've chosen well. *Courage!* You're in good hands. When we meet again, all will be changed. *Adieu, Adieu.* I am afraid little Genia has drunk too much and twirled too much. I must take the dear child home and put her immediately to bed."

Davide and his officer had vanished entirely.

Without asking where I might wish to go, M. Tartuffe ordered his driver to take us to Dominic's, a posh restaurant near the Passazh. I admired the indifferent authority in his voice, though I immediately began to worry about my appearance. It was one thing to appear in Majesté's garb at a private party, quite another to flaunt it to the world at large! When I stammered out my qualms, M. Tartuffe only laughed and said, "Oh, you'll pass well enough, my lovely. Trust me, I know perfectly well what I'm doing."

The night that had descended on a slumbering St. Petersburg was frigid and absolutely clear; the moon shining down on us seemed miraculously enlarged. I began to shiver uncontrollably, though the cold was scarcely the sole cause. M. Tartuffe arranged heavy tartan blankets over us, and wrapped an arm around me and drew me close to him. I could feel the warmth of his body; each jolt of the sleigh threw us together in ways he contrived to exaggerate, and which I did not resist, so that my various jewels had been fairly well mauled by the time we arrived at Dominic's.

He immediately ordered a private room, into which I was bustled, followed by French champagne and an accompanying platter of iced oysters.

"A slip like you must be famished," he told me. "Please eat. And drink this fabulous champagne, so much better than the sweet stuff your countrymen swill. I can see you're a young lady of refined inclinations, and will appreciate a taste of my homeland."

I wondered how long he intended to sustain the absurd fiction of my sex.

He wished to hear all about my school, my classmates, my hobbies. He was most intrigued by my tales of La Karsavina, which made me regret having divulged them. Given his initial reaction, he was exceedingly patient with my stutter.

He also told me about himself, how he had grown up in Paris, and from an early age had adored the works of Tolstoy and Turgenev. All the happier, then, when he found himself posted, after a lively stint in Teheran, as cultural attaché under the employ of Maurice Paléologue, France's ambassador to the Imperial Court.

Seeing he was a diplomat, or at least posing as one, I asked if he had ever known my Uncle Ruka.

"Why, yes," he told me. "I knew him quite well, in Bokhara. We were guests of the Emir, and once hunted antelope together in the Tien Shan mountains. And when we returned, the Emir provided for our entertainment a band of itinerant singing boys of a type quite common in the region. *Bachi*, I believe they were called. They wore lovely bright costumes, and groomed themselves as finely as women."

I was virtually certain my uncle had never been anywhere near Bokhara, as he professed a horror of our Central Asian territories; furthermore, I could scarcely imagine him hunting. But M. Tartuffe, whoever he was, spoke with such assurance that I hadn't the heart to call his account into question.

When we had consumed most of our bottle, and all but a few of the oysters, he instructed the waiter, "Leave us for half an hour."

"Now," he said, moving closer to me on the banquette. "Our little moment of truth. What say you to that?" Gently, with finger and thumb, he held my chin and drew close to me, and with the other hand began to disarrange Majesté's carefully arranged folds and pleats.

The reader will imagine that I closed my eyes and awaited the long-awaited inevitable. I did not. Suffice it to say that at the very moment M. Tartuffe brought his lips to mine I revolted. Why? Perhaps my head swirled with a surfeit of images gleaned from the evening. Perhaps the champagne began to nauseate me. Perhaps Dr. Bekhetev and his hypnotic wand made a spectral appearance, urging me to abjure such base temptation. Whatever the case, the Russian Army's retreat from Galicia was accomplished with scarcely less haste or disarray than my own flight from that private suite at Dominic's—to the ribald amusement, I am sure, of the patrons in the main dining room.

13

I HAD FONDLY IMAGINED THE ABYSSINIANS MIGHT be brought closer by our escapade, but this was not to be the case. Genia was swept so decisively into Yuri Yurev's orbit that Davide and I seldom saw him anymore. It was as if our friend had moved to a foreign land.

Things between the two remaining Abyssinians began to alter as well.

At the Crystal Petal one afternoon, after many coffees and cigarettes, Davide confided, "I don't do it for the money, you know, but for the pleasure of slaking a vicious thirst. Do you follow what I'm saying, Seryosha?"

Strangely enough, in my still-innocent way, I did.

"Haven't you ever wished to peer beyond this city's Potemkin façade? I can take you there. I can be your guide. Just the two of us, and whatever adventures we find. Say you will. Or if not, leave me. Get up this moment, walk away, and do not look back."

He said this quite theatrically, as was his wont.

I grasped his hand even as my heart fluttered dangerously, and said, "But how could I possibly say no? You've always mattered..."

"Careful," he warned. "We mustn't get sentimental about what promises to be, after all, a nasty business."

The next day, with very little in the way of second thoughts, I kept my appointment with perdition.

Huddled together by the washbasins of a dim, aromatic public loo near the Anichkoff Bridge, the stalwart remnant of the Abyssinians smoked cigarettes and observed the variety of men who came, did their business at the urinal trough, shook themselves dry, and left. Most paid us no attention, though now and again one would linger for a few minutes when finished, finally buttoning himself up in disappointment. One elderly gentleman, who had dawdled quite a long time, treated us to an exasperated sigh as he took his leave.

My initial nervous excitement having faded, I began to wonder whether I might not have spent my time more profitably reading a book. I had only the vaguest idea, really, what Davide intended, and was no longer certain I wished any part of it. But then a decent-looking sort would happen through and my interest would return, only to be deflated by his brisk departure.

The already dismal light was fast dwindling when a soldier entered, a handsome dark-haired fellow wearing the distinctive uniform of the Volhynian regiment. I was surprised when he stayed on, looking from time to time over his shoulder toward where we stood. "Finally lightning strikes," Davide murmured. He flung his cigarette to the floor, crushed it, and sauntered over to the urinal trough. The soldier stood motionless, staring straight ahead. Davide unbuttoned his trousers. The soldier turned his head, looked down, then pivoted his body slightly toward Davide, who mirrored his movement. "You're a lucky one today," Davide said in a perfectly reasonable voice. "There's two of us for you."

"Your friend's quiet over there," the soldier observed. "You sure he's game?"

"He's not done this before, but he'll quickly loosen up. Take my word for it. Let's go along to the Baths, shall we? You'll soon have ten rubles to spend however you like."

Out in the open air, the soldier seemed wary. "Perhaps you two should walk ahead," he suggested.

"There's nothing to worry about," Davide assured him. "We're not your common types, by any means. You'll be most satisfied."

"Walk ahead," he insisted, and Davide and I complied. The baths lay just past Znamenskaya Square.

The door was open; inside, seated on a stool, a bulky man with a large mustache, his meaty arms crossed over his chest, glared at us, then made a gesture as if shooing away flies.

"Don't fear. We'll pay handsomely for the convenience," Davide announced. "Old Wealth and New Wealth go hunting together. And we don't need your catalog of beauties; as you can see, we've brought our own." To me he confided sotto voce, "Though be well advised, there are two rather exquisite twin brothers from Kaluga to be had here at a modest price. If ever you're interested."

Still impassive, the gatekeeper rented us soap and a towel and showed us to a room with a bench, a low wide bed, a washbasin. Davide ordered champagne, but before it even arrived he had begun caressing our soldier, who, when coaxed, gave his name as Kolya.

He was not half so handsome as Oleg, but handsome enough, a rough-hewn specimen blessed with a strong jaw and desperate eyes. He said he came from a village west of Arkhangelsk, which explained the provincial accent.

We stripped and, wrapped in towels, made our way across a slick floor to the pool. Steam rose from the surface of the oily water. Several big-bellied older men congregated at one end, smoking, tapping their ashes out onto the tiled edge of the pool. Otherwise, the pool was deserted. I love nothing more than a warm solitary bath in a tub. Now I squeamishly immersed myself in unhygienic communal waters. Davide and our soldier seemed unfazed, splashing water on each other, giggling like schoolboys, and at once I was back on the red clay banks of the Oredezh, watching two boys dismount their steeds to cavort in its pure waters. Oblivious to my presence, Davide and Kolya ceased their commotion and moved toward each other to embrace with almost ceremonial gravity. They did not kiss, but leaned their foreheads together, the soldier's large hands kneading Davide's thin buttocks. Slipping from his grasp, Davide took Kolya by the hand and led him from the pool. With a backward look he beckoned me to follow, but I hesitated as the two disappeared into our cubicle. I had as yet done nothing. I could put on my clothes, I could walk out of this dark place into the pale sunlight, I could yet look Father and Dr. Bekhetev in the eye.

But of course my clothes were folded neatly on the bench beside the bed Davide and Kolya had already mounted. I shut the door behind me and sat meekly as they hugged and fondled.

When I reached out to touch Davide's flank he said sharply, "Seryosha, no! Your turn's next."

As if bitten, I retreated to the bench. I had not realized the extent to which my Abyssinian brother was truly depraved. I watched, first with considerable ardor, later with increasing melancholy as he yielded himself to our soldier's brawn. Nothing had quite prepared me for the shock of that act—the raw exertion, the messiness.

When our soldier had finished with Davide, who sprawled spent across the bed, he beckoned me over. I shook my head. If I had not had the courage to leave, even less had I the courage to venture forward.

"Don't be a fool," Davide said. "You've already fallen into the lion's den. You might as well enjoy your martyrdom while it lasts."

Given the circumstances his logic was, I suppose, impeccable. Soon enough Kolya had me on all fours and was using his lion's tongue to thrilling effect.

Once the sweet ordeal was over, Kolya drank champagne from the bottle as Davide and I dressed. We pooled our money, tipped him stupendously, and left him sitting naked, still supernaturally excited and unashamed, poor scoundrel, and looking rather cheerful. Outside on the wooden pavement Davide grinned and announced, "Well, I feel like quite the shriven sinner. And you?"

But I did not know how I felt. Abjectly sorry, deliciously manhandled, rapturously fallen, defiantly unguilty, well-nigh shattered, I walked through the streets of an unchanged city a changed person, a traveler returned from a foreign and fantastical land. But unbeknownst to me, the city had changed in my brief absence as well. A great crowd thronged the square in front of Our Lady of Kazan. Many held tapers. Hymns were being sung. I was in such a daze of my own wonder that for a moment I imagined the assemblage somehow had something to do with Karsavina. Then I realized that strangers were embracing each other, soldiers were kissing civilians, well-heeled gentlemen were dancing with the meanest of droshky drivers. A very solid babushka threw her arms around me and, shaking with sobs, buried her head in my chest. I asked her what was wrong.

"Wrong?" she said. "There's nothing wrong. They've found Rasputin's body drowned in the Neva, God be praised!"

14

SUCH WERE MY CONFUSIONS AND EXHILARATIONS as the annus horribilis 1917 began to emerge from its hibernal lair. Snow and cold were exceptionally abundant that winter; food and firewood were not. Nearly every day saw a procession through the streets of red banners bearing the slogan BREAD AND PEACE! By late February, an unnerving mix of panic and gloom pervaded the city.

Davide and I had shared more expeditions into the dark continent he called "infernal Petrograd," but I sensed that he had come to see my presence as a hindrance to his more daring investigations. I gleaned from various hints and asides that he had fallen in with a rowdy crowd of officers; I noted that of late his hands had begun to tremble, and that his gaze had turned strangely vacant.

I had not realized how much I depended on my friends' company till they began to abandon me. We were to be together as Abyssinians one last time. Forget the gathering storm of rumors and pamphlets: for months *my* St. Petersburg had been abuzz with the news that the great director Meyerhold was staging Lermontov's legendarily unstageable *Masquerade,* and that the male lead was to be undertaken by none other than Yuri Yurev. The arrival of an invitation, on Yurev's stationery but in Genia's hand, to the Alexandrinsky première brought my already considerable excitement to a fever pitch.

My mother adamantly opposed my venturing out that February evening. Her attitude toward the developing crisis had recently swerved from indifference to near hysteria. Father did his best to assure her that the witches' kettle had yet weeks before reaching a boil—if it ever did. "I wouldn't worry, Lyova," he said. "People will talk this revolution to death long before it ever comes to pass."

"Perhaps if you were to accompany him," she said, but immediately regretted her words. "No, no, you must both remain here, where you'll be safe."

Father replied that he had no intention of attending the performance, as the lead actor's private life was the stuff of sordid rumor. Then he turned to me and said gently, "But I don't suppose there's any danger in your watching him from afar. He's undeniably talented."

Eventually a compromise was reached: Volkov would convey me to and from the performance in the Benz.

Save for the occasional Cossack patrol, the streets proved reassuringly deserted, the only hint of civic desperation being the long queues already forming in front of bakeries that would not open till dawn.

To my surprise, Volkov addressed me, a liberty my parents strongly discouraged in our servants. "Only hours ago," he told me hoarsely, "Nevsky was full to the brim with humanity. You wouldn't have believed it. Such a clamor. Such a sea of red flags." Then he fell silent, as if wishing me to ponder the import of his observation. But as he pulled into the square, the sight of dozens of black automobiles drawn up in rows provoked a further exclamation. "Like coffins!" he said in a tone of awe. "Like the rows of coffins after the Tsar's coronation, when all those poor revelers died in the stampede in Khodinsky meadow, and His Majesty didn't even cancel the Imperial Ball!"

As recently as a month before, Volkov would never have dared utter such a potentially traitorous aside.

Gaily dressed, my beloved Abyssinians stood on the steps waiting for me.

"Thank God you've made it through safely," Genia said breathlessly. "Meyerhold was shot at. Soldiers stopped Yuri and me, and weren't going to allow us through, until the captain of the guard recognized Yuri and apologized. But I'm told a man has been killed at the far end of the square. That's all I know. It happened before we arrived."

Davide, who had laughed nervously at Genia's report, sat down on the steps and put his head in his hands.

"He's begun taking morphia," Genia whispered in my ear. "The officers procure it from the doctors at the military hospitals." He crouched beside our companion and put an arm around him. "It's become quite epidemic, you know."

I hadn't known, and was about to inquire further when, much to my surprise, Majesté emerged from the theater, looking extraordinary in ostrich feathers and mink. "Ah, my dears, I've been sent to chaperone. We must proceed immediately to our seats. All is about to begin."

As the opening night had been designated a benefit in Yurev's honor, a special box was reserved for the actor's entourage.

"All eyes are upon us," Majesté announced rather implausibly as we entered. The others in the box rose to be introduced. Maurice Paléologue, the French ambassador, bowed gallantly, and as he did so, I was mortified to recognize in the man standing directly behind him none other than M. Tartuffe, introduced a moment later by the ambassador as his chargé d'affaires,

M. Tristan LeJeune. This was a peril I had failed to anticipate. A glance from M. Tartuffe warned me to acknowledge nothing. Fortunately, I recognized no others from the pederast's ball, though Grand Duke Nicolay was visible in the Imperial Box, along with Grand Dukes Mikhail and Boris. Neither the Tsar nor the Tsarina was present.

Majesté, who had shed her mink to reveal a rather daring décolleté, settled herself and began to survey the theater with a pair of opera glasses she drew from between her padded bosoms. Apparently satisfied with the *haute société* she no longer traversed, Majesté whispered to us, "I've been told an 'imperial surprise' awaits the end of the performance. Imagine that, my children. Our Yuri's sins are widely known, and especially displeasing to Her Majesty the Tsarina. It happened well before your time, *mes petits*, but let me tell you: it was no scantiness in the divine Nijinsky's costume that caused the Imperial Ballet to fire him. No, no. It was pretty Vatza's, shall we say, *unusual* relations with Diaghilev that reached the Tsarina's ears. Of our Yuri's predilections she is said to have complained, 'Yurev is like the ocean, and mothers with sons must live in fear of oceans.'"

The rise of the curtain interrupted Majesté's revelations. The theater lights had not been turned down. Nothing separated us from the stage: the opulent, oversized set was the space of our own homes and palaces stretched to dreamlike proportions, lit by a thousand candles and backed by mirrors that reflected the dazzling audience back to its own dazzled self. Vases and pots and tubs of the most fragrant hothouse flowers—jasmine, camellia, gardenia—bloomed everywhere on that stage, sweetly corrupting the hall with their scent.

Much has been written about the extraordinary production, at once fantastical and disquieting. Beneath the precisely scored patter of the dialogue (Meyerhold's famous "biometrics"), Glazunov's melodies slithered like black serpents beneath bloodred roses. As the murderous lover Arbenin, Yurev seemed to have distilled into a clear and bitter cordial those elements I had earlier remarked in his character—Byronic nonchalance, a slightly sinister corpulence combined with a weightless darkness where one imagined his soul should be.

From time to time I permitted myself to glance over at Genia, who sat engrossed by the spectacle before him. What did he see as he gazed so intently at the stage that was no longer a stage, really, but our own unreal world? Of everyone in this audience, he alone had been chosen to enjoy awful intimacies with the actor who mesmerized and, truth be told, frightened us all. *Yurev is like the ocean, and mothers with sons must live in fear of oceans.* Wasn't drowning the most gorgeous of deaths? As I watched his delicate profile, his upturned nose and long eyelashes, I pitied Genia, I envied him, I felt the current sweep him so far out into perilous waters that no one could any longer rescue him.

Beside me, Davide had fallen asleep, or passed out, his head resting on Majesté's bared shoulder.

What I could not see, however, preoccupied me as much as what I could—namely, the presence of M. Tartuffe, whose coldly amused gaze I could feel taking liberties with the defenseless back of my neck. Once the performance was over and the applause began, how was I to escape without being accosted? At the same time, I entertained the feverish notion that should M. LeJeune speak to me afterward, I should be unable to resist, and would acquiesce in whatever wickedness he might propose.

Thus my thoughts roiled as the climactic masked ball commenced. The stage filled with Harlequin and Columbine, Pulchinello and Pierrot, a host of masked men in fezzes and turbans, a wild tribe of women in harem garb. I suddenly sensed that the entire performance was a reenactment, for my benefit alone, of the infernal pederast's ball. Indeed, I suspected in Yurev's invitation of LeJeune to his box the laying of a deplorable trap for which I began to feel almost grateful.

Scarcely had I stumbled upon that thought when, to music gone suddenly quiet and disquieted, the figure known as The Stranger strutted onstage. Clad in black domino and white mask, self-possessed and vile, he enticed the motley crowd into an increasingly lascivious orgy of pantomime. I conceived the tormenting notion that, were The Stranger to remove his mask, he would reveal himself as none other than M. Tartuffe, and it was all I could do to restrain myself from turning around in my seat to make certain that M. LeJeune had not vanished from our box and reappeared onstage. At the height of the frenzied music and miming, Davide woke with a start, letting out an alarmed little cry, further taxing my nerves. Drawing two fingers across my brow, I discovered I was sweating.

At once the music ceased. The Stranger turned, glaring at his foolish followers, freezing them instantly in their tracks. In a weirdly staccato voice he dispensed his famously ambiguous advice to Arbenin, and now his band of maskers swirled like irrepressible thoughts around the tormented husband, even so far as to hide him completely from our view.

Then the end. The anguished atonement. The church bells and somber choir. From the audience, rapturous applause, that ponderous rhythmic Russian applause I have not heard in years and never expect to hear again. Bouquets of roses handed all around. Laurel wreaths bestowed. When Yurev came out for his bow, the audience rose as one. Then the solemn announcement from a red-liveried imperial deputy: Nikolay II, Tsar of all the Russias, Tsar of Kazan, Tsar of Astrakhan, Tsar of Poland, Tsar of Siberia, Tsar of Georgia, Grand Duke of Smolensk, Lithuania, Volhynia, and Finland, Prince of Samarkand, etc., etc., hereby bestowed upon his loyal and valued subject Yuri Yurievich Yurev a gold cigarette case emblazoned with a diamond-studded, double-headed imperial eagle.

"Well, my dears, now what do you think of that? Isn't there a fascinating moral here somewhere? Isn't it a perfect coda to such a strange vision? Theater and life blend so seamlessly sometimes." Majesté beamed at us, looking as proud as if he were Yurev's own mother. "Come, Genia," he cooed. "I am charged with escorting you directly to Yuri's dressing room. He has his own surprise waiting for you there."

Genia smiled at us, frail and slight, as Majesté took him tenderly by the hand.

But now I must face my own ordeal, and indeed, M. Tartuffe accosted me the first chance he saw. When I boldly met his eyes, the expression I saw there, cold and taunting, shocked me.

"I'm truly gratified to see that mademoiselle made it home the other night without incident," he murmured.

I had expected a wolf's gleam in his eye, a kindling of warmth. His abrupt manner brought out the worst in my stutter. I stood frozen, unable to utter a word as that look of consternation he had initially exhibited toward my affliction returned, and I saw whatever confused reveries I had entertained throughout the last two hours evaporate, much as the unreal world of the stage had shortly before. With a beautifully correct about-face he left me there, and I distinctly remember the smart click of his heels as he walked away.

"Ugh!" Davide consoled me as we left the theater. "I saw you with him at the ball. What an ape. You can do much better for yourself, I should think. You must meet my officers, I've decided, and soon. You won't recognize yourself any longer, once they're through with you."

Glimpsing Volkov standing in the crowded square beside our Benz, I offered my dear friend a lift.

"No, no," he said. The trams were still running, and in any event he surmised a brisk walk would do him some good.

"Well then," I told him, "till we meet again." We gazed on each other for a long moment. He surprised me by kissing my cheek. With a pang of distressed affection I watched him cross the emptying square.

"The sooner we get you home, the better," Volkov admonished. "I've been looking around, and I don't like the things I see."

The bread lines I had noticed earlier had strangely disappeared, and the trams seemed to have stopped running. Davide would have a longer walk than he had planned.

Normally a cautious driver, Volkov seemed agitated, accelerating and slowing in fits and starts. In the distance I heard what sounded like a gunshot, but the sound did not repeat and so I was not certain what I had heard.

Volkov broke the silence. "Will you look at that?" he said. The unsteadiness in his voice struck me. I saw him shake his head and point, but I could see nothing. We drove through one intersection, then another before I realized what he had remarked. On rooftops overlooking each crossing, Cossacks had begun setting up machine guns.

15

BERLIN
NOVEMBER 30, 1943

ALL AFTERNOON, LEADEN SKIES HAVE OFFERED the prospect of an evening's respite from the RAF, and they do not fail to deliver. Snow begins to fall around eight and continues nearly till dawn. No one heeds the curfew; the streets of Berlin are thronged, young and old alike taking advantage of this lull. The atmosphere, despite everything, is festive. Cafés and dance halls stay open long past midnight. The coal fires burning out of control in backyard after backyard seem cheerful rather than ominous, though the loss of the city's recently delivered winter fuel supply will be grievously felt later on. But for now it scarcely matters. We are alive, we are alive. People gather around those pyres, warming themselves as they have not been warmed in their homes for weeks, singing hymns that normally would be *verboten*, and praying to a God who has been distinctly absent of late.

I walk the night, momentarily free from fear, ravished by this ruined city's ghastly beauty as snow settles everywhere, softening the blackened debris, obscuring the mortal wounds, and suddenly I am remembering, helplessly, a late spring afternoon high in the mountains, somewhere along the flanks of the Grossvenediger, where Hermann Thieme and I are surprised in our sunny ramble by a glittering snow squall blown in from nowhere, and Hermann in a transport of sheer joy lifts his arms into the air to welcome this whim of Nature, and as he does so his shirt rides up, exposing to view an expanse of smooth stomach, and impulsively, gratefully, in pure tribute I kneel before him and kiss him there on his taut belly, grazing my lips along smooth skin, savoring that narrow furry trail that leads southward from his elegant little navel, and there has never, I think, been a more perfect moment in the history of the world.

Love of my soul. Heart of my heart. It is two years since the police escorted us from our fool's paradise in Castle Weissenstein. Two years since Hermann was sentenced to the 999th Afrika Brigade. Penal battalions are valued as "tramplers" in minefields. They are useful in spearheading suicide attacks. They make excellent decoys, and are superb at drawing enemy fire. Wehrmacht doctors are not permitted to treat the wounded. It is forbidden to bury the corpses. Those few who survive their sentence earn the right to serve as regular infantry on the Eastern Front.

I will not see Hermann again. Never, never, never, never, never.

16

ST. PETERSBURG

FOR THE NEXT SEVERAL DAYS NO ONE DARED venture forth. Father spent hours in his study, conferring by telephone with Miliukov and other members of the Duma. Every now and again he would descend the stairs to announce another bit of rumor or news: the police had fired on workers; certain army units had refused to fire on those same workers, and had begun firing instead on the police; the entire Volhynian regiment had massacred its officers and gone over to the workers; scores of police stations were in flames; the Peter and Paul Fortress was under siege; the prisons had been emptied; strikers occupied the Winter Palace. General Khabolov had informed the Tsar that he could no longer maintain order in the city.

Then the final blow: the Cossacks of the Escort and the Regiment of His Majesty, the elite of the Imperial Guard, abandoned the Tsar and joined the rebellion.

I have never been the least bit brave. I remember, as a child, how I feared carriage rides on rough roads, a swing pushed too high, Golliwog in the picture books, candles flickering in an unfamiliar bedroom. But I had never known terrors like those which surrounded us that February afternoon as sounds of gunfire from the street penetrated every part of the house.

For several hours, just outside our front door, a body lay on the pavement. I could not bear the sight, and yet somehow I could not bear the thought of that body unattended. I kept creeping up to the window and peering down, as if my intermittent vigil could offer either of us any consolation. The poor soul had lost one of his shoes in the melee, and the sight of his stockinged foot was somehow the most shocking aspect of that scene. Though I now daily walk past scores of corpses in hideous states of desecration, that image remains imprinted on my memory: I had never seen anyone dead of violence before.

On the third day of the crisis we could hear prolonged machine gun fire from farther up the street, toward Maria Square. From the oriel in my mother's boudoir we could see smoke and flames in the vicinity of the Astoria Hotel.

Soon refugees from the fighting began to arrive at our door. The first was Yuri Rausch's mother and her second husband, Admiral Kolomeytsev. While Aunt Nina wept in my mother's arms, the imperturbable old admiral told a horrifying story: a mob had gathered in front of the Astoria, demanding that any officers within who remained loyal to the Tsar should be turned over. Their demands were met with machine gun fire. With dozens of their comrades wounded or dead, the enraged crowd stormed the hotel, seizing several officers even as they tried in vain to disguise themselves by tearing off their epaulettes. They were summarily dragged down to the square and executed, courtesy of the same machine guns that had earlier inflamed the crowd's bloodthirst.

Bundled in old cloaks, the admiral and his wife had made their escape by a servants' entrance in back.

Not long after, an English officer known to my father arrived to hand into our care a frightened Belgian family with small children, whom my mother suggested my brother and I divert as best we could. Having scarcely stirred all day from the sofa where he lay composing a poem, Volodya felt roused enough by the children, two ringleted girls and an adorable dark-eyed boy, to demonstrate some magic tricks I had not seen him perform in years. He quickly lost interest, though, and clambered back inside the impregnable shell of his poem; I remember him lying there immersed in reverie, oblivious to the occasional rattle of gunfire.

As I have never mastered even the most rudimentary magic trick, and the children remained in dire need of attention, I fell back on a piano game, a sort of "name that tune," which the children found highly unsatisfactory. Before long I had abandoned our refugees to their own devices in order to pace fretfully from room to room. In the downstairs vestibule, a blue vase held a bouquet of ivory-hued roses; throughout the day I kept revisiting those lovely flowers, and as their pale hothouse petals dropped off one by one, I would press each to my lips.

As I passed by his sofa for the hundredth time, Volodya emerged from his Olympian preoccupation to remark, "You're acting quite the fool, you know. We either live or die. It's out of our hands. What matters is how we spend the time we're given."

After several anxious days the turmoil in the streets subsided. Father decided the time had come to make his way to the Tauride Palace, where Miliukov and other members of the Duma were gathered.

"I shall be perfectly fine," he assured my mother. "I'm no general, no grand duke. No one on the street will recognize me." He thought it best, however, to set out on foot, and alone, in order not to call attention to himself. The rare automobile that raced down Morskaya was invariably festooned with red flags. "Idiots," Father said. "They're fooling no one. Sooner or later they'll be pulled from their—"

Seeing my mother's look of alarm, he desisted. He kissed her gravely on the forehead, then made over her the sign of the cross—a gesture which, since he so seldom performed it, filled me with dread.

With a shameful wail I rushed to him and embraced him, butting my head into his chest as I used to do when I was a child. He took a step backward, clumsily patting me on the back, saying in his crispest English, "Now, now, old boy. Buck up."

With Volodya he shook hands in the best English manner.

As I had thoroughly convinced myself I would never see Father again, I spent most of the day at the piano, playing snatches of operas he and I had attended together. Once, when we had gone to the Narodny Dom to hear *Boris Godunov*, I had felt him in the seat next to me shudder as the dying Tsar—his wretchedness magnificently embodied by Chaliapin—dismissed the boyars, called for a monk's robe to be brought for him, and with an unearthly sob expired. The memory of that shudder—the palpable feeling of it—kept returning as I played through bits of *Boris*.

Late in the evening Father returned, weary but with an unmistakable lightness about him. We crowded around. He spoke solemnly. "Something great and sacred has occurred," he told us. "The Romanov dynasty is no more."

The Tsar had abdicated both for himself and his son in favor of his brother, whom the Duma soon persuaded to abdicate as well. Father himself had penned Grand Duke Mikhail's abdication.

"The Tsar seems quite relieved," Father reported. "We'll see what the Tsarina has to say when she discovers what's happened.

No doubt she'll be livid. For his part, he wishes only to retire to his estate at Livadia and grow flowers."

After three weeks' suspension school resumed, albeit with thinned ranks. I eagerly watched for Davide, but after several days it was clear he would not be among those returning. Thinking it likely his family had been forced to flee the city, as war profiteers had become targets of the mob's fury, I made my way one afternoon to the headmaster's office to inquire of Gonishev what news he might have of my friend.

I had not stood in that book-lined room since the spatterdashes episode three years before. The portrait of the Tsar above the desk had been removed, replaced with a scrap of red bunting. Upon hearing my inquiry, Gonishev gestured for me to be seated. He removed his spectacles, rubbed his eyes, replaced his spectacles on his nose, and asked, Had Gornotsvetov and I been especially good friends?

I affirmed that we were.

Gonishev considered this statement. Where the Tsar's portrait had hung, the wallpaper remained unfaded, and I could easily make out the ghostly outline of the frame. I wondered if the red bunting was meant to express genuine enthusiasm for the recent changes, or whether our headmaster simply thought it advisable. "I see," Gonishev said after a long pause. He stood and went to the window. "I'm so very sorry to have to report this, Nabokov, but your classmate perished in the disturbances. I understand he was returning home from the theater. How inadvisable to have ventured out on that night, of all nights—but who amongst us could have known?"

He turned to face me, and I was astonished to see his cheeks were streaked with tears. Only then did the nonsense he had just uttered seem possible.

"Perished—but how?" I managed to stutter.

"Pierced through the eye by a stray bullet. Absurd, really.

He was very nearly home. That's all I know. I believe his parents are no longer in Petrograd. You'll understand, I trust, the present need for discretion. I intend to post poor Gornotsvetov's obituary on the announcement board in due time, but that time has not yet come.

"When you're older," Gonishev went on, "you'll see that a brave future doesn't come without grievous expenditure. Your father understands this. I hope he understands as well the danger posed to the Provisional Government by the Soviet. Kerensky, Miliukov, your father: they serve at the Bolsheviks' pleasure. I fear the enemies of democracy bide their time. But enough. We must remember what little any of us matters, we who are in the hands of Fate. Your friend Gornotsvetov is no doubt in Paradise with the saints and martyrs. In any event, think of him that way, and pray for his soul!"

I thanked Gonishev as best I could, and wept uncontrollably in the school lavatory for some time after, scarcely bothering to conceal my state from the occasional boy who stuck his head in and promptly fled, nonplussed by my animal wails.

A clammy fog of grief enveloped the next several weeks. I could not very well complain to anyone I knew, since no one save Genia was even aware of my friendship with Davide—and for some reason I stayed away from my fellow Abyssinian.

Among the many boys who no longer attended the Gymnasium was Oleg, who I supposed had returned to his father's estate in the Ukraine. I was therefore startled one gloomy March afternoon to encounter him in the street.

"I must say I'm very happy to see you, Nabokov. I've been thinking much about you."

A few flakes sifted down in the dim light, the beginning of what would be the last heavy snowfall of that bitter winter.

"I imagined you'd left for home," I said.

"Soon. The end of the week. What a terrible mess Russia's

got herself into! Still—any day now, the British will rescue the Tsar and his family. They'll restore the monarchy in short order—and then Bolshevik heads will roll. You'll see."

He slid his arm though mine. The blizzard was intensifying rapidly, obscuring even the buildings on the other side of the avenue.

"Anyway," he went on, "I've decided to give you what you want. I've been terribly rude to you, and all you've ever been is kind to me. Mad times call for mad actions, don't you agree?"

I had no illusions. I knew he was a bully. I knew he cared not a whit for me. Nonetheless—perhaps the boldest thing I have ever done—I leaned in and kissed his cheek. Wrapping an arm around me, he drew me close.

"Then let's find suitable shelter," he murmured. "This shouldn't take long, and I do want to make you happy, Nabokov."

An archway led into an empty carriage court. He faced me against the wall, and with alacrity undid my trousers and then his own. "This is what you want, isn't it?" he whispered roughly. "Isn't this what you've been dying for? See? I'm not such a bad fellow after all, now am I?"

It was over quickly enough. For a brief moment Davide's death receded to a small spot of black in my soul, though it roared back as soon as we had finished.

"Pray for me from time to time," Oleg told me. "I'm certain we'll meet again in a better world."

I started to speak, but he warned, "You're better, Nabokov, when you're silent."

And with that he left me. I stood there trembling and sore, still aroused, still astonished, full of that precious improvident life Davide would never again know.

With some trepidation I finally called on Yurev's apartments on the Fontanka Embankment. Though it was the middle of

April, the afternoon was bitterly cold; the Neva, which had earlier begun to thaw, was once again encumbered by ice floes. Red banners flew from most every building. I had still not gotten used to strangers hailing one another on the street as "comrade!"

Genia met me at the door. He wore a white peasant smock embroidered with colorful birds over black trousers and emerald slippers. A dreamy look lit his gray eyes; a drowsy smile played across his lips. His hair had been teased and tinted, and that more than anything seemed proof that he was no longer the Genia I had known.

He told me Yurev was away at the moment, conferring with the newly formed Revolutionary Council of Actors, but would be home soon. My visit would have to be brief.

"Are you free to leave?" was the first question I asked.

"Perfectly free, but why should I want to? My parents have disowned me. I've no desire to return to that wretched school of ours. The world has quite simply broken apart. Really, I'm quite happy here in this refuge, Seryosha."

I asked him had he heard the terrible news about Davide?

He had not. Sitting on a divan with one leg coquettishly drawn up under him, he seemed oddly unmoved.

"Things were bound to end badly for our friend," he said. "He kept many of his secrets from you, no doubt many from me as well. He feared you'd despise him were you to know everything. So I'm afraid it's better this way."

He spoke with brittle certainty, and I was surprised to see how quickly he had grown into his new role. When I first knew him he was still a child, I thought. Now he had become a professional catamite—reserved, indifferent, rather cruel.

He had his own piece of startling news.

"You won't have heard. It's been kept quiet. But Majesté as well is no more. She took arsenic. No one knows why. They found her in her chambers after no one had seen her for several days. They found a note as well, which said only: *I thank God for this life which I never asked for.*"

"And how will things end for you?" I asked.

He shrugged his frail shoulders. "It's not how things end, Seryodushka. It's how they are. I'm alive. Yuri is monstrously kind to me. I've always asked only for some measure of kindness in my life, so I'm very grateful. There's nothing more to say, really."

I could see my visit had come to an end.

"Give my respects to the great Yurev," I told him.

"Do you realize," Genia said as he showed me the door, "that the Tsar's gift to my friend turned out to be the very last official act of his reign? Isn't that strange? It must auger something, though for the life of me I can't ascertain what it might be. Yuri's been teaching me to read Tarot. So perhaps one day..."

"I wish great happiness for all of us," I told him. "But I'm afraid, for the moment, I can see it no more clearly than you."

Those were the last words I ever spoke to Genia Maklakov. I have often wondered what became of him. I must confess I fear the worst.

17

IF THE FEBRUARY REVOLUTION HAD WORN AT least some of the trappings of a regular crisis, the October Revolution unscrolled with all the excitement of a shift change at a sewing machine factory. Mostly, the revolution appeared to be an excuse for everyone to get drunk: if anything can be said to have been liberated, it was the wine cellars of the Winter Palace and the city's restaurants. Soldiers and sailors who had never downed anything but vodka got roaring drunk on stately Burgundies and fabulous Tokays laid in during the reign of Catherine the Great. Dominic's resorted to guarding its cellars with machine guns, but a crowd overwhelmed them and an ugly scene ensued. Similar rampages occurred at the Great Bear and Coutant's.

A few days later, as the collective hangover brought a welcome pause to the revolutionary debauchery, Father called Volodya and me into his study to announce, quite matter-of-factly, that he thought it no longer advisable for the two of us to remain in St. Petersburg. Lenin had announced the immediate formation of a new Red Army into which the likes of Volodya and me were likely to be conscripted. "You'll go south, to Crimea, which so far has escaped Bolshevik control. The Countess Panin has generously offered you refuge at her estate outside Yalta. The weather should be lovely. It's quite near Livadia, where the Tsar, poor man, wished he might be allowed to retire.

"For the time being I remain behind, but I shall be sending the rest of the family to you soon. I've nominated myself for the Constituent Assembly. Elections will proceed as scheduled. The Bolshevik hold on power is so tenuous, Miliukov jokes that at their meetings they stand rather than sit, ready to bolt." He paused to chuckle, but his expression betrayed him.

The following day he accompanied us to Nikolaevski Station.

The train's departure having been postponed, he sat at a table in the station restaurant, drinking coffee and drafting, in his fluent script, an article whose prospects for publication, all liberal journals having been shut down by the Bolsheviks, seemed as dubious as our train's departure.

To keep my mind off our circumstances, I leaned against a pillar and watched the pigeons perched in the iron girders high above our heads. Every now and then, with a noisy flapping of wings, one would sail out in a lazy circle and return to its companions; how I envied those ordinary birds, unaffected by the human stupidities taking place below. It never for a moment occurred to me that I would never see St. Petersburg again, that the bleak sight of those pigeons in the cold damp of Nikolaevksi Station would be among my very last memories of home. A few weeks of anxiety, I thought, and all would be resolved. Father would see to that. His busy scribbling seemed to promise nothing less.

Looking smart in dark flannels, Volodya loafed about, scornfully scrutinizing the Bolshevik placards plastered about the station. Occasionally he poked at one with his walking stick, and made himself more noticeable than was prudent. The cane had once belonged to Uncle Ruka; now Volodya was using it to tap the nose of V. Lenin.

At last, after hours of delay, the Simferopol Express began venting steam. Father rose, stuffed his papers in his briefcase, briskly made over each of us the sign of the cross, and then added, almost as an afterthought, "My dear boys, I shall quite possibly never see you again."

As he walked briskly away, a figure of heroic nonchalance, Volodya exchanged with me a look I shall never forget. All his high spirits seemed to leave along with the father we loved. The gravity of our situation was inescapable.

Once sequestered in our cozy first-class sleeper, however, we opened the bottles of mineral water and Madeira, the foil-wrapped chocolates, almond biscuits, and hothouse peaches our mother had so thoughtfully supplied, and grew a bit more cheerful. As it smoothly left St. Petersburg, the express seemed little different from those *trains de luxe* we had taken in the past to Biarritz or Abbazia, and it was hard not to imagine we were once more bound to a pleasant seaside spot.

After Moscow, however, everything worsened. At each successive stop more and more soldiers, mostly drunk, scrambled on board. We gathered that news of Lenin's coup had led to widespread desertions all along the front. Homeward bound, the soldiers lolled about in the corridors singing rowdy anthems. Soon they were pounding on the flimsy door of our compartment, determined to share their high spirits with us. Volodya was equally determined that we should retain our compartment against all intruders.

"This is a quarantine compartment," he called out to our unwanted guests clamoring at the door. "Beware. There is a typhus patient in here. Can't you read the official warning posted on the door?"

In frantic pantomime he urged me to appear ill. A burst of inspiration came to me, and I took from my bag some lipstick I had almost left behind. Stippling my face with bright dots, I wrapped myself in both our woolen coats and huddled in a corner, trusting my natural scarlet flush for once to come to my aid and simulate the effects of high fever. When, a moment later, the door flew open with a crack and a young deserter staggered into the room, I was moaning in opulent misery.

"Typhus," Volodya pointed. "I've been exposed as well. You'd best protect yourself."

Behind the intrepid first soldier I could see the vacantly grinning faces of several others as they peered in.

"Believe me," Volodya continued as I launched into a further fit of moans and trembling, "we have papers here from Dr. Bekhetev. I wouldn't wish this condition on any of you."

The soldier, stupidly handsome in his way, looked doubtful, but already his wiser comrades were seizing him by the shoulders, tugging him out of harm's way. When it became clear that we had prevailed, Volodya smiled at me and said, "Well done, Seryosha." I was seventeen and a half years old. He had never in that many years said such a thing to me, and the gift was welcome and sweet.

Our cheer was soon cut short by a distressing new development. The soldiers had somehow managed to climb onto the roof of our compartment, where they renewed their efforts to oust us by urinating into the ventilation hatch. Eventually they tired of their sport, and departed by twos or threes at the interminable stops we made at every small station along the route, so that by the time we reached Kharkov the morning of the third day, our tormentors were nowhere to be seen.

It was later that day that I nearly lost Volodya. The Simferopol Express, which had long since become entirely local, had stopped at yet another dreary station. Against my nervous wishes, Volodya insisted on getting off to stretch his legs. From the window I watched him and Uncle Ruka's estimable cane promenade up and down the platform, where other, less sympathetic eyes watched as well. All at once the train gave a start and began to pull from the station. Volodya made for the steps but stumbled, propelling Uncle Ruka's cane onto the tracks. He looked up at me, holding up his hands in what seemed both surprise and wonderment. "Come on," I shouted, but he stood where he was, an impossibly stylish and forlorn figure receding slowly as the train began to pick up speed.

Never have I felt at such a complete loss. I considered leaping from the train to join him, but the thought of consigning our luggage to certain oblivion was unthinkable. Thus I did nothing, refusing to admit, in my shock, that in an instant everything had changed forever. Scarcely a quarter of an hour earlier I had been preoccupied with what would happen to my schooling, and Volodya had been speaking of returning soon to St. Petersburg to retrieve the butterfly collection he had left behind. Now that sullen row of muzhiks who had watched from their benches as he promenaded gaily about the platform were no doubt beating him bloody, stripping him of his finery, taking revenge for the very existence of thoughtless families such as ours in their newly ascendant world. With that thought I quickly finished off the half bottle of Madeira that remained.

How could we have been so foolish—all of us?

Numbly I tried to word the cable I would be forced to send from Yalta to my disbelieving parents. That strange exercise calmed me a bit.

From his leather portmanteau I removed on impulse the single thing Volodya had brought along from his precious collection: a sphagnum-filled larvarium—all that was left me of my brother save the words with which I would convey his demise. In the box, like shrouded mummies in a tomb, lay several fat pupae he had been nurturing.

Then with amazement I saw a wriggle of movement. In the

warmth of our compartment, perhaps jostled out of its sleep, urged forward, like us all, toward difficult metamorphosis, a brownish moth was hatching, wet-winged and dazed, before my eyes.

"What have you there? Careful. Well, what do you know." Volodya was beside me, peering into the box, prodding with his finger, not acknowledging my incredulous whoop of drunken joy at the sight of him. "You little fellow." He addressed the creature by its scientific name. "What a world you've decided to come into."

"But how…?" I stammered.

"Simple. I waited till the last car had passed, snatched my walking stick from the tracks, and relied on a strong-armed hero of the revolution to lend me his outstretched hand from the caboose. Unfortunately, the knob is all smashed now. By the way, where's the rest of that Madeira? I feel I really must go make him a gift."

18

CAMBRIDGE

"LET'S BEGIN AT OUR FRONT DOOR," SAID VOLODYA. "Number 47 Morskaya. We'll be walking in the direction of Nevsky Prospect. At Number 45 we pass Prince Oglonski's, then the Italian Embassy at 43, and the former German Embassy at 41. We reach Maria Square. Beyond the lindens in the small park on the north side of the square you can glimpse the dome of Saint Isaac's. To the south stands that mediocre equestrian statue of Nikolay I. Past the eastern edge of the square we come to the Hotel Astoria. And then—"

He paused. In reality, we were strolling The Backs in Cambridge, England. Two and a half years had passed since our escape from Russia; Volodya and I were beginning our third year at university.

"And then—but what comes next?" he asked me. "What's the building next to the Astoria? I can't visualize it at all."

I laughed and told him I wasn't sure either.

"But it's no laughing matter," he exclaimed. "Don't you see? Already it's beginning, that hideous process of decay. Our beloved Saint Petersburg is beginning to disappear before our very eyes. Seryosha, we must face the appalling truth."

I reminded him that the city itself remained firmly ensconced on the banks of the Neva, the shores of the Bay of Finland.

"Pah! Today's Petrograd isn't the Saint Petersburg we once knew. Were we to sneak across the border and make our way to its once-familiar streets, we'd recognize nothing. No, what concerns me is the Petersburg preserved in here"—he touched his forehead, then his heart. "And that indelible city is vanishing as we speak, and stroll, and sip tea, and very soon, I fear, I shall be left with nothing but a few stray phantoms, misremembered relics, the odd bit of déjà vu, then nothing at all."

I told him I was content to enjoy our autumnal walk.

"Yes, yes, it's perfectly fine," he said, as if observing for the first time the lawns, the willows, the towers and spires in the distance. "An entirely plausible landscape, except for the lethal fact that it's so relentlessly crowding out the past I love. Not just the material landscape of buildings and rivers and trees, but people's faces as well, the scent of Russian lilacs at dusk, the noontime dance of sphingid moths among the allée of oaklings at Vyra, the sound of the warmhearted Russian language speaking incessantly through my dreams."

I foolishly mentioned that I, for one, welcomed the opportunity to gain a richer, more supple English. "What use is Russian to us now, anyway?" I asked.

He looked at me as if I had slapped him across the face.

How difficult to convey the strange tenor of those eighteen months during which we scattered Nabokovs gradually regrouped in Crimea, where we perched precariously, swimmers about to dive into exile but still hesitating, clinging to the ever-diminishing hope that events might yet relieve us of that necessary plunge. They did not.

In January 1918, the sailors of the Black Sea Fleet mutinied, massacring their officers and declaring allegiance to the Bolshevik regime. In Yalta, on the elegant esplanade, sailors tied stones to the feet of native Tatars and refugees alike, dispatched them with pistol shots to the head, and threw the bodies into the water.

Then in April the Reds suddenly withdrew, to be replaced, courtesy of the Treaty of Brest-Litovsk, by a well-provisioned, smartly uniformed army of Germans. Overnight, chaos gave way to order. Handsome soldiers handed out cigarettes and sausages. On the emerald lawns of public parks neat little signs warned one to keep off the grass. Cafés and restaurants that had shuttered themselves in terror reopened, and it was once again safe to travel from Countess Panin's estate at Gaspra into Yalta, where we gazed into the shallow waters of the harbor at the ghoulish crowd of upright corpses gently swaying in the back and forth of the tides.

In July news arrived that the Tsar had been executed in Yekaterinburg, soon followed by rumors that his entire family had perished as well.

When November came, the orderly Germans effected an orderly disappearance and were replaced by the Whites, whose occupation, despite the nominal fact that they were "on our side," proved nearly as frightening as that of the Reds had earlier.

The ordinary and the perilous mingled farcically. There was the afternoon when my piano playing was interrupted by the arrival at our door of a clutch of sailors who had evidently been drinking and debauching for days; heavily armed, with ammunition belts slung across their chests, they also sported brooches and diamond tiaras and long strands of pearls. Their uniforms and faces were ominously smeared with blood. As our trembling servant Ustin explained, "Our friends here were drawn by your melody. They wish to enjoy it again, if you'd be so kind. They wonder if you might sing for them as well."

Uncertain whether I could accurately recall the words to Uncle Ruka's barcarole, but reminding myself that, since the verses were in French, it did not particularly matter, I began the gently undulating figure in the left hand, then added the delicately scented melody, and as if by a miracle the words came: "*Un vol de tourterelles strie le ciel tendre / Les chrysanthèmes se parent pour la Toussaint.*" I held my own till the song had come to an end in a cadence of three bittersweet chords. Two of the sailors were sobbing like girls. "Again," Ustin urged, and I complied. I believe I played and sang Uncle Ruka's unforgotten song half a dozen times before the sailors, almost comically unsteady on their feet, lurched at Ustin, my father, Volodya (the women in the house had hidden themselves upstairs), embracing each in turn with clumsy hugs and slobbering kisses. I remember meeting Volodya's eyes as he stood stoically, clasped by a lipsticked young murderer who insisted on kissing my brother's neck, his cheek, his bitterly compressed lips, leaving a blood mark everywhere his own rose-red lips touched. Then merrily, they staggered out of the house and down the road, hooting as they went their rough approximation of Uncle Ruka's fastidious melody.

Against such a baleful backdrop, I found myself from time to time slipping into one of Yalta's humble Orthodox chapels. I did not consider my impulse religious so much as the simple need for momentary refuge from too much reality. I knelt before gilded icons and tapers lit by pious old ladies. Always I left those dim, aromatic sanctuaries feeling as at peace as it was ever possible to feel in those distinctly unpeaceful days.

In the meantime, I had a brief and unhappy fling with a young dancer named Maxim, and an even briefer but rather more satisfactory liaison with a German officer. Volodya had more affairs than anyone could keep track of, lyrical spasms he converted with great efficiency into the poems he regularly recited behind closed doors to my parents. Occasionally we would be visited by Yuri Rausch, who was with Deniken's army in the north as they attempted to stave off the Bolshevik effort to retake the peninsula. He was more charismatic than ever, but disappointingly aloof, on one occasion rudely rebuffing my attempt to resume our conversation about friendship from some years before. Instead he chose to spend his time discussing the volatile political situation with Father, or taking long walks with Volodya in the hills above Yalta. Then one terrible day came the news that he had been killed in action.

I remember knocking on the door of my brother's bedroom, expecting to find him sitting in the dark, perhaps gazing out the window, alone with his grief. Instead he was at his desk, intently fixing a butterfly specimen to a board, the beginnings of a new collection to replace the one he had been forced to leave behind.

"I'm very sorry," I told him.

He did not turn to look at me, nor did he speak. With precision he pierced a beautiful brown-and-orange butterfly's thorax with a pin. I wondered whether I should continue with the course I had rehearsed. Foolishly I decided to.

In limpid, unstuttering, astutely memorized prose I recounted to him the story of my friendship with Davide Gornotsvetov, its shocking end, my grief, and how, over time, that grief had faded into a belief that the dead do not vanish entirely but remain with us, watching over us.

When I had finished, he turned around and looked at me strangely.

"Seryosha," he said, his voice uncommonly gentle. "I appreciate your attempts to comfort me. Really I do. But please, don't persist in inventing a past for yourself."

I asked him what on earth he meant.

"If what you say happened, why have none of us heard of

this Gornotsvetov? Did he ever come to our house? Was he ever introduced to our parents? How well could you have known him? And wouldn't you have at least mentioned his death at the time, if it indeed occurred as you say it did?"

It was true: suspecting they would not have pleased my parents, I had kept my friends to myself; I had suffered my grief in lonely silence. Still, I protested to Volodya that he had seen me with Davide any number of times. Our paths used to cross all the time in St. Petersburg, afternoons after school when he was out strolling with Valentina. Didn't he recall the tall, slender boy by my side? The Abyssinians, we called ourselves. The Left-Handed Abyssinians.

"I remember no tall, slender boy. I've never heard of any Left-Handed Abyssinians. Please, Seryosha, you'll end up evaporating into thin air if you keep replacing reality with your own wistful inventions. Now, please, I've got some work still to do this evening. So if you wouldn't mind..."

Thus I was again left alone with my grief. Yuri Rausch had astonished me one summer afternoon, when he and my brother had bathed in the Oredezh. He had kissed me once. He had listened, sympathetically I thought, to my dream of friendship. And he had afterward neglected me so studiously that I came to suspect he knew my secret and was repulsed. He had been Volodya's great friend, never mine—but I wept tears for him that were as real as if he had been.

19

NOT LONG AFTER, AS THE SITUATION DETERIORATed into desperation, we exchanged Yalta for Sebastopol, but were soon forced to flee aboard a Greek steamer bound for Constantinople and thence Piraeus. After a sojourn of some weeks in bright, dusty Greece, during which Volodya managed to cultivate three separate love affairs and I none, we eventually made our way to London. Father's elder brother Konstantin, who had been the chargé d'affaires at the Russian Embassy until the Bolsheviks stripped him of his position, met us at Victoria Station, and set the family up in an alarmingly expensive flat in Kensington. Soon, Volodya and I were enrolled at Cambridge, he at Trinity and I at Christ's, thanks to a scholarship that had been established to aid indigent émigrés. Hard to believe that is what we had become.

But what a paradise my new home seemed! How I loved the mellowed stone, the venerable rituals. I loved the academic gowns worn by dons and undergraduates alike—as if we were all participants in a medieval pageant at once whimsical and perfectly serious. I loved that pale, long-haired Milton, "the lady of Christ's," had written poetry under the mulberry tree in the Fellows Garden. Even the battered old bicycle that served to transport me from lecture to lecture in halls scattered across the narrow-laned town seemed well-nigh timeless.

I found the English on the whole to be quite sympathetic, despite their tiresome desire to discuss "the Russian Crisis" with every Russian they came across. Most showed themselves to be hopelessly gullible; Bolshevik propaganda, crude though it was, found in them an ideal audience. But my only real complaint about England was this: I was cold all the time. It may seem an odd complaint for a denizen of arctic clime to lodge, but in Russian houses wood fires blazed warmly throughout the winter; I was woefully unprepared for how parsimonious the English were with their coals.

I quickly fell in with a very gay crowd, and if the world around me had admirable depth, my loves in those years were blessedly shallow. All that anguish expended on the likes of Oleg and Davide had taught me a valuable lesson. No more would I fall deeply for anyone—and since no one else in my set did either, all was well.

There are few things more heavenly than drifting in a punt on a lazy summer afternoon. *Hat Trick*, *Sheet to the Wind*, *Careless Destiny*: I still recall their whimsical names. My friend and I and a portable gramophone playing Al Jolson crooning "Coal Black Mammy" or that foxtrot we couldn't get enough of during 1921, "Forty-seven Ginger-headed Sailors." My friend changed with the season: Francis Snell, so delightfully musical; brilliant Stanley Haycroft; Percy Duvall, who was, come to think of it, something of a bully; Maurice Upton-Grainger, exhibiting even then aspects of the dipsomania that would kill him prematurely; gallant Nigel Hebbelwaite. In those halcyon days, among that bright young crowd, an affair could mean anything from protracted deep gazing into another's pupils to the full-throated reenactment of fondly remembered Etonian high jinks. I asked little of these charming and varied relationships, and I got exactly what I asked. Of them all, the loveliest was Hugh Bagley.

I fell in with Hugh one night at the Portland Arms, a pub forbidden to undergraduates (as they all were). A certain set I found congenial frequented its paneled rooms, drinking Brandy Alexanders and listening to jazz played on a phonograph set up behind the bar. Hugh's gray eyes and luscious lips immediately attracted me, as did the chic figure he cut in his black-and-white-checked "stovepipe" trousers. That he was quite drunk and had been stood up by a dear friend made my conquest of him, rather excitingly undertaken in a punt moored near the Trinity bridge, absurdly easy. That might well have been that, but he sent me the next day a vase of beautiful jonquils with a gallant card expressing the hope that he had not been too forward, and wondering if we might soon lunch together. Surprised that he even remembered my name, given his advanced state of inebriation, and frankly astonished to find that he thought *he* rather than I had been the aggressor, I accepted his invitation. We had just enough in common to ensure some jolly times together.

He made it quite clear from the beginning that his destiny, as the eldest scion of the Bagley clan, was marriage and family—the fortunate girl, one of the Morris-Stanhopes from Buckinghamshire, having already been determined. Nonetheless, it is to Hugh that I owe one of the most deeply serious experiences of my life.

In 1921, toward the end of spring vacation, I traveled down to Somerset to stay with him for a few days at his family's Westbrook House. I had never ventured into England beyond Cambridge and London. We drove round to a couple of Norman churches, had pints in the local pub, visited an elderly friend of his who restored antique clocks and another who, though stone deaf, managed a lively conversation while serving us crumpets and sherry. We took his Irish Wolfhounds, Hansel and Gretel, for long, muddy walks. On the final afternoon of my visit, informing me that he had saved a great treat for the very last, he walked me down to a small barn at the edge of a field. Two farmhands waited there. When they threw open the large double doors, Hugh invited me to peer inside.

In the semidarkness startled doves flapped. I was not at first sure what I was seeing.

"Her wings are folded. We'll put them right when we bring her outside."

"She" turned out to be a de Havilland Moth—a handsome, bright red, two-seater biplane. Her attendants pushed her out into the sunlight and began the task of moving her wings into place.

"You're proposing we go up in this machine? Can you fly it?"

"Of course and of course. Unless you're too frightened. I've been up two dozen times or so, with nary a hitch."

I told him the "nary" made me a bit anxious.

"I've gotten much, much better on landings. Trust me."

He had thoughtfully brought along a flask of whisky for encouragement, and had halfway fitted me into a leather flight jacket, cap, and goggles before the enormity of what I had agreed to do fully struck me.

"You never told me you had an interest in aeroplanes," I told him.

"I'm many-faceted, as I hope you know by now. It'll be surprisingly cold up there, and the wind is terrific. We won't be able to converse. So if you've any last words for me, say them now."

I laughed nervously. Were the two young brutes not in attendance I would no doubt have told him, "I love you, crazy Hugh," but in their presence I asked only, "Have you taken your betrothed up?"

"Never. She refuses to go. I suppose there really are certain pleasures one can only enjoy with other men!"

On that merry note, the laborers having secured the Moth's fragile-looking wings in place, we finished off the flask, climbed into our respective cockpits, and strapped ourselves in. The motor turned over, sputtered, caught. Hugh taxied slowly onto the grassy airstrip. With dashing sangfroid he gave a thumbs-up to his groundsmen and we were off, jostling along the uneven turf as the elms at the far end of the field rushed nearer (so this was how I would die), and unsteadily at first, then with more assurance, we found ourselves airborne. The air streamed past us, we climbed, we banked, the green earth upended itself, then straightened out. My heart was beating like a racing stallion's; any moment now it would burst. Fear did not leave me, but instead commingled with jubilation. The sky was a cloud-flecked blue. Below us lay the house, the gardens, the road leading to the village, the village itself, and beyond the pied roofs the irregular chessboard of fields dappled with earthbound sheep safely grazing, farther on the darker woods, purplish low hills, and in the far distance what must be the Bristol Channel and Wales: our world as angels see it.

As far as I knew, no one else in my family had flown—with the exception of Uncle Ruka, whom everyone thought was half mad. And so he was, I thought giddily, and so am I. What heights we had known, Ruka and I, what exhilarations—while all the proper, normal world slumbered unaware. Thus in his honor I said a little prayer to the martyred Saints Sergius and Bacchus, those secret Christians, soldier friends whom I had always imagined were lovers as well. For a few fanciful moments I pretended Hugh and I were Sergius and Bacchus ascending to our reward in heaven: at any moment the winged hosts would come down to welcome us. But then I remembered that Hugh, too, had chosen the proper, normal world; Uncle Ruka and I were alone in our fugitive ecstasy, and Uncle Ruka of course was dead, so I was very much on my own. So be it. In my delirium I could practically imagine casting off the straps that secured me, hoisting myself out of my seat, perching for a moment on the wing, unnoticed by my pilot, before launching myself into the illimitable azure. Would God's hand gently lift me up? Rather than rush toward me, would the world recede, the fields and woods and rivers knitting together in a shrinking tapestry till the whole became a blue-green orb, a dot of dim light, then nothing at all?

With a shiver I tried to imagine the presence of God, which was all at once not so difficult, as Hugh had sloped the plane into a perilous-feeling turn and to the right all was heaven's cerulean abyss, and to the left the mottled fundament of terra firma. Soon enough we righted ourselves, and my giddiness calmed. Enough of God's dazzling lure for one afternoon!

The flight of the Moth lasted fifteen minutes at most; then we were back on the solid ground that is, after all, our birthright. Staggering out of the cockpit, helped down by one of the muscular gardeners, I fell on impulse to my knees, and like my mother on her annual return to Vyra kissed gratefully the dark earth of Somerset while everyone else stared.

"You're hilarious," Hugh told me. "But you did all right, didn't you?"

"Splendidly," I spluttered. "I think I'm going to have a heart attack now. I can't thank you enough."

"Isn't it marvelous? As a hobby you absolutely can't beat it."

"Hobby?" I exclaimed. "I'd say—more like a vocation!"

20

"YOU SEE," SAID MY UNCLE KONSTANTIN, SITTING erect on the sofa in his small London flat, "the abdication of the Tsar placed me in a very difficult position. Having held the Liberal view since long before the revolution that a change in the autocratic methods of the government was a necessity, I thus stood in complete sympathy with the new Provisional Government. However, almost immediately that government began to make the series of mistakes which would ensure its eventual collapse. Miliukov's ill-conceived call for the immediate repatriation of all Russian citizens who had fled persecution by the old regime, no matter what their political affinities, meant an influx of Bolsheviks at precisely that moment when the fragile new government could least afford their presence. I can't say precisely who allowed Lenin to return from Germany, or who authorized the release of Trotsky-Bronstein, but I warned Kerensky and Miliukov time and again: if you continue to allow this indiscriminate immigration, then you cut the branch upon which you are sitting. And we know too well how they continued to cut, and how the branch came crashing down! They were men simply unfit for the task before them, Miliukov with his contempt for the uniformed generals and Kerensky with his *mania grandiosa*..."

Thus he would go on, till half a bottle of Madeira had vanished, rehearsing his litany of frustrations and disappointments. Volodya found all this intolerable, especially our uncle's dogged insistence that "under Lenin, most government posts were assumed by Jews concealed under Russian names." After a few visits, I found myself calling on my uncle alone, as Volodya suddenly had other appointments to pursue. (The names Marianna, Paola, Nina come to mind.) I would have lapsed as well, had I not soon discovered there were other, more pleasurable aspects to my uncle Kostya.

He shared, for instance, my passion for the ballet, and regularly attended the London seasons of the Ballets Russes. He had known Diaghilev since the heady days of *Mir Isskustva;* though he distrusted the impresario's silken guile and naked ambitions, he nonetheless admired his accomplishment in general, and his having brought ballet to Britain in particular.

"The man's completely devoted to the world of art," he told me. "His energy is boundless, as is his charm. Why, he could charm a dead man back to life. But if you get in his way, or oppose his will, then he'll destroy you without a moment's regret. No one's indispensable. Look at Nijinsky, look at Fokine. Now Massine's the apple of his eye, but we shall see. One must be very wary. Even *I* keep my distance, and I'm a highly trained diplomat!"

I told my uncle I should very much like to be introduced to the great man.

"He'll try to borrow money from you," my uncle warned. "For the sake of your pocketbook, I intend to keep you far from his clutches!"

With his own diminished pocketbook my uncle was

wonderfully generous, and I soon was coming up to London with a regularity I could not otherwise have afforded. And what riches there were to be discovered: *Schéhérazade*, *L'Oiseau de Feu*, *Les Sylphides*. Perhaps most remarkable was *Parade*, which had had its Paris première two years earlier and was now gracing—or sullying, depending on one's point of view—the stage of the Empire Theatre. Nothing had prepared me for that brilliant little confection, which I first saw in November 1919: Picasso's astonishing cubist costumes; Satie's droll music with its clattering typewriters and aeroplane drones; Massine's clever choreographic commentary on gestures familiar from the circus and vaudeville. Massine himself danced the Chinese Conjuror, and in the role of the Little American Girl was none other than Karsavina, escaped from Russia and looking more beautiful than ever. Nothing like it had ever graced the Russian stage. The Abyssinians' long-cherished dream of seeing Diaghilev's troupe had at last become reality. Davide and Genia would have loved the inspired irreverence of *Parade*.

"Pretty shallow stuff," Uncle Kostya said once the tepid applause petered out. "*Épater les bourgeois* is what it's all about. This Cocteau who's behind it all is frightfully conceited, I gather. Some waggish reviewer wrote that while Cocteau is perfectly aware that the sets and costumes are by Picasso, and that the music is by Satie, he nonetheless wonders whether Picasso and Satie aren't by *him*. Dreadful fellow. I believe Serge Pavlovich has now distanced himself from that little charlatan."

I told my uncle I had thought it all rather witty at the expense of things no one should take too seriously.

Uncle Kostya was nothing, however, if not serious. Father, an Anglophile himself, referred to him as "my Englished brother," and indeed my uncle had so thoroughly absorbed a special type of English solemnity that he easily out-Englished the English, as so often happens to refugees who embrace too gratefully their refuge.

"I suppose the younger generation finds all sorts of fun in improbable places. At least we now know what the fuss is about. It can't be said we're behind the times any longer!" he allowed as we headed from the theater toward a cheap but very English restaurant off Leicester Square that he frequented now that his wealth was gone. ("And to think I used to dine regularly at the Savoy!" he would exclaim wistfully.)

We had scarcely tucked into our chops when, to my surprise, I saw Karsavina herself enter the humble dining room, in the company of Massine, Nemchinova, and other members of the troupe. They proceeded to a table in the corner. Only later did I learn how continually cash-strapped was the Ballets Russes, how it was all nothing more than a glorious sham, desperate magic cobbled together nightly before the financial abyss.

After several minutes of internal struggle, I laid aside my fork and knife, excused myself from my uncle's company, and made my way to the dancers' table.

"Pardon me," I announced, blushing as I bowed. "I don't wish more than a moment of your time. Some years ago, in Saint P-P-P-P."

Of course my curse chose that moment to descend on me. Everyone at the table stared. I had no choice but to abandon my intention of invoking those long-ago midnight rambles, the discreet Abyssinian Guard that had watched over their idol so attentively. Instead I said only, "Thank you. Thank you for having shown me I was alive."

Karsavina looked at me politely, nonplussed by this stuttering, scarlet-faced stranger; then she held out her delicate hand, which I daringly raised to my lips and kissed, ever so reverently—for all the Left-Handed Abyssinians.

Still smiling a stage smile held past its natural span, she slowly withdrew her hand.

"You are very kind," she told me. "I do not know precisely what you are talking about, but you are very kind."

21

OF ALL MY PLEASANT YOUNG MEN AT CAMBRIDGE only Bobby de Calry—or to give his incomparable name in full, Count Robert Louis Magawly-Cerati de Calry—was to prove problematic. In his red shoes, Oxford bags, outrageous cravats, and fur gauntlet gloves he cut a remarkable figure even by the standards of my dashingly eccentric set. A trim mustache that would have made anyone else look à la mode on him seemed vaguely old-fashioned. There was a haunted cast to his blue-gray eyes. His eau de cologne—rumored to be made exclusively for him by Irfe, Prince Yussupov's Parisian *parfumerie*—left a distinctive fragrance in his wake. How tantalizing it was to visit Volodya in his dreary rooms and detect traces of that scent lingering in the air. For Bobby and my brother had become, improbably, the best of friends.

"He's awfully amusing," Volodya explained in that offhanded way he had acquired. "A pathetic fellow, perhaps, but remarkably droll and affable. Besides, all my Russian friends have been sent down, so I've dubbed Calry an honorary Russian. It's not too far-fetched. His mother's Russian, and he speaks it a bit himself—astonishingly badly, if you must know."

I was quite pleased to know, in fact, as I had developed a terrific smash on the young man. For several weeks that fall he had hobbled about on crutches, having broken his leg while skiing at Chamonix. This mishap lent him an attractive air of vulnerability. No doubt he was spoiled, affected, naturally moody as well. Had I spoken to him early on—and how easy it would have been to remark casually on his cast—I would not have quietly worked myself into the infatuation that ensued. By the time I realized my mistake it was too late. An unspannable gulf seemed to separate us. Did he feel it as well? Our paths would cross. We would look at each other wordlessly. Something smoldering or disconcerting or hostile—it was impossible to know which—would pass between us, sealing our mutual silence. And all the while he was on free and easy terms with my brother. It was maddening.

"But what on earth do you two *do* together?" I asked Volodya.

"Well, like normal men our age, we mostly hunt girls."

His eyes twinkled with what I could only interpret as cruel mirth while I hastened to assure him that Calry wasn't my type at all. Besides, I went on, I couldn't imagine Bobby would be the least bit interested in me.

"No," Volodya agreed, "I can't imagine he would be. It would be perfectly useless to try to know him, if that's what you're conjuring. He's perfectly normal that way."

I would see them on the tennis court, or gadding about in Bobby's powerful and illegal red Rover. (The Motor Proctors never seemed to catch him.) I would encounter them punting on the Cam beneath the horse chestnuts, my brother poling while his glamorous friend—now freed of his cast—trailed a hand in the indolent stream.

It seemed impossible Volodya had no clue as to either Bobby's history or proclivities. To me, and to many of my falcon-eyed set as well, it was all too clear that poor Bobby was mad about his Russian friend. Was Volodya simply basking in the adoration? He had begun to publish regularly under the fairy tale pseudonym "Sirin" in Father's new journal, *The Rudder.* Was he enjoying the first temptations of literary renown? Was that why he tolerated Bobby's slavish devotion?

Bobby seemed eager to do anything for his friend. He put himself and his Rover at Volodya's disposal. He had his maid take in Volodya's laundry. He stopped by in the mornings to make my brother tea, and took him out in the evenings to dinner. It was even said that Bobby regularly gave my brother his notes from the lectures Volodya never bothered to attend. That their relationship might be in any way reciprocal never occurred to me. I knew my brother too well.

All this made my jealous head throb.

It was in this disheveled state of mind that I went up to London in November to attend, with Uncle Kostya, the première of Diaghilev's much-anticipated *The Sleeping Princess.* Having recently dismissed Massine from the company, as Uncle Kostya had predicted, and thus finding himself without a choreographer, the ever-resourceful impresario had decided to revive Marius Petipa's 1890 masterpiece, *La Belle au Bois Dormant,* the very cornerstone of the "old school" Russian ballet that Diaghilev had so dramatically broken with. Stravinsky had rearranged and reorchestrated Tchaikovsky's music, and my parents' friend Léon Bakst had updated the costumes and sets.

I dressed especially well for the occasion in a secondhand dinner jacket borrowed from my brother (who had it from Rachmaninov), finishing my ensemble with a black opera cloak lined in scarlet silk I had recently purchased for a criminal sum of money. With a touch of Helena Rubinstein I deepened my colorless lips; with a dab of lilac powder I cooled my cheeks. All of this my uncle noted, and none of it did he seem to mind.

"I hear Serge Pavlovich changed the name from *Sleeping Beauty* to *The Sleeping Princess* because he claims there are currently no beauties in his troupe," he offered. For someone who, since his resignation from the Embassy, claimed to have foresworn all dinner parties, he managed to hear quite a bit about town. "Well, we shall see," he went on. "He's risked everything on this venture, poor fellow. *Sleeping Beauty* was the first ballet he ever saw. It was one of the first I ever saw as well. The great Cecchetti danced the role of the evil Carabosse, and Brianza was the good Princess Aurora. I understand that Diaghilev has coaxed Brianza out of retirement to undertake Carabosse. A splendid symmetry, don't you think? Aren't all beauties fated, eventually, to become the witch?"

With such musings, we arrived at the Alhambra in Leicester Square. In the air was all the palpable excitement that surrounds a première, and a notable one at that. I scanned the audience in the hope of glimpsing Diaghilev—the unmistakable white streak in his ebony-black hair—but he was not in evidence.

I did, however, lay eyes on the ever-elegant Bakst, who greeted me warmly; I reminded him of the fine portrait he had done of my mother, which to our great regret we had had to leave behind in our flight from Russia.

"But there is good news, Sergey Vladimirovich," he told me. "Our friend Benois has had that drawing, along with some of his own works, transferred from your former house to the new State Museum where they are now perfectly safe, or at least as safe as anything in our poor Russia can be. I've been meaning to write your parents, but as you can imagine I've been terribly overworked."

I told him how pleased they would be to hear that news, though my own emotions were unpleasantly stirred by the thought of our belongings—my father's books, my mother's beloved prints, even my brother's carefully mounted butterflies—so duly disposed of in our absence.

"Have you said hello yet to Serge Pavlovich?" asked Bakst.

I told him we had never met.

"How can that be?"

"My uncle is under the impression I should be kept from him."

"But your uncle is most fond of Serge, are you not, Konstantin Dmitrievich? I don't understand at all. At the risk of creating a scene, I'll take you to him immediately."

"That won't do," my uncle said. "Our Serge is no doubt in the green room as we speak, clutching his Saint Anthony's medallion and crossing himself like the most superstitious of old babushkas, repenting his sins and beseeching protection from all the saints and holy martyrs. I once called on him in his hotel room. When I set my hat on the bureau, he cried out, 'No! No! Do you want me to face financial ruin?' So I set it on the bed, and he cried out, 'Do you wish me disaster in love?' I set it on the chair—well, you can guess what ensued. So I ended up holding my hat for the entire visit."

Bakst laughed. "Then you must come around afterward to the Savoy. There's a dinner party in his honor. All his fears will be calmed by then, and he'll be most delighted to make your acquaintance, I'm sure."

Though I was disappointed Karsavina was no longer performing—she had recently married a diplomat who had been posted to Bulgaria, and decided to put the rigors of marriage before the demands of dance—two other favorites of mine graced the stage: Olga Spessivtseva as Aurora and the luminous Lydia Lopokova, who brought the Lilac Fairy to rich, warm life. I did not know Tchaikovsky's score, but was soon won over by its dandyish charms. Bakst's sets were superb, especially the Enchanted Palace where the princess slumbered on an enormous bed canopied with cobwebs and brooded over by two giant, thoughtful spiders. The fairies bearing their gifts for the infant princess were ravishing: how I loved the subtle way each set of gestures was later incorporated into Aurora's repertoire—their gifts nothing but the gift of dance, which is to say life itself! Everything the wicked Carabosse would destroy...

Only the occasional mechanical malfunction marred the magic that first evening: at the end of the Birthday Party, when the Princess Aurora has pricked her finger and fallen into a sleep, and the Lilac Fairy conjured a thicket of roses to protect her, the roses failed to rise from the ground at her command; and in the next scene, as the gondola bearing the Prince made its way toward the sleeping princess, the descending veils of gauze meant to indicate a gathering fog caught on a protruding pipe and piled up clumsily rather than descending gracefully. But no matter. What really mattered—the dancing—was perfection. Despite all my modern prejudices, Petipa's choreography was a revelation: here was a world of noble and harmonious form, full of lucid gestures: a bold movement here contrasted with a subtle one there, a flurry of motion was answered by the most eloquent of pauses. Through everything shone such calming certainty about what is beautiful in the world that I found myself transported to a place where beauty seemed nothing less than a birthright.

For once, Uncle Kostya and I were in perfect agreement over the merits of a performance; however, we were in less perfect agreement over Bakst's intention to introduce me to Diaghilev.

"He thrives on young men," my uncle warned me as we entered the dining room of the Savoy. "Observe his latest specimen." He pointed out a slender youth. "His name is Boris Kochno. Seventeen years old, can you imagine? And already he's aping his mentor's mannerisms. You may always tell Diaghilev's young men by their clothes. He dresses them as he dresses himself. They all wear homburgs, and their collars high, and tuberoses in their buttonholes. They even become hypochondriacs in honor of the master!"

Bakst, it soon became apparent, had been a bit too eager in extending his invitation. I could tell by his gesticulations to the maître d' that his spur-of-the-moment guests would not be admitted, even if he *were* the great Léon Bakst.

Bakst returned to us livid. "He presumes to tell me that only Serge Pavlovich or Madame Sert, who is bankrolling this little fête, can admit guests who do not carry an official invitation. And both of those individuals have simply *vanished!* There's really nothing I can do. I can labor like a slave, I can throw my soul into sets and costumes the Ballets Russes can barely afford, and for which I have not been paid a centime, but I can't bring my two friends to dinner."

My uncle seemed quite relieved, assuring him there was nothing to apologize for, that it was the thought that had counted. Disappointedly, I did the same.

"Please remember me to your dear parents," Bakst reminded me. "*Au revoir!* I must live with my great shame."

He turned his back on us and marched into the dining room, calling out merrily to the seventeen-year-old whom Diaghilev had claimed, "Borya, how are you?"

"My liver's a bit congested, I'm afraid," I could hear Kochno complain as waiters whisked past us platters of luscious-looking smoked salmon and caviar. "Otherwise I'm pretty well..."

"Fate has intervened," said my uncle, wiping his face with a handkerchief. "I shall happily treat you to some claret and a nice steak-and-kidney pie at our usual haunt. Who knows? We may well meet some of the dancers there."

We had just left the hotel when a black Hispano-Suiza pulled up to the curb. Out tumbled an absurd-looking little man whom I recognized at once as Stravinsky. He was followed by Madame Sert, a woman of striking, bird-of-prey beauty, and she by a corpulent, sweating Diaghilev.

"Kostya Dmitrievich!" He cried out in his high-pitched voice.

I could see my uncle quail. Nonetheless, he managed a cordial "Sergey Pavlovich. Greetings, my old friend."

"What news of Russia?"

The question seemed to bewilder my uncle, but Diaghilev did not appear to notice. I saw that he had been weeping, and had only just now pulled himself together. His huge dark eyes were bloodshot, his cheeks still streaked. I felt embarrassed, as if I had stumbled upon a scene never meant for my eyes.

He peered at me through his pince-nez. "And who is your young companion?" he inquired of my flustered uncle. "Yet another recent acquisition?"

My uncle bristled. "This is my most esteemed nephew, Sergey Vladimirovich."

"*Enchanté,*" said Diaghilev, clearly less interested than he had been a moment before. I bowed respectfully, and told him how beautiful had been the production, how much I had adored it in every respect.

"Nonsense!" he bellowed. "The fact is, I'm ruined. Pure and simple. There can be no recovery from this catastrophe. The entire enterprise is now cursed. I should never have attempted to revive the glories of a bygone age. What you've witnessed tonight is nothing less than the beginning of the end of the Ballets Russes. Mark my words. Within three months, you shall see me a broken man, my company scattered to the ends of the earth. Fate holds sway over us all. We're at its mercy, and it shows us no mercy, none at all."

This rather took me aback. Stravinsky and Madame looked at me as if I were somehow to blame for precipitating this outburst.

With great tenderness Stravinsky took Diaghilev's arm. "You're exhausted, my dear friend. You're making too much of too little. By tomorrow night all shall be remedied; no one will remember a thing of these little mishaps. Some champagne, the company of your friends and ardent admirers, you'll soon see that all isn't lost. Far from it: you've created a stupendous triumph tonight."

Madame Sert began to soothe him as well, murmuring into his ear words I could not make out, and the three of them began to move slowly toward the entrance of the Savoy, having already forgotten who we were, or that we were ever there.

"Well," sniffed my uncle. "He's in rare form tonight. He's the most childish of men, really. I suppose that's the price of his greatness, but it can be most dismaying. My relations with him aren't what they once were. No, not at all."

But he would say no more, neither then nor later. My uncle, I dare say, went to his grave with many more secrets than most of us.

22

BERLIN
DECEMBER 5, 1943

CERTAIN INDIVIDUALS ONE RECOGNIZES AT ONCE as Nazis. That is the case with my latest caller. He just misses being handsome; a battlefield of old acne scars desecrates his lower face. For a moment I think I know him from somewhere, but that is likely not the case. He is blunt with me.

"You are Sergey Nabokov?" he asks, showing me his warrant disk.

"I am."

"Then I must inform you that I have questions for you."

"As you wish." I motion for him to be seated in the frigid semidarkness of my room. For some reason I think it wise to offer him a drink.

"Where did you get this?" he asks once I have poured. I have forgotten that brandy is only available on the black market.

"Oh," I say, "I've had it for quite some time. I saved it for a special occasion."

"I'm no special occasion," he says, "but I'll take a drop anyway."

"Special occasions seem to arrive unexpectedly these days."

"What do you mean?"

"Never mind," I tell him. Through his stupidity, he senses I am mocking him. I know my behavior is reckless, I know I still have many pages to write, but I cannot resist. He is all the tormentors I never sufficiently resisted in my youth. "Why have you come?"

"I've been sent to ask you a few questions."

He sips his brandy. Then deliberately removes from the pocket of his coat a document which he carefully unfolds. He studies it with a frown and a squint.

"You are Russian?"

"Well, yes, quite obviously."

"Nothing is obvious," he tells me.

"You're quite right. Yes, I am a Russian émigré. I carry a Nansen passport, if you wish to see it."

"Not necessary. You arrived in Berlin on May 18, 1942. From Prague. And before that you were in Ostmark. You had been held in the jail in Lienz. For what reason, may I ask?"

"Your documentation seems quite thorough," I tell him. "I'm surprised you need to ask."

"I wish to hear it in your own words."

"I was arrested under Paragraph 129b of the Austrian Penal Code."

"And what is Paragraph 129b?"

"It's rather like the Reich's Paragraph 175. You know, criminal sexual relations with persons of the same sex."

"And what did you plead?"

"It really doesn't much matter, does it? I was convicted. I served out my five-month term and was released."

"Why did you come to Berlin?"

"I sought employment. The office where I worked briefly in Prague was shut down. My cousin suggested I come here, as various ministries were seeking qualified translators."

"And you have been employed by the Ministry of Public Enlightenment and Propaganda?

"Correct."

"Is it common for the Ministry to employ Russians who are not citizens of the Reich?"

"Quite a few Russians work at the Ministry."

"Doing what?"

"Document translation, for the most part. We're an invaluable resource. The Reich needs us for its campaign in the east."

He frowns. "Germans are not trained to do this?"

"We were in Berlin for twenty-five years, but no one bothered to learn any Russian from us. So yes, the Reich needs us. You might say the Reich depends on us."

"The Reich depends on the strength of the German people," he seems compelled to say. "That is sufficient."

"Are you questioning the wisdom of the Ministry's employment policies?"

He ignores that impertinence. We sit in the semidarkness. Seeing the papers on my desk, where I have been interrupted in my writing, he asks suspiciously, "Is this Ministry work?"

"Yes," I tell him. I show him a page. "Hold it up to the light. See? The Ministry's watermark." I do not tell him that I have been pilfering these precious blank pages one at a time over the past several months, the way my colleagues take toilet paper home.

"But this is neither German nor Russian."

"English," I tell him. "I also translate into English. My language skills are quite cosmopolitan. As you may know, the Reich is presently fighting a war on several fronts."

"And winning on each of them, heil Hitler! Then you are still employed by the Ministry?"

"Of course," I lie. "We've been asked to work from our lodgings, a way of dispersing our vital contribution to the war effort lest the Ministry, God forbid, is hit. So far it has been fortunate."

"Our antiaircraft defenses are superb. The British are losing their bombers and crews at an unsustainable rate."

"I'm glad to hear that."

"I understand you were educated in Britain."

"I was. I spent some lovely years there."

"And would you say you retain fond memories?"

"I believe I was closer to God there than I have ever been, before or since."

He looks puzzled. "Explain, please."

"Oh," I tell him, "there's nothing to explain, really. I went up in an aeroplane, quite high into the heavens."

"I see. Then that is a joke you are making."

"I suppose it is. Though it doesn't feel like a joke."

"You are religious?"

"I'm praying even now."

He frowns. In reality, he is not at all handsome.

"And about Russia," he says. "Do you have fond memories of Russia as well?"

"It hardly matters. My Russia no longer exists. Rest assured, I owe absolutely nothing to Stalin and his thugs."

"And to the Reich?"

"I've always loved Germans," I say truthfully. "My very first love was a German boy who operated the lift in a hotel in Wiesbaden. I loved a German officer in Yalta, much to my brother's disgust. I was sent to jail for loving a citizen of the Reich. But I must tell you this, lest there be any doubt where I stand. Hitler's Reich is no more Germany than Stalin's Soviet Union is Russia. They're both murderous phantoms masquerading as reality. Now, is there anything else I can enlighten you about?"

He writes on his pad, but does not look up at me. "That will be all for now," he tells me when he has finished. "You will be contacted further as necessary."

I rather wish he had said, "if necessary," but I am under no illusions. As soon as he leaves, I swig freely from the brandy bottle, till all its false promise of relief is depleted. Then I pray some more.

23

CAMBRIDGE

AT CHRISTMAS, WHILE VOLODYA VACATIONED IN the Alps with Bobby, I joined my family in Berlin, where they had moved after England proved too expensive.

Though I found Berlin depressing, evenings at our flat were enlivened by a steady stream of émigré writers and artists. Miliukov was often there, irritating my father as usual; he had begun a journal in Paris, *Latest News*, as a rival to Father's *The Rudder.* Other frequent visitors included Stanislavsky, Chekhov's widow Olga Leonardovna, and Iosef Hessen, *The Rudder's* coeditor. My cousin Nicolay, a budding composer of impressive talent, was staying with us, courting my sister Elena, which *our* mother fully approved and *his* mother did not. That rift lent the whole enterprise a tragicomic tone he exploited in full, even going so far as to assert that our grandmother Nabokova should be the final arbiter of all romantic predicaments within the family.

That truculent old lady (whom my cousin Nika drolly dubbed "La Generalsha") had recently joined us, having followed her own circuitous route out of Russia; now she and her ever-faithful Khristina commandeered a small room at the far end of the hallway. They had both aged shockingly in the last few years, but physical frailty did not in the least dim my grandmother's spirit. "Seryosha, I'm virtually held prisoner in this room," she complained. "Your mother insists on taking the chaise longue in the parlor for her own, so what choice do I have? But it's for the best. Such squalor out there! Don't say you haven't noticed. Your poor mother always was an inept *maîtresse de maison*, but now she's become *completely* hopeless."

I too had noticed with some consternation the apartment's general disarray: the overflowing ashtrays and unmade beds, the stacks of dirty plates and glasses in the kitchen.

"How your father can endure such chaos is beyond me," Grandmother went on bitterly, "but then so much about your father is beyond me. He's only brought it on himself. And the food, my dear! Sauerkraut! Wurst! Klopsen! Bah! In Russia we ate beautifully, we dined like royalty, we *were* royalty. It breaks my heart!

"At least you, my dear, still make the effort to dress well. But you're so terribly thin. You look lovesick. Can this be? How's dear little Kostya, by the way? Still the starched Anglomaniac? Does he still have his soldier friends about him? Has he told you about his dalliance with a well-known officer in the Life Guard Mounted Regiment? How he scandalized his father in those days. But I intervened; I protected him. Oh, your grandfather had no power where I was concerned. I knew everything. I could have exposed him at will. One day I should set down my memoirs. Then wouldn't everyone squirm?"

My days passed pleasantly enough. In the mornings I often went with Father and Nika to rehearsals of the Philharmonic;

in the evenings we would stand at the back of the hall, as we could not afford seats. Sometimes, afterward, I would visit the Adonis Club in Bülowstrasse, which Nika had helpfully pointed out to me, though I was too distracted by the thought of Volodya and Bobby in Switzerland to give my full attention to any pleasures near at hand. Try as I might, I could not reach the bottom of my strange and tangled jealousy. Finally we received a postcard announcing that the pair had commenced their journey north to Berlin.

Volodya, however, arrived alone, announcing that Bobby had opted at the last minute to go to Parma to visit his mother. Thus thwarted—but what exactly had I wished for?—I had to content myself with the company of Svetlana Siewert, my brother's latest flame. One thing could certainly be said about Volodya: he had become far less secretive in his amours over the years, perhaps because one had only to open the pages of *The Rudder* to follow, in verse, the tumultuous pageant of "Sirin's" latest emotions.

I warmed to Svetlana with remarkable ease. Five years younger than my brother, she had just turned seventeen, a dark-eyed beauty full of sweet and touching vitality. Her bold laughter echoed in our parlor, her musical voice cascaded down the corridor. I have never seen a young woman wear a cloche quite so perfectly.

When the weather was rotten, as it often was, she would play Brahms on the old Becker piano; sometimes I joined her for a four-handed round of Schubert while Volodya looked on with that air of indifference he assumed whenever forced to listen to music. On days when the skies cleared, we would play doubles on the deteriorating public tennis court next door, Volodya paired with Svetlana and I with her sister Tatiana. Afterward, there were visits to the konditoreis on Kurfürstendamm, or to the Russian cafés that had sprung up in Charlottenburg.

One evening my curiosity overcame me, and I pestered Volodya with a flurry of questions. Had he enjoyed himself in

Switzerland? Had Bobby had a good time? Would they repeat their adventure?

My desperation must have caught him off guard, for he said brusquely, "Calry can be a most mercurial and melancholy fellow. Now, if you please, I'm heartily tired of this subject."

For several weeks after my return to Cambridge I glimpsed Bobby scarcely at all. Then one raw evening toward sunset, as salmon clouds scudded across a sky of heart-stopping blue, our paths crossed. We looked each other over, but this time he startled me by speaking.

"I gather you're Vladimir's brother," he said.

"Quite."

"Well, I thought so." He seemed at a loss as to how to continue. For once in my life I spoke without hesitation.

"I was just on my way home to a pot of tea. Would you fancy some?"

The poverty of my rooms embarrassed me, but Count Magawly-Cerati de Calry seemed not at all discomfited. Shedding his gown to reveal a canary-yellow blazer and sapphire-blue shirt, he made himself at home by collapsing into a wicker chair that received him with an arthritic crackling. While I busied myself with a pot of Darjeeling, he lit his pipe and began to inspect my bookshelf.

"Lermontov can be quite wonderful," he said. "Still, he's completely outdone by his contemporary Leopardi. Do you know Leopardi?"

I told him I did not.

"Oh, you must read Leopardi! *Così tra questa / Immensità s'annega il pensier mio; / E il naufragar m'è dolce in questo mare.* For those lines alone, Italian is well worth mastering. I'd tutor you happily. I've tried to interest your brother, but he insists that all he wishes, these days, is to perfect his Russian—which already seems to me rather perfect."

"He's deathly afraid his Russian will be corrupted," I explained. "It's the only thing of our past that remains him."

Bobby replaced the Lermontov. "And do you fear being corrupted?" he asked, looking up at me most charmingly.

I laughed at the impertinence of his question. "I'm fast becoming a cauldron of English habits, both bad and good."

It was his turn to laugh.

"Never fear. You'll never be entirely English," he said. "Nor will I. Irish, Italian, and Russian blood mingles freely in these veins, but not a drop of English. We're both gentlemen of the greater world."

I asked him if that was different from our being worldly gentleman.

"Oh yes," he said earnestly. "Quite a bit different. For my part, at least, I'm hopelessly unworldly. I take it that could describe you as well."

I told him I certainly wasn't *otherworldly*.

"Oh no, no, not for an instant to think *that*."

This was pleasant enough, if rather opaque. It was as if the delicate artifice of some long-vanished court found itself preserved in his manner. I was relieved when our tea was at last ready.

As I poured, I asked nonchalantly how he had enjoyed his winter *vacances* in the Alps.

A shadow passed over his refined face. "Has your brother spoken of it?" he asked.

"Very little. I suppose he had a perfectly fine time. My brother always manages to."

"Perfectly fine!" Bobby exclaimed, getting up and pacing my narrow sitting room. "Perfectly fine!" he repeated, as if he found the phrase somehow offensive. "Well, yes, I suppose it *was* perfectly fine. I paid for the hotel, I paid for the meals, I lent him my skis. I showered on him my largesses. And why not? A small price! And what do you think came of it? What do you think *could* come of it? He loves only women. But you're not the least like your brother, are you? I'd thought that might be true. He never speaks of you, but I had the sense... Do you think Fate is laughing at us right now? We really must celebrate, don't you think?"

"But what are we to celebrate?"

"Oh, I don't know," he said with that curious resignation of his. "Everything, I suppose. Life, love, madness. Misery. Despair. Hilarity. All the things that keep one going."

I was dumbstruck to see that he had quietly begun to shed tears. There's something vaguely clownish about him, I thought. At the same time, I found myself moved by the grandeur of his mood.

I broke a lengthening silence by asking why he had ignored me for so long.

"Fear of exposure. Guilt by association. It wouldn't have done at all for Vladimir to associate me with you. But now the game's up. He's been perfectly cool to me ever since the term began. Not rude, but I've been cut off. What more can I lose?"

We stared for a long moment into each other's eyes; tears were still seeping down his cheeks.

"Shall I complete the ruin, then?" I asked delicately.

"You *do* resemble your brother in a good many ways," he murmured, clearly trying to convince himself of the truth of that observation. "Do you fancy a bit of supper? My valet can arrange a most soothing meal."

His rooms in Trinity were grand indeed, and I wondered what he had made of Volodya's seedy digs. But then he had been in love with Volodya.

There was nothing much to our congress and, after some exquisitely prepared Huîtres de Whitstable and a very fine bottle of Meursault, we turned out to be comically incompatible. When, afterward, he remembered an urgent appointment with a friend, I felt more relief than disappointment. As I dressed to leave, he pressed into my hands a slim volume he had withdrawn from his bookshelves. "In remembrance of the great never-to-be-had," he said. "Leopardi. First edition."

With a queer feeling of contentment I made my way back to my own wretched lodgings. I inserted the elegantly bound Leopardi between Lazhechnikov and Lermontov. I poured myself a warm bath in my beloved zinc tub, and lay there soaking for quite some time, my curiosity slaked, my vanity caressed, my infatuation abated.

24

AN ORDINARY FAMILY DINNER AT THE NABOKOVS' flat, Sächsischestrasse 67, Berlin-Wilmersdorf. The date: Monday, March 27, 1922. Volodya and I were down from Cambridge for the Easter vacation. Joining us at the table were Svetlana Siewert, our cousin Nika, and Iosef Hessen. The guest of honor was Pavel Miliukov, recently returned from a visit to the United States and scheduled, at my father's invitation, to address an audience at the Philharmonie the following evening.

Usually conversation was general at our table, but on this night my father and Miliukov engaged each other exclusively while the rest of us, conscious of a momentous duel between the old friends and rivals, remained silent and alert.

"More and more," declared Miliukov in that pompous way of his, "I'm convinced that despite the perils, we must think seriously of returning to Russia. There are a quarter million Russians in Berlin alone. Add to that the tens of thousands in Paris, and Prague, and Constantinople. The *crème de la crème*. How is Russia ever to survive Lenin and his hooligans without our vital lifeblood flowing through her veins?"

"But don't you see, my friend?" asserted Father. "It's all over. The Russia we loved, the Russia not of pogroms and police but of a culture so remarkable and tender the world has never known its like, *that* Russia has ceased to exist. I shall never return. I shall never cooperate with the Soviet regime. Nor shall I ally myself with the Social Revolutionaries, as you so foolishly propose. They've already indicated their unwillingness to work with the Cadets. Your uprising of the peasants is, alas, little more than wishful thinking."

"Ah, my dear Vova. Beware exile's bitter allure. It tempts you into fatalism. Russia is lost only if we say she is lost."

"She is lost," said my father. "We must give her up the way the Jews long ago gave up Jerusalem. For us as well: the Diaspora."

"Not all the Jews have given up Jerusalem. Even as we speak, Zionists by the hundreds are reentering the Promised Land."

"And their efforts will end in folly and worse."

"But you're a friend of the Jews. The Jews have no greater friend than you."

"Yes," said my father, "I'm a great friend of the Jews."

I had never before heard Father speak in such a pessimistic vein, and he seemed aware of the gloom he had cast on our table.

"But enough of this," he said. "We must remember how very much we should be thankful for. We have our health, our happiness, we've kept our souls intact, we're surrounded by the ones we love. And around this humble table"—here his tone began to change from one of heartfelt seriousness to mock-academic grandiosity—"we possess an almost endless fund of knowledge. In the best spirit of our Soviet brethren who believe that everything must proceed collectively, let us endeavor to tap into that knowledge. Comrades, we must adapt to the future! I shall ask the first question of Volodya. If you'd be so kind as to divulge to us, Comrade Lody"—he paused portentously—"what was the name of the Pomeranian in the famous Chekhov story?"

Volodya did not hesitate. "The lapdog is nowhere named. Unless"—he smiled to himself—"one wishes to consider that its name is Gurov."

Father nodded appreciatively. "Excellent. Proceed."

Volodya scanned the table. His gaze lingered on me. "Seryosha, what name did Achilles take when he hid among the women?"

Years of practice had honed my skill at fielding these rounds of questions. Some were spurious; others led to real answers. No one at the table was immune. The questions came fast and furious.

"Describe Plyushkin's garden in *Dead Souls*."

"What did Napoleon say when he crowned himself emperor?"

"Who was the world champion in chess before Lasker?"

"What caterpillars feed on privet leaves?"

"The Astapovo Station, where Tolstoy died, was located at the intersection of what train routes?"

This breakneck game of sense and nonsense invariably cheered my father up. His face flushed with pleasure, his tired eyes regained their old glitter. My mother looked from guest to guest with nervous solicitude, sometimes crying out, "But that is too diabolical!" when she felt someone had been unfairly interrogated.

I saw that Miliukov sat perplexed, hoping he might be forgotten amid all these familial fireworks. Chain-smoking Hessen, on the other hand, seemed thoroughly amused; he kept my mother, who sat next to him, and whom Father often scolded for smoking too much, supplied with expensive Goldflakes which he tipped out in a steady stream from their yellow packet.

Having answered correctly, and with quiet triumph, the most recent of Father's questions ("Kozlov-Volovo and Moscow-Yelets"), Volodya turned his attention to Olga.

I had seen relatively little of my sisters in recent years. While Elena had blossomed into a poised, lovely girl, Olga had grown strange and moody, a flower bud clenched tight. Often she stared distractedly into space, and hummed monotonous snatches of melody. She read widely in Madame Blavatsky and other Theosophists. When Volodya asked her, "What books had Emma Bovary read?" she shrank into herself and glared blackly at him.

"Of course you've read *Madame Bovary*?" he prompted when no response was forthcoming. "Our esteemed Mademoiselle Hofeld hasn't neglected your education to that degree, I presume?"

"You quite liked the book, didn't you?" said Mlle. Hofeld helpfully.

"A single title will suffice," taunted my brother.

"The Brother Who Died," said Olga between clenched teeth. "An execution in three volumes by Olga Vladimirovna."

"Sorry," said my brother. "Your choices were—"

Father intervened; resorting to a time-tested method, he threw pellets of bread across the table to try to cheer her up, but this time it had no effect. Olga burst into tears, and rose from the table in a fury. "I hate you!" she cried. "I hate everybody in this cruel family! I wish you all would die!" Throwing down her napkin, she ran sobbing from the dining room.

Across the table, Svetlana's squirrel eyes gazed steadily at mine, a connection we did not break for several seconds as the general commotion around the table rose ("Olga, my dearest," Father called after her) and gradually subsided (my mother and Mlle. Hofeld excused themselves and hurriedly followed Olga from the room). What Svetlana wished to communicate, exactly, I do not know: what I saw in her gaze was alarm, disapproval, a sense that her worst, unnamed fears about her lover and his fantastical family had somehow been confirmed.

None of us could know that this would be the last evening we would all be together.

The next day I slept late, and read a bit from *Splendeurs et Misères des Courtisanes,* which I was quite enjoying despite my brother's belief that it was not literature at all but only a crude attempt at social history. In the evening I went out to the Adonis Club. The mood there was uncommonly festive. The center of attention was a stocky, middle-aged gentleman, fashionably dressed and sporting a prodigious walrus mustache of the kind in vogue among a certain generation of Germans. Flanking him like bodyguards sat two muscular young men, one short-haired and blond, the other a brunette, both looking as if they had come directly to the club from a boxing ring. Hovering about was a girlish-looking lad whose long bony hands fluttered with even greater alacrity than his long dark eyelashes.

"Come to Papa." The mustachioed gentleman patted his lap, and obediently the flitting youth perched there. I recognized one of the men at the table as Bruno, with whom I had had several amiable conversations on other occasions; he recognized me as well, and motioned for me to join the group.

I asked him what was being celebrated.

"Oh, but you don't know? It's the twenty-fifth anniversary of the Scientific-Humanitarian Committee. Dr. Hirschfeld"—he nodded toward the mustachioed guest of honor—"is being fêted far and wide. He's the toast of the town these days."

I told him that, regrettably, I knew nothing of the committee nor its work, and reminded him that I was seldom in Berlin.

"Then you must learn about us. We're a group dedicated to the repeal of Paragraph 175."

I asked politely of what this paragraph consisted.

"Dear God," he said. "You really are a stranger. Dr. Hirschfeld is a great pioneer in the realms of human freedom. Our petition's been signed by some very prominent men. Thomas Mann, Hermann Hesse, André Gide, Albert Einstein. The tide of history is with us, and we may be proud that Germany has proved the most enlightened of all nations in regard to the advancement of human sexual liberty. Our future here is very bright indeed!"

Hirschfeld himself, at the far end of the table, held forth, richly and fervently, for some time. I cannot now fully recall all that he said, but I remember that he ended by declaring, in his gruff and kindly baritone, the resolute voice of a general, "We are citizens not of a nation but of the world, Plato's invincible army of lovers. What a tomorrow awaits us, *mein Kinder.* Nothing—nothing!—shall keep us from our destiny."

I could not help but contrast his words with Father's melancholy prognosis of our émigré plight the night before. I wondered if Father knew of this Dr. Hirschfeld, and determined to ask him at the next opportunity. It might even provide us with an occasion to address certain aspects of my life he seemed set on ignoring.

Just as the political conversation chez Nabokov had given way to fun and games, so merriment in the Adonis Club also became general once the doctor had finished speaking. A small band of musicians began to puff and wheeze its way through a polka. Had the Germans not yet heard of jazz? Some couples danced. I found myself talking to a curly-haired tailor who told me proudly that he specialized in reconfiguring military uniforms into evening wear. When he began to disparage the Russians flooding the city and undercutting honest men's wages, I was relieved to be able to pass for English. Had it not been for his attractively upturned nose I would have turned heel and walked away. But it amused me, as did something humorous in his blue eyes, and I resolved to kiss him before the night was through.

He wished to introduce me to a chap who'd been to

England once, and I obliged, seating myself at a table slick with spilled beer while the fellow regaled us with a preposterous story involving the Victoria and Albert Museum and an Egyptian mummy. My tailor—I believe Maximilian was his name—contented himself with massaging my thigh with his large hand. It was all very jolly, even if I do dislike the smell of beer and cigar smoke, and the inane drivel that is polka music. I watched Dr. Hirschfeld move with great ceremony about the room, stopping here and there to receive congratulations from well-wishers.

"Tante Magnesia is in her element tonight," drawled the fellow who had been to England.

"Oh, don't be rude," Maximilian told him. "Not everyone appreciates the professor's work," he explained to me. "*Some* small people are positively jealous."

"Why should I be jealous of a self-aggrandizing old queen who abuses her medical privileges for the sake of bedding clueless young thugs? It's reprehensible, really."

"My, we've developed a stern case of morals since we returned from London. Is the fog there really so thick that it clouds one's libido?"

I could see that these two had for far too long been sparring partners.

Impatient, I asked if I could have a word with Maximilian alone.

Maximilian shot his friend a haughty look. I took him around the corner to an alley and proceeded to kiss him. It was nothing but a lark, that kiss, harmless mischief of the sort I had been pursuing with some vigor since my arrival in the city ten days before. Unlike London, which was all great innocent fun but little more, Berlin invited one into more immediately naughty embraces.

My new acquaintance seemed at first startled and then gratified by my assertiveness, and he answered in kind.

What happened next is difficult to describe. Even as I relished the taste of his mouth, the firm organ that was his tongue, his buttock-clutching tailor's hands, there suddenly descended on me a desolation so profound that even now I shudder to recall it. The feeling lasted scarcely a moment, but in that moment all satisfaction in kissing this pleasingly available Berliner with the snub nose evaporated. He seemed surprised by the abrupt cessation of my advances, even going so far as to mutter, "Hey, what funny business is this?" as I broke our embrace and thrust him from me.

I told him I had forgotten an appointment of paramount importance. All I knew, with eerie certainty, was that I must at once go home.

"Well that's a fine thing, for sure," my snubbed companion complained. "Leaving a poor fellow in the lurch. My friend always warned me the English have no real manners."

"Russian," I corrected as I hurried away.

At Nollendorfplatz I waited some minutes for a streetcar, but as none was forthcoming, and my agitation had not abated, I began to walk.

Somewhere along the Hohenzollerndam my arrival at a streetcar stop coincided with the approach of a tram, and I gratefully boarded the empty car that would speed me homeward. The conductor wore frayed gray gloves, and swayed drunkenly as he made his way up the aisle to where I sat.

I calmed a bit. My strange sense of urgency seemed absurd, and I set about thinking how I meant to scold Olga for using such uncommonly violent language at the table the night before. It was bad luck to say such things, and she of all people should know better. From Olga my thoughts turned to my German tailor, toward whom I had behaved abominably, and who no doubt was now besmirching me to his colleagues at the Adonis Club, perhaps even to Dr. Hirschfeld, about whom I really must remember to ask Father....

I am recounting all this in some detail, as it is, even to this day, etched with awful clarity in my memory.

I got off the tram at Sächsischestrasse and walked the remaining few blocks. Outside my parents' building I passed the elderly gentleman who nightly patrolled the neighborhood, tapping at the curb with his cane, ever on the lookout for discarded cigarette butts.

A sepulchral quiet greeted me as I entered our flat—and yet the room was far from empty. Several of Father's friends—Hessen, Kaminka, Shtein, Yakolev, all of whom must have returned with him from Miliukov's speech at the Philharmonie—sat silently. Hessen had been handing around cigarettes when I walked in, but froze when he saw me. No one spoke a word. I noticed that the men looked pale and exhausted. Father had said last night, after Miliukov left, that his speech was sure to be dreadfully dull—but had it been as bad as that?

Mother raised herself from the divan where she had been reclining.

"Seryosha, we were so worried. Where have you been? How could you have stayed out till such hours?"

"It's not all that late," I said, though it was well past midnight, "and besides—"

Volodya, whose presence I had not till that moment registered, took me firmly by the arm. "Seryosha," he said, "you must know immediately. Father has been shot."

"That's not possible," I told him, and indeed, I fully expected Father in the next instant to come leaping into the room, flicking pellets of bread, delighted at this bit of sport he had arranged at my expense.

All eyes watched me as Volodya continued to grasp my arm. "This is no dream," he told me. "Father's dead. He's been murdered."

* * *

The facts, the immutable, incontrovertible, to this day barely comprehensible facts: at the crowded Philharmonie that evening Father introduced Miliukov, who spoke for an hour or so on "America and the Restoration of Russia." He had just finished his speech when a gunman rushed the stage, crying, "For the Tsar's family, and for Russia!" He fired off several rounds at Miliukov. Each missed. My quick-thinking, fearless, doomed father seized the gunman's wrist, and along with his friend Avgust Kaminka succeeded in wrestling him to the floor, whereupon a second gunman emerged from the pandemonium and fired three times, point-blank, into Father's back, piercing his spine and heart.

The gunmen, who were apprehended, were pro-monarchist thugs who had long nursed a political grudge against Miliukov. As it turned out, Peter Shabelsky-Bork and Sergey Taboritsky had no clue as to the identity of the man they actually succeeded in murdering.

I knew Father had had many enemies—his life had been in danger for many years—and yet I had convinced myself, once we had fled Russia, that the danger—the immediate, physical danger—had at last subsided.

Losing Russia was not half so hard as losing Father. Gone were the conversations we might have had, the concerts we might have attended, the friendly disagreements over Wagner and Stravinsky we might have entertained. Gone forever was the hope of regaining his respect, which I knew I had lost through my aberrant ways. My actions the evening of his death seemed shamefully frivolous. Father had given his life for Russia while I had been seeking to kiss a German in whom I was not even very interested.

25

SOMEHOW VOLODYA AND I MANAGED TO COMPLETE the second part of the Tripos in June, and both of us took degrees with seconds in Russian and French. After that we returned to Berlin, where our fellow exiles treated us with great tenderness, offering us various unsatisfactory jobs from which we had difficulty extricating ourselves graciously. Funds were low, my mother's store of jewels long since depleted, but Berlin was ludicrously inexpensive in those days, and we were able to subsist by doing a bit of translation work, tutoring the occasional pupil in English or French (no one wanted to learn Russian), and in Volodya's case giving the odd tennis lesson. We were, as he put it, two young gentlemen selling off the surplus of our aristocratic upbringing.

My unexpected estrangement from Volodya began with two happy announcements. We had taken a tram out to the Grunewald one bright afternoon to stroll in the pine woods. Dappled sunlight sifted through the latticework of green needles above onto the carpet of brown needles below. A butterfly dogged us delicately, dipping around our shoulders, fluttering before our noses. Volodya can identify that butterfly, I thought to myself, and I cannot.

"Angle wing," he said, as if reading my mind. "Our sweat attracts it." Then: "At the aquarium, yesterday, I proposed to Svetlana, and she accepted."

I clapped my hands together in delight, and told my brother what wonderful news that was. "Cherish her," I admonished him. "She's beautiful, charming—above all, wise." His confidence touched me; was it possible, after the recent shock we had endured, that our fraternal bond might be maturing into something less fraught?

"There's one condition, however, dreamed up by her impossible parents. I must find myself a proper job. As you know, I refuse to be shackled to a desk. Keats's 'delicious diligent indolence' is what I must protect above all else if I'm to coax my ever-reluctant muse to sing."

I laughed and told him his indolence was liable to make Svetlana jealous.

There had always been moments when I felt I had stepped across an invisible line: this was one. He looked at me with furrowed brow and narrowing eyes. "Svetlana must know where my first loyalty lies," he said. "If she doesn't—then God help her. But that brings me to my second bit of good news.

"Gamayun has commissioned me to translate *Alice in Wonderland.* Isn't that splendid? I've always loved poor Alice's adventures. I pity her real-life counterpart in the clutches of that dull, depraved mathematician—but what glorious imaginings his dreamy and deranged mind was capable of."

"It's perfect for you," I told him. "How much is he paying?"

"My advance was an American five-dollar bill. I would show it to you as proof of my great wealth, but unfortunately I had to change it yesterday on the tram; I had no other money for the fare."

"In other words, it scarcely constitutes a proper job in the Siewerts' eyes."

"Her father's a mining engineer. It's maddening to have to deal with such cautious, unimaginative folk. How Svetlana sprang from those two I'll never know."

He paused to look around us. On the shores of Grunewaldsee, Berliners had spread themselves—singly, in pairs, or in larger family groups—and were enjoying the fine summer afternoon.

"Speaking of vacancy—what a scene. I'm not sure which are more repulsive, those who've shed their clothes or those who've retained them. Surely the Germans must be the most repellent of God's inventions."

There were moments when I hated my brother.

To our left, two laughing youths were cavorting in a game that seemed to involve grabbing each other's wrists. They had been in the water, and their bathing trunks clung to them tightly.

"Come," said Volodya. "I know a lovely nook nearby." I followed, and soon we had entered a secluded glade which retained a view of the sparkling lake. He began immediately to remove his clothing. My brother was by both inclination and avocation something of a naturist. Already his flesh had extracted from the stingy summer sun a golden hue unmarred by that band of ivory that exposes the infrequent nudist.

"Oh, come on," he said. "The sun releases us from all those artificial obligations. Rejoice! Let the sun translate you into another language altogether!"

He was in a good mood.

Settling myself on a clean spot of sand, I declined his invitation. One or two embarrassing incidents in my youth had taught me the wisdom of remaining clothed when in the presence of other males, a caution I extended even to my brother. Was he deliberately provoking me—or was he indeed oblivious to my liabilities?

"You remind me of an old pensioner," Volodya complained. "At least remove your jacket and shoes, for God's sake. Don't you have any capacity at all for pleasure?"

I told him I had my own pleasures, thank you, which he very well knew about. I suppose that provoked him, but then I was feeling rather bullied.

Volodya lit a cigarette without offering me one. He exhaled expressively, staring skyward, where a small biplane had appeared in the fathomless blue. "Father spoke of you his last night on earth."

I found my own pack and lit one. This was something I had not known. I had seen very little of Volodya since Father's death.

"Just as we were going to bed. We were speaking of *Boris Godunov*, Father was recalling the scene where the Tsar, hallucinating the face of his murdered son in the clock face, cries out in guilty terror and then begs God for mercy. He said he always found that moment in the opera disturbing. Then he began to speak with bewilderment of your inclinations. I believe they weighed much on his mind."

He turned his head to look at me. "I've never asked," he said. "I suppose I'm curious. Where were you that night?"

"If you must know, I was at the Adonis Club. You can guess its nature by its name. I don't apologize for my inclinations, as you call them, though I do regret that I wasn't with you and Mother when Hessen telephoned with the news. But I have to tell you—even there, at the Adonis, I knew. It's as if God's shadow fell across me, as if I could feel Father's soul sweep past me. I believe his spirit paid me a final visit. Why, I don't know. But then, what is *Boris Godunov* but a tale of a father's guilt?"

Volodya responded sharply. "Father had nothing to feel guilty about. He never mistreated you in any way! If anything, he was extraordinarily lenient. Imagine what our grandfather would have done in similar circumstances."

I asked him if he thought it no mistreatment for a parent to withhold love from his child.

"I won't hear of this," he said. "You're impossible. You're worse than Olga!"

For several silent moments that accusation hung between us. I tried to take pleasure in the shouts that came from the two lads on the beach, but I could only feel a sadness as I realized the awful gap between what we say and what we mean to say.

"I've had a letter, by the way, from Bobby de Calry," Volodya resumed. "He tells me he's taken a mistress in Paris—as if that somehow absolves him. I'm given to understand that you and he… Well, I can only hope it was more satisfying for you than it was for him. He confessed all at the end of term, and I forced myself to hear him out, for his sake, since he seemed so distraught. I have little to say. I don't see that you've conducted yourself honorably, but that's not my business. I'm curious, though. Why poor Bobby? Or does your kind simply take advantage whenever it sees advantage to be taken?"

I was of course quite taken aback by this latest thrust—and by Bobby's betrayal of a secret whose necessity I had sternly impressed upon him.

"Has it never occurred to you that he might've sought *me* out?"

"No, frankly, it hasn't. Bobby's a lovely, weak, pathetic soul. He's easily taken advantage of."

"I presume you know this firsthand?"

Now, I think, it was his turn to be surprised.

"I beg your pardon?"

I pressed on. "Didn't you take advantage of his infatuation with you? You know perfectly well that Swiss vacation was financed not so much out of his pocket as out of his heart."

Volodya had sat up. "How deeply troubled you are, Seryosha. But rest assured, I do pity you. As did Father."

I stood up, dusted off the seat of my trousers, and told him

I must be going. I had had enough of this pointless conversation.

"As you see fit," he said. "Now that Father is no longer with us, life will be much more difficult for everyone."

The séance was Svetlana and Tatiana's idea.

Tensions in our gloomy household ran high that autumn. My mother spent her days chain-smoking on the divan, leafing through old photograph albums. My grandmother rarely left her room. "My son was the only principle of order in this madhouse," La Generalsha would fulminate. "Now the lunatics are left to run the asylum." Olga was becoming increasingly sullen. Kirill was doing poorly in his studies. Of all of us, only Elena exhibited a sweet and irreproachable demeanor. She even went so far as to assist our hapless *Putzfrau* with her chores—a saintly deed that earned her grandmother's scorn: "So you aspire now to be a chambermaid? Who wishes to marry a chambermaid? Can't you see that's the real reason your cousin Nika no longer comes around as often?" (To his mother's delight, Nika had begun courting Princess Natasha Shakhovsky.)

When Volodya departed in late July for Bad Rotherfelde, where Svetlana and her family were summering, I breathed a sigh of relief, hoping that our unfortunate afternoon in the Grunewald would be forgotten. But when he returned in a surly mood, my sundry attempts at a rapprochement were summarily declined.

As mysticism is most plausible when systematically practiced, the Siewert sisters had strict rules: the séance must take place at midnight; it must involve the lighting of twelve candles; it must be introduced by appropriate music. Tatiana, having had some practice in the dark art, would serve as medium: the spirits of the departed would speak through her.

At the appointed hour, we gathered around the dining table: Svetlana and Tatiana, Volodya, La Generalsha. Refusing to participate, Khristina sat apart and observed. To my surprise, Mother wished to take part. I had brought along a fellow I had recently been seeing, an unassuming young man named Willi who worked in a flower shop near Potsdamer Platz. He spoke neither Russian, English, nor French, and I feared the bloom of our fledgling romance was already beginning to fade—though my German, of necessity, was blossoming. As I would never have dared do when Father was alive, I made a show of including Willi in family occasions whenever possible, though I knew the presence of a German, let alone an invert, was bound to rankle. Let them take umbrage. Dr. Hirschfeld's revolutionary ideas were beginning to take hold in me.

The candles shed their unsteady light. "Spooky chords, please," Svetlana commanded, and I obliged by vamping a few, minor-key. Then I joined the rest of the group at the table, taking my place between Mother and Willi.

As instructed, we held hands and closed our eyes. Silence followed. Beyond the windows, we could hear the occasional racket of a tram, a barking dog, the passage along our street of an automobile.

The first spirit to arrive, via Tatiana, was a Bavarian farmer who had died of the plague. He was concerned about a goat that had gone missing. When Svetlana asked our spirit to tell us his name, he replied "Pigeon."

Our collective giggle must have frightened him off; he was replaced by a character speaking in a high treble who proclaimed that she was Almaden of Peru. Had we all heard of Lady Almaden of Peru?

We had not. She seemed miffed, and began to recite her considerable but highly improbable accomplishments—social, political, sexual. When we asked her which century she hailed from she replied, 'Why, the twenty-first, my dears!'

And so the merriment continued, as we asked questions of the spirit and the spirit, through Tatiana, responded. There was

Matilda, a lace-maker in Bruges who went through five husbands in fifty-five years, and Boris, a young rake in Novgorod who had met his end on a burning bridge on Christmas Day while pissed as an owl. I had never credited my partner in doubles with such an inventive imagination—for surely this was all a product of her imagination. It was a pity she had never been at our table when Father had unleashed his game of questions: how splendidly she might have answered the nonsense queries.

But then, just as I was admiring her talents, and regretting that poor Willi must sit through all this without comprehending a word, something truly strange happened. As she was in the midst of regaling us about the court of Catherine the Great, as seen through the eyes of a scullery maid, a second voice interrupted the breathless chatter—casting aside the poor scullery maid and holding forth in sepulchral tones that to this day I have difficulty believing Tatiana's vocal chords were even capable of producing.

"Someone is coming," announced that voice. "Clear the stage. Someone has arrived. Someone wishes to speak."

We waited, breathless and thrilled. Tatiana was a genius of improvisation; there was no doubt of that. Just when the game had become a bit routine, she had chosen to liven things up. Even Willi, I gathered from the way he squeezed my hand, was impressed.

The silence lengthened. Someone among us cleared his throat. Outside, it had begun to rain, a cold windswept rain tapping against the windowpanes. We waited.

I am not certain, even to this day, what got into me. All I know is that I began to speak. And what everyone there attests is this: I spoke with no stutter at all.

"How nice of you finally to call on me. I've been waiting. But don't worry, I've not been bored. I realize you're all very busy. I've been quite busy myself. You see, things are rather different over here. We have our own interests."

Mother released my hand and began to sob. Afterward she swore I had mimicked Father's voice with uncanny perfection.

"Seryosha, stop it," Volodya commanded. But I could no more stop speaking than I could stop my heart from beating. My pulse raced; I broke out in a cold sweat; my face burned.

My grandmother was unperturbed by her son's appearance. "What interests?" she asked me—or was it Father she asked?

"You can't begin to imagine. Once you become an adult, try as you might, you can no longer be fascinated by rubber balls or jackstraws. Still, there are times when Lody interests all of us here very much. His remarkable investigations. My colleagues and I—"

Volodya silenced me by springing up from the table. "Have you no decency?" he asked, leaning across as if he meant to cuff me.

Wherever the words had come from, they ceased as abruptly as they had commenced. Emptied, I looked around in a daze. I had never in my life called Volodya "Lody." Only Father ever called him that.

"Sergey." Willi touched my upper lip. "*Kuchmal. Du hast Nasenbluten. Was geschieht?*"

What had happened, indeed?

"It's the work of the devil," Khristina muttered as I applied my handkerchief to the crimson flow of blood that issued from my left nostril. "Demons enjoy masquerading as the souls of the departed. There was a time when everyone knew that. Now people have forgotten." She shook her head sadly.

Not long after, other developments sent further shocks through our household's precarious balance. My grandmother announced that, as she was unappreciated, she had decided to move to Dresden in order to be near an old flame of hers, a former senator from one of the Baltic provinces. Then came far worse news: in January, Svetlana's parents summoned Volodya to a conference regarding their daughter's engagement. He returned home in a rage. Though he did not tell me the details himself, Mother reported that Roman Siewert had informed Volodya that, as his prospective son-in-law had no serious prospects before him, he could no longer sanction the marriage. Svetlana herself was present at the interview and, despite her fiancé's appeals, raised no objections to her father's pronouncement. "Volodya is as furious with her as he is with her father," Mother reported. "And I must say, I'm surprised as well. I thought she was a girl of far more spirit than that."

In March, Olga became precipitately engaged to the penniless Prince Sergey Sergeevich Shakhovsky, a mad and charmless young man perfectly suited to my equally mad and charmless sister. By April, outraged by the light sentences meted out to Father's murderers, Mother had begun to talk of moving the rest of the family to Prague, where the Czech government was offering pensions to émigrés.

When, a month later, I received from Paris an offer to join the staff of Miliukov's *Latest News*, the time seemed ripe to bid Berlin *auf Wiedersehn* and set out on my own.

26

PARIS

THE HOUR WAS MIDNIGHT. JEAN COCTEAU'S notorious nightclub, Le Boeuf sur le Toit, throbbed with its formidable menagerie of poets, painters, and pederasts. Courtesy of an ebony-hued saxophonist and his ivory-pallored pianist, an ebullient tide of jazz washed over the bar. I felt immediately at home. It was the end of May 1923.

From the sleepy-eyed bartender I ordered a glass of champagne, and as I waited, my gaze attached itself to the painting above the bar—an enigmatic, staring eyeball surround by a storm of graffiti. Above it, crude letters spelled out "*L'Oeil cacodylate*."

"Picabia," the bartender told me.

"'The arsenic eye'?"

"It's Dada. They say arsenic cures syphilis." He shrugged. "Perhaps you should ask Picabia himself. You may find him right over there, having cocktails with Tristan Tzara."

I told him that sounded like something of a dare, and he smiled. "You're perhaps American? The Americans adore presenting themselves to famous strangers."

"English. As for myself," I confessed, "I'm here for Monsieur Cocteau."

The bartender gestured toward the musicians. Looking like a spindly seahorse plucked from its aquarium and set on a piano stool, Cocteau stroked the piano keys with long, bony fingers. He had folded his cuffs back from his slender wrists. Eyes closed, he threw back his head in feigned ecstasy, exposing a prominent Adam's apple on his stalk of a neck. He wore pale face powder and darkish lipstick.

Abruptly, though, he relinquished the piano, and was replaced by a plain little woman in an even plainer dress who proceeded to launch herself into a mad pastiche of tangos, waltzes, and ragtime.

Cocteau made a quick tour of the crowded room, ending at the table occupied by Picabia and Tzara. When he was done with them, he slid in beside me at the bar and observed, "Have you noticed how immensely superior jazz is to alcohol? Alcohol befuddles the brain while jazz intoxicates the soul. My musical talent is nothing compared to Madame Meyer's"—he gestured in the direction of the confoundingly inventive pianist—"but it's as important to me that I play jazz as well as I draw. They're the same thing, really, but with one glorious exception: when you play jazz you become the god of noise himself. That's why I adore it so."

He took my arm with thrilling familiarity. "And you? Are you musical as well?"

I told him I feared my musical skills were purely classical.

"You're British, I imagine."

Correcting his flattering presumption, I introduced myself properly.

He scrutinized me. "But you are dressed *à l'anglaise*, no?"

"Old Cambridge habits die hard," I allowed, unwilling to confess how severely my present funds limited the scope of my wardrobe.

Leaning in close, he murmured, "Are you here alone? Shall I abduct you for a bit?"

I stuttered that nothing would be more welcome.

He waved away my attempt to pay the bar bill. "Please," he said. "If I'm no longer to be taken seriously as a poet because, as my enemies like to say, I've found my true calling as a nightclub manager, then at least allow me the occasional benefit of my degradation. Of course," he continued as we emerged into the pleasant air of late spring, "it was precisely *because* I was afraid of being taken too seriously in the first place that I undertook this little venture. Always remember: to be taken seriously is the beginning of death.

"But now I'm in no danger *whatsoever* of being taken seriously!" He beamed like a child, though he was some twenty years older than I.

Our stroll took us down through the Place de la Concorde; as if to make good on his promise of abduction, he nudged me into the leafy shadows of the Tuileries, murmuring, "A park in the city's like a patch of pure sleep in the midst of dreaming, don't you think?"

We walked along graveled paths intermittently illuminated by circles of lamplight. A gap in the chestnut allée revealed the Tour Eiffel shining like a beacon on the far side of the Seine.

"Ah!" Cocteau exclaimed, "I'm afraid our poor Eiffel is past her prime. Once she was the Queen of Machines, Notre Dame of the Left Bank. Now she's nothing but an Art Nouveau artifact blemishing the skyline. She should be retired at once. Imagine a Brancusi Tower in her place! How the future would remember us then!"

Gripping my arm tightly, he brought us to a stop and stood perfectly still.

"I must ask you. Do you worship at the altar of the Terrible God? I scarcely know you, my child, but I believe you very well may."

"The Terrible God," I repeated uncertainly.

He laughed. "Usually my young men come to me much more egregiously. Some of them even send me their photos. Sometimes in the nude! Can you imagine? How much more do I admire your frank and straightforward approach. For what have you done but made a *pilgrimage!* So very tasteful, but then all the Russians I have known, and I have known quite a few, have exhibited an exquisite—might I say Oriental?—sense of decorum. Even that oaf Nijinsky was God's *dazzling* oaf. But speaking of Russians—Stravinsky's latest marvel opens at the Gaieté-Lyrique tomorrow, followed the next evening by a party thrown by my American friends the Murphys. You must grace us with your presence. Though I do not yet know your considerable talents, I suspect I shall discover them very soon. Do you write? Do you paint? Or do you make sublime music? Speak to me of your own life. I beg you."

After such a cascade, how was I to begin? I stammered out that I had adored *Parade* in London, that meeting its maker was a great honor, that I had recently fled Berlin and only yesterday acquired lodgings in Paris, and that I was sorry my impediment had made the preceding exposition so torturous.

"Not at all." Cocteau patted my hand fondly. "You speak like a reluctant angel. But how reluctant are you? Come. Let's dispense with merely carnal distractions as soon as possible, shall we?"

So that was the Terrible God. Seldom in my life have I been so swiftly taken in hand. Nearby shrubberies abetted us.

"Moderately endowed," Cocteau appraised. "Generally I prefer them larger, but an artist works with whatever he has at his disposal. At least it's eager enough. Yes, it's marvelously responsive, almost too much so. Oh dear! Are we done already? Never mind. You needn't attempt to pleasure me, my dear. You've already given me all the pleasure I require of an evening."

Thus we soon reemerged onto the graveled path.

"Dear me," he observed, taking advantage of the nearest streetlamp to consult his pocket watch. "My flock will think I've abandoned them. Paris isn't too strange for you, I hope. You can find your way home from here?"

As I would have many occasions to witness, everything about Cocteau seemed to take place at five times the speed of life. My various senses were still spinning when he bade me, "Goodnight, my tender Hyacinth. Do come to the concert and party. Where do you live? I shall have an invitation sent first thing tomorrow."

27

WITH GREAT ANTICIPATION I BOARDED THE *Maréchal Joffre*, a barge turned restaurant that our rich American hosts had rented for the evening. I wore the better of my two battered suits, shiny at the elbows, its silk lining in tatters; a neat stiff collar with a crimson tie; smart dove-gray spats. I had toned down my rosy flush with lavender powder. My lips bloomed, in contrast, with a touch of geranium rouge (Helena Rubenstein!). I had adjusted a lock of hair to fall just so over my left eye. At least, I thought, if I was not to be the handsomest devil at the soiree, I would nonetheless prove one of the most debonair.

Gerald Murphy met me at the bottom of the gangplank—an open-faced, unassuming fellow, hardly my notion of a rich American. (His family owned a leather goods empire.) Later I would come to admire the very few but highly original paintings he would produce before lapsing into the painterly equivalent of silence.

Fortified with a flute of champagne from the bar, I stationed myself by the railing to await Cocteau's arrival. Happily, he was not long. And what an entourage he had brought! There stood Diaghilev, pale and bloated, with handsome factotum Boris Kochno on his left arm and shockingly beautiful Serge Lifar on his right. Behind him, Véra Nemchinova, the troupe's *prima ballerina*, was accompanied by Ernest Ansermet, under whose baton *Les Noces* had sprung so thrillingly to life the evening before.

Lifar and Nemchinova bounded aboard, but Diaghilev remained quayside. Despite the urging of Cocteau and Kochno, he balked at making his entrance.

"Please, Sergey Pavlovich, it's time to come aboard," Kochno urged.

Diaghilev shook his huge head, on which a tiny derby balanced precariously. He adjusted his monocle, chewed his lower lip. "Why wasn't I told?" he demanded.

"It's perfectly safe," Kochno reassured him. "I offer you my word."

Drawing a handkerchief from his pocket, Diaghilev dabbed at the sweat on his brow. "When they said 'restaurant'..."

"Perfectly safe," Kochno repeated.

Diaghilev's voice grew shrill. "Why could no one be bothered to tell me? Isn't there a single soul here I can trust? Go! Summon Lifar. Can't I count on a single one of you ungrateful little bitches?"

"Honolulu," serenely chanted Cocteau, who until now had been silent. "The most soothing word in any language. Simply repeat after me: Honolulu."

Diaghilev ceased to pat his brow, and bestowed on Cocteau an extraordinarily charming smile. "I'm hardly assured by such foolishness, Jeanchik. Nevertheless: should today prove my appointed day, well, then, so much the worse for my creditors." And with that, gripping his walking stick with one hand and Kochno's arm with the other, the portly figure crossed over the gangway and onto the deck.

Safely delivered, he paused to survey the crowded scene before him. I felt a tremor of anxious excitement as he recognized me. "Ah, my dear fellow exile," he said, approaching and clasping my hand. He seemed to have forgotten entirely the inauspicious circumstances of our earlier meeting. "What news of the holy motherland? My great condolences on your father, my boy. An irreparable loss for our tragic country." For a moment, tears seemed to glisten in his watery eyes. Then he turned to Cocteau. "My dear," he purred, "have you made this youngster's acquaintance?"

"We've taken to one another like kittens to milk," Cocteau affirmed. "Isn't that true, *mon cher*?"

"Quite," I managed to stammer out.

At my side appeared Kochno bearing two flutes of champagne he held out to his elders. Sergey Pavlovich took one daintily, a bear sniffing a golden tulip.

Cocteau fluttered his lashes. "Oh my, but I detest alcohol, my pretty child. A terrible vice. Please take it away. Give me a mouthful of Negro jazz instead. Can our Gerald and Sara have neglected to hire an orchestra? What good are Americans if they can't provide music? We simply must have music. Otherwise, my dears, the evening's doomed. Forgive me. I've got to find music."

Diaghilev watched him dash away, then remarked to us, as if it had just occurred to him, "He's found his true calling at last—as a nightclub manager!"

Left alone with Diaghilev and Kochno, I giddily gulped champagne as Kochno murmured to his master, "He's not attracted to her in the least. Have no fear."

I looked in the direction of their stare: Lifar and Nemchinova surrounded by admirers.

"No, of course not," Diaghilev said bitterly. "He's only attracted to himself."

"That's not true," Kochno assured him. "You're everything

to him—as he, in return, wishes to be to you. He confessed that happy state of affairs to me only this morning."

"Yes, yes, of course," muttered Diaghilev.

In an attempt to bring myself into the conversation I said, "I bear greetings from my uncle"—a sentiment true in spirit if not strictly in fact. I suspected my uncle would be alarmed to find me unchaperoned before the great man.

"Ah, yes. Dear Kostya. Our country's great debacle ruined many fine men, but none so completely, I fear, as he. Is he still smarting from the various blows to his pride as well as his pocketbook?"

"My uncle has a long memory for slights."

Diaghilev laughed amiably. "Our Kostya has conveniently forgotten far more than most men remember. Ask any number of regimental officers! For that matter, ask two or three striplings from my own troupe. He's never forgiven me for one of them, though he'd never deign to admit it. But I can tell. I know when someone has turned against me! It's happened so often."

Cocteau's return ended this illuminating line of talk. He had somehow managed to exchange his cream-colored summer suit for the navy-blue jacket and white trousers of a ship's captain.

More guests were arriving. First came Misia Sert. "The only female our woman-hating Serge Pavlovich can abide," Cocteau whispered in my ear. "We all thought they'd eventually marry, but Serge is only in love with his work and Misia, it turns out, is only in love with his work as well."

The mannish figure with the aquiline nose was Princesse Edmond de Polignac, née Winnaretta Singer, heiress to the American sewing machine fortune turned patron of the arts; it was she who had commissioned *Les Noces.* And with her? Natalia Goncharova, who designed the sets, and Bronislava Nijinska—yes, sister to you-know-who—who had done the choreography. That handsome fellow greeting Diaghilev? Oh, that was Etienne de Beaumont, who threw the most fabulous *bals masqués* in Paris.

A small, dapper man with bulging eyes turned out to be Picasso, accompanied by his very solemn, very Russian-looking wife. Did I want to know how Picasso finally won the hand of Olga Khokhlova? Was I aware she was the only dancer in Diaghilev's entire corps de ballet who would have the cocky little Spaniard, and only after Serge told him, If you want a Russian girl, Pablito, you'll have to marry her first.

"And Picasso took his advice!" Cocteau exclaimed sotto voce. "Isn't that mad?"

The brisk jangle of a ship's bell interrupted his highly informative chatter. In American-accented French, Gerald Murphy announced that dinner was to be served below decks. The last of the evening light was so pacific we were all reluctant to forsake its balm for the dimly lit *salle à manger.* And yet, as we descended the stairs, the banquet tables, set with pale blue china and soothed by candlelight, offered another kind of beauty. In lieu of flowers, a small pyramid of toys adorned the center of each table. From the ceiling had been hung a great laurel wreath with the inscription "*Les Noces—Hommage*" in golden script.

Radiating elegance, Mrs. Murphy directed guests to their seats. At her side stood Stravinsky, every so often amending her directions in a way that made it clear he had been rearranging the place cards.

On seeing me, Mrs. Murphy looked blank, but I hardly registered her confusion, so utterly caught off guard was I by my sudden proximity to greatness. Though an exhilarated "*cher maître*" was ready to spring from my lips, Stravinsky's indifferent gaze silenced me completely.

"Last minute substitution," he told Mrs. Murphy. "I gather Monsieur Radiguet's gone missing, so Cocteau has enlisted this myrmidon in his stead."

The remark puzzled me, but Mrs. Murphy smiled with such

unaffected warmth that I was immediately reassured. With a gracious gesture she motioned me to the most remote of the eight tables.

"Marvelous!" Picasso exclaimed, seating himself at the first table and beginning to pick through the piled-up toys like a child opening his stocking at Christmas. He lifted each piece, then began balancing them one on top of another.

Cocteau had taken up a position at one of the barge's portholes. "We're sinking," he announced to an inattentive crowd. "I'm afraid the *Maréchal Joffre* is doomed. I can't tell you how honored I shall feel to perish alongside such celebrated company."

Stravinsky, meanwhile, evinced exaggerated surprise at finding himself seated between Mrs. Murphy and the Princesse de Polignac. Next to the Princesse, Diaghilev took his place, and next to him Madame Sert and then Serge Lifar and Olga Picasso and Gerald Murphy and Natalia Goncharova and finally the industrious Picasso, still putting the finishing touches on his whimsical construction, brought the circle back around to the beautiful Mrs. Murphy.

I was thrilled to see, on arriving at my own table, that Cocteau's place card was next to mine. I could also see that my new friend was still hovering rather forlornly about the main table, as if searching for the little rectangle of cardboard that would allow him to evict an overreaching guest.

"I believe you are down there," Stravinsky told him, gesturing in my direction.

"Surely there's a mistake," Cocteau appealed to Mrs. Murphy, who was explaining to Picasso how she had forgotten that the flower market sold toys rather than flowers on Sunday, and rather than return empty-handed...

Cocteau looked around in vain for some higher authority to whom he might appeal; there being none, he made an insouciant shrug and marched over to another porthole. "I regret to report," he announced, "that we continue to sink. Who knew the Seine was infested by serpents?"

It made those nearest him laugh, which seemed to mollify him a bit.

Our table was populated by Americans and other nonentities like myself.

"I'm Mrs. Cole Porter," chirped the woman next to me. "So very pleased to meet you." She extended a small, limp hand. She was very beautiful, and seemed to know it. The name Cole Porter meant nothing to me, though she seemed to assume it should.

"My husband"—she indicated a polished-looking fellow at the next table—"and Gerald have known each other since Yale, where they were the best of pals."

I asked her how she liked *Les Noces.*

"Dear me, such a clatter. But so modern! Don't you think so? So very modern and yet so very Russian. Those peasants in their smocks. And four pianos! What a bold idea, don't you think? I'm going to ask Monsieur Stravinsky if he might give my husband some composition lessons. My husband writes marvelous music, to be sure, but Monsieur Stravinsky could teach him any number of things, I think, counterpoint and syncopation, all the things you have to do to be taken seriously. It's not enough these days just to carry a tune. I think my husband capable of writing the Ballets Russes a show sure to be an even bigger hit than *Hitchy-Koo of 1922.*"

She waited for my response, but since I had none, though I cast about desperately for one, she went on, a bit plaintively, "You've at least *heard* of *Hitchy-Koo*?"

I told her that I regretted that I had not.

"In America it was huge. Gilbert"—she addressed a rather staid-looking man across the table—"wasn't *Hitchy-Koo* a huge smash?"

"The hugest," he confirmed.

"See?" she told me. "But what I'm really dying to know"—she discreetly lowered her smoky voice—"is what Monsieur Stravinsky's compatriots think of his portrait of their native land. Before this evening is out, I intend to ask one of the Russians here *exactly* what they think."

I told Mrs. Porter the ballet had reminded me of Russia not at all.

"*You're* Russian? Why no—that can't be." With her delicate hand she covered her mouth's surprised *o*. "Your English is so very good."

I told her I had had English governesses and had spoken English my whole life.

"How fascinating. It would certainly be fun to travel to Russia one of these days. But we're not to call it Russia anymore, are we? The Soviet Union. How grand that sounds, and so very modern, but also rather forbidding, don't you think? My husband says—"

Waiters descended with plates of lovely food. Not having eaten since morning, I was grateful to turn my attention from the fascinating Mrs. Porter to other nourishment.

"Do you observe," Cocteau said, "that we are the only two men in this room who have been seated together? What message is our amusing Igor trying to send?"

Ignoring his food, he glared in the direction of the head table, but after a few minutes his fury at having been demoted to the American table seemed to abate. He pushed his untouched plate away and observed that I seemed to have watched with interest Diaghilev's reluctance to board the barge.

"Rather a dramatic hiatus, no? Aren't you curious?"

"Most curious," I admitted.

"Gentle Narcisse will reveal all. You see, when our Serge was but a boy, he suffered a most unfortunate encounter—with a woman! Now, don't be shocked. It's not what you think. Oh no: it's far worse. This woman was a gypsy. Serge was twelve, thirteen. He has never told a soul the full story. One can only imagine how this wretched gypsy accosted our innocent lad, took him by the wrist, led him down a dark, foul-smelling alley. You're Russian, you can picture these things much better than I! With one filthy hand she held open his milk-white palm, with the other she stroked it. Cunningly, she then uttered the words, never to be forgotten: *Beware. You will die on the water.* And with that, my dear, she released him. He ran all the way home, but no matter how fast he ran, he could not outrun her words. No, he is still running from those terrible words. *You will die on the water.* And what do you know? Many successful years later, when it came time for the Ballets Russes to sail to South America, why, our Serge simply could not accompany them! The prophecy was too much for him. He stayed behind. With his great blessing—I can see him make the sign of the cross over his beloved, and bestow upon the troubled youth a medallion of Saint Anthony of Padua he has had specially struck—he sent the blessed Nijinsky forth to his doom. To Romola, that is—a Hungarian gypsy herself, who deftly seduced Nijinsky away from our poor Serge. I wonder, sometimes, whether it was not Romola's own grandmother who first uttered the prophecy, knowing full well it would one day deliver unto her granddaughter a prize at the time not yet even born."

Leaping to his feet, Cocteau said, "But do you believe such a ridiculous tale?" He made for the nearest porthole. Peering through a pantomimed spyglass, he reported, "Still sinking," though no one save me looked his way.

With a theatrical shrug, he returned quietly to his seat, where he resumed his scabrous chatter. No one in the whole room, it seemed, escaped his keen eye.

"And what do you make of our host, Gerald? But of course you've only just met him. He's altogether sweet, but there's a loneliness in him that sings its plaintive little aria just beyond the range of common hearing. But listen—listen to the way he talks—can you hear?"

Cocteau dropped his voice to a whisper. "It's said he had a terrible schoolboy crush on Mrs. Cole Porter's husband back in their tour of undergraduate duty at Harvard, or was it Princeton? Some ivy-infested excuse for American higher learning. Never requited, of course, though I think Mr. Porter, for all his tuneful wit and delightful marriage, may yet prove his allegiance to the lonelier realms. Mark my words. Inverts,"—and here he reverted to his normal tone of voice—"they do after all recognize each other, you know. Just as Jews do. Only sometimes, life's mean little joke, they manage to recognize everybody but themselves."

From a piano that had hitherto lurked unremarked in the corner of the dining room came a burst of music. At the keyboard I recognized Madame Meyer from Le Boeuf.

"My own father, I believe, failed to recognize himself," Cocteau continued. "I've often thought that had he seen through his own malaise to the occult arrow that had so grievously wounded him, the result may well have been that I myself would never have been born. Imagine that! One could build a religion on such a lovely paradox, don't you think?"

I said it sounded rather like his tale of the gypsy and her granddaughter, only somehow in reverse. But what about the Princesse de Polignac, whose mannish bearing had attracted my suspicions?

"So you do have a gift," said Cocteau. "Our *Tante* Winnie, as she likes to call herself, has been quite mad about any number of women—and not without reciprocation. I could name names, but I doubt they'd mean much to you, my boy. In time, perhaps."

"And Mrs. Murphy?"

"My dear Mrs. Murphy. But just look at her, *mon petit.* Those eyes the blue of cloudless prairie skies, that hair the color of wheat fields under a summer sun. No, my dear. Mrs. Murphy is beyond reproach. In fact, as I look around this room, I might well be forced to conclude that, of all of us, Mrs. Sara Murphy is the only one entirely beyond reproach. Unless, Mrs. Porter—" He leaned past me to gaze on my companion. "I may safely assume that you, Mrs. Porter, as well are beyond reproach."

"Quite," she told him. "I have no idea what you're talking about."

"Of course not. Neither do I. I never, on strict principle, have the slightest idea of what I talk about."

Madame Meyer having concluded her aural shape-shifting with a final, definitive chord, those last words hung in a sudden silence.

"Dear me," Cocteau mused. "Was it something I said?"

But everyone's attention was drawn not to him but to Madame Sert and Serge Lifar. As if on cue, they had risen from their seats to take up positions at the piano—Lifar, to everyone's astonishment, climbing on top of the instrument. For a very long moment the two remained motionless: Lifar reclining, eyes shut, dreaming; Misia attentive, poised, prepared. Then Lifar tilted back his head, touched his thumb to his lips as if to sip some exquisite unseen elixir, and Misia obliged with that languid melody curling into sultry chords by which Debussy so unforgettably conjures *L'Après-midi d'un Faune.* Half crouching, Lifar slowly, liquidly shed his jacket, then crept down from the piano. From Misia's neck he uncoiled her ivory-colored scarf. At the touch of his hands, her chords faded into silence. In the room's awed hush he began to dance—a sinuous, deeply mysterious communion between himself and the fortunate scarf. It was charming, it was shocking, it was very beautiful.

Applause accompanied knowing laughter. "He's certainly the bold one," Cocteau remarked, applauding along with everyone else. "The faun is dead—or at least hidden away in a Swiss asylum. Long live the faun. I wonder how long our latest ingenue imagines it will last. He's heir to such a distinguished lineage. Did you hear what Stravinsky said when Nijinsky first danced that prurient faun? 'Of *course* Vaslav made love only to the nymph's scarf. What more would Diaghilev have allowed?'"

At the head table, as Sert and Lifar resumed their places, Diaghilev, the wounded, the all-powerful, the unquenchable, rose to his feet and raised his glass to propose a toast—an old-fashioned Russian toast—to the lovely and brilliant Princesse de Polignac, dear *Tante* Winnie; to our refined American friends Gerald and Sara Murphy; but most of all (he spoke hectically, stumbling over words, even leaving words out altogether), most of all (his voice rising to an almost hysterical pitch), most of all to *notre cher maître* Igor Stravinsky. "I have loved with all my heart *L'Oiseau de Feu*, I have loved *Petrouchka,* I have loved the holy *Sacre*—but I have never loved, as I love now, this *Les Noces,* this wedding that is so... How can I say it? How can I tell you, if you are not Russian, how..."—he seemed to search in vain for words—"how..."—he gestured futilely, as if holding in his outstretched palms the fertile soil of the motherland—"how *Russian* it is." I saw, to my astonishment, that tears were streaming down his fat cheeks. "*Merci,* dearest Igor," the great Diaghilev sobbed. "*Merci, merci, merci.*"

Stravinsky stared at the tablecloth.

Our waiter brought yet more champagne. More music poured from the piano as well, a cascade of improvisations that swung from waltz to fox-trot to polonaise and back again. Madame Meyer was in splendid form, and soon dancing got under way.

Cocteau resumed his tour of the portholes, declaring loudly, in a deadpan voice, "We're sinking, my fellow travelers. Rejoice, we're still sinking. May we continue to sink without end."

At a table in the corner, by the flickering light of a raft of candles, Natalia Goncharova read palms.

"I detest these Russian diversions," huffed Diaghilev, strolling among us. "She does it as a joke, but she only invites trouble."

Memories of that disastrous Berlin séance still haunted me, but on this evening I surrendered to a bit of Russian nostalgia, and when my time came I too sat before Goncharova and allowed her to palpate my palm with her slender, bejeweled fingers.

"Nice young man from Petrograd," she addressed me. "What I see I see clearly. You will marry a princess from an eastern kingdom. You will sire a gallant son and a beautiful daughter. You will live in a castle high in the Himalayas and become wise, you will love sweet music, you will die in great happiness at the age of one hundred and forty-five!" Then she lowered her voice to a whisper. "Meanwhile, beware the prancing admiral! He's an *homme fatal* for such as you, my mooncalf. You'd do best to find other company."

With a smile, I slowly withdrew my hand from hers, though she seemed to wish to prolong her claim on me.

"I rather believe I can take care of myself," I told her.

"Nice young man from Petrograd," she said, smiling steadily, "I do hope that's true. He is right about one thing. The river is full of serpents."

A commotion at the far end of the room brought an end to our disquieting intimacy. The dishes having been cleared away, Kochno and Ansermet clambered onto the head table and began unhooking the commemorative laurel wreath from the ceiling. Giddy with champagne, they leapt down, holding their trophy between them. Stravinsky removed his shoes, and in socks whose twin holes revealed his yellowish heels, sprinted the length of the room and, executing an ungainly jeté, leapt through the proffered wreath to great applause before crashing comically into the wall.

That inspired act signaled the end. Soon everyone was

saying good-bye. One of the Americans passed around a menu, asking each of us to append our names. "I never, ever want to forget this," he proclaimed. "I want all my friends back home to know. This truly has been the most beautiful evening of my life!"

28

BERLIN
DECEMBER 6, 1943

I HAVE NO PARTICULAR WISH TO VENTURE OUT TO my niece's wedding. I would prefer to stay at my desk as the grains of sand slip inexorably through the neck of the hourglass, but obligations are obligations, and I am, after all, the best man, even if my gift of brandy is no more. The bride's mother is my cousin Onya, Nika's sister, who married a German career officer and thus chose loyally to remain in Berlin. Her husband, like all German husbands, is at the Front—in his case, guarding the Atlantic Wall against the threat of invasion, which Onya is certain will not happen. "The allies would be insane," she says. "The coast is so well defended, they would be slaughtered. Even Churchill is not so mad as to order that. Mark my word—there'll be a negotiated settlement. Before you know it, we'll hear the news that the British Fleet has been handed over to the Reich."

I do not know the groom particularly well, but I like him; a fellow exile, he is a composer of church anthems, the leader of the Black Sea Cossacks Choir, a gentle, intelligent, cultivated man, and a good quarter century older than his bride, about which Onya is not entirely pleased. A church ceremony being out of the question, the wedding is a modest, even forlorn affair held in a basement reception room in the heavily damaged Hotel Adlon.

It is difficult to watch this vestige of normal life through the eyes of a ghost, for that is what I am. I do not of course for a moment let on to that assemblage that I am a ghost. It is their happy day, after all.

The Black Sea Cossacks Choir, much reduced in number, sing several austere hymns that take me back to my childhood, and I am grateful for the excursion.

Onya confides to me that she is wearing a brand-new hat. Do I like it?

"Very much," I tell her. "Where on earth did you find a new hat?"

"There's a lovely shop in the neighborhood I used to frequent, but for the longest time there's been nothing in the window. Then last week I went by and saw the most extraordinary collection of hats. I was too busy to stop, but the next day I went back. As I turned into the block my heart sank, for I could see buildings burning on both sides of the street. But the shop hadn't been hit, though the plate glass was shattered, and the shopkeeper was sweeping up the shards. I asked if the shop was open, and he said, 'By all means!' So I went inside and tried on half a dozen hats—what fun! It's been such a long time since I did anything like that, and I thought I might never have the chance to do it again. And so I chose this one. It was covered in ash, but then so was I. It dusted off quite nicely, I think."

"You look marvelous," I tell her.

"We all look marvelous these days," she says. "Everybody

who's still alive looks marvelous, even the most bent-over crone or hideously mutilated cripple. I mean, when you think of the alternative. On my way here I passed a downed Lancaster, I suppose from last night. It was still smoking. They'd laid the charred bodies out on the sidewalk. I pity the RAF boys still alive who fall into the hands of the locals. I don't imagine it's pretty."

"No," I tell her, "I don't imagine it is."

The wedding puts me in a dismal mood; perhaps it is the sense that life will go on perfectly well without me, perhaps also the feeling that everything I do, I do for the last time. The refuge I have sought in composing this account of my past no longer seems sufficient. I have lived, certainly—my pages attest to that—but I am also still alive, and Onya's new hat makes me think there are certain things I too would like to do once more before I leave this earth.

I have heard that the Milchbar, where I used to while away some hours, continues despite everything to entertain a clientele. As the evening promises to be clouded, and the chances of another raid thus fairly slim, I determine to see for myself if this furtive oasis still flourishes in the desert the British have made of Berlin.

Though a nominal curfew is in effect, there are plenty of people on the streets: those ubiquitous crews of POWs clearing rubble, families scavenging their belongings from heaps of stone and brick, twelve-year-old boys in uniform heading to or from their antiaircraft batteries.

The city resembles the mouth of an old man—most of his remaining teeth are blackened stubs, and in between are gaps and bare ravaged gums; nonetheless, here and there, inexplicably, a single tooth, though stained, remains undecayed. Such is the Milchbar. So many churches destroyed, and yet God has left this cozy little den intact. I am, as ever, thankful for His mysterious ways. Indeed, I resist an urge to kneel and cross myself as I step across its threshold. What have I expected to find? At most, a handful of depraved old men, those too feeble or demented to serve in defense of the Homeland. Instead I survey a dimly lit room thronged with men and boys. I hear a murmured host of languages—German, Russian, Polish, Italian. There is no music, only a libidinal hum that seems to me heavenly. In one corner two men are kissing; one has shoved the other against a pockmarked wall, and their legs intertwine as their mouths feed on each other. Men sit around tables, their arms draped over each other. Champagne from occupied France is available, but so, I see with astonishment, is wine from the Rothschild cellars. In all wars, it seems, some suffer and some live well—if only for a time. A painted boy of fifteen or sixteen moves flirtatiously from table to table, allowing himself to be fondled shamelessly.

And then I see him, standing alone, one elbow resting on the bar. For a moment I am certain I am mistaken. But there is that lock of hair hanging down over his eyes. He is still wearing his waiter's uniform; he must have come directly from work. I have learned not to question Fate's strange mercies. Without a moment's hesitation I take my place at his side.

"Hello," he says in lightly accented English.

"Hello yourself," I tell him.

With a little laugh, he reverts to German. "My English is really very terrible. I only know song lyrics, and it's rather difficult to string them together into much of a conversation, don't you think?" He peers at me in the dim light. "Do I know you?"

"No," I tell him. "But I've seen you at the Eden."

"I seem to remember. Well, actually, I don't, but I believe you."

"I suppose the obvious question is, what's a fit young man like you doing working in a hotel?"

"I'm not so fit, actually. I've a bad heart. I used to think it doomed me. Now, what do you know? It might actually save my life, at least in the short term. There really isn't any long term anymore, is there?"

Unable to resist, I brush his hair from his eye.

"Hangman's lock," he says in English.

"Very nice," I tell him. "Very handsome. Are there others of your kind around? Or are you the only one who hasn't been arrested?"

"Swing boys?" he says. "Oh, there's a few of us left. No one seems to care anymore."

"Do you have a name?"

"Let's call me Hansel, shall we? And you?"

I think for a moment. "Svetlana will do."

"I see." He runs an inquisitive hand up my arm and then down again. I take his hand in mine and examine his tidy, lacquered nails. His lips are plummy, and there is a dark beauty mark just above, on the left. He removes his hand from mine and slides it down the front of my trousers. "So, is Svetlana feeling a bit romantic?"

It seems a miracle I can be aroused, given my daily quotient of terror.

"You're trembling," he says.

"I know."

"I'm trembling as well."

"I know."

He takes me by the hand and leads me down a short, darkened corridor. Suddenly we are outside in the cold air, and I realize that the entire back of the Milchbar has been sheared away. We stand amid rubble, shattered furniture, a shredded mattress. We are not alone. In the darkness I can make out other figures, can hear murmurs and groans as men grapple together in a tableau of the damned. A bit of commotion near my feet causes me to look down: an obese rat scuttles out of sight. At least someone is living well these days. Then Hansel the swing boy's lips are pressed to mine, his hands roaming restlessly, grabbing, caressing, tugging, all of which I meet in full. His breath is quite noxious but I do not care in the least. I revel in all his odors. How my heart goes out to him, this Abyssinian in all but name whose very doubtful future I take gratefully in my traitorous mouth. As I receive his gift I am as certain as I can be that I shall never on this earth taste love again.

29

PARIS

THOUGH MY FRIENDSHIP WITH COCTEAU blossomed like an origami flower, I soon came to understand that our romp in the Tuileries had been more a welcoming handshake than anything else. His real love he reserved for an erratic young man still in his teens named Raymond Radiguet.

I met this Radiguet only rarely when visiting Cocteau in the flat he shared with his mother on rue d'Anjou. My friend would usually still be in bed, in his lilac pajamas—this was his preferred way of receiving guests. The room was awash in stray papers, curios, sketches, little abstract sculptures he would devise from pipe cleaners while he chatted with you. Without any announcement, a young ruffian would barge in to borrow whisky money or read aloud a review he'd just penned for the *Nouvelle Revue Française*. He looked as if he had been discovered asleep in a stable and subsequently manhandled by the groom.

His lips were chapped, his fingernails unkempt, his haircut atrocious. But he had written a novel, *Le Diable au Corps*, which had been a succès de scandale; Cocteau had christened it "the greatest masterpiece in French literature since *La Princesse de Clèves*."

He talked of Radigo constantly, a steady stream of latest news and well-founded apprehensions. "Radigo's lately becoming much more regular in his habits," he reported, "though he's not renounced whisky, and spends too much of his time with eager American pederasts and egregious French aristocrats. I suspect he's sniffing out ideas for a new book, about which he tells me nothing, but which I sense will be more brilliant than anything he's accomplished so far. He's borrowed Georges Auric's typewriter and spends hours clattering away."

Or: "He's been telling everyone he plans to marry that girl he keeps out in Clichy. He claims to be terrified of waking up one day as a forty-year-old 'Madame Jean Cocteau.' How ridiculous! I fear he's dreadfully unhappy, but his work goes well, which is all that really matters. He's at last becoming less stupid in his habits. He's numbering his pages, he's copying out legible drafts. What people don't understand is this: art's only half intoxication; the rest is paperwork. Only a fine line separates the artist from the accountant—but as in drawing, the placement of that line is everything."

And then one day—quite suddenly, at the age of twenty—Radigo was dead.

Cocteau was beyond devastation. He kept to his bedchamber. He answered no one's letters. He rebuffed any attempt to visit; only Maman was allowed to tend to him. Finally, after weeks of this tombal silence he summoned me.

The room was darkened. He lay propped on his side, thin legs folded under a coverlet. An elusive odor hung in the air: grass and damp earth. He held his pipe over the opium lamp and breathed in the delicate fumes that wafted toward his nostrils.

"How very nice of you to come," he said. "Most people avoid ghosts out of superstitious fear, but you, *mon cher*, are supernaturally brave. Tell me: do they still speak of me in the world beyond these walls? Or have they already forgotten that a beautiful genius has simply ceased to exist?"

For a moment I could not tell whether he referred to Radiguet or to himself. I did not volunteer the news that the smart set at his nightclub had taken to calling him, this sad spring of 1924, "*le veuf sur le toit*"—the widower on the roof. It seemed too cruel. The young man's death had disconcerted everyone, even those ill-disposed toward him. But in Paris tongues will wag, and fingers point, and I was beginning to learn that cruelty is everywhere, especially among the great and talented. It was whispered that Radiguet should have known better, that it was common knowledge Cocteau spelled doom for young men, that this was hardly the first time such a tragedy had happened on his watch. With a shudder I remembered Goncharova's "*C'est un homme fatal.*"

He seemed well aware of the scurrilous gossip.

"You needn't worry," he told me. "No one should. I've put myself under quarantine—*lifelong* quarantine. I've drawn too many young men. Who knew I was such a lethal candle, I whose flame is so very dim? But my beautiful moths, those with the hyperacuity to detect my pale flickering fire—they plunge headlong. No more. Never again. Only those who are already doomed shall be allowed to remain close to deadly Narcisse."

He packed another opium pellet into the bowl of his pipe and rocked it gently over the flame.

"Listen to something terrible. These were Radigo's last words to me: 'In three days God's firing squad will execute me.' I told him, nonsense, the doctors had said there was an excellent chance the fever would break. Despite his weakness, he interrupted me with such anger in his voice that it took me aback. 'Your information's a lot less good than mine,' he told me. 'The order's been given. I heard the order given.' Three days later he was dead. No one was with him at the end. That's the worst of it. He told us all that what he feared most was the prospect of dying alone. Then he banished us and did just that. I couldn't bear to go to the funeral. I knew his beautiful corpse would sit up in the coffin and ask, 'What on earth have you done to me?' I know too well what I've done to him."

"But that's absurd," I told him. "Everyone knows he died of typhoid. There was nothing you could have done."

"All those months he was ill—in secret. How could I *not* have known? Perhaps whisky masked the symptoms. Perhaps opium prolonged the veneer of health. I never smoked while he was alive, you know. It's only to soothe my grief that I indulge now. Do this in remembrance, as our Savior said."

He inhaled the rising smoke. I contemplated his pipe, a finely made item with a bulb of blue-and-white porcelain. Of course: even in the mindlessness of grief Cocteau would be mindful enough to use only the most pleasing of artifacts to court forgetfulness.

He murmured, "Do you know what Picasso says? 'Opium is the least stupid smell in the world.'"

Several minutes drifted by.

"It's a living organism, you know. The person who doesn't smoke will never comprehend what kind of beautiful flower opium might have unfolded within him.

"But you listen so patiently. Really, your stutter has blessed you. It's bestowed on you the genius of listening, a much under-appreciated gift in our noisy times."

I laughed nervously.

"Of course you're right to laugh. But you're very good for me, *mon cher.* I feel great affection for you. In the old days I'd have invited you to share my bed. But the genius of opium is that it clears away the sexual instinct. Come now, kiss me. With lips parted. Just so."

I leaned close, touched my open lips to his. He breathed into my mouth a delicate fume of smoke.

Not long after, having received an urgent summons—*Expedition necessary. Yr. expertise required. Total secrecy essential*—I found myself accompanying my convalescent friend to Boulogne-Billancourt, where he had an appointment with one of my countrymen who went by the name of Shanghai Jimmy.

When I told him that the name hardly sounded Russian, he clucked at me. "It's clear you don't understand the first thing about espionage!"

What was abundantly clear, however, once we arrived at Shanghai Jimmy's spacious but dismal rooms, was that they doubled as some sort of laboratory. He and two coarse-skinned babushkas were so engaged in their work that they scarcely looked up when we entered. Poured into a fantastical assortment of vessels—trays, bowls, casseroles, even a chamber pot—fragrant, brownish residue steamed above spirit lamps. One of the women was straining the material through a cloth. The smell was so fresh and exciting, the sight of the opium fudge, especially in the chamber pot, so suggestive and nauseating that my head was instantly light.

"Shanghai Jimmy spent many years in Irkutsk, where he studied and perfected certain venerable practices of the Chinaman," Cocteau said by way of explanation.

"That's as good a story as any," averred Shanghai Jimmy, noticing us at last. His brusque manner seemed to indicate a military background; an imperial double-headed eagle tattooed on his left bicep confirmed it.

"You'll only acquire the finest from me," he told us. "No adulterants here. Only the purest stuff: poppy and good, rich earth. See for yourself."

As he and Cocteau conducted their transaction, I wandered about the high-ceilinged rooms. It seemed this building had once been a factory, and artifacts from its former incarnation, hulking metal skeletons and curious small wooden gadgets, lay all about, though I found it impossible to determine what, exactly, had ever been produced here.

"I am but a simple soldier," Shanghai Jimmy was saying when I returned, "loyal to the last to my dead Tsar and his family, God rest their martyred souls. Still, desperate times call for visionary solutions. If we can't return to our homeland by ordinary means, then we must coax it to come to us. Imagine: a hundred, no, a thousand chambers in which we émigrés lie dreaming our lost motherland. Who can say that the force of all those dreams won't alter reality itself? Who can say for certain that one day a new Russia—the only real Russia—may not be observed floating in the blue skies above Paris for all to see? We'll wave to the Parisians, bless their souls, and they'll wave to us, and then our sainted Russia will slowly drift heavenward, out of sight of the sad old earth entirely. The Bolsheviks can continue their murderous rampage. We won't care at all. God will be so surprised when we draw near His heavenly throne."

I was relieved when we were once more in the street, and yet saddened by this latest evidence of my fellow exiles' ongoing refusal to face reality. It was why I avoided the émigré salons hosted by Miliukov, the Vinavers, the Gippiuses—all family friends whose havens of Russian culture and politics I might have been expected to frequent as soothing reminders of home. Mother often asked after them in her letters, but I had nothing to report to her. I could not bear the endless talk of "how Russia was lost." I saw no point to the question "Which is preferable, Russia without freedom or freedom without Russia?" Seven years into our new lives, my countrymen still circled around that old, useless quandary.

Once we were in his bedchamber, Cocteau wasted no time in lighting his lamp and packing his pipe. "It's the least addictive of substances," he assured me. "So have no fear, *mon cher.* You're perfectly safe—in fact, safer than safe, as taken in moderation opium is the healthiest of practices. I know doctors who recommend it to their patients. You'd be surprised who smokes. The Princesse de Noailles, for instance. The Comtesse de La Rochefoucauld. Coco Chanel, who I believe is *centuries* old by now, and doesn't look a day over twenty-nine. Come, *mon petit.* Inhale."

The effect proved subtler than I might have expected. I felt a comfortable torpor, both mental and physical. My eyes had not closed, but before me appeared a scene as palpable as if it really were there. Behold the Oredezh, speckled with nenuphars, on which blue demoiselles alighted, resting motionless before resuming flight. The landscape was caught in a lovely pause, as if something were about to happen—stallions, perhaps, were about to thunder into the shallow waters—but I was able to prolong the moment indefinitely, and savor the stillness, the languor, the burning midday scene before me.

Not for an instant did I take the hallucination for anything other than what it was, and I was rather proud of myself for maintaining my mental clarity throughout.

When I told Cocteau that it had been quite interesting, though not so remarkable that I intended to pursue it as an avocation, he hastened to declare, "Then we needn't repeat this experiment. I've no wish for anyone to accuse me of attempting to ruin you."

30

AS NEVER BEFORE, I MUST EARN MY KEEP. AN occasional review for Miliukov's *Latest News* brought in spare change, but most of my meager income derived from English lessons. For several months I shared with the painter Pavel Tchelitchew and an American pianist named Allen Tanner an apartment in rue Copernic so tiny we called it "The Doll's House." They were amusing company—Pavlik high-strung, paranoid, exuberantly ambitious; Allen self-effacing to a fault but indispensible to his companion, who was far more concerned with Kabbalah than with paying the rent. We were a threadbare lot, but soon mastered the fine art of making a brandy and coffee last a whole evening in the cafés at the Raspail corner. We became expert at "dining on fumes," as Pavlik dubbed the practice of absorbing the delicious aroma of a proper meal being consumed at the next table. Once or twice a week we would pool our scant resources and venture to Madame Wassilieff's *cantine* on the avenue du Maine, where four francs bought cabbage soup, vegetable pie, a glass of white wine, and a cigarette. The day after our feast, we would fast.

As Pavlik had no money to pay for models, I posed for him on occasion.

He talked as he worked.

"There's the most scrumptious boy lingering at the street corner," he informed me, dancing back to the window. "He's a leopard in boy form. No, don't move. It's what Diaghilev must have seen when he first glimpsed Nijinsky."

He improvised a pirouette. "What I wouldn't have given to see him dance. They say Diaghilev keeps him locked away in a guarded flat in Passy. The clown of God, he calls himself these days. He's quite mad. Be still, kitten. I like that look on your face just now. Resolute but bored. What's the color of your soul, I wonder? Like me, you're part woman. Isn't that true? But don't answer. Don't say a word."

For a full minute he painted, then leapt back to the window.

"Oh, dear God, that boy makes me so hungry. The only boys more scrumptious than French boys are the American ones, don't you think? But this one's so purely French. Surely he senses the gratitude streaming down on him from this window. See? I myself am sometimes like the famous faun. *Sans pitié du sanglot dont j'étais encore ivre.* There's something wrong with this painting. Or perhaps I'm what's wrong. It should be possible, you know, to execute an entire painting without the tip of the brush ever leaving the surface. That's how God created the world. But we poor humans must dip and dip, and dawdle, and go again and again to the window.

"No, don't say a word. You'll ruin that beautiful look on your face. You're quite the Russian princeling. Don't look at me that way. Why, the Nabokovs are nearly as old a family as we Tchelitchews. Next to us, the Romanovs were johnnies-come-lately. Do you know that when Grand Duchess Marie saw my father at the theater, she exclaimed to a friend, 'Now there's someone who's even nobler than we.' It's a fact. Our line traces itself back to a brother of Caesar Augustus. And I hear that you're descended from a great Tatar warrior. Tell me, Seryodushka, is it true what I've also heard—that the blood of Peter the Great flows in your veins? Speak. I've granted you permission."

"It's old family gossip," I admitted with a trace of a stutter. "Grandmother Nabokova conducted her amours at the very highest levels of the imperium. Alexander the Liberator was a particular friend."

"And here we are, penniless, desperate, in exile. And longing for a boy who won't even look this way."

When he had finished the painting, I was a bit chagrined by the image the canvas conveyed: a figure ridiculously gaunt, more jester than princeling. Nonetheless I felt gratitude, even a strange sense of relief, that I had been recorded. Unfortunately, as Pavlik had no money for new canvases, that portrait was soon covered over by a new painting—an arrestingly garish basket of strawberries.

Later, when Pavlik was famous and I no longer knew him as well, I regretted that none of my portraits survived. But no matter.

Though my poverty was dreary beyond description, my reviews did afford me the luxury of otherwise unaffordable seats at symphony concerts or my beloved Ballets Russes. And I was not without other diversions. For a while I took up with Claude, a sweetly pathetic, big-bottomed lad from Reims. When that faded, I spent several weeks achingly enamored of Hervé, a handsome mannequin maker's apprentice, only to discover, upon finally attaining his bed, that he was entirely impotent.

After each of these episodes I was left feeling somehow duller than before.

Then, in the fall of 1925, I met an American from Cleveland. Heir to a department store fortune, Weldon Bryce III was keen on jazz, French cuisine, and Byzantine icons, roughly in that order. I seemed to fall under the latter category, and he was happy enough to add me to the collection of smoke-darkened saints and martyrs that adorned his well-appointed chambers in rue Montparnasse. That they had mostly been looted from churches by the Bolsheviks gave me pause, but not enough to reject his advances. He had a large mouth and delicious lips, and he turned out to be well endowed in more respects than one.

We quickly settled into a pleasant enough routine. He was always immaculately clad in strange American threads, and inordinately fond of the expression "Wow!"—which Paris evoked in him with some regularity.

My friends found Weldon impossibly handsome and hopelessly naive. "I am mesmerized by *l'américanisme*," Cocteau confessed to me after meeting him, "as by a man pointing a revolver directly at me."

A tender day in early spring. Standing at a third-floor window of the Thermes Urbains, ashen and gaunt, clothed in a robe of regal purple, Cocteau bestowed on us an unhurried papal wave, his long slender fingers held rigidly together.

"*Mes enfants!*" he cried. "So heavenly of you to come. But do not approach. You must remain at a distance. The wise doctors insist."

For a moment I could not repress the sense that he was being held in quarantine—the *homme fatal* at last found out by the authorities. In reality, he had checked himself into the clinic for an opium cure—a brutal regime, if his occasional notes to me could be believed, of purges, cathartics, and enemas, all paid for by the indispensible Coco Chanel.

"But tell us how you are," Weldon called out.

Cocteau cupped his left hand to his ear while continuing to wave with his right.

"How *are* you?" Weldon repeated, responding in kind by cupping his hands around his mouth like a megaphone.

"Marvelous," Cocteau told us. "My memory is returning. I can remember...telephone numbers! And bits of poetry I thought I'd lost forever. An angel comes every night and sits on my chest as I sleep, though the nurses claim this can't be so. But what do they know? He touches my lips with his fingers which are feathered like the wings of birds."

A nurse appeared by his side. "Monsieur Cocteau," she urged. "You're disturbing the other patients. Perhaps you could return to your bed. You need your rest."

"I'm so invigorated," Cocteau told us—and the nurse as well. "All my sexual energy has returned. I sweat, I piss, I ejaculate. These are miracles." At this the nurse looked positively miserable. She was joined by a second, even more formidable sister. Firmly they took our frail friend in hand. "*Adieu, mes amis,*" he cried like a child carried off to bed. "*Adieu, adieu.*" Then he disappeared. The window shut behind him. We remained where we were, looking up at the spot he had vacated.

Then the window opened, just barely, and out sailed a flimsy aeroplane of folded paper. The breeze caught it, sustained it till it landed almost at our feet. Unfolded, the page torn from a notebook revealed an alarming sketch: Cocteau, his eyeballs protruding at the ends of long stems, his slender fingers likewise stems, as if his whole body were in the process of metamorphosing into a grotesque bouquet of opium pipes.

His own antique pipe and lamp he had bequeathed to me on his entry into the asylum. Even as I scrutinized that horrible drawing, a part of me longed to be out of the wonderful sunlight and sequestered in my wretched room in rue St.-Jacques. I had not counted on succumbing so readily to the drug's lures. I reassured myself that my habit was hardly regular enough to be habit—an indulgence, rather; a sometime refuge from the dull daily march toward oblivion.

It was the only cause for quarrel between me and Weldon. Indeed, I suspected he had brought me to the Thermes Urbains to absorb in full the terrible, disfiguring vision Cocteau had sketched for our benefit. It struck me that my desire for opium mimicked my other desires: my thirst for the ballet, my hunger for old books, my fevered quest for various ill-starred loves. Weldon, for instance: I loved the mere fact of his skin. But what, in the end, did I wish from him? What did I want from any of them? It was a conundrum I pondered increasingly.

After a hearty meal at the Closerie des Lilas, we parted at the corner of boulevard Montparnasse and the boul' Mich. I am loath to admit it, but I remained with Weldon in part because he was happy to treat me to dinner at such restaurants, and I was tired of dining on fumes.

When I arrived home, the concierge handed me a letter from my mother.

My dearest Seryosha, she wrote from Prague,

> *Perhaps you will have heard the news from Berlin, though knowing your brother I suspect he has neglected to inform you: he has married one Véra Evseevna Slonim. You are not to feel slighted. There was no ceremony; they told no one of their plans, and no one from the family attended. I am of course happy for him, as we all must be—happy for his happiness, that is. As for this Véra, she is a rather strange creature, I think (though I hardly know her, and mostly through your brother's taciturn remarks) but in many ways I believe her to be quite well suited to our Volodya, and utterly devoted to him and to his art. She is both muse and typist—and, by my count, the fifth woman he has asked to marry him. Perhaps now he'll settle down. Your aunt Nadezhda, by the way, is quite beside herself at the thought of having a Jewess in the family. Of course, as usual, she blames your father's liberal attitudes for this turn*

of events. I must say I relish her discomfiture, as would your father. Your Uncle Kostya has not yet weighed in, but I can imagine his reaction as well.

All is well enough here. Your sisters and little brother send their love, as do I, my dearest.

I had become used to following my brother's life from afar, whether through Mother's missives or the increasingly frequent appearances of "V. Sirin" in émigré journals. The news was not so much startling as melancholy, and I realized how I still grieved the silence that had become so entrenched between us. If only he had married Svetlana Siewert—*she* would not have allowed this estrangement to continue.

Before retiring to my bed to enjoy a consoling smoke, I wrote my brother a friendly and congratulatory note. Several weeks later I received in return a printed announcement:

Monsieur Vladimir Nabokov
Mademoiselle Véra Slonim
Mariés le 15 Avril 1925
Berlin, 13, Luitpoldstrasse

The handwriting on the envelope was unfamiliar—Véra's, no doubt. No personal message was attached.

Weldon and I got on famously. In August we traveled south to the Côte d'Azur, where Cocteau had established himself at the Hotel Welcome in the small harbor town of Villefranche-sur-mer. There, cured, he was writing and drawing by day, and by night invoking the god of music by playing jazz in the hotel bar.

We arrived early in the morning, having taken the night express from Paris, the *train bleu* that he had recently immortalized in his ballet for Diaghilev. A stern-faced concierge—one of those formidable women one seems to meet behind every counter in France—took us up to Cocteau's rooms, but to her repeated knocking there came no response. She opened the door onto a familiar scene of chaos—books, papers, sketches everywhere, but no Cocteau.

We returned to the lobby, where a lugubrious young Algerian woman appeared from the kitchen to inform us, "He is out there." We followed her pointing arm to the lapis lazuli ocean and there he was indeed, seated in a small dinghy and rowing madly. In the prow of the boat stood a bare-chested lad no older than twelve; from his frantic gestures, he appeared to be urging Cocteau, who was clad in a terry cloth robe, to apply himself more forcefully to the oars. Behind them loomed an immense American warship—as if bearing down on them in hot pursuit. That was an illusion, of course; the ship was still far out and no doubt unaware of the small craft making for shore.

We helped drag the boat ashore. The boy jumped out—he was wearing nothing but a loincloth, and the remains of a laurel wreath perched on his head. His lips and cheeks were gaudily rouged.

"The Americans come by sea *and* by land," Cocteau greeted us, "while my wise Russian sticks to land. I'm most happy for all invasions. You've arrived just in time. You shall see. Tonight will be magnificent! Never underestimate the benefits of a deep harbor!"

He was not wrong. By noon the American battleship had docked, by midafternoon the quayside was swarming with giddy sailors, and by early evening the Hotel Welcome, which turned out to be a bordello as well as a hotel, was replete with them. Liquor flowed freely. Cocteau accompanied a local accordionist, violinist, and trumpeter on the hotel's out-of-tune Pianola. The whores, who seemed to have been selected to appeal to an impressive range of tastes, lured their increasingly inebriated clientele into increasingly libidinous dances.

Weldon and I sat at a small table near the entrance, away from the commotion, and drank pastis with two of Cocteau's latest "*enfants,*" Jean Bourgoint and Maurice Sachs.

Sachs was a familiar face, a habitué of Le Boeuf, but Bourgoint was new to me, and I found it difficult to take my eyes off him. Alas, the more he talked, the more vacuous he seemed, whereas Maurice—pudgy, ill-shaven, disheveled—exuded considerable conversational charm. He soon had us all in tears of laughter with his story of having to smuggle his mother into England, as she faced arrest in France for having passed a bad check.

Weldon asked Sachs if it was true, as we had both heard, that the walls of his bedroom were covered in photographs of Cocteau.

"It *is* true," he affirmed sweetly, "and there is one particular photograph to which I pray every night."

Bourgoint seemed to find this inordinately funny.

"At least I don't sleep in the same bed as my sister," an offended-looking Sachs told him.

"Jeanne and I are twins," Bourgoint said. "Why shouldn't we?"

"I happen to know as a matter of fact you're not twins. Your brother is her twin."

"We're spiritual twins," Bourgoint countered, as if that somehow settled it. Cocteau would some years later immortalize those "twins" in his *Les Enfants Terribles.*

"Depravity of all kinds fascinates me," Weldon said. "If you're in love with your sister, you shouldn't be ashamed. I left America in order to discover people like you. And you as well." He turned to Sachs. "I think it's marvelous that you worship at Cocteau's shrine. Where I come from, everyone is so boring. It repulses me."

Sachs looked perturbed. "I'm not sure how admirable it is to be a tourist in other people's misery," he said.

"Oh, come," Weldon said, "it's what we Americans are good at. Besides, we can afford it. That's certainly what Sergey likes about me."

I told him his finances had nothing to do with my affection for him.

Arching his eyebrows, he gave me a look. "Let me get this round," he offered. "And the next as well. I know perfectly well you're all penniless."

None of us, I am sorry to report, declined his offer.

31

IT WAS VERY LATE. THE AMERICAN SAILORS HAD returned to their ship; the whores were having a nightcap in the bar; Weldon had gone to bed, as had Bourgoint and Sachs. As requested, I knocked on Cocteau's door. I found him lying in his large bed, atop the coverlet, scribbling madly. Without glancing up, he patted the mattress to indicate I should join him. When I had slipped off my shoes and settled in comfortably beside him, he flung aside his writing. "Beastly muse," he said. "Well, I'm done with her for the evening. And now I have you, *mon petit*. How lovely to see you here in the splendid south. It must all seem wonderfully strange and heaven-kissed."

I told him my family used to summer in Biarritz, but that I had been very young and scarcely remembered a thing.

"I too came as a child, but most assuredly not with my family," he said. "No, when I was fifteen I ran away to Marseille. Such a foolish little romantic I was, besotted by the likes of Jules Verne and Pierre Loti. An old Chinese-Annamite woman found me lost on the docks and took me to the rue de la Rose, in the old quarter. I explained to her that I didn't want to go home, telling her my family was monstrous, which wasn't true at all. For a year I lived there under a false name: a boy had drowned and I had his papers. I worked in a Chinese restaurant that was also a *fumerie* and a brothel. Everyone smoked; the opium was of the finest quality. But I was young then, and had no need to smoke; however, the other pleasures on offer I certainly did investigate."

As he spoke, he caressed my thigh, and in return I petted him as well. We were two children, sleepy, at perfect ease with each other.

"It was the happiest year of my life," he continued dreamily. "But enough of the past. Let's speak instead of the present. How has the God of Love treated my favorite Russian?"

I told him that Weldon was amusing, impetuous, earnest, though I worried sometimes that he considered me an exotic specimen, an extension of the Russian icons he collected.

"But you *are* exotic, my dear. All you Russians are. We never know quite what to make of you, which keeps us tantalized."

"Still," I said. "It can be rather tiresome at times."

"You sound unhappy," he diagnosed with discomfiting certainty.

"Not at all," I told him. "Why should I be?"

I was still smarting from Weldon's remarks earlier in the evening. Cocteau had gradually worked his hand higher up my thigh till he had found the spot he sought. I surrendered without resistance to his long, kneading fingers. When I reciprocated his attentions, he purred, "You see, I'm fully brought back to life. How terrible those weeks in the clinic. And how little I knew what lay in wait for me upon my release. You've heard the news, I imagine. *Everyone*, it seems, has heard the news, and everyone has his own opinion. Not that I care that some profess to be scandalized by the return of a loyal if prodigal son to the Church and its sacraments.

"I've never renounced my faith, after all. Shall I confess this to you, *mon cher?* I, the most frivolous of men, have often surprised myself by slipping into out-of-the-way churches, to offer up a solitary candle to our Lord. I don't think I fully understood, at the time. Indeed, I thought nothing of it. But God knew. What is that marvelous line by your countryman? 'God sees everything, but waits.' For me He has indeed waited—and then He made His move. It was at a dinner party at the home of Jacques Maritain, that most exquisite of Thomist philosophers. One of the guests had come straight to Paris that very evening from a mission to the Bedouins. He might as well have been an angel sent straight from the Lord. As he spoke of his work in Arabia, I was knocked for a loop. Punch-drunk, as they say of boxers. Room, books, friends: nothing existed any longer. I was *caught.* Yes, my dear, it's true. A priest gave me the same shock as Stravinsky and Picasso. Three days later I made confession and took the sacraments in Maritain's private chapel in Meudon."

I felt a queer shiver at his words. It was years since I had last been in a church, save once to peek inside St.-Séverin, which lay just a few doors down from my current lodgings—and that only to admire the architecture. I associated those occasional visits I used to make, during that horrible time in Yalta, with a kind of cowardice, a cringing animal fear of imminent extinction I had not been afflicted by in quite some time. Enveloped in European safety, my soul had grown fat and indolent. For years I had had the luxury of neglecting its condition entirely. Now that I regarded it, I was not sure I liked what I saw.

"You can't imagine what Radigo's death did to me," Cocteau continued, though I only half listened, absorbed by my own thoughts. "Left alone and half mad, I knew in those weeks and months that I should raise my hands to heaven for help, but I simply couldn't. So I sought instead Baudelaire's artificial paradise. It's excruciating, *excruciating*, to be an unbeliever with a spirit that is deeply religious. And speaking of excruciating, what delicious release, finally, to... Well..."

He regarded the aftermath of the mutual convulsion he had brought us to. "We've made quite a mess of ourselves, haven't we? And yet I've thoroughly enjoyed our little chat. I shall remember it for a good long while. I hope you will as well?"

Later that night, after I had slipped into bed beside the peacefully snoring Weldon, I dreamt of God as I had not in many years. In the dream He invited me into His wood-paneled study and was showing me a map. He no longer looked like Michel Fokine; I have no clear impression of His face in the dream. He had shed Father's military uniform for a plum-colored smoking jacket. Instead of a desk there was a card table, and on the card table was laid out, much as Mother used to lay out jigsaw puzzles, a collection of Tarot-like images connected to each other by intricately embroidered filaments. The images were like small motion pictures, busy scenes that I failed to make out clearly, despite His urging me to do so. "Fate," said God. He touched the map with His fingertip, and the images changed—but from what to what, exactly? Try as I might, I could not see them clearly. "Providence," He said. He touched the map once more, and again it changed. "Free will," He said. I had the sense that He was growing rather exasperated that I could not make any of this out for myself.

Our month in the beautiful south drew to a close. The night before we were to leave, I stopped by Cocteau's room to thank him for his gift of sun and sea. As I approached his door, Picasso's least stupid smell in the world brought me up short.

I hesitated before knocking, but my desire to take proper leave of my friend overcame my reluctance to discover him in this lapse.

"By all means enter," he said from within. When I opened the door I could see, by the dim light of a lamp over whose shade a silk handkerchief had been draped, Cocteau propped on his elbow in bed—and beside him, likewise recumbent, Jean Bourgoint.

"Ah, welcome, *mon petit.* I knew you would come. The flame draws many a lovely moth, does it not?"

When I said nothing, he went on. "Are you surprised? I suppose you must be. How complex this life is! Yes, I'm perfectly aware I was saying only yesterday that opium resembles religion about as much as an illusionist resembles the Christ. But it's so easy to get lost among these distinctions, isn't it? Come. Have a little of my pipe. This is very fine, infinitely better than Shanghai Jimmy's famous mud."

Bourgoint said nothing, merely stared glassy-eyed in my general direction.

"Come," Cocteau repeated. He stretched out his hand to me. "Please."

"Weldon will have what the Americans call a 'fit.'" I said. "Despite everything, he's quite the Puritan."

"Americans," Cocteau replied. "I'm so tired of Americans. America reminds me of a girl who's more interested in her health than in her beauty. She swims, boxes, dances, leaps onto moving trains—all without knowing she's beautiful. One suspects she doesn't even care. Enough of it, I say. I so much prefer my Jean-Jean here, who knows one thing, and one thing only, which is how to be beautiful."

Bourgoint gave Cocteau an ineffectual little shove. Cocteau ignored him, taking instead another delicate effusion of smoke into his lungs. There was something so charming about the two of them, something so calming in the scene before my eyes, that I realized how very much, these past months, I had secretly longed for opium's solace.

"You *understand,*" Cocteau told me as I slid into bed beside him. "Of all my friends, you *understand.*"

Weldon was not as understanding.

"You've been smoking," he said when I returned to our room.

"I can smell that horrid smell on you. You've been dishonest with me, and that dishonesty has ruined our final night here."

I attempted to explain the circumstances.

"I despise that little Frenchman," he told me. "And I don't understand your infatuation with him. He ruins young men. Forget the religious blather; *that's* his true vocation. He plans to completely destroy that poor Bourgoint fellow, who's really too innocent to live. He's clouded Sachs's head with incense and mumbo-jumbo—a shame, because at least Sachs has an intelligent head on his shoulders. The man exults in chaos. Just look around us. We're living in a brothel, for God's sake."

"I thought you found all this pleasingly exotic."

Weldon paced the room. "What do you want from me?" he shouted. "What have you ever wanted, besides all the little luxuries I can provide you with? Admit it: you're still very angry about what happened to you and your country. You haven't even begun to come to terms with what it means. That's why opium holds such a damnable attraction for you; it allows you to neglect what you don't want to face up to. I thought I could somehow replace opium in your affections, but clearly your grief is much, much deeper than I can assuage."

I wondered how long he had been rehearsing this particular outburst.

"I don't think you know yourself at all," he went on. "You pretend not to be serious about anything, but you're completely blind to your own predicament, Sergey. It hurts me to have to speak this truth to you."

"What would you have me do, then?" I asked him.

"Oh, I don't know. This is so tiresome. *You're* so tiresome. I wish I'd never met you. Or no: I wish you'd turned out to be real. But there's nothing there. There's just a flicker, and then on closer examination there's nothing."

We got on famously, Weldon and I, and then we no longer got on so famously. And then we no longer got on at all.

32

"THE JEWS HAVE PRODUCED ONLY THREE originative geniuses," announced the grand figure seated on her throne. "Christ, Spinoza, and myself." A sandal dangled precariously from her big toe. I watched to see if it would fall, but it did not. None of the young men seated in a semicircle around the throne seemed willing to contradict her pronouncement.

"You see, Pussy?" The regal figure addressed the small, dark woman who had admitted us. "They agree with me."

"Lovey certainly knows very well these things she knows," said the small dark woman.

"But what new faces are these?"

"Tchelitchew and Tanner, and another young man who is unknown to us."

"Why yes. The Russian painter and his American friend."

Now she peered at me. "And they have brought along an unknown young man of inscrutable intent."

All the young men eyed me, as if eager to witness my

peremptory eviction. But Miss Stein only laughed—a cordial, infectious, mirthful cascade of notes that settled into a prolonged jolly chuckle. "Very well," she said. "I like unknown young men, as long as they intend to become well known."

I bowed, and haltingly introduced myself.

"Why—a stutterer! How marvelous," Miss Stein exclaimed. "You see, I also stutter, though only on paper." She laughed again. The young men laughed as well, though their laughter was but a pale shadow of her capacious chortle. She was massive, continental, American; they were wisps of cirrus drifting across that landscape.

Blushing, I told her I very much wished to read her work.

"No doubt you shall, one day," she said, adding, in a rather melancholy tone, "all in good time. You see, the world's not ready just yet for my genius. Even my young men are struck half dead by it—and they're the chosen ones. But in the meantime, tell me what you are, what you do, what you dream. You must be another Russian, I presume. Where do all these Russians come from?"

I told her I gave English lessons, and the occasional Russian one. That from time to time I reviewed concerts for an émigré newspaper.

"You write about music?" She frowned.

"Yes."

"And in Russian, I imagine."

"Yes."

"I see. I really don't wish to fathom Russian," she said. "It's got the temper of saints and the tongue of bears and the sweet stench of great smoking candles. I fear it, really I do. I would compare it to a wild forest into which I might wander and be lost—and end up changed into a beast or maybe a bird."

As that had never occurred to me, I was left momentarily tongue-tied. Her young men murmured approvingly. Evidently she took my silence for assent, or perhaps she had grown bored with the direction our conversation had taken; in any event, she nodded toward small, dark Miss Toklas, who took me by the arm and led me to a circle of chairs in a far corner of the room, away from the charmed circle, where two fashionably dressed American ladies balanced plates of cakes in their laps and observed the imperial proceedings from afar.

"You'll be much happier here," Miss Toklas confided.

Miss Stein, leaning forward from her throne, was telling Pavlik, "So you're our young genius. Well, well. I like young geniuses so long as they are young."

"Don't be crestfallen," Miss Toklas continued. "You see, Lovey thinks music is something for adolescents, and since she's fully adult, she has no need of such amusements. Here. Sit by me. I shall manage to entertain you perfectly well."

Producing needlework from a bag by her chair, she commenced her work, all the while peppering me with questions. How did I know this Mr. Tchelitchew? What did I think of my compatriot's work? Or that of his friends? She bandied about the names of Bérard, Berman, Tonny—painters with whom Pavlik had recently been associating in exhibitions and cafés. Who was the leader of that band of young Romantics? That was what they were, weren't they? Young Romantics bent on overturning the ancien régime of Picasso and Matisse? As for Mr. Tanner: did he have any talent as a pianist? Was he the next Paderewsky or Rachmaninov? If so, why had he not gone further? Did he lack ambition? Surely Mr. Tchelitchew did not lack ambition. Miss Toklas had seen the wolf gleam in his eyes.

I answered as best I could, sensing that every word of mine would find its way back to "Lovey." I caught the phenomenal laughter booming forth occasionally across the atelier, and Pavlik's high giggle in echo.

"Lovey so admires Mister Tchelitchew's *Basket of Strawberries*," Miss Toklas divulged to me. "So fleshly ripe, so refreshingly shocking, really, for plain adorable old strawberries. When she saw it in the Salon d'Automne she said immediately to me, 'This is why there is no flower, this is why there is no flower in color, this is why there is why.' And she wondered whether there could be more where that delightful impertinence came from. We do think Mister Tchelitchew paints like one paints who paints what's real."

Throughout our "conversation" the two American ladies had said not a word, and Miss Toklas had evinced no interest in them whatsoever. Now, taking advantage of a break in Miss Toklas's narrative, one of the ladies complimented her needlework, and asked where she had found the pattern. "It seems so unusual," she said.

"Picasso designed it for me," Miss Toklas told her matter-of-factly, without glancing up from her work.

The Americans—it dawned on me they were tourists drawn to the famous spectacle at 27 rue de Fleurus—looked at each other wide-eyed, as if every slight of the evening had in that instant been redeemed.

"Lovey has her business to attend to, but soon," Miss Toklas revealed, "there will be plenty of time to mingle. I've made some cakes to be eaten, and a liqueur to taste, and soon we'll all be talking among ourselves. You must be curious who these young men are with whom you will soon be talking.

"There is Juan Gris, who is not young but who is the only true painter in the world, all the others are mere artists, and he is talking to an artist in many different ways, Monsieur Crevel, who is young and drawing and writing and living in ways that are unexpected and dangerous and inspired like driving a Ford along country lanes at much too great a speed but enjoying all the while a passionate view. There is Monsieur Bernard Fäy the professor of wit and morals who is a most indispensable presence. Mr. Anderson the American writer who is also not young but has been writing for many years in a way that is very American and thus youthful even if no longer young. There is Elliot Paul who is also writing and is said to play the accordion like the very devil and has begun a very fine magazine which publishes only the literature of the future which is what the literature of today should be whether it is American or young or anything else. And another American who writes the music of the future which we admire but do not enjoy, his name is George Antheil, and he is always plotting his fame. They are all very musical, the modern young men of America. That one as well, Virgil Thomson. Lovey declares him a variety of apple, crisp but sweet, available for brandy-making. And finally, by the fire, Bravig Imbs, he is new to us and he aims to please, and we very much like him at the moment despite his aiming to please."

Struck by her curious way of talking, I was uncertain whether my leg was being pulled—and that uncertainty would remain with me for all the many evenings I spent in their company.

My conversation with Cocteau that night in Villefranche lingered, as did that perplexing God dream I could not get out of my head. I had other dreams, which I remembered in snatches when I woke: heavenly hallucinations, indistinguishable in their way from the dreams opium fosters, and yet different, as they were not artificially induced but sprang, I fully believe, from my deepest soul. God, I was convinced, was attempting to show me something, only I was too stupid to understand.

In the wake of Weldon's disappearance from my life my smoking grew much worse. Meanwhile, Cocteau's admission of his longtime habit of ducking into churches had encouraged a recurrence of my own religious practice. I began to frequent St.-Séverin, which was in the neighborhood, but soon I ranged farther afield, to St.-Sulpice in the faubourg St.-Germain, La Madeleine in Cocteau's neighborhood, St.-Roch near the Louvre. I told no one that I had begun to pray in earnest to the nearly naked man who hangs bloodied from the cross.

St.-Roch was my favorite. Le Mercier's masterpiece. Framing the main altar was a baroque sculpture of the Nativity, Mary and Joseph flanking the infant Christ in the crib. In a stroke of theatrical genius, one's gaze was directed beyond that tableau, through an aperture, to the Calvary Chapel where the adult Christ hung crucified. As if thirty-three years were telescoped into a single instant, one took in at once the whole awful drama, from ignominious birth to ignominious death, all framed by Mary and Joseph, who leaned inward very much like two hands cupped in prayer. I do not know why this moved me as much as it did. That afternoon when I first paid a visit, I felt somehow closer to life's mystery than I had ever been—only I was still too stupid to understand. The words came to me: *For God so loved the world that he gave his only Son, that whoever believes in him should not perish but have eternal life.* I thought of Davide, of Yuri, of my father—all lovely, beloved sons, all prematurely dead, hideously tossed away. Fate. Providence. Free will. Just as in the dream, God who so loved the world asked me to understand what I had not felt capable of understanding. I gazed through tears at Christ's beautiful, broken form. I never saw Davide's corpse, but I had seen Yuri's, and Father's: undeniable evidence that they were no more, the same evidence Jesus's followers saw when they put His body in the tomb. And yet—when the women went to the tomb, it was empty. And the angel said, Why do you seek Him here? He whom you seek is not here.

Weldon had accused me of failing to come to terms with my grief. What if it were true? What if, beyond all the superficial pleasures in which I all too happily engaged, there was at my core an unassuageable grief? Grief for those I loved who had not loved me in return, grief for those whose death made our failed relationships forever irreparable, grief for Volodya, to whom I could conceivably still make amends except for our estrangement, which felt as absolute as death. Grief perhaps most of all for the self I had failed to become: the generous, abundant, joyful self I avidly turned my back on as I longed, even now, for the pipes I would smoke when back in the tombal safety of my room.

They were not here, those whom I sought. Be they ever so battered, they were not any more battered than our Savior Himself had been when they took Him down from the cross. It was improbable, illogical, scarcely to be believed; yet without that hope—that all the dead, and all that love, would somehow live again, and forever—life as I understood it could not be borne. And I was suddenly, absolutely, irrevocably convinced, there on my knees in St.-Roch, that God would not, indeed could not, have created lives for any of us that cannot be borne.

Thus, in the fall of 1925, unbeknownst to any of my family or friends save Cocteau, who graciously agreed to be my sponsor, I began to prepare for the Rite of Christian Initiation of Adults in order that I might, at Easter, be received into the sacraments of the Holy Roman Catholic and Apostolic Church. Weekly I attended a course of instruction with a gentle and most sympathetic priest at St.-Séverin who encouraged me to pray to Mary, the blessed Mother of God, for guidance and assistance.

"We say, 'From Mary, straight to Jesus,'" he counseled. "Your friends and family may fall away, but Mary remains your most steadfast ally and advocate."

When eventually I addressed her in prayer, I felt a remarkable sensation, which I find difficult to describe even now, for no sooner had I begun my prayer than three images sprang into my heart. The first was La Karsavina as she knelt in the vast cathedral before the Icon of Our Lady of Kazan, offering up to God her gratitude, her devotion, her sublime artistry. The second was my mother, kneeling to kiss the dark earth at Vyra—an act she performed each summer when we arrived in the countryside. The third was myself, in abject gratitude at having been returned safely to earth, courtesy of Hugh Bagley, after my ascent into the heavens over Somerset.

33

ON A BLUSTERY AFTERNOON NOT LONG BEFORE Easter, on the boul' Mich, where I had been browsing among the secondhand bookstores, a taxicab pulled up to the curb beside me. I paid it no heed, I walked on, it kept pace with me, then a voice called in Russian, "Hey, you there, don't you want a ride, Nabokov?"

I turned and looked at the driver, whose voice I had recognized with a dreadful thrill. Oleg Danchenko's face was fuller and coarser than it used to be; a nasty scar marred his forehead, just above his left eyebrow, but his gold-flecked eyes remained undimmed.

"*Bozhe moy*!" I cried. "Is it really you?"

"In the flesh. Come on and hop in. Where are you going?"

"Nowhere in particular," I told him.

"Still stuttering, I see. Well, no matter. Let's go nowhere, then. Let's sit at a table and drink some wine and catch up for a bit. How's that sound? Are you glad to see me?"

"Delighted, actually," I told him in all honesty. "I'd no idea you were here. Why haven't our paths crossed?"

He appraised my tweeds, courtesy of Weldon's still-recent largesse. "I don't imagine we move in the same set," he said. "I'm in the taxi all the time, except when it's in the garage, which is too bloody often. I spend half my hard-earned pay keeping her running. But what can a fellow do? I'm obligated to keep the wife in a style she's accustomed to, don't you know?"

We ended up out in Passy, at a bar filled with émigrés smoking, playing chess, killing time. I so seldom came out here to the so-called Russian suburbs that I felt strangely alien among my countrymen.

"I'm really very happy to see you," I told Oleg. "I always wondered whether you'd made it out alive."

"Yes, we got out, even my aunt in Smolny. Then my father had a heart attack a month later in Constantinople. Dropped dead in Taksim Square. Probably for the best. It would've killed him to have to live like this. After Constantinople we were in Sofia for two years, and now here since the spring of twenty-four. And what about you? What exciting adventures do you have to tell me about?"

The exchange of escape tales is de rigueur whenever émigrés meet, and I narrated my own, including my current straitened financial circumstances.

"Have you heard the joke?" he said. "Two men are sitting at a café. One of them says, See that bartender? Well, he used to be a banker in Moscow. And the other one says, See that waiter? He used to be a colonel in the Russian Army. And the first one says, See that dachshund? It used to be a Great Dane back in Ukraine." He laughed. "We've all sunk low. I feel like a paper doll here, a thing of no substance at all. I often go to the Russian church on rue Daru. How that takes me back! And yet I doubt I'll ever be going home. It's all gone, you know. Leningrad isn't Petrograd. In Leningrad they've been burning books and furniture for fuel. That would never have happened in Petrograd. There's nothing in Leningrad but misery and suffering. And all because of Germany and the Jews."

Wishing to head off *that* tiresome topic, I said, innocently enough, "So you're married. Congratulations are in order. Since when? And who's the lucky girl?"

"Nearly five years. Can you believe it? Valechka Nikolaevna. An adorable little kitten I fell in with after my father prudently recalled me from Petrograd to the family farm. You'll meet her soon enough. She's vivacious, a good head on her shoulders—a heart of gold, as they say, somewhere underneath that sarcastic wit. We'll have you to dinner very soon. She'll be pleased to meet one of my oldest friends. She's heard lots about those days, all my school pals, but so few of them are still around. So few made it out. Ilya, Vassily, Lev: all gone. Butchered like animals. I think Valechka sometimes doubts whether I even have a past. But what about your pals—what did you call yourselves, the Assyrians?"

"Abyssinians," I said, surprised and touched he remembered. "Likewise dead."

He slid his large hand over my own. I noted that his thumbnail was blackened, a detail I found at once repellent and arousing. "We've truly suffered, haven't we?" he said. "And yet here we are, you and I. It's quite mad when you think of it."

For a moment there was a lull. He did not remove his hand. I dared not look him in the eyes.

When I could stand the silence no more I withdrew my hand and said, with forced gaiety, "But we forge on, don't we? I have quite a few friends these days. Rather well-known friends, in fact. Cocteau, Diaghilev, Stravinsky. Gertrude Stein. Our illustrious compatriot Tchelitchew, who will soon be quite a famous painter—famous enough to rival Picasso, whom I also happen to know." When I had finished reciting these preposterous boasts I was thoroughly ashamed of myself.

"Half those names mean nothing to me, and the other half

I'd call a real rogues' gallery. Do you really go about with the likes of Picasso?"

"He's a difficult man to know well," I fabricated. "Once, at a dinner party, I watched him create a most marvelous sculpture from a pile of children's toys. It was like watching a magician at work."

"I was never much for art of any kind, I must say," Oleg said. "Give me something practical to do: that's all I've ever asked. Why, I should be overseeing the most productive wheat fields in all of Ukraine right now. But you're right. We forge on. And I suppose I've done well enough. I have a respectable wife, I keep my head above water, I haven't lost my self-respect. And today I've discovered an old friend I thought I'd never see again."

He had drunk several glasses of wine in quick succession, and now called for vodka. I told him I had an English lesson scheduled for four o'clock, and asked if he would mind giving me a lift back to the Latin Quarter.

He seemed disappointed, but said, "Right you are, we mustn't piss the afternoon away. We've all got to earn our keep these days. But we'll be seeing each other again, won't we? We'll exchange addresses."

He hesitated before climbing into his ancient Taxi de la Marne. "Perhaps you'd like to drive," he offered. "Would that amuse you?"

I told him I had never learned to drive.

"What a shame. It's one of life's great pleasures. I'll teach you one of these days." I noted, with some bemusement, that he kept trying to contrive future opportunities for us to meet. How satisfying it would be to tell him, once and for all, "I've got quite the life myself these days. I'm not sure I can find room for a distant acquaintance from the past." But I resisted the temptation to be cruel.

When he dropped me off on rue de Vaugirard, he reached

out and grasped my arm. "I'm glad Fate has thrown us back together, Nabokov. You'll be hearing from me soon. My wife is quite the cook!"

I gave his hand a quick, friendly pat and turned away toward the crowded sidewalk. There was a small florist's on the corner selling lilies for Easter, and on impulse I squandered several precious francs in honor of the approaching Holy Week.

And thus the happy day arrived—the happiest of my entire life. I woke at dawn eager as a schoolboy; all day I was good for nothing, so focused was my soul on the evening ahead. When night finally fell I put on my most exquisite makeup, wore my opera cloak, and took along my fanciest walking stick. I was, after all, going to be received into the House of the Lord.

Cocteau and his claque of six or seven *enfants* joined me at a café near St.-Séverin. It quickly became apparent that some or all of them had smoked beforehand, and though I felt momentarily bereft, I soon decided that that was their affair, not mine. I would stand before the Lord with clean heart and clear conscience.

"Isn't it grand?" said Cocteau, thrumming his long fingers on the tabletop as if it were a keyboard. "It's like attending some young girl's *début.* So seldom do we have an opportunity in this life to become virginal again!"

"I haven't been so excited," Bourgoint admitted, "since the première of *L'Enfant et les Sortilèges.*"

"But confess: you thought Ravel's opera was going to be about you," said Sachs.

"I still do," Bourgoint told him.

Having entered the Carmelite seminary some weeks before, Sachs wore a soutane. When, in all seriousness, I told him how becoming it looked on him, he sighed and said, "Yes, black *is* slimming, isn't it?"

"When we learned you were at the seminary, we thought it

must be a new nightclub," opined a languid, curly-haired *enfant* whose name I have forgotten.

"*I* always thought you were Jewish," sniffed Bourgoint.

"Well I was," Sachs told him. "I was born Maurice Ettinghausen. So there."

What followed was pure enchantment: the hushed procession of the Paschal candle through the darkened church, the celebrant stopping three times to intone "*Lumen Christi*," the congregation responding "*Deo Gratia*" as each of us received his own candle so that gradually the darkness was beaten back, the church filled with light and life, which is of course Christ Himself. Then the magisterial Liturgy of the Word, followed by the Mass of the Resurrection with the singing, for the first time since Lent, of the *Gloria in Excelsis Deo*. The organ and church bells pealed joyously, and the statues that had been draped during Passiontide were one by one unveiled. The first solemn Alleluia since Septuagesima led to the Gospel of the Resurrection, and then it was time for my confirmation.

All the jumbled pieces of my life arranged themselves into a kind of whole—and the whole, I saw clearly, was love. I thought of my mother, and La Karsavina, and I consecrated the moment to Davide Gornotsvetov. All my prayers were for the salvation of his soul.

They flanked me at all times, my lovely brothers in Christ. Cocteau kept murmuring, at intervals, "I love you, oh, how I love you." Bourgoint, on my immediate left, sweetly clasped my hand through most of the ceremony.

Never had I felt so protected by so many disparate forces.

It was theater of the highest order.

34

NEVER WILL I FORGET THE AFTERNOON IN LATE spring 1926 when I espied, prominently displayed in the window of the Russian bookshop on rue Pierre-le-Grand, a poster advertising MARY—A NOVEL OF ÉMIGRÉ LIFE BY V. SIRIN. Never will I forget the excitement with which I carried away my precious copy, the avidity with which I devoured those pages.

I of course recognized immediately the bitter world of present-day émigré Berlin our hero Ganin inhabits: even more did I recognize the sweet world of his memories, the happy summer of 1915, a boy and girl's first ardors amid the arbors of a family estate. Here was the delicious heart of the novel, and I relived with strange intensity that adolescent romance on whose edges I had often inadvertently found myself. Yet certain details perturbed me. There was that tryst—which I had quite unintentionally witnessed—"on the six-columned porch of a stranger's closed mansion." To demote our uncle Ruka to the status of a mere stranger—well, I did not much like that.

Nor did I particularly like Sirin's description of a "lecher who was always crossing their path in avenues of the park." True, the wretch is described as foul-mouthed, orange-haired, and twenty, the son of the watchman; still, I winced to see myself thus transmuted.

It was all fiction; I reminded myself. Volodya certainly had never bestowed on me the swift punishment our hero Ganin metes out, sans brass knuckles, to the cowardly voyeur. But the dark question lingered: had he on occasion wished to?

A tricky thing, this parsing of reality and invention.

But a far greater shock lay in wait. The room adjacent to Ganin's in that sordid Berlin pension is occupied by two ballet dancers: mannered, mincing nancies, both giggly as women. We see one of them, Kolin, as he applies coral varnish to his fingernails, splashes himself with sickly-sweet toilet water, powders his face and makes up his eyes, then flicks the tip of his fancy cane up and down as he goes for a walk. Of the other, who bears the heart-stopping name Gornotsvetov, we read: "His features were dark and very regular, and long curled eyelashes gave his eyes a clear, innocent expression. He had short, black, slightly frizzled hair; he shaved the back of his neck like a Russian coachman and had grown sideburns which curved past his ears in two dark strips."

A deep flush came to my cheeks. I found it difficult to breathe. This was, of course, none other than Davide Gornotsvetov who had tutored me in the use of nail varnish, Davide Gornotsvetov who had showed me how to employ a fancy walking stick, Davide Gornotsvetov in whose very existence Volodya had once refused to believe and whose likeness he had now transferred to the page!

It left me with a nasty feeling of sham and mockery, of stale unreality that a long nocturnal walk in a very real Paris under a lightly falling rain did little to dispel.

* * *

That summer of 1926, enduring the tiresome nonsense that always accrues to anyone cursed with a Nansen passport, I traveled to Prague, where my mother and younger brother Kirill shared with the ever-loyal Evgenia Hofeld a small flat on the west bank of the Vltava. I had not seen my mother in three years, and though she was but fifty, I was shocked by how diminished she seemed. Her hair had gone completely gray. Her mouth quavered, as if she were never far from tears. The flat, with its shabby furniture and unemptied ashtrays, was crowded with mementos—the books Father had written, the journals he had edited, albums in which she had lovingly copied out my brother's poems, framed photographs of all of us on every surface.

Volodya and his new wife had visited some weeks earlier. Mother reported, "I've never seen your brother looking happier or more content. Finally he's settling down. Still, I would never have imagined such a one for him! I know, mothers are always critical of their son's choices. You may have guessed that your grandmother Nabokova never entirely approved of *me*. I've heard from her, by the way, six months ago now. She's left Dresden for Romania, at the invitation of Queen Marie. I didn't even know they were friends. But then your grandmother enjoyed cultivating her secrets. Evgenia, if you'd be so kind, I believe the letter's on the stand beside our bed. Really, she's a most extraordinary woman, this Véra Slonim. Very intelligent, very literate, but then the Jews have always been so, haven't they? That's why they're so envied, which is the real reason they're so despised. Would I have chosen her for my son? No. Has he chosen well? Yes, certainly. She adores him, and he adores her. I know from my own marriage what a happy state of affairs that is. Oh, thank you, dear. Now if you could find my specs, I think I left them over there—really, Seryosha, I've gotten very forgetful recently—thank you again, my dear—let's see, ah, here it is. Your grandmother writes, 'Khristina is impossible. She still forgets to flush the toilet. I think it's from spite. But then everything is spiteful here. Get me out of this gypsy hole. Romania is not a nation, it's a profession.' As you can see, she remains in inimitable form. I can only imagine what mischief she's getting up to."

For the first time since my arrival, I heard Mother make a sound that could almost be construed as laughter.

The only other time she came fully to life was when I brought up *Mary*. "Isn't it beautiful?" she enthused. "I wept when I read it. How very proud his father would be."

I mentioned that I found it curious that the hero, though only sixteen, appears entirely unattached, as if he has no family at all.

"Oh, your brother's very discreet. I suspect he felt reluctant to bring us into it."

I did not mention my other misgivings.

When, with some trepidation, I told her about my conversion she nodded vaguely. "Yes," she said, "we all seek what comfort there is. *My* great comfort is that I was once so very happy. Unlike others, I don't look forward to Paradise as a hope; I gaze back on it as a fact."

My second visit that summer took me to England; first to Uncle Kostya, whose ever-worsening finances had forced him to leave his rooms in Kensington for cheap digs in Battersea. Nonetheless, I found him in as cheerful a mood as I had ever seen him. Not once did he talk bitterly of German Jews and their Bolshevik puppets, nor did he rehearse the many slights and disappointments he had endured. On several occasions he referred cryptically to a young lieutenant in the Royal Engineers, stationed at Aldershot. I left London without ever meeting the lieutenant, though I was shown his handsome photograph, which had taken its place among the other handsome photographs, most dating from the happy years during which my uncle had been posted to India, long before everything fell apart.

After London I nipped down to Somerset to pay a brief visit to Hugh Bagley, who had remained a faithful and affectionate correspondent over the years. I found him living the sort of unhurried idyll only possible in the English countryside. Married life had clearly agreed with him, and though he had added a half stone or so, he was handsomer than ever. Filling out the bucolic scene were the plumpish, merry-eyed wife (Lucinda of the Morris-Stanhopes), two cherubic little girls, and three rambunctious border collies.

As our time together at Cambridge had been so uncomplicated, I felt nothing but happiness for Hugh's present happiness. During a stroll along the river, he alluded to our old times together freely and without regret.

"Still," he said, "one grows out of such youthful fun, into greater responsibilities."

"I haven't grown out of it," I protested. "Nor do I imagine I ever will. For some of us it's not a passing fancy."

"But don't you wish, sometimes, for the comfort of a wife, children—the knowledge that at the end of the day you've done your bit to continue the family name?"

"As long as the human race continues, I suppose I'm content. I've never felt my own particular blood was anything special."

"Forget the future, then. I still heartily recommend married life to any man. I never knew what joy women could bring till I married my beloved. Out of my absolutely undying affection for you, I wish you the same joy, Sergey. Really, I do."

"Oh, you're just weak-minded," I teased him. "You've been booted out of Plato's army, and for good reason."

Playfully he shoved me. I shoved him back. One thing led to another—all in jest—and soon enough we were grappling like schoolboys till he tripped on a rhododendron root, gripped my arm to catch his fall, and suddenly we had both plunged down the muddy bank and into the shallow waters of the Frome.

He was not the least bit upset. Instead he whooped like an Apache—the old captivating Hugh I remembered so well—vigorously splashing me as I spattered him back. We stood in three feet of turbid water, facing each other, panting, grinning.

"The adventure I remember most of all," I told him, "far more than any bits of drunken misbehavior, is our flight in your aeroplane. That I shall never, ever forget. You showed me my soul that day."

"You see then why I love it so much. I'd take you up again in an instant. I've even got a brand-new machine—the latest in De Havilland's smashing Moth series. Alas, the motor's being overhauled, so we're earthbound for this visit. But you'll come again, Sergey. We're not done with soaring, you and I. Our destiny's in the air."

He opened his arms to me, and I moved toward him through the waist-deep water till he had enfolded me in an embrace; we clung to each other, our hearts both beating madly, and I could feel his warm breath on the side of my neck, then the light graze of his lips along the same spot, and his grip all at once tightened and he released me. He wiped a tear from his eye.

"Were you crying?" I asked him.

He laughed. "I do that sometimes. You stutter. I cry."

For the space of forty-eight hours Hugh's happiness—by which I mean the whole happy sphere of Westbrook House and environs—became my own. Rolling Somerset is not at all like flat Cambridgeshire, but I was ambushed by nostalgia for something ineffably "English." It was nostalgia completely unlike that which I only occasionally felt for Russia—a sense of what might have been, another life I might have been happy in, a different destiny just as real as the one I have followed, but in which I would not, one day, in a Berlin half obliterated by British bombs, have uttered aloud my own death sentence.

35

BERLIN,
DECEMBER 8, 1943

"I MUST SAY, THE RAF'S PLAN TO 'HAMBURGERIZE' Berlin doesn't seem to be working particularly well."

Felix and I have met, by prior arrangement, at the corner of Wilhlemstrasse and Prinz-Albrechtstrasse—imprudently close to the Ministry and the Gestapo offices, I objected, but he only repeated, "In plain sight, my friend, in plain sight."

"No," he continues, "it's not so easy to erase us from the map. It turns out Berlin's no Hamburg. Wide avenues, spacious parks, sturdy masonry—so very unlike that crowded, timbered, medieval city. We offer too sporadic a fuel for the firestorms to get fully under way. Already the British have inflicted about as much damage as they can, while continuing to sustain very heavy casualties themselves. Have you noticed? One sees more and more British POWs in the work crews.

Not that your friend will be among them."

"You have news, then?" I ask.

He frowns and strokes his neat little mustache. "No news, only leads. And they require us to venture in *there*." He points to the Gestapo headquarters.

"Surely you must be joking."

"Do you wish to discover the truth about your friend or not?"

"But why must I accompany you? Surely this is madness. I might as well simply turn myself in."

"Have the Gestapo come round yet?"

"Yes, as a matter of fact, a dressmaker's dummy did stop by. He seemed more a census taker than anything else. He asked me a few questions he already knew the answers to."

"The Gestapo can afford to take their time. They will come for you when they wish to do so. In the meantime, cherish your freedom. Between now and then, after all, anything can happen. Anything at all."

He is testing me, of course.

I feel I must ask him point-blank: "Are you Gestapo?"

He laughs. "What an amusing thought. Of course you're suspicious of me. We must all be suspicious of each other these days. That's the worst of it. Were Jesus himself to appear, one would have to be suspicious."

"I thought you'd lost your religion."

"I've lost so much, it's difficult to keep track of all I've lost. But what I do have"—he pats the breast pocket of his jacket—"is a very valuable pass signed by none other than Count Wolf-Heinrich von Helldorf. With it we're practically invincible. Don't ask how I acquired it. I have many friends who owe me many favors."

As Count von Helldorf is Berlin's chief of police, I am somewhat mollified, though Felix continues to become more rather than less mysterious. It occurs to me he is not so much challenging me as challenging himself to venture into Gestapo headquarters. It also occurs to me he is merely using me to further some incomprehensible private aim of his own.

I do not have much choice but to follow him.

"Those work crews, by the way," he says as we mount the steps. "They're most phenomenally efficient, don't you think? Within hours fires are doused, seemingly impassable streets reopened, electricity reinstated, telephone lines repaired. The Führer takes extraordinary care of his Reich."

The building appears to be under evacuation. Clerks carry boxes to waiting military transports. Armed guards loiter, but seem indifferent to our presence. Felix approaches one, and when they have conferred for a bit, he returns to me and indicates we should go upstairs.

As we venture further into the darkened building, I have the dreadful feeling that I am being led into a labyrinth from which I shall not escape.

"I believe this is the department we seek," Felix says.

A small man sits behind a desk stacked with paper halfway to the ceiling. The room is filled with the clatter of typewriters. No sooner has one sheet finished than it is whisked off the roll, another inserted, and the rapid-fire process begins anew.

"I come with a priority request from Count von Helldorf regarding a certain POW taken into custody near Hamburg on 29 July of this year. Flight Sergeant Hugh Bagley, serial number 658465, RAF Group 4, Squadron 78, based at Middleton Saint George, Durham."

I am stunned by this information Felix has somehow managed to gather.

"That would be a military matter," the small man says.

Felix is undeterred. "Our records show he has escaped from detention and is currently being sheltered by subversive elements, perhaps even here in Berlin. I wish to request that you track any pertinent information you may have about him."

As he fills out—with apparent relish—various complicated forms, I watch the infernal battery of typists at their relentless work. They are mostly young women, very professional in appearance, with smart haircuts and good legs, though many are dressed in the sort of motley one sees on people whose apartments have been destroyed. I have a very bad feeling that they are typing arrest warrants, or perhaps transfer orders to labor camps. I wonder whether at this moment my own fate is being typed somewhere in this room.

At last Felix is finished with the paperwork, and we retrace our steps along busy corridors to emerge into the gray afternoon light.

"I insist you tell me," I say. "What have we gained by that? Has Hugh Bagley really escaped? And if so, haven't we in fact made matters worse for him?"

Felix is calm. "Oh, I have no evidence whatsoever that he has escaped. The problem is, I have no definite information as to where he is being held. I am merely trying to work in reverse. If the Gestapo can confirm to me that your friend is not actually on the lam, they may reveal inadvertently where he is currently detained."

"I don't understand why you continually put yourself in jeopardy like this. And others too, I might add."

"Simply because I can," he says. "Ah, Nabokov. It's really not complicated. I don't know whether you've shown great courage or great foolishness in your recent actions. What matters is, I know I have shown neither."

"And perhaps all this gives you a chance to show it now?"

"Listen to my great fear, Nabokov. Worse than my fear of dying under bombs is the fear that I shall die without having taken a stand. That owing to caution and conformity, which I always thought would ensure my survival, I have instead muddled my way into something unspeakable. The men who have brought this war on us are beasts. And yet I fear I have done my bit to sustain this war as much as anyone. You must have that fear as well. And yet you've spoken your mind."

"God tells us there's no such thing as a human beast," I say. "It's a contradiction in terms. Whoever has started this war, whoever continues it, is as fully human as you or I."

"Perhaps that's why I no longer believe in God."

"Perhaps that's why I still do. The alternative is simply unacceptable."

"Yes," he says, looking at me dolefully. "The alternative is unacceptable. I will leave you now, Nabokov. Expect to hear from me soon. We shall see if my little plan yields results."

There is a very beautiful and ancient hymn, "Salve Regina," and as I begin again on these pages, once more at my desk in this frigid room, I sing it quietly to myself. *Salve, Regina, Mater misericordiae, vita, dulcedo, et spes nostra, salve! O clemens, O pia, O dulcis Virgo Maria.* It calms me. It comforts me. It nourishes me. It contains the whole of my life even now, from the nativity I have forgotten to the crucifixion that ineluctably awaits me. Everything, I remind myself, has already been paid in full by the beautiful young man nailed to a cross. All that is left for me is to complete the paperwork.

36

PARIS

I AM NOT CERTAIN EXACTLY WHEN I BECAME AWARE I was being shadowed. I would be walking down rue de Montparnasse or rue de Vaugirard and sense a presence gliding patiently behind me. When I turned around to confirm my suspicions, the red-and-black taxicab that had been following some fifty paces behind stopped and allowed me to go on without interference. The same taxi—I could see it from my fourth-floor window—would often be parked across the street from my building on rue St.-Jacques. It was preposterous, really. Of course I knew it was he; he made no attempt to hide his identity. At last I summoned the will to confront him.

"You'd make a dreadful spy," I told him. "You must have learned your tricks from the Tsar's secret police."

That made him smile.

"What is it you wish?" I continued.

During the weeks following our initial meeting, Oleg had sent me various scrawled notes I had been reluctant to answer. What, after all, was the point? Our friendship, as he liked to call it, had never existed. Our acquaintanceship had consisted of half a dozen brutalizing encounters.

He seemed agitated. "You see, my old friend, it's like this. Driving a taxi day in and day out, thoughts get inside a fellow's head and he can't get them out—like mealybugs in the flour."

"I imagine that's so," I told him.

"Well, it so happens you're one of those more persistent thoughts, Seryosha."

"I see," I said, failing to resist the little leap of excitement those words stirred in me. Had he ever called me Seryosha before?

"I'll admit it. I've not been decent toward you in the past." He stared down at the sidewalk. "In fact, I see now how beastly I've behaved. I'd like to make it up to you."

I was surprised to find him meeting my gaze at those last words.

I spoke very carefully. "And how does one, as you say, 'make up' the past?"

"If only I knew how." He laughed—though it was clear his derision was directed solely at himself.

"You're in quite a mood today," I ventured.

"I've been in quite a mood for some time now. I've made a decision. I wish to teach you how to drive."

Now it was my turn to laugh.

"That's very kind of you, but really, I have no need of driving lessons."

He leaned in close. "Still," he murmured, "I'd like to teach you."

How absurd! I glanced from Oleg to his ancient taxi and back to his lovely imploring eyes, and fully conscious that I was taking my life in my hands in more ways than one, I acquiesced.

★ ★ ★

On Sunday afternoons he would pick me up in front of my building and drive us out of Paris, to Fontainebleau, or Rambouillet, where on empty country lanes he would instruct me in the fine art of motoring. To my surprise, he proved a patient teacher, and I a quick learner.

Sometimes we brought with us bread and pickles and a bottle of wine and made a picnic in some tranquil spot we found. Our conversations seldom touched on our past, dwelling mostly on our current lives. He talked incessantly of Valechka, her cunning intelligence, her voluptuous charms. For my part, I narrated the latest goings-on at 27 rue de Fleurus: how Pavlik, thwarted in his desire to paint a portrait of Gertrude to rival Picasso's masterpiece, had painted Alice instead. How he insisted to everyone that Alice despised the result but Gertrude adored it, when in reality Alice liked the way he depicted her and it was Gertrude who found the result objectionable. "He's painted Pussy without a mouth," she complained. "Everyone knows Pussy has a mouth, and a very intelligent mouth full of very intelligent words. Why, I wouldn't be surprised if Pussy wrote her own autobiography one of these days. What things she would say! Everyone would be very surprised."

"Tchelitchew." Oleg spat. "I had some encounters with him in Constantinople. Conceited snob. A charlatan if ever I met one. I don't understand why you would want to spend evenings with the likes of him—or any of them for that matter. They seem a ghastly crew."

It took me a few moments to formulate an answer. "You're absolutely correct," I told him. "What happens there for the most part is simply rot. Nothing anyone does in that room matters. What matters happens elsewhere, in the solitude of painters' studios, at writers' desks. Gertrude and Alice's salon is merely where they come afterward, after the holy tasks are done, to burn off excess energy, to flush from their system all the petty grievances and anxieties that are the furnace slag of the creative process. Of course there's always the hope Gertrude may somehow 'make' them, as she's believed to have made Picasso and Matisse and Gris, all that earlier generation who are now banished from her good graces. Of course I know perfectly well what you'll ask: 'But *you* don't paint, *you* don't write, *you* don't compose operas with cheeky titles like *Four Saints in Three Acts*. So why do *you* go there?' Well, I'm very conscious of my failings. With a brother like mine, how could I not be? I'll only say this: I go to pay homage to those who are greater than I can ever hope to be."

"Did you once have artistic aspirations, Nabokov? Is that your secret?"

We reclined on a patch of long grass that sloped down to a pond where five identical ducks floated above their reflections. We had finished our bread, our pickles, our bottle of wine.

I thought for a moment of telling him I had once, as a schoolboy, in a world that had since disappeared, begun a novel in the style of Bely. Instead I said, "I wished to be like Volodya. I adored him so. Not just for himself, but for how much he was loved. I wrote my own verse, thinking I might duplicate his standing with our parents. But then I realized it wasn't his gift alone that endeared him to them. It was something else; the gift was merely the expression of that other unaccountable thing. I could compose all the verse I might and I'd still never succeed in unraveling the mystery of it. But you've turned me quite philosophical. You once warned me of the dangers of being too philosophical. Besides, you were only supposed to give me driving lessons, not a session on Doctor Freud's couch."

"You never know, with me, what you might get," Oleg said. He reached over and stroked the threadbare cuff of my jacket. "That's what's always intrigued you, isn't it? It's what's kept you coming back."

"As I remember it, I didn't so much keep coming back as you kept turning up."

"And I've turned up again, haven't I?"

"You've turned up again," I said, understanding perfectly well how dangerous the moment had become.

"Then perhaps it's my turn to take the couch. I might as well begin by confessing: my marriage has seen better days. Valechka's making a cuckold out of me—perhaps even as we speak. There, I've said it. The ugly truth's out in the open. And on top of it all, I owe astonishing sums of money to my friends and acquaintances. Let's just say, most of my former friends are now acquaintances, and my former acquaintances no longer speak to me. As you can see, life's taught me bitter lessons. I'm not the boy who used to treat you cruelly. Still, I wager your own needs haven't changed. Am I right? Look: my wife's often out for hours—where, I don't even like to think. The flat's empty in the afternoons. Can you picture some arrangement that might be mutually agreeable? What do you say, Nabokov? For old times' sake? We could get up to things properly, for once."

In those gold-flecked eyes was a plea I could scarcely ignore. How much I would have given in 1915 to witness this abjection, but it was no longer 1915, and as Oleg was fond of observing, the world had changed. With a cruelty all my own I savored the moment.

"You're quite a handsome fellow," I told him. "Can't you find a mistress? I'd think there'd be plenty of prospects for someone like you."

"Sometimes a man doesn't want a mistress. Sometimes a man needs something else."

Remarkably enough, I laughed. "As I've told you before, I've got quite the life these days—"

He lunged toward me, and before I could register what had happened he had kissed me on the lips.

Five identical white ducks floated above five reflections.

From the Paris–Fontainebleau road, one would have seen only them, and a battered old Taxi de la Marne parked at an angle on an unkempt bit of grass.

At 27 rue de Fleurus, Alice served thimbles of a liqueur she had made herself. Pavlik was purring at Gertrude, who was purring back. Despite everything, she had purchased his portrait of Alice for a considerable sum.

Alice was in a friendly mood as well. She beckoned me over, pulled from the large Spanish armoire a blue *cahier*, the kind schoolchildren use, and said, "Tonight Lovey wishes you to have a look at what she is writing when she is writing."

I told Alice how very honored I was. Though I seldom talked to Gertrude, Alice assured me that the great woman found me to be a nice young man, and that she very much liked nice young men.

"It's a lecture she's intending to give at Oxford," Alice explained, handing me the notebook with all the care of a priest handling a reliquary. "You've studied at Oxford. You must tell me exactly what you think of the insights she is proposing."

"Actually, Cambridge," I told her, "Not that it makes a bit of difference. But yes, certainly, I'll tell you what I think."

"You have an honest stutter," Alice said. "And we are always counting on you for that."

I opened the notebook and began to read the surprisingly childish scrawl: *Composition is the thing seen by every one living in the living that they are doing, they are composing of the composition that at the time they are living is the composition of the time in which they are living. It is that that makes living a thing they are doing.* I wondered whether Alice had perhaps substituted absinthe for her homemade liqueur. Several times I read the sentences, but they made no sense to me whatsoever.

I could hear Gertrude chastising a young man Virgil Thomson had brought; he had committed the unforgivable sin of admitting that he was reading—and even worse, liking—*Ulysses*. "Why do you waste your time?" Gertrude asked, her lovely volubility gone steely. "That Irish drunk—he's nothing but a second-rate politician masquerading as a fifth-rate novelist. Why are all the young men still reading him? Can anyone tell me?"

The young man was blushing, but naively determined to hold fast to his opinion. "Surely, Miss Stein, you must—"

"Good evening to you," Gertrude told him.

Nonplussed, the young man remained seated.

"Don't you understand? I said 'Good evening to you.'"

He did not, in fact, seem to understand until Thomson whispered in his ear, took him by the arm, led him to the door—which Alice had leapt up to hold open for him.

"We do not wish to see you again," she said, her unpainted mouth a grim flat line. "People must understand. We do not sanction impertinence or stupidity in this house. You are guilty of both."

Barely had the poor American gotten through the door before she shut it with a loud report.

It so happened that I too had read *Ulysses*, and thought it a most remarkable novel, but I knew well enough when to keep my honest stutter to myself.

Thus reminded of the delicacy of the task at hand, I turned back to Gertrude's pages. They seemed to me at best inspired gibberish, at worst an amateur con job. I desperately formulated what I might say to Alice.

Fortunately, she conferred for quite a while with Virgil Thomson, who kept shaking his head and holding out his hands in a gesture of bewilderment, and then with Gertrude, whom the incident had clearly plunged into a dour mood.

When at last Alice returned to her favorite chair and had taken up her needlework she asked, "So what has the bright young man made of Lovey's thoughts?"

I laughed nervously. "The bright young man is not so very bright tonight, I'm afraid."

"Isn't what she has written perfectly clear?"

"Clear? Yes, well, perfectly clear. Beautifully, magnificently clear. Would that an Oxford audience were half so clear."

"She is taking elocution lessons to improve her delivery."

"Yes," I stuttered less than honestly, "the delivery is no doubt very important. I would say, much depends on the delivery."

"Yes, indeed," Alice confirmed, wresting the notebook from my hands. "When the time comes, I can assure you, Lovey's delivery will be absolutely perfect."

That spring of 1927 I received two letters, only days apart, both written on black-edged stationery. The first came from my mother, who passed along the news that my grandmother had died—had in fact been dead for nearly a year, though word from Romania had only now reached her circuitously, via our former Berlin address.

She wrote: *Maria Ferdinandovna was a most extraordinary—and extraordinarily difficult—lady, an unrepentant relic of an era whose time will never come again. It is hardly a secret that we found each other trying, and I have often contemplated the extent to which your long-suffering father did his best to keep the peace between us, and to honor his mother who persisted in criticizing nearly everything he attempted in his noble career. With each year that passes, I understand his selfless generosity more and more deeply, and I trust you appreciate how fortunate you were to have had his unerring guidance when you were young.*

She then ended with a familiar complaint. *The Miliukovs, the Gippiuses, Benois—they tell me no one ever sees you. They miss you, dear Seryosha. They worry that you have cut ties entirely with your fellow countrymen. Please do call on them and assure them their fears are unfounded.*

I expected the second letter—from my Aunt Nadezhda in London, also written on black-bordered notepaper—to reiterate the news contained in my mother's letter, but my aunt seemed curiously unaware that her mother had died; I could only conclude that my mother's missive and hers had crossed somewhere in the English Channel. Instead, shockingly, my aunt informed me that her brother Konstantin had recently been taken ill with a liver complaint and admitted as a precaution to Charing Cross Hospital, where he promptly caught pneumonia and died.

He was a very lonely man, she wrote obtusely, *a bachelor to the end of his days. It was a life I'd have wished on no one. Now I have the sad duty of settling his affairs, disposing of his furniture and photographs, burning his diaries and correspondence. He never recovered from the loss of his beloved Russia; nowhere else did he ever feel the least bit at home. But then how true that is of so many of us. Can my heart ever forget St. Petersburg under snow on a winter's day, when everyone went out driving in a sleigh along the Neva quay, past the magnificent Senate Building, and Falconet's statue of Peter the Great riding his wild horse, and the Winter Palace, the Admiralty, the dear jardin d'été with its lovely old paths and trees, and, embracing everything, the red winter sun setting toward the Islands behind the outline of the Fortress of St. Peter and Paul, the clear frosty air and scurry of falling snowflakes…*

My aunt always did fancy herself a writer.

One never chooses one's allies, at least not within a family. But these two, La Generalsha and Uncle Kostya, had been mine. Both had been intimidating, and eccentric, but they had not shunned me upon learning my secret. Their deaths left me feeling alone in a way I could not have anticipated.

He called me his afternoon wife. I would come to his shabby flat in Passy once or twice a week. The single room was made even smaller by the imposing matrimonial bed which, along with a table and two unsteady chairs, constituted its only real furniture. When winter came, a small black stove in the corner kept the temperature just above freezing.

How curious to possess, finally and fully, the object of one's dreams. Was there a sense of fulfillment? Absolutely. Was that longing which seems the very condition of the heart assuaged? Not in the least.

In bed Oleg was robust, rather unimaginative, endearingly clumsy—exactly what I might have suspected. He was always the husband, which suited me perfectly well, though every once in a while I would be struck by the suspicion that he secretly wished to be mastered. But to ask for that was beyond his courage.

He talked endlessly of Valechka.

"She's so untidy," he complained, holding up a stocking latticed with tears. "And forgetful, too. She goes out shopping, and returns having failed to purchase half what she intended, so out again she goes. You're better off without them, Sergey. You're lucky that way."

I was not particularly surprised when, one dismal drizzling afternoon, he produced a cheap opium kit from underneath the bed.

"I suppose you must know Shanghai Jimmy," I said.

"Of course. Everybody knows Shanghai Jimmy. But how do you know him?"

When I failed to answer, he punched me lightly in the shoulder. "You bastard," he said. "You too, eh? What do you know? We *are* the queer pair, aren't we? Imagine that."

I asked him if Valechka was aware of his habit.

"Oh, Valechka doesn't mind at all. I could go to hell for all she cares."

We lay curled on our sides on his matrimonial bed, the opium lamp between us; lazily we passed the pipe back and forth, holding it over the coal, letting the ravishing smoke drift up to our nostrils. It was stupidly dangerous, the lamp was unsteady, a sudden movement could tip the whole thing and the bed would instantly be in flames. As such, it was oddly emblematic. We would smoke in contented silence. I would feel a closeness to him I had never felt before, not even in the most physically intimate of moments.

37

BERLIN
DECEMBER 9, 1943

A DREADFUL THING HAS HAPPENED—OR PERHAPS it is the answer to my prayers.

Last night the skies were clear, a bright moon out, the waves of bombers relentless. From night to night the RAF refine their diabolical repertory, whose signatures we have learned to recognize—the sharp crack of canister explosives, the doves' rustle of magnesium stick bombs, the wet smack of the phosphorous incendiaries spreading their inextinguishable green lava across roofs and down walls. The suction pressure is almost unbearable; it takes the air right out of our lungs.

Once more the sweep of the firestorm. Once more the benumbed relief afterward. When we emerge from our cellar at dawn, we see the most astonishing sight: the rear of our building remains; the façade is completely sheared away. One can observe the contents of the building's various floors. There is the sofa in the parlor. There is the floor lamp. There is the kitchen, with its scrubbed pots hanging above the sink. There is Frau Schlegel's ironing board, still upright. But of stoic Frau Schlegel who ironed her way through many a raid, there is no sign.

Her daughter is distraught. Well, we are all distraught. Theodor and I climb the precarious, mangled staircase to search the floors one by one, but she has vanished without a trace. Frau Schlegel—imperious, intrusive, opinionated, resourceful. Our lives have depended on her, and now she is gone.

We shall have to find other lodgings. And in this I detect—though I may simply have lost my mind—the hand of God scattering the chess pieces that would have led all too quickly to checkmate. Now the Gestapo will have difficulty tracking me down. I am unexpectedly afforded an extra chapter, and I will prove a fool if I do not hasten my narrative along as the clock, blessedly reset, begins once again to tick.

38

PARIS

LIKE THE PRINCESS, I HAD FALLEN INTO A DEEP slumber, watched over by spiders, protected by thorns, concealed in a fog of opium. How to convey how weeks, months, even years disappeared? Much happened, but nothing changed. My finances remained as precarious as ever, and though I found myself remembering Weldon and his American dollars with great fondness, I made no attempt to find myself a benefactor. Indeed, the effects of opium had so suppressed my libido that weeks would go by without my registering a single throb of desire. As Oleg found himself in the same foundering boat, we came to resemble, in our desultory exertions, nothing so much as two castaways seeking in each other the battered mast that might keep them afloat after the ship has disappeared beneath the waves.

My attendance at 27 rue de Fleurus began to flag, till

there came the inevitable moment when Alice, at the end of an evening, took me aside and asked pointedly, "Why are you here at all?"

I told her—with an impertinence that would have been unthinkable two years before—that I had lately been wondering the same thing.

"Perhaps a young man shouldn't any longer come to a place he wonders whether he should be."

I bowed politely. I thanked Alice for her wisdom. On my way out I thanked Gertrude for a magical evening, as ever. That great inscrutable shameless pretender inclined her head, assessing me one final time. In her eyes I could see that I had already disappeared.

My expulsion distressed Pavlik and Allen, who were ready to campaign for my reinstatement.

"I'm no match for the ambitions of that world. I'll be content to hear about it from afar," I told them. What I did not say was that I would rather spend my Saturday nights smoking a few pipes in the indolent solitude of my room, and attend mass at St.-Séverin the following morning in order to repent my sins.

As it happened, Pavlik and Allen did not last much longer at Miss Stein's salon either; in the spring of 1928, the pair was informed that their presence was no longer welcome.

Though ever on the verge of bankruptcy, the Ballets Russes thrived as never before in those years. Diaghilev scooped up talent like a giant child gorging himself on sweets: Balanchine, Lifar, Dolin, Markova; even Pavlik, who had always expressed a fear of becoming decorative, got swept into the fold, designing overwrought sets for *Ode,* whose pleasantly forgettable music my cousin Nika composed.

In the fall of 1928 Sirin's second novel, *King, Queen, Knave,* was published. I had not seen my brother in five years, and increasingly I resigned myself to the possibility that our paths might never again cross. The novel was a brilliant performance, but very cold. That self-portrait toward the end, inserted in the manner of old Flemish painters, lingered in my mind: the girl with the delicately painted mouth and tender gray-blue eyes, her husband elegantly balding, contemptuous of everything on earth but her. Mother had said she feared Véra brought out some of Volodya's worst traits. Unkind thoughts, courtesy of Aunt Nadezhda and Uncle Kostya, crowded around me, and the more I thought about it, the more I began to fear for my ensnared brother's soul.

I considered sending him a letter; I sat down on several occasions to write one, but my attempts were mawkish. Who was I, after all, to lecture anyone on the state of his soul? Thus, with a dejected groan, I lit myself a pipe instead.

Then everything changed—not all at once, of course; many months were to pass before I would finally muster the courage to seize Fate's invitation.

It all began inauspiciously enough at a reception in June 1929, given by fellow-exile Nicolas de Gunzburg at his *hôtel particulier* in the faubourg St.-Germain.

His Jewish father having prudently moved both family and bank accounts abroad some years before the Bolshevist debacle, the Gunzburgs' wealth survived where sturdier fortunes had evaporated. As the adored son and heir, witty, erudite, spectacularly handsome Nicki cultivated a dizzying cast of friends and hosted extravagant costume balls that rivaled those of Étienne de Beaumont. A few years later he would star in Dreyer's celebrated horror film *Vampyr.* He had a serious side as well, and was one of the Ballets Russes' more generous patrons. It was to honor Diaghilev, in fact, that he had arranged this particular occasion.

Among those in attendance: the Princesse Anna de Noailles, Coco Chanel, Grock the clown, a young American acrobat named Barbette whose transvestite performances at the Casino de Paris had been enthralling audiences; Jean and Valentine Hugo; the painter Bébé Bérard, whose presence was certain to infuriate his rival Pavlik, who had not been invited; a fat, ebullient gossip columnist from America named Elsie Maxwell; Count Harry Kessler, a dapper German diplomat, along with an entourage of his fellow countrymen; my cousin Nika; and another composer, the sympathetic and touchingly unhandsome Henri Sauguet.

Misia Sert arrived with Serge Lifar; she could often be seen promenading him around Paris the way others might go about with a leopard on a leash. Stravinsky had been invited but declined, as he and Diaghilev were currently not on speaking terms. (Stravinsky had committed the unpardonable sin of composing a bit of music for a rival company.)

Cocteau sent his regrets from Villefranche, where he and his current *enfant,* Jean Desbordes, were summering.

As usual, the guest of honor arrived very late. When he finally made his entrance he was accompanied by the indispensible Boris Kochno on one arm and a feral-looking youngster named Igor Markevitch on the other. Even if one had missed the latest rumors about Markevitch's adoption into Diaghilev's inner circle, a quick glance at his outfit—the white tuberose in his buttonhole, the walking stick, the homburg—would have revealed all.

Though I spent much of the evening in those gilded chambers longing to be free of that urbane crowd and shut away with three or four heavenly pipes, the reception produced three memorable encounters.

The first was with Lifar. I had never had much to do with him. He had grown as a dancer—a stunning Apollo in the 1928 season, and most recently a transcendently abject *fils prodigue.* Still, I had always found him unnerving offstage. There was a bored patience in his gaze that reminded me of a sleek racehorse that submits patiently to being petted.

On this evening, however, he seemed in an uncommonly communicative mood. Nodding in Diaghilev's direction, he said, "He's not looking well, do you notice?" The master was showing off Markevitch to the Germans. "He's fifty-seven years old. His debts are enormous. The money's already spent long before it comes to him. He has one suit only, and if you look closely you'll notice how threadbare the cuffs are. Art, beauty, and youth are the only things he's ever cared about. Thirty years of living in hotels, and being turned out of many: it's taken a toll, even on one so resilient as he.

"And yet, what an epoch-making life he's led. To have been even a small part of that is a very great honor for me. And it almost didn't happen. Please, do me a favor. Let's switch places. I'll stand with my back to the man. I'm craving a cigarette. I can ash in the potted palm. He forbids me cigarettes, you see. He'd forbid me every pleasure not connected with dance, if he could! How I remember those early days in the company, when he showered me with such kind words—'little flower,' 'little berry,' 'my darling boy.' I could scarcely imagine my luck. I'd heard whispers about his unusual life, his 'favorites' and so forth. Could it be possible, I said to myself, that I was to be one of those favorites? I remembered the girl I'd left behind in Kiev, to whom I'd promised to be faithful. Would I remain faithful if Diaghilev were to choose me? There was only one solution. I'd abandon the Ballets Russes. I'd abandon dance, the dream for which I'd abandoned *her*, and become a monk."

Lifar laughed with a sort of ghastly mirth as, discreetly, he stubbed out his cigarette. "Of course I didn't become a monk. The very next time I saw Diaghilev he said to me, 'You must do what you must do, my dear boy. But I'm going to Italy next month, and if you wish to accompany, you may.' In an instant it was all settled.

"And now, in spite of his diabetes, he's determined to tour Germany with little Markevitch, even though his doctors have warned against travel. I wish the boy well. He has no idea what he's in for, but I wish him every happiness. It won't be easy, but it will be worthwhile, for his life will have been changed forever. I hope he finds a tenth of the happiness Sergey Pavlovich afforded me."

Lifar had scarcely left me before the great man himself, entrusting his "favorite" to Mme. Sert, walked over to where I stood sipping a newly refilled glass of champagne. He no longer intimidated me as he once had; I had come to see the fundamental sweetness, generosity, and civility his haughty manner and famous tantrums sometimes masked. He always inquired after my mother, always had a kind remembrance of Father, and always asked, at some point, "What news of Russia?" though it had long since become apparent that I had no news whatsoever of Russia anymore.

"I saw you talking to Lifar," Diaghilev said. "Did he smoke a cigarette? He's forbidden to smoke! I shall speak with him later. In any event, what on earth was he going on about? He looked quite unusually earnest. But don't be deceived. There's not a single thought in his beautiful head. Oh, he's a superb beast, an athlete of the highest caliber—but you don't go to our Lifar for any ideas!"

"He was talking of you," I said. "Of all you did for him."

"I'm a great fool!" he exclaimed, his large doleful eyes welling up at once with tears. "Of course he loves me. He's always loved me. And I love him. I love all my dancers, my musicians, my artists, without whom none of this"—he gestured around the beautiful room as if to indicate how easily it might vanish into thin air—"none of this would exist."

"But the great miracle is that it *does* exist," I said.

"Ah, the great miracle." For a moment Diaghilev seemed at a loss. We stood in silence. Then he said, with an anguish that took me aback, "The Markevitch boy is simply madness, I'm afraid. Especially at my age. What scandal! Even I know it. How people must laugh behind my back. Yes, I don't mind if I do have another"—he plucked a petit four from a tray offered him by a servant—"and I'll have more champagne if any can be found." His eyelids half closed in pleasure as he bit into the sweet. "And yet there it is," he went on, "the pure hopeless blissful reality of the situation. So very beautiful. So very talented as well. I've scheduled him to perform his Piano Concerto in London next month. And I've commissioned him to write a ballet for me. His music is the music of the future. Even Stravinsky has acknowledged that. Mark my word, without a doubt Markevitch is the next Stravinsky."

He gazed longingly in his beloved's direction. "My God, look at him. And he's only sixteen!"

I did look at him; the youngster stood next to a potted palm, a glass of orangeade in hand, and chatted up the Princesse de Noailles. Clearly he was charming her. Clearly he was entirely normal, not a bit of the invert in him. And for Diaghilev—I could see this with such bittersweet clarity—there would be only heartbreak ahead. He was simply lying down on the tracks, like the heroine from one of yesteryear's silent movies, sans villain, sans ropes, sans struggle, in order to await the arrival of the oncoming locomotive.

The final encounter of that evening occurred as I waited in the foyer for the servant to bring me my trilby and walking stick. One of the Germans whom I had seen earlier in Count Kessler's company arrived to retrieve his items as well.

"Retiring early?" I asked.

"No earlier than you, it would appear."

"But I've come alone. Your comrades..."

He ignored my stutter. "You're mistaken. I've come alone as well."

"Forgive me. I assumed you were with Count..." My affliction had never been worse.

"With the Germans?" He laughed. "No, I'm afraid I'm from

the other Germany—the new, artificial one the war created. I mean Austria, of course. I'm old friends with Nicki; that's why I was invited. I'm just up to Paris on business. I wouldn't, by the way, have guessed you were Russian from your accent."

"But how then did you know I was Russian?"

"Let's just say I made a few discreet inquiries. I'm Hermann Thieme. You're Serge Nabokov. I'm very pleased to meet you."

He held my gaze. His eyes were rather wonderfully blue, lavender, periwinkle, lilac. I had no sense that there was any particular intent in his gaze. It is a manner some men have, and in their presence one becomes aware just how seldom one actually looks one's interlocutor directly in the eye.

He was tall, very slender, impeccably dressed in a bespoke suit with lemon necktie. He wore ivory spats. He and Nicki would make a very handsome pair, and I wondered, idly, whether they ever had.

From the salon came the lilt of a waltz: Nika had seated himself at the piano. Hermann hesitated at the open door.

"Very nice," he said. "Very apt. Do you recognize it?"

I did not immediately, though I told him it sounded incongruously old-fashioned and Viennese in this Parisian setting.

"Precisely," he said. "It's *Der Rosenkavalier.* It was Count Kessler who first passed on to Hoffmannsthal that wisp of an anecdote about the Marschallin who renounces her love for a younger man so that he might be free to pursue a clueless girl his own age. Of course Hofmannsthal and Strauss turned it into their masterpiece. Few know the Count's part in it. What a lovely tribute. The Count must be very pleased."

We emerged onto the street. A pleasant light rain was falling. Our destinations lay in opposite directions—his the Hotel Bristol on the Champs-Elysées, mine rue St.-Jacques in the Latin Quarter—but he seemed oddly unwilling to part just yet. I, on the other hand, was dying for my first pipe.

"By the way," he said, "I've been reading a novel by one

of your countrymen. Not in Russian, of course—my Russian is nonexistent—but in German translation. It's quite good. Perhaps you know it. It's by a writer named—"

I knew the instant before Hermann named him who it would be. Mother had recently written me that Volodya had sold the German rights to *King, Queen, Knave* for a small but very welcome sum of money.

"Actually, I know V. Sirin quite well," I said. "He's my brother. Sirin's a pseudonym, obviously."

"Someone told me it meant 'firebird.'"

"No," I said, feeling a spasm of dread. "More like 'siren,' though the Russian siren has wings and lives in the forest rather than on the rocks of the seacoast. I thought it quite an unpleasant novel, actually. Perhaps it reads better in German."

"Perhaps. It's what Germans say about Shakespeare as well. What's he like, your brother? On the basis of this piece of evidence I'd say he's fiercely intelligent, an exemplary stylist, a coolly detached observer of the human condition, an uncompromising moralist. Am I at all on the mark? I'm fascinated by what a writer reveals about himself in his work, whether consciously or unconsciously. Is there any correspondence between the author of those bracing pages and the brother you know in real life?"

As he spoke, my anxiety had increased exponentially. My underarms went clammy, sweat dampened my brow. "I'm sorry to disappoint you," I said, hearing a hardened tone come into my voice. "I haven't seen my brother in several years. I probably wouldn't even recognize him if I did see him. Indeed, I recognized very little of him in those heartless pages."

My anxiety all at once swelled into full-fledged distress. I was already late for my pipes. The street started to spin, my stomach heaved, and with no warning I was bent double, spilling a noxious mess onto the sidewalk. Poor Hermann took it with gallant aplomb, touching my shoulder sympathetically, sliding his hand beneath my elbow to steady me when I straightened back up. As I wiped my befouled mouth with a handkerchief he asked gently, Did I need to sit down on the curb? Was I feeling faint?

I shook my head. "I've got to go now," I told him. "I'm sorry."

He hailed a cab—one of the Taxis de la Marne that still plied the streets. The evening having rapidly degenerated into grotesque farce, I was certain the shabby vehicle that pulled to the curb couldn't possibly be piloted by anyone other than Oleg.

But Fate had already had its fun; the driver turned out to be a crusty old man with a thick Breton accent. I failed to dissuade Hermann from paying my fare, and reassured him that I would be quite all right, he shouldn't concern himself any further on my account.

"Well, that's someone I'll see no more of," I told myself with a strange sensation of relief, as the taxi pulled away.

The next day I received a note, written on letterhead from "Castle Weissenstein," expressing Hermann's great pleasure in meeting me, and looking forward to our seeing each other again in the near future. There was nothing in the note that was not polite, even charming—but it provoked in me such unreasonable dread that I could not bring myself to reply.

Each time during the next several months Hermann announced an upcoming business trip to Paris and his desire to see me, I shied away with all my heart. Perhaps I sensed I was wholly unworthy of the gift Fate proposed—or threatened—to bestow on me. I found myself returning again and again to the devastating realization: were anything to be possible between us, I would first have to change. I could not face Hermann Thieme as the man I presently was.

39

ONE SWELTERING AFTERNOON IN AUGUST 1929, the concierge handed me a telegram: *Diaghilev est mort ce matin. Lifar.*

Later I would learn the details: how the great man had gone to Venice, broken after the failure of his trip with Markevitch; how Lifar and Kochno tended to him in his last days; how Coco Chanel and Misia Sert arrived just before the final curtain fell. Sergey Pavlovich Diaghilev, whom the gypsy had long ago predicted would die on the water, had breathed his last in that city known as Serenissima, Queen of the Sea.

As I read the telegram, the memory that came to me was of the evening in 1928 after the triumphant première of *Apollon Musagète*, when Diaghilev had fallen to his knees before Lifar, who was still costumed in his tunic. Solemnly he kissed the dancer's bare thighs, saying, "Remember this always. I am kissing a dancer's leg for the second time in my life. The last was Nijinsky's, after *Le Spectre de la Rose!*" And I remembered Lifar looking pleased and proud and a touch uncomfortable, for he loved Diaghilev, but never in a way that could be in the least commensurate with Diaghilev's electrifying, abysmal, impossible love for him.

Diaghilev's death announced the end of an era two months short of the collapse of financial markets. As with the arrival of the evil Carabosse at Aurora's christening ceremony, the effects were instantaneous. Overnight the Americans disappeared, scurrying back to their wounded republic. Shops, cafés, hotels, restaurants that had depended on their largesse went dark. In what clubs remained open (Le Boeuf did not) the jazz turned melancholy. At 27 rue de Fleurus, Gertrude and Alice cast out the few young men who remained in the charmed circle, turned out the lights, and abandoned Paris for a country house in Bilignin. Lifar, Kochno, and Balanchine struggled to keep the Ballets Russes afloat, but it was as if the troupe had lost its heart.

The only one who seemed to profit was Shanghai Jimmy. "You can't imagine the clients I see these days," he told me in his brusque way. "Businessmen, lawyers, bankers flock to me to assuage their well-earned misery. The times have turned spiritual on us. It's a great blessing."

Cocteau was particularly despondent. "It's all been for nothing," he said. "As far ahead as I can see stretches only a gray, featureless landscape, uninterrupted by any flash of beauty, tenderness, kindness. There must be a new art for this desolation, but I have yet to find it within me. I invented the twenties. Must I invent this new decade as well?"

As the world flagged, my brother thrived. From some insatiable hunger in him poems, short stories, novels poured forth as never before. Even though I avoided émigré literary circles, I heard his name spoken with reverence in bookshops and cafés; he had become the hope of the emigration, the figure who would save us from ruin, obscurity, futility, even from ourselves. My brother! I scarcely recognized him in all the delirious talk. With each new production he won over powerful new admirers: Fondaminsky, Aldanov, Khodasevich, Berberova.

In the fall of 1929 *Luzhin's Defense* began to appear in installments in Fondaminsky's *Contemporary Annals*. I read it with unmitigated awe. How wonderfully Sirin manages his plot; how nimbly he evokes a sense of lives overheard, urgent voices in other rooms, a slammed door somewhere, confirming one's nagging suspicion that life's real narrative, its fateful pattern, is always going on in secret, only vaguely apprehended by its human participants. And how marvelous the series of happy near misses—the mysterious pleasure of a conjuror's trick, the fantastical misbehavior of numbers, the brain-twisting challenge of jigsaw puzzles—by which young Luzhin, our strange but sympathetic protagonist, is gradually brought to the fateful harmonies of chess. Here was my astonishing, maddening brother's promise utterly fulfilled, a tale throbbing with all the life, tenderness, perplexity and, yes, transcendent beauty that had been so furiously scrubbed from his previous novel.

Other novels followed swiftly: *The Eye*, a macabre riff on Gogol; *Glory*, with its romantic Cantabrigian ethos in which Bobby de Calry is to be found unexpectedly memorialized as "kindly, ethereal Teddy" who has a "graceful, delicate fluttery something about him"; the darkly cinematic *Camera Obscura*, whose opening paragraph rivals anything in Dickens or Tolstoy.

I read them with bemusement. In their pages I found—or imagined—odd coincidences and correspondences, the stray shared memory, queer borrowings as if from my own most secret soul. The *artist* my brother had become I could see perfectly well, but beyond the tricky elisions, the diabolical fracturings and grotesque recastings, the beautiful outpouring of words, I wished to glimpse the *man* he had become. I did not succeed.

* * *

In defiance of social and economic reality, Nicki de Gunzburg's parties grew more extravagant. "The Country Ball" took place in June 1931, at a pavilion in the Bois de Boulogne. As usual, his instructions were explicit. Guests were to be costumed in accordance with the rustic theme. They were to be suitably masked. They must arrive by horse-drawn carriage or bicycle. They must be witty and gay at all times. Any hint of reality would mean instant expulsion.

Boris Kochno and his new lover Bébé Bérard had shrouded the pavilion in shimmering silks, littered the gardens with tissue-paper poppies, papier-mâché farm animals, huge wire-and-fabric vegetables, even a full-size hay wagon. Bathed in beams of light, the scene had all the enchantment of one of the more elaborate Ballets Russes sets.

Kochno had dressed as Little Bo Peep, Bérard as Shakespeare's Bottom (a notion with which those who spoke English had great fun). Elsie Maxwell came as a Breton milkmaid. Mr. and Mrs. Cole Porter arrived in a Sicilian donkey cart festooned with orchids and gardenias. Jean and Valentine Hugo were sunflowers. Coco Chanel and Anna de Noailles looked adorable as two matching lambs, which Boris quickly claimed as his own. Edmée, duchesse de La Rochefoucauld and Comtesse Marthe de Fels seemed to have stepped directly out of a Watteau canvas. Tchelitchew and Tanner impersonated two barefoot farm boys—"Hucklesberries Finns," according to Pavlik's colorful English—while the English poetess Edith Sitwell, who was carrying on a mad platonic affair with the painter, much to Allen's consternation, looked more like a Plantagenet queen than the American Gothic farmwife she claimed to be.

Nicki de Gunzburg was resplendent in a thematically inexcusable toreador costume. "I made the rules, I break the rules," he explained with an exquisite shrug of his shoulders.

Misia Sert attended as Misia Sert.

I had originally contemplated transforming myself into a muzhik with a scythe, but then in Poupineau, the lovely circus shop by the Musée Grévin, I discovered a yellowed wedding gown of provincial vintage. A wig, tiara, and Venetian-style mask completed my disguise. Helena Rubinstein did the rest. In case anyone asked, I was the Sleeping Princess.

A gasp from the crowd marked the arrival of Serge Lifar, mounted on a white stallion and wearing nothing but a leather girdle, his muscular body covered entirely in a sheen of gold paint.

A Negro jazz orchestra played. Sitting wonderfully erect on a garden stool, Edith Sitwell narrated to anyone who would listen an implausibly Dickensian version of her childhood. Bérard nudged me aside in order to begin a separate conversation. He had removed his ass's head, and held it under his arm. I saw that some green oil paint remained encrusted in his reddish beard.

"Cocteau sends you greetings. I saw him in Toulon, where I smoked with him and *l'enfant* Desbordes."

I asked his impressions of Desbordes, whom I hardly knew.

"In a word, infantile," pronounced Bérard. "Cocteau praises him to the heavens, but there's nothing there. His so-called poetry's simply embarrassing, a snail's trail of semen on a mirror that has been gazed into far too admiringly. Really, our brilliant friend's judgment these days has gone steeply into decline. I understand he's made a movie, though no one's seen it yet. Or if there's been a screening, *I* haven't been invited. Have *you*?" he asked with suspicion.

I told him I had not, though Cocteau had enlisted me to help paint the stage sets for *Le Sang d'un Poète*, which I had done with a rare sense of accomplishment.

"Well, either it'll resuscitate his fading career or be the end of him. Movies! What on earth is he thinking! Of all his *enfants*, the one I wish I'd known is Radiguet. I've read his two marvelous novels. Such promise—though he's already totally forgotten. I wonder which of us from this generation will be remembered? Perhaps we'll all be forgotten, and this era will be seen as little more than a wasteland."

There had been a momentary lull in the music. Now through the humid night air came the sound of a soprano saxophone eerily usurping the voluptuous flute melody that begins *L'Après-midi d'un Faune*. The queerness of the arrangement—Debussy was really quite ill-suited to jazz band transcription—made the music sound crudely rather than shimmeringly seductive. Still, it cast its pagan spell.

A dais had been set up—and there, languorously reclining, near-naked and fully golden, head tilted back, his thumb held to his lips as if to sip that longed-for elixir that never quenches thirst, was Lifar. He stretched sumptuously, rose on his haunches—the immortal, aching, libidinous faun in the heat of the midday sun.

A crowd had gathered. Misia Sert, looking pensive, stood apart from the others. An emptiness opened in me. Even at the Murphy's barge fête, nearly ten years ago now, there had seemed something vaguely corrupt about Lifar's appropriation of Nijinsky's famous role. Cocteau had pointed out the sheer cheekiness of it. But I had been younger then, and his performance had not struck me as nearly so crass as it did now.

"What a beast," I heard Boris tell Bérard. "Lifar has no morals whatsoever. He'll sleep with anyone if it'll advance his career. Right now he's trying to sleep with us all."

Strangely disconsolate, I withdrew into a shadowy corner of the garden, where roses bloomed in beds quadrisected by sandy paths. Though it was night, their scent still lingered. The reds were lost to darkness, but the whites floated mothlike out of the obscurity.

I could hear the orchestra as it ardently scaled its summit, then descended in those ravishing triplets, but the sound was distant, as if the rose garden had walls which shielded its occupant from the disappointing world without. A spider had begun to spin a web from one rose bush to another, across the path, and as I brushed against it I broke its fragile, clinging filaments. Presently I realized I was not alone.

A fellow I had noted earlier—a strapping young man dressed in a Tyrolean cap, open shirt, colorful braces, and lederhosen which exposed, beginning mid-thigh, the muscular legs of a cyclist—had quietly entered the garden.

The orchestra and Lifar having finished their sultry desecration, fireworks lit up the sky, like petals borne aloft and then spilled down upon us.

"So, at last," said the stranger. "I thought I might find you here."

He strode over to me and before I could say a word, planted a kiss on my lips.

He wore a black half mask. As he removed it, a burst of gold and green spangled the sky and I found myself looking into a pair of eyes the most exquisite shade of blue.

"Oh," I said.

"Don't act so startled," said Hermann Thieme. "I'm not going to scold you, though it *was* rather rude never to respond to my notes."

"Why did you run from me?" he asked later, as we lay together in the matrimonial bed in the Hotel Bristol.

"There's no guarantee I won't run again," I told him. "No guarantee at all."

"I won't lock you in a tower and throw away the key," he said. "If you wish to flee me once again, now that you've seen I'm not an ogre, I won't stand in your way."

"You're certainly not an ogre. It's never been the ogre I've feared; it's the prince that might break my heart."

"Well, if it eases things between us, I'm no prince either, even though my parents own a castle. Quite a modest castle.

My father bought it a few years ago, not so much because he desired a castle as because it was in dire need of restoration, and he couldn't bear to see it decline any further."

"That was decent of him."

"Father's a decent man. I'm lucky that way."

"My own father—" I began to say, but Hermann put a finger to my lips.

"Your father was a very *great* man. I already know a good deal about him."

"But how?"

"I was curious. It wasn't difficult to find out. There are many people eager to share their memories of him. And your brother's fame doesn't hurt."

There it pounced again: that panic that had seized me on the street outside Nicki's town house. Feeling very much the cornered animal I looked about the opulent room half convinced that it was about to dissolve before my eyes, and that the handsome man next to me would in the next instant tear off his human mask to reveal a gloating demon. But of course none of that happened.

"What's wrong?" Hermann asked, placing his palm on my bare chest. "I can feel your heart thumping."

"It's nothing. It's just that—there are moments when everything seems completely unreal to me."

"And this is one of those moments?"

"Yes," I said. "It is."

He nestled in close to me, spoke with his lips against my ear. "But I'm quite real, Nabokov. This room is quite real. The city outside the windows is indisputably real."

"I don't doubt those things at all. It's my own unreality that frightens me."

"But that's absurd!" Herman exclaimed. "I need another cigarette for this." He reached to the nightstand to fumble with his pack.

"Do you really," he asked, exhaling a wraith of torpid smoke, "think I would have pursued a phantasm for two years? Yes, that's how long it's been. You may not have been counting, but I have. And now to have you here, flesh and blood, body and spirit..." He inserted his cigarette between my lips, and I took a puff. "If you're not real, Nabokov, then I'm utterly mad. And I've never once in my life been even tempted to consider I might be mad. So there. It's settled."

To prove it he stubbed out our cigarette, and the passionate empiricist in him began once again to investigate my reality.

40

THERE WAS NOT TO BE A LILAC FAIRY'S MAGIC wand. A lifetime of unreality is a devilish legacy to undo.

I did not attempt to hide my vices entirely. I confessed to smoking opium—on occasion. ("A nasty habit!" Hermann exclaimed. "We'll have to see what we can do about that.") I confessed to an occasional bit of afternoon naughtiness with a Russian schoolmate—for old times' sake. ("I promise I won't hire a gangster to do him in!") I confessed to my very serious lapses as a Roman Catholic ("And I'd assumed you were Russian Orthodox. Well, that's a bright bit of news. All is not lost after all.")

Our first weeks together were exhilarating. Business brought him frequently to Paris, and the Hotel Bristol became my home away from home. Not since Russia had I found myself in such luxury, and though I had told myself again and again I did not miss all that, to find myself coddled was delightful. It was always a shock to return to my own flat whenever, after a magic week, Hermann traveled back to his parents' castle in the Tyrolean Alps.

Had I fallen in love? Yes, indubitably. Though he assured me that his parents were perfectly ordinary *bürgherliches Volk*, that the family business, which involved the manufacture of wooden cigar boxes, was as humdrum as could be, nonetheless Hermann's taste and manners were exquisitely refined. He was erudite and kind. At university, he had become vegetarian. He was a great champion of animal welfare, and though he was the most mild-mannered of men, I once witnessed him fly into an astonishing rage upon seeing a farmer beat an emaciated donkey that had fallen and could not rise to its feet. Though fit, he was hardly a fighter and the farmer was a red-faced ox of a man, yet Hermann thrashed him so thoroughly that the fellow soon fled the scene entirely while the donkey, having finally hoisted itself up, munched on some roadside clover.

When he was in Paris we dined superbly, spent our evenings at the ballet or opera, and afterward made the rounds of the jazz clubs. He loved Django Reinhardt, and thought Josephine Baker extraordinary. I very much enjoyed these diversions as well.

He had always been an avid athlete—swimming, cycling, skiing, tennis. I was no match for Hermann much of the time, but on the court I managed to surprise him enough to make things competitive.

He was not only Catholic but devoutly so. He adored Baroque architecture, and I took great pleasure in being toured around La Madeleine and St.-Roch and St.-Sulpice, those great roiling testaments to divine ecstasy I already knew well. In the midst of dispensing a torrent of information he would suddenly become as self-conscious as a precocious schoolboy. At such moments he would emit a shy, nervous laugh; dimples would appear by magic in his cheeks. He'd blink several times, as if trying to refocus on the dull, ordinary world those eyes whose blue seemed in certain lights to overflow the iris and spill into the whites.

After his too brief Paris sojourns I reentered my own world with the noblest of intentions, resolved to live up to the high ideals of our relationship. When he was in town I had taken to eating opium rather than inhaling it, a despicable option but necessary, as I could not, obviously, shut myself in the lavatory, and indulge in a pipe or two while in his company. And I found that I missed Oleg—absurd as that may sound. I missed his dismissive but oddly caring "So, Nabokov, what new outrages have you been up to in that pompous world of yours?" I missed his caresses, made all the more poignant by their rough, clumsy reluctance which would suddenly, with a groan of surrender, yield to something more genuine, desperate, heartbreaking. He had become, over the years of our liaison, much more willing to reciprocate, though it was nothing we ever spoke of; it simply happened. And it meant the world to me.

I could not relinquish him, however much I wanted or needed to.

Hermann never asked about my old school friend. I told myself, "He'll expect me to have cleared that matter up." That I was unable to do so only deepened the secret misery I felt.

After several months of seeing each other with some frequency—usually every fortnight—Hermann proposed that I accompany him back to Austria for a visit. I agreed, though inwardly I felt a little rumble of trepidation, not unlike the ominous trill in the bass that keeps interrupting that lovely opening melody in Schubert's B-flat Sonata.

We traveled—first class, of course; how long had it been since I last traveled first class?—on the Paris–Munich Express, and thence by chauffeured car into the Tyrolean Alps. Winter's first snows had fallen a few days earlier, thickly blanketing the countryside; it had been many years since I had seen so much snow. Matrei in Osttirol was situated at the convergence of three valleys, and guarded to the east and west by the stupendous peaks of the Grossglockner and Grossvenediger, both barely visible that afternoon through lowering clouds. On a crag just beyond the village perched the squat, unprepossessing Castle Weissenstein.

"Not exactly Neuschwanstein," said Hermann with a self-deprecating laugh, "but then what were you expecting?"

"What indeed?" I said. "It's magnificent. It's like a dream. I can't believe I'm here. Frankly, I'm terrified."

"There's nothing to be terrified of. My parents are very old-fashioned, deeply warm-hearted, and adorably clueless. You don't have a thing in the world to worry about."

Though he had affirmed that countless times, still I did worry. I should not have. His parents greeted me affectionately, as did two enthusiastic Alsatians that nearly knocked me to the ground.

"Sigmund! Sieglinde!" Herr Thieme called out, clapping his hands together briskly. "Don't murder the poor fellow with your kindness. You've got to press back against them. Stand your ground and you'll have won them over entirely."

When they had exhausted what novelty I had to offer, they turned their attentions to Hermann, who had settled into a crouch, the better to receive their sloppy adulation full in the face. "Good dogs," he cooed sentimentally. "Very, very good dogs."

Once the canine introductions were over, I met the parents properly. Though both were white-haired and ruddy-cheeked, Anne Marie seemed a good deal younger than Oskar. She was dressed simply but smartly; he wore a rather shabby, out-of-fashion tweed jacket and a distinctly old-fashioned mustache. They beamed when Hermann called them "my beloved parents," and nodded approvingly when he described me as "a great good friend." When our luggage had been conveyed indoors, and Hermann and his mother had conspiratorially vanished, I found myself being led by Oskar on an elaborate tour of the castle. The various buildings were a patchwork of egregious disrepair and elegant restoration. He took me though the history of the structure, from its modest twelfth-century origins through its enlargement in the fourteenth century, its decline into an almshouse in the eighteenth, its refurbishment in a romantic English style in the nineteenth, and its purchase by the Thiemes in 1921. We visited the cobbled courtyard with its ancient cistern, and the old stables where the family's automobiles now resided. We climbed the battlements and looked out over the village, the parish church of St. Alban, the much older St. Niklaus, the soul-stirring panorama of mountains.

"I hope the dear man hasn't exhausted you," Hermann said when at last I found him in his bedroom. A fire danced in the hearth to the strains of Bix Beiderbecke on the gramophone.

"Not at all," I told him. "He was thoroughly charming. He even showed me the trophy head of the first boar you ever shot. You never told me my favorite vegetarian was once a keen hunter."

He sighed. "The first of many embarrassing secrets that will no doubt come to light. I *was*, actually, quite the huntsman. Bear, boar, deer. I can't set foot in that room these days. But I loved being in the forest with Father at dawn on cold November mornings. I've never felt so close to him as I did then. My decision to abstain from meat—and, obviously, hunting—quite puzzles him. I think he's never gotten over the disappointment, but I'd like to think that's the worst disappointment I've given him. Well, that and my bachelorhood, which I've sustained about as long as is feasible. You'd be doing me a grand favor if you occasionally mentioned Sophie."

"And who's Sophie?"

"The nicest thing about her is she doesn't exist. Other than that, she's the cold-hearted woman in Munich I've been desperately in love with for several years, and who simply will not return my affections. Don't you think I'm coping well with my disappointment?"

"Admirably," I said. "Strange coincidence, though. I once had a Sophie myself. Cultivated her to excellent effect for the sake of the physician who was attempting to 'cure' me at the time. But that does beg the question, doesn't it? Eventually you'll have to get over dear Sophie and find someone else."

His merriness left him. "I'm well aware of that. If my parents were ever to discover their son is a nancy boy, it would kill them."

"Well, if it's any consolation, there's nothing about you that seems the least bit nancyish. You could almost fool me. Aren't you worried my presence here will compromise you?"

"No. As you can see, my parents are the gentlest of creatures. They'd never think unkind thoughts about anyone I brought home."

He had spoken before of his friends—Karl the mathematical wunderkind from university, Marco the clock restorer, Herbert the pianist. Each episode had come to an amiable conclusion, and he continued to maintain cordial relations with them all. At least, that was his story. I could so scarcely believe my illustrious predecessors had somehow fallen by the wayside that I suspected, in my darker moments, that some flaw must exist in Hermann which I had not yet detected. My occasional query would elicit only a shrug: "Who knows?" he would say. "There's luck, and then there's luck. And then there's you."

But how lucky was he to have me? I wondered, as I calculated anxiously whether I had brought enough opium to get me through the visit. Given that I was to be under constant observation for the week, I had purposely cut back as much as I dared, and already was feeling a maddening restlessness in my limbs, a disagreeable sensation in my chest. Nights were the worst; I suffered indescribable dreams—wonderful, deranged, epic—that seemed to last for hours, but when I woke with a start I would discover that scarcely a quarter hour had elapsed. I was perversely grateful that Hermann thought it imprudent for us to spend the night in the same bed, and it was with relief that I retreated to the privacy of my own room once our nightly session of tenderness had concluded. My fairly consistent failures to perform did not humiliate me as much as they should have, for he insisted, no doubt disingenuously, that "simply to have you in my arms" satisfied him sufficiently.

By day we traipsed about the snowy village accompanied by Sigmund and Sieglinde; attended mass in the parish church of St. Alban (one glimpse of Zeiller's marvelous ceiling frescoes and I understood whence came my friend's love of the Baroque); sipped Italian coffee and ate beautiful but tasteless pastries in the konditorei. We strapped on skis, and under Hermann's expert tutelage I was soon able to enjoy off-piste forays into the silent countryside.

The Austrian Alps were not nearly so cold as the Russian flatlands, and did not resemble the landscape of my childhood, though among Matrei's traditional Tyrolean timbered houses, a Baroque building glimpsed out of the corner of my eye would sometime conjure a half-remembered Petersburgian scene. At such moments it seemed not impossible that Oleg would come around the corner—not the ruined Oleg of today but Oleg as he was at fifteen or sixteen or seventeen.

I found myself involuntarily revisiting Volodya and Bobby de Calry's alpine vacation as well.

Now and again I would catch Hermann looking at me strangely, as if he sensed my unease.

In the evenings we dined with his parents. Despite my first impression, Oskar turned out to be rather reticent unless he had something strictly material he wished to discuss—a range of paneling that needed to be replaced, a particular bird he had observed, thoughts about the menu for the coming week.

Anne Marie, however, was a prodigious talker on a variety of subjects, and I listened with interest to the stories she told of Hermann—how, for instance, he had rescued Sigmund and Sieglinde as puppies from the village tobacconist, who intended to drown them since they were not pure-blooded Alsatians. Her accent, and on occasion her choice of words, betrayed a humble upbringing; her father had been a farmer, she was the youngest of seven children. She had moved to Linz at nineteen, found a job as a secretary, and surprised everyone, herself most of all, by becoming engaged to her employer, eleven years her senior. "Can you imagine?" she would say with a mirthful smile, tapping Oskar reprovingly on his wrist. "He married his secretary. It's truly the worst thing I know about him!"

After dinner we played cards as Sigmund and Sieglinde slumbered at our feet. I have never been much of a card player, but neither was Hermann's mother, and thus we made common cause while Hermann and his father battled it out with great intensity and verve.

Watching the two of them spar could put me in a wistful mood, and I found myself recalling those poker games my mother and Uncle Ruka would play late into the night at Vyra, as well those drives home from the opera in St. Petersburg when Father and I would argue spiritedly about music. All vanished—and yet here I was, disorientingly welcomed into the bosom of this contented Alpine family.

One evening, after poker had ended and the Thiemes had gone off to bed, I remarked on the marvelous harmony between son and parents. Unexpectedly, my remark plunged Hermann into gloom.

"You don't know how I envy you," he told me. "Nothing I have is substantial. It's all based on lies. You may rue your poverty, your estrangements, but at least, Sergey, you've nothing to hide."

I was on the verge of confessing my own dissimulations

when we both heard a sound outside the door of his bedroom, as if someone had dropped something in the corridor,

"That's strange. There shouldn't be anyone about at this hour," he said.

"It's a gnome," I whispered. "At night those hideous little statues I see in all the gardens come to life."

"Don't laugh. The villagers actually believe the gnomes are descendants of the Nibelungs. There are spots in the mountains they're said to haunt, certain grottoes behind waterfalls. You'll come across little mounds of stones the locals have built in order to appease them. If you haven't noticed, the place flickers with magic."

"Hermann," I said, "we don't believe in gnomes or Nibelungs or anything like that."

He laughed. "Of course we don't. Still, I do wonder what that noise was. I would like to investigate."

The corridor, however, was empty.

41

AT THE END OF THE FORTNIGHT I RETURNED TO Paris alone—though still first class; kind Hermann had seen to that. He could not, alas, relieve me of the headache of my Nansen passport. I spent the journey mired in grief, certain that there was only one course of action available to me. The next day I wrote him a careful letter in which I explained that his parents had been wonderfully welcoming, his dogs memorable, the castle a thing of beauty, his own behavior toward me loving, kind, impeccable, but that I regretted beyond words that I would be unable to see him again.

Two days later Hermann stood on my doorstep.

"What a great waste of time," I told him. "I've made my decision. Please have the decency to respect it."

He smiled. Those wonderful eyes never left mine. "What's time for, if not to waste? The only question is how. In any event, I understand perfectly well that it's not you who made this decision. I may be quite the provincial, but I spend enough time in Parisian circles to know what's what. I refuse to allow myself to be bested by some beastly flower from the Orient. It's a dreadful scourge, and I don't blame you in the least. I don't even blame Cocteau. He's as much in its thrall as anyone. In any event, I've made some inquiries. There's a hospital in Meudon willing to receive you this very evening if you'll consent to come with me."

He said all this with such poise and assurance that all my shored-up bulwarks gave way, and I burst into tears. He put his arms around me, and I put my arms around him, and we both sobbed and bawled and eventually, yes, even laughed brokenly there on the landing outside my room. I saw the concierge stick her head out her door to see what the ruckus was and abruptly withdraw.

"Say you'll consent," he said after several minutes had gone by.

"Yes. Yes, of course, by all means. Let's go at once, without another thought."

"The taxi," he said, "is waiting downstairs."

I packed a small bag and we descended to the street. As promised, a Taxi de la Marne idled at the curb. Oleg Danchenko was not behind the wheel.

Every hellish thing Cocteau had told me about the cure was true. Constipation, diarrhea, sleeplessness, nightmares, cold sweats. Purges, enemas, electric baths. The doctors were unfeeling brutes, the nurses bullies, the orderlies sadistic—and to them all I owe a great debt of gratitude. I have undergone other tribulations—five months in an Austrian jail, for instance—and I fear even worse adversities ahead, but what I discovered in that hospital of God's grace and mercy will see me through whatever lies in store for me. That I know, even in my present abject terror.

I was in for eight weeks. Allowed no visitors, I could nonetheless receive mail. Though for obvious reasons I wished the news kept from my mother, I told Hermann to otherwise make no secret of my rehabilitation. Besides his own letters, which arrived sometimes twice or even thrice daily—charming little notes that he often illustrated with amusing drawings—my only other regular communication was with my cousin Nika and the American Allen Tanner. Seeing his days with Tchelitchew numbered, Tanner still—out of habit, I suppose—continued to report his beloved's activities as if they were transcendent events: Pavlik was painting scenes from the circus; he had rediscovered the secrets of magenta; he was reading Horapallo and rereading the Kabbalah; he had still not forgiven Cocteau for having exclaimed, at his latest exhibition, "This isn't painting, this is puzzle making." I read all this with indifference.

That Cocteau never once wrote disappointed me, but I knew that he was having difficulties of his own, smoking in Toulon with Desbordes and Bérard and mourning the continuing financial *crise* that had turned his once gay world gray. According to Hermann, Cocteau was miffed because I had missed the January première of *Le Sang d'un Poète.* That by then I had already entered the hospital made no difference. "It's quite simple to let oneself out," Cocteau was reported to have said. "What are bed linens for but to make a rope from which to swing down from a high window?" I do not know if any of this was true; it is quite possible Hermann had already begun his campaign to separate me from Cocteau's influence. If that is the case, I forgive him.

I emerged in March, marvelously renewed. I could urinate without difficulty, my nerves had calmed, my pupils had redilated, my libido had returned. Hermann whisked me away to Matrei for several calm weeks. We took long hikes along verdant valleys and rocky ridges. As the weather warmed we ascended higher into the mountains, reaching vertiginous heights from which the serrated Alps lay all before us, a panorama unequaled since my aerial adventure over the gentle swales of Somerset.

Hermann asked many questions about my boyhood, made me recall things I had hidden away. He flushed with anger when I told him about Dr. Bekhetev and my "treatments." He laughed at my exploits with the Left-Handed Abyssinians.

The only topic I avoided was Oleg. Several times I came right up to the precipice and stared down, but I could not take the plunge. And the more I filled out the story of my life, the less easily I could double back and include this essential item I had so inexplicably omitted.

On the subject of Volodya Hermann was delicately circumspect, sensing my reluctance to probe the tender bruise of our estrangement. Father, on the other hand, stirred his imagination. An avid reader of history and politics, Hermann suggested that I should write the biography of Vladimir Dmitrievich Nabokov. Who, after all, was in a better position to do so than I?

I was much taken by this idea, though my congenital indolence kept delaying the actual commencement of that noble exercise.

I returned to Paris in late summer to put my affairs in order. After much discussion, I had decided to forsake cosmopolitan toil and hardship for life in the gentle provinces. I was not without doubts, but I was in love—and perhaps more to the point, I was loved, as I had never before felt loved. It was a bit unnerving, to tell the truth. For so long I had sought just such a relationship. Now I found myself gasping for breath. Something Father Maritain had once said haunted me: "God's love can be an awful thing to bear. And just think: in Paradise, there'll be nothing but God's love. Perhaps that's why so many people spend their lives on earth doing everything they can to sabotage that daunting prospect."

This, in other words, was a rehearsal. Thus I screwed up my courage and paid a visit to Oleg. The weather had turned sultry. I mounted the narrow staircase to the fifth floor and with no little trepidation knocked on his door. There was no answer. My heart leapt at the prospect of a reprieve. At least I had tried. I knocked once more, and then a third time, just to be sure, and as in the darkest of fairy tales the door swung open.

He had neither bathed nor shaved recently. Within their still gorgeous irises his pupils were pinpricks. But he seemed overjoyed to see me, embracing me affectionately and covering my face with rough kisses.

"Nabokov! You devil! I've been worried out of my mind. I thought, Surely something nasty must have happened to him. But here you are, looking fit as a fiddle. How could you abandon me like that?"

"I was kidnapped by fairies," I told him. "Held captive by a ring of fire."

He stared at me. "For once," he said, "I choose to believe you. Otherwise I'd have to thrash you."

The least stupid smell in the world hung in the close air.

"Look," I said, "Are you hungry? Let me take you to a café."

"I'll have to make myself respectable. I've been ill the last few days. I haven't been able to work for a week."

I sat on his bed and smoked a cigarette as he stripped, washed himself, shaved while peering into a smudged bit of mirror. His hair was sorely in need of a trim.

"Here," I said impulsively, going over to him. "You're a bit untidy. Do you have a pair of scissors?"

"Somewhere," he said, and after a moment's search found a pair.

He chafed a bit as I snipped stray strands. "Careful," I said. "I don't want to cut your ear off."

Slivers of auburn hair fell to the floor. I brushed a couple of wisps from his bare shoulders. I touched his neck, where a vein throbbed. Through the open window came the sounds of traffic. Oleg whistled a bit of melody as I clipped. Something seemed wrong, out of place—I kept glancing about the room, trying to make out what was missing.

Having put on a clean shirt, decent trousers, a frayed but presentable summer jacket, he proclaimed himself ready to venture forth. Flush with Hermann's money, I proposed Le Sélect, where the artists and writers went, where I had once, in another life, been an habitué.

"It's not really the sort of place I fancy."

"It's August. There'll be no one there. I'd like to treat you."

Despite the season, he wanted oysters, so willfully we settled in to two dozen marrenes and a bottle of Pouilly-Fuissé, followed by tournedos béarnaise, and a bottle of Châteauneuf-du-Pape.

He ate ravenously. I have never in my life so enjoyed seeing someone eat. As he feasted I told him of my weeks in the hospital, my recuperation in the Alps. I told him of Hermann's affection for me, and mine for him.

Oleg grunted noncommittally. When he had finished devouring his meal, he leaned back in his chair, patted his belly, and said, "You know, you needn't see me anymore if you don't want to."

"What's wrong?" I asked.

"Nothing at all," he said.

"Something's wrong," I insisted. "I know you well enough."

"You don't know me at all. No one does. But if you must know, Valechka's left me."

"For all practical purposes Valechka left you a long time ago," I told him.

"You've never been married," he said. "You've never loved a woman. You've no idea what it's like."

A prolonged bout of coughing seized him. "My lungs are shredded," he said with a ghastly grin. "But my heart's shredded as well, so what's the difference? And about my soul I dare no longer inquire. I pawned it some time ago, along with anything of else of value."

"You really needn't talk like that," I told him. "It doesn't do anyone any good."

"And who are you to talk? What's any better about your life? Oh, you've won yourself a temporary stay of execution—but for how long, Nabokov? We've both wrecked ourselves, though I daresay it's not entirely our fault. Do you know a single Russian who isn't ruined in one way or another? We who escaped are every bit as doomed as the ones we left behind. Maybe *they* were the luckier ones, in fact. At least for them, the end came quickly. They didn't have to wait around fooling themselves that everything was going to be fine again one day. No, when the patient's doomed, it's best to put him down immediately. Anyone who knows horses knows that."

"I should be perfectly honest with you," I said, "It's the least I owe you. I'm in love with this Hermann Thieme."

"I'm not an idiot, Nabokov. Of course you are. Don't you think I can see that? And do you think I care anymore than you care that Valechka left me? I admire you, my friend, really I do. If anyone knows when to jump ship, it's you, old chum."

"I'm not jumping ship. I'm simply telling you something I should have told you some months ago. I owe you that."

He looked at me intently across the table. "But you've never owed me a thing, Nabokov. For better or worse, you've never owed me a single thing."

Strange how a very long chapter in one's life can finally close. We parted on friendly terms, if one can be said to part from a ghost on friendly terms. On the corner of the boulevard Montparnasse and the boul' Mich, Steerforth held out his hand. Copperfield returned the gesture. Neither drew the other into an embrace; no bright tear glistened in either's eye.

"For a pair of outlaws," Oleg said, "we've been brilliant."

Then he bestowed on me, one last time, that unforgettable smile.

I watched his figure disappear down the glittering street. He did not look back.

42

BERLIN
DECEMBER 11, 1943

"EXPECT TO HEAR FROM ME SOON," FELIX SILBER has said, but that now presents a grave difficulty. I have no way of contacting him save through the Ministry, which would be madness, and to chalk my new address on a ruined wall on Ravensbergerstrasse for everyone, including the Gestapo, to see would be madness as well. So I am stymied. I have moved into a room in Onya's comfortable villa in a relatively unscathed neighborhood past the Grunewald, in the direction of Potsdam. There is a bomb shelter dug in the back garden, but we have not so far had to seek shelter in it. At night the bombers come—we hear their rumble in the distance, we see the sky to the north-east lit up in an infernal glow. One morning we emerge to find the ground littered with strips of tinsel the RAF has begun dropping to confuse the German radar; it looks as if the whole neighborhood has been decorated for Christmas. And there has been snow as well. It would all be oddly festive were it not for the reality of everything.

I tell Onya that I have quit my job at the Ministry. No more ration coupons, she points out. I tell her I may be in some difficulty with the police. She frowns, but says nothing. I offer to find other lodging, but she tells me, "Don't think of it. We are Nabokovs." I do what I can to make myself useful. I spend one morning scavenging coal from a bin up the road, and come back with my last suit thoroughly ruined.

One day, as she is attempting to eke some tea from thrice-before brewed leaves, she says, "I'm so thankful Nika moved to America when he did. And Volodya. We all had the chance. What were the rest of us thinking?"

I contemplate that question for a moment. "We were certain we were loved," I tell her. "I refuse to think we were wrong."

After several days I can stand this hiatus no longer, and make my way into the battered city, nearly a two-hour ordeal, as very few trams or buses run any longer. When I pass POW cleanup crews I scrutinize their faces, though I know Hugh will not be among them. What would I do if he were? My intention is to catch Felix as he leaves the Ministry without attracting the attention of any of my other former colleagues. I muffle my face in my scarf and loiter in the vicinity as inconspicuously as possible. At least the bitter cold subdues the pervasive odor of death. Funny that I should come to have some sympathy for the Tsar's secret police who used to stand outside our house on Morskaya Street on winter afternoons. A steady stream of people comes and goes from the Ministry building. I realize I have no idea what entrance or exit Felix uses, which way he turns as he leaves the building, where he might be lodging now that his home has been destroyed. I realize once again how very, very little I know about this unassuming man to whom I have become so oddly attached. I am fully aware that my attempts to assist Hugh Bagley are pure folly—as Felix must have been aware all along. But without the distraction of these attempts I should soon yield to complete despair, for I realize that my obsession with aiding Hugh is in part a substitute for my utter helplessness with regard to Hermann's terrible fate.

Eventually dark settles. No Felix. I am cold, and hungry, and absurdly disappointed, and in fact begin to cry like a frustrated child. The prospect of a very long walk back to Onya's is disheartening, but I realize I have nowhere else to go.

But I do not return immediately to Onya's; instead I make my way to the Milchbar. My parting from Hansel the swing boy was studiously casual—"See you around, Blisters," he said with weary glamour, hitching up his tight trousers. Why raise any hopes? One must remind oneself daily: to hope is to be crushed. Still, the prospect of seeing him again stirs me.

When I reach the Milchbar I see that it is utterly gone, the entire street reduced to rubble. Soon enough the air-raid sirens on the city's outskirts begin to keen like Valkyries. It is not too many blocks to an S-Bahn shelter, and those have held up remarkably well during the bombardment.

43

PARIS

AN EVENING IN LATE NOVEMBER 1932. THE MAIN hall of the Musée Social on rue Las Cases filled to capacity with Russian literary Paris: Khodasevich, Berberova, Aldanov, Bunin, Adamovich, Zinaida Gippius. After a longish wait, V. Sirin entered.

By sheer accident Hermann and I had been in town and seen the announcement in a bookshop window. At first I was hesitant about attending—after all, I had not seen my brother in nearly a decade—but Hermann was adamant. "By all means we must go. I'm most curious to hear your brother read, even if I won't understand a word of it! You'll have to translate for me afterward."

In the end, of course, I was even more curious than Hermann to hear Volodya read.

Balding but otherwise looking fit, my brother sauntered to

the lectern, arranged his papers, paused, looked beneath the lectern, cleared his throat. Could a glass of water be made available? Another longish wait (staring at the ceiling) while water was brought. He sipped. Stirred his papers. Looked straight ahead—defiantly, as if somehow daring the audience to attend. An anticipatory hush fell over the hall.

Never looking down, Sirin began to recite in a strong, even-keeled voice. I held my breath. He held his audience rapt. When he had ended the poem, rapturous applause ensued. He looked about, now seeming a bit abashed at the intensity of the response he had provoked. He sipped once again from his water glass. Again he brought forth a poem. Again the tempest of approval. After several poems he seemed to relax. He could see he had his audience firmly in hand.

He sipped more water. I studied him avidly. He looked handsome, confident, worldly in his ill-fitting dinner jacket. The lights gleamed on his balding forehead. His cheeks sagged, pulling down the corners of his mouth, making his eyes droop. He looked like a sad but still regal hound.

I used to hear him, through a closed door, reciting his latest melodious effort to our parents. The poems were still melodious, but they were no longer parlor songs: they were by turns stern, powerful, hypnotic, ironic. Like Pushkin, they sparkled. Like Fet, they sang. Like Blok, they delved wondrously deep.

After another swell of applause he mumbled what I presumed was meant to be a transition or explanation or joke—something to do with the water he had been sipping, and the title of the story, "Music," he proposed now to read—but few if any in the audience seemed to grasp his intent, so diffident was his delivery of his impromptu lines. Nonetheless, as soon as he dove into the first sentence of the story he was once more in his element. He read, he declaimed, he chanted—clearly he retained the story fully in his head, glancing only occasionally at the pages before him, perhaps to assure the audience that the words had actually been written down, butterflies seized out of thin air, deftly ethered, pinned permanently to the page.

The reader will recall that Volodya had no ear for music. Neither does the protagonist of "Music." In a salon he sits, indifferent as a pianist storms through his flurry of meaningless notes. As his gaze travels around the room he realizes to his dismay that his former wife, whom he has not seen in two years, is in the audience as well. Tender, painful memories of their brief marriage ensue. He feels imprisoned by the music, the room, her presence. He will not look her way. He recalls his discovery of her infidelity, his decision to live without her. It is all simply intolerable. But now a wholly surprising tenderness replaces his feeling of entrapment. *Come, look at me*, he thinks. *I implore you, please, please look. I'll forgive you everything, because someday we all must die, and then we shall know everything, and everything will be forgiven—so why put it off?*

Had my brother any inkling I might be in the audience? All I could know was that the author of those imploring words could not be altogether heartless, that at the very least he must see their relevance to his own estranged brother.

The music ceases. The protagonist notices, with a pang, that his former wife is taking an early leave of their hostess; clearly she has seen him as well. And suddenly the music, which had seemed such a prison, becomes a magic glass dome under which he and she have lived together, breathed together for a short blissful time that is now ending, that is now, since she has left the room, gone forever.

The switch from poetry to prose had not diminished the audience's enthusiasm for Sirin's art. Beside me, Hermann too applauded energetically, though I knew he had not understood a word.

"Marvelous. It's like listening to Boris Godunov," he confided, his face flushed, his forehead glistening with sweat.

(The hall was quite overheated; the crowd had been much larger than anticipated that evening.)

There followed a half hour's intermission. If I had thought to speak to the acclaimed author, the spectacle of dozens of people crowding around him quelled that notion. Only at one point, near the end of intermission, did the mob subside, and I saw my chance—but at that instant a woman rushed up to him and began to harangue him fiercely. I could not hear what she was saying, but she seemed to be lecturing him with great agitation. Clearly she had once been a great beauty, but her looks now were coarsened. Though she seemed vaguely familiar, try as I might I could not place her. He withstood her onslaught impassively, finally directing his eyes heavenward and lifting his upturned palms before him in a gesture of helpless if amused surrender.

"He certainly seems to be getting an earful," Hermann observed. "One hardly needs words when a pantomime's as expressive as that."

The second part of the reading consisted of the first two chapters of his latest novel, *Despair.* He read with ironic detachment, deliciously emphasizing the cluelessness of the narrator (named Hermann!) as he confidently, hilariously misconstrues everything in the world around him. That the whole was headed for heartbreak somewhere down the line quickly became apparent, but the astute clowning of those opening pages—the narrator's spectacular inability to begin his tale, his mad dash to arrive at his meeting with his supposed double Felix (a kind of premature ejaculation in narrative terms, masterfully managed for full psychological effect), the slow hatching of Hermann's odious and improbable scheme—provided the audience with considerable opportunity for merriment, with only the occasional sensation of the bottom dropping out from underneath everything.

It was splendid, it was triumphant. It was a quarter till midnight. He had read for more than two and a half hours, and had kept his audience spellbound the entire time. As far as I could see, the only ones in the whole hall who defected midway through were Adamovich, Ivanov, and Gippius—no surprise there, as they regularly savaged Sirin in print—as well as the mystery woman whose scolding my brother had endured.

Seeing that his band of admirers was not likely to disperse anytime soon, I told Hermann we should leave. I rather fancied a drink.

"No," Hermann said. "Speak to him, by all means. Stay as long as you need. Trust me, he'll be very pleased that you came. I'll just be outside having a cigarette. And then we can go get that drink you crave."

I waited. I spoke briefly with Miliukov, whom I had not seen in months, much to Mother's consternation, and who always seemed to feel it his duty to commune with me. I spoke at greater length with Nika, which was always a pleasure. "There's talk of adjourning to a café afterward," he told me. "You'll join us, I hope."

"I've got a friend waiting outside. I think he's made plans for us. Tell Volodya I'm sorry to have missed him, but by all means congratulate him on his reading."

"It *was* quite brilliant, wasn't it? I somehow feel we've been present at a historic occasion. But will the greater world take any note? There wasn't a single non-Russian in the whole hall."

"Well… One, actually," I said. "My friend Hermann."

"And what did he think?"

"He couldn't understand a word. Otherwise I think he quite enjoyed it. Take care, Nika." I kissed him affectionately on both cheeks. "No doubt we'll see each other soon."

As I turned to leave, Volodya came bearing down on me.

"Ah," he said. "Planning to sneak away like the guilty fox? How very nice to see you."

"I wouldn't have missed it," I stammered. "You were superb."

His face registered the old involuntary dismay he used to show whenever a word would catch me up. "That's very kind of you," he said. "It did go off quite well, didn't it?

"Absolutely."

For a moment we stared at each other, both at an awkward loss.

"Well," he said. "I find these occasions very tiring. Necessary, I suppose, but tiring. I'm very much looking forward to heading straight back to Nika's and getting a good night's sleep."

I took a deep breath. "Look, Volodya. Things have been very bad between us for a very long time. Perhaps they're fated to remain so. But as you yourself so beautifully wrote, 'Someday we all must die, and then we shall know everything, and everything will be forgiven—so why put it off?' If you'd only give me the chance to explain myself, to see if by some means we can find our way past the obstacles that have divided us for so long. I have to think that our estrangement would have saddened Father, as I know it saddens Mother. I think this is something Father would have wished. Just one meeting. The two of us."

He studied me coolly. "My schedule's very crowded," he told me. "I leave tomorrow afternoon for Berlin." He coughed, scratched his forehead distractedly, took a deep reluctant breath and said, "Still, I will meet you for lunch. On one condition. You must pay. I'm afraid I have no funds at all at the moment."

44

WE MET AT MICHAUD'S, ON THE CORNER OF RUE Jacob and rue des Saints-Pères, in part because Hermann was underwriting the meal, but also because, as I told Volodya once we were seated, James Joyce and his family could often be seen dining at that table in the corner.

"Mr. Leopold Bloom," said my brother, "who eats with relish the inner organs of beast and fowl, is the most thoroughly decent figure to stroll through literature since Lyovin, though his sexual tastes are far more depraved. As for myself, I must confess I'm entirely indifferent to food in all its remarkable forms, beast, fowl or otherwise. As far as I'm concerned, it's fuel—necessary, but hardly to be praised or pampered or paraded, which I sense the French are inclined to do. Left to my own devices, I'd be perfectly content to eat scrambled eggs three times a day. I do like champagne, though."

With a satisfying *pop!* our waiter uncorked the bottle I had ordered.

"Yes, I like champagne very much," he repeated. "This is

so much better than the sweet Russian stuff, which is fit for children and old ladies and no one else."

I told him he must find Berlin congenial, then, given its undistinguished cuisine.

"Berlin doesn't exist," he said, "any more than a movie exists. Unreal City, as Eliot calls London in that flimsy pastiche of his. *That's* why I find Berlin, as you say, 'congenial.' I needn't bother with it at all. Some would say we émigrés live as ghosts amid the cities we find ourselves in. I assert the opposite—it's *we* who are real. Yes," he said, seeming to warm to that line of thought, "that's our predicament. We're real citizens doomed to inhabit phantom cities. A parable, really: the fate of rich, real consciousness in a sham-material world."

To draw his attention a little closer to earth, I congratulated him once again on the previous night's triumph.

"I presume you noticed who stalked out? At least Bunin stayed to the end. He even managed to find one or two vaguely complimentary things to say, much as I'm sure it pained him. He's really the dullest man alive. As for the others, Ivanov is a complete nobody; someone should seal him into his mousehole for good. And that grotesque old fool Gippius never liked my work, nor did her husband, despite his claim that he taught me all I know about literature; besides, she's a lesbian, or hermaphrodite, or some such unpleasant thing. As for Sodomovitch, the less said the better."

"And there was another," I said. "The woman who accosted you at intermission. She seemed vaguely familiar. I've been trying ever since to place her."

My brother laughed. "Oh," he said. "I'm astonished you remember her at all, since your memory's so often faulty. But yes, you did meet her once—rather embarrassing circumstances. The Acropolis..."

At once I remembered: it had been during our short stay in Piraeus, an interval of repose between Crimea and England. I had gone with Nika and Onya to see the Parthenon by moonlight. All at once a voice rose from amid the ruins, singing first a pulsing aria from Verdi, then a plaintive Russian song. We later learned it was the celebrated diva Cherkasskaya, serenading the stone maidens of the Erechtheum. At almost the same time, as if stage-managed by an invisible hand, there emerged from other shadows my brother and a strikingly beautiful young woman whom I did not know, and whom I was not to see again in Piraeus, but whose moonlit looks and poise in a potentially embarrassing moment must have imprinted themselves in the nether regions of my consciousness.

"Novotvortseva was her name," Volodya said. "I've been trying to recall her first name. She was married, I remember, and fancied herself a poet. She's not aged well, and she should bathe more often. She took umbrage with that story I read—seemed to think it was addressed exclusively to her. As if I'd known she'd be there. And in the meantime, she'd had absolutely no idea that Sirin and I were one and the same. Comic, isn't it. Now what was her first name?"

I told him I was afraid I could be of no help there.

"It doesn't matter," he went on. "I must get her out of my head. On the whole, I seem to have found my footing here in Paris quite nicely. They apparently find me English—that is to say, high-quality. Already some of my better bons mots are coming back to me. And increasingly I hear a word beginning with the letters *g-e-n*... I've written to Véra telling her we really must move here as soon as possible. We're practically the last Russians left in Berlin. How marvelous it was to look out at that sea of literate faces! All of literary Berlin could—and on occasion does—fit into a modest sitting room. I've been making valuable contacts as well. I've met with the translators who are metamorphosing *Luzhin's Defense* and *Camera Obscura* into French. A professor from the University of California has offered to show several of my books to American publishers."

I had never heard my brother speak at such length—about anything, and certainly not about himself—and I began to wonder whether his literary successes had begun to swell his head, until after some minutes it began to dawn on me that it was instead his nervousness at the prospect of our beginning a real conversation, the sort of conversation I had asked for, that accounted for his uncharacteristic volubility.

Only the arrival of our food stemmed the torrent of his narrative. Though we had not yet finished our first, he wondered if another bottle of champagne might be in order. I assented with some relief. He tucked into his *foie de veau* with methodical zest while I took advantage of his momentary preoccupation to say, "Mother conveys to me in great detail whatever she gleans of your life from the letters you send. I have no idea whether she does the same regarding my news. I've gone through some turbulent times, but things have been sorting themselves out." He continued to eat without looking up. Feeling a bit queasy, I went on, "I'd like you to know, for instance, that I've converted to Roman Catholicism." He stopped eating, laid down his fork and knife, tipped his napkin to his lips, and looked at me curiously.

"I did not know that," he said. Then he picked up his fork and knife and resumed his meal.

"Mother's known of my conversion for quite some time," I told him. "I broke the news to her when I visited back in twenty-six. I suppose I'm not surprised she neglected to pass it along. It was almost as if she hadn't heard me. Not that I blame her. She had quite a lot on her mind, I'm sure."

"I'm afraid Mother tells me very little about you in her letters. Don't take it personally. She's very distracted by her financial situation, which as you know is frighteningly grim. I've been doing what I can, but I've no money whatsoever. My books may be acclaimed, but they earn me nothing. Recently I've begun to give the occasional by-invitation-only reading in an attempt to raise funds to send her, but most in my circle are as penniless as I. How you can afford to bring me to this restaurant, by the way, I have no idea."

"I'll explain that a little later," I told him, daunted by how much territory I wished to cover, and aware that his schedule severely limited our time together. "It's another chapter entirely. Have you no response to my conversion?"

He shrugged. "What am I to say? I should think it provides you with much-needed consolation and hope. It can't be easy for someone in your condition. I imagine there's much to be sorry for. If belief in an ancient and long-lasting system of practices eases one's suffering, I am hardly one to criticize it—just as I'm not about to criticize Mother's taking up Christian Science, which I presume offers similar benefits."

Now it was my turn to be surprised.

"But I've heard nothing of that!" I told him.

"She's dabbled in it for some time now. She and Mademoiselle Hofeld both. It's helped her spirits immensely, though to me it's all hopelessly vague. It reminds me of those depressing séances one attends in hopes of actually learning something tangible about the dead. I've never quite forgiven, by the way, that cruel prank you pulled."

"It was no prank," I said. "To this day I still can't explain what happened. But I swear to you, I had no ill intent; what happened was entirely beyond my control. How can I make you believe that?"

He studied me. The waiter poured more champagne. "I don't know that you can. It was a very long time ago. It's hard to know anymore what one knew then. There was a time when I made it a hobby to investigate the other world. How many séances I endured, obscure messages from the Great Beyond spelled out one letter at a time by a lazy teacup on a painted board, spectral knockings in darkened parlors, proper ladies making fools of themselves in sham basso profundo to resurrect the spirit of

Frederick the Great or a slave from the time of Vespasian. I was rummaging through all that dismal magic in the hope that, somehow, Father might have found a way to send me a sign. We made a promise that whoever died first would have a solemn duty, through whatever means possible, to breach that barrier separating this world from the next. But though I upheld my end of the bargain, I was never contacted by anyone remotely resembling Father. Though there was one spirit who professed to know my future in great detail. Claimed I would one day teach schoolchildren in Kaluga. 'High above Kaluga's waters,' as the spirit poetically put it. But I shall never return to Russia. All through the twenties I never ceased to believe that one day we *would* return. But it's like a love that has gone. I shall never return to Russia. I shall never have the opportunity to speak to Father again. At thirty-three, that is where I find myself."

Obviously he had dismissed out of hand the notion that I might have been the conduit by which Father reached him.

"Do you still believe?" I asked. "I mean, in a world beyond this one? Any kind of life after death?"

He spoke carefully. "I know more than I can understand. I understand more than I can express."

Unfortunately, at that moment our waiter returned to clear away our plates and, in the process, the fragile communion between us. When he had gone I said, to salvage the moment, "You'll be interested to hear that I've thought seriously about writing Father's biography. A friend who's a great admirer of Father's has urged me to do it. He thinks I'm uniquely suited for the task."

Volodya's reaction was immediate.

"And what do you imagine you might produce?" he asked. "Some dry, learned rehearsal in which Father's public 'accomplishments' float unattached to the ultimately unknowable texture of his private life? An allegory of the liberal spirit undone by its own idealism? A sham *biographie romancée* where an infinitely graduated life is reduced to an artificially crafted plot, complete with characters and dialogue and dramatic scenes that never happened—and worst of all, sentimental detours into the subject's psyche, his innermost thoughts and emotions. No, I think I'd rather see poor Father's corpse thrown to a pack of feral dogs."

I had never seen him quite so agitated, though he rapidly enough seemed to recognize that the ferocity of his response was out of all proportion to my innocent proposal. He went on, more mildly, "What I mean to say, Seryosha, is that I don't know if a conventional biography is the best approach to the task. It seems to me there must be a better way, a way more attuned to Father's particular genius—though what that way is, precisely, and if it would be at all available to an amateur such as yourself, or even an artist such as I, I don't yet entirely know. I must give it some thought. But I'd strongly caution you against plunging too hastily into such a challenging project."

"My great regret," I said, "is that Father and I were on such uncertain terms at the time of his death. Indeed, I've always regretted your account of his worry about me the night before his murder. But what was I to do? Can any of us, even for the sake of the ones we love, be someone we simply are not? People speak of my 'attitude,' as if it's something I've willfully adopted. I assure you that's not the case."

"My views have changed somewhat," Volodya told me. "I've become aware of the extent to which such an attitude runs in our family, though I still fail to understand how heredity is transmitted by bachelors, unless genes can jump like chess knights."

"You're thinking of Uncle Ruka, and Uncle Konstantin, and, according to Grandmother Nabokova, at least one other. Speaking of the failure to understand—*I've* never understood why you were so cruel to Uncle Ruka, who clearly loved you dearly."

"Uncle Ruka was a vain, vile monster, who, were there a hell, would deserve to burn there for eternity."

"But why?" I asked, aghast.

"Why? Because he habitually took advantage of those who were younger, weaker, more vulnerable than he, whether servants or stable boys or Arabs or anyone else he fancied. His appetite knew no bounds. Were you blind to all that reprehensible behavior? But then he never wished to cuddle you every chance he got; he never forced you to play the stallion game. He never humiliated you with his kisses and caresses in front of everyone. You were fortunate, Seryosha. Very fortunate."

"What I'd have given for a kiss or a cuddle—anything that might have shown he was halfway conscious of my existence," I said.

"I'm perfectly aware you admired him—far too much for your own good. And because he never took liberties with you, perhaps I'll allow him one single day every year to walk in the green fields of Paradise. But only one! I must confess, Seryosha: I hated seeing you become one of his kind, though I suspect you're infinitely kinder, more moral than he. But are you any less unhappy? He, too, adopted Roman Catholicism in his endless search for relief from his urges, but I don't think it did him any good. I can only hope you're more fortunate than he."

The remark gave me pause; I had forgotten entirely my uncle's long-ago conversion. "You were often quite cruel to me," I found myself saying. "The way you and Yuri teased me, when I was Louise Poindexter and you and he were Apaches and mustangers. Or when you showed my diary to our tutor, knowing that he would most certainly show it to Father. Or when you denied me my grief for Davide Gornotsvetov, practically accusing me of having invented him—and then to read in *Mary* a description of a character named Gornotsvetov who resembles Davide in so many ways. What am I to think of that, Volodya?"

"I never knew this Davide Gornotsvetov. Readers are always

finding uncanny coincidences in my work. Art has a discomfiting way of sending its tentacles out into so-called reality. That's all there is to it."

"It doesn't matter. It was all a long time ago, as you say, and I don't mean to rehearse old grievances."

"I really don't remember any of these things you accuse me of, but then I'm all too aware I was a bit of a brute and a bully in those days. For that I'm truly sorry. But you have to understand, dear Seryosha,"—here he smiled—"as the butt of a practical joke now and again, you really were irresistible. I hope you can forgive me."

"Of course I forgive you. I forgive everybody who, whether inadvertently or not, made my boyhood so miserable. Father, Mother, the teachers at Tenishev and the Gymnasium, my treacherous classmates, that villain Bekhetev."

"Bekhetev? Our physician?"

"An ass and a charlatan," I said. "Now there's someone who should be consigned to hellfire."

"I can't imagine a more decent, benevolent gentleman. I'm terrifically grateful he's in Prague these days, where he can attend Mother even if her Christian Science asks her to eschew proper medicine. Even today, Olga and Elena swear by his care. They won't see anyone else."

I proceeded to tell him in some detail of my "cure" at Dr. Bekhetev's hands, those weekly sessions of pseudoscientific cruelty that ended only when the civilization that had mandated them ended as well.

"I never knew," he said when I had finished. He looked vaguely perplexed. "But then, most of your life has necessarily been mysterious to me. Even when we lived under the same roof."

"Why 'necessarily?'" I asked.

He thought for a moment. "I don't know, really. I suppose I've never given it any thought."

"I've never wished to be mysterious, and I certainly don't wish to be mysterious any longer," I told him. "My only wish at the moment is that you'll consent to know me as you know any other human being. I'm no less real for having been your shadow."

"You were never my shadow."

"I'm afraid I was. I know I was born too soon. I know I followed you too quickly into this world. It's neither my fault nor yours. But from the beginning, I think, you resented me."

He smiled, scratched his head, leaned back in his chair, put one hand inside the English-style waistcoat he had worn ever since his Cambridge days.

"Ah, Seryosha, I'd like to tell you you're quite mad, but since a mood of 'honesty' seems to be upon us this afternoon, and since my train leaves soon, I'll instead tell you this. You may do with it what you will. As you undoubtedly know, I'm plagued by merciless insomnia. One of my earliest memories is of lying awake at night, listening to your contented breathing on the other side of the bedroom screen, feeling both envy and—shall I confess it?—a certain sense of superiority to the ease with which you could forsake consciousness. Even today, when I do eventually manage to drift off, I'm assailed by nightmares so torturous as to make my slumber seem hardly worth the effort. One nightmare in particular repeats itself. I've never told this to anyone. Probably it doesn't bear telling even now. But it would seem to involve you, or some dream twin of yours.

"It's one of those particularly horrible dreams in which one dreams that one is asleep and then one wakes, but only within the dream, though it passes for reality. In this case I rather unpleasantly 'wake' to find myself lying facedown on top of someone. I attempt to roll off, but find I cannot, because I'm joined at the navel, see, face to face, nose to nose, lips to lips, with my twin, who turns out, Seryosha, to be you. For a moment I'm confused, but then in the next moment comes the terrible realization that this is a normal state of affairs, however revolting—that you and I have always been conjoined, that only in sleep is it possible to escape for a few hours that almost unendurable attachment. You're still sleeping when I 'wake,' and I examine your too familiar face for the millionth time, knowing each pore and nostril hair and pimple, feeling your breath, breathing in your odor and spittle—and then suddenly your eyes spring open, and I stare full into them. I try to wrest myself away but we're permanently attached, remember, there's no turning away, this is our life and will be our life day after day till the end of our days." A fastidious shudder coursed through him.

"For what it's worth, I've never had a similar dream," I told him.

"I'm relieved to hear that. It would have been too hideous if you had. One of the awful aspects of the dream is my knowledge that the shared blood coursing in our veins forces us to share the same dreams, the same thoughts, the same emotions. Or at the very least makes us susceptible... I'm not, by the way, in the least interested in what the Viennese witch doctor and his disciples might make of the random firings of my cerebral cortex, nor should you be."

It was my turn to smile—though admittedly it was a troubled smile. A thought had occurred to me. Struck me, rather, with considerable force. "In the meantime," I said, "I've had dreams as well—dreams I never fully understood until this moment. But now they make a certain kind of sense."

As I spoke I was aware that a certain someone had entered the dining room, as planned, and seated himself at the next table. My back was to him, but he had a clear bead on Volodya—as Volodya, were he so inclined, would have on him.

"It's a very curious dream," I went on, "arriving in a number of guises. It wasn't so much a recurring dream as an unfolding dream—unfolding, that is, over many years, unsystematically.

In short, from time to time, I dream I'm in the presence of God. He's always disguised: once he looked like Michel Fokine,"—that provoked a chuckle from Volodya—"once he wore Father's imperial uniform, another time he sported a smoking jacket. He spoke evasively, as God always seems to speak. But the general theme in those dreams remained the same. He wished to apologize for having run out of souls when it came to making me, for having bestowed on me a counterfeit soul, a negligent act even He could not undo.

"I've never believed that it was actually God who appeared to me in those dreams. Sometimes I've thought it some diabolical trickster. At other times I presume we merely dream what our natures incline us to dream. But now I wonder whether I wasn't, all the time, dreaming about you."

"What a peculiar thought," Volodya observed.

"Not really. The longing to fully know you—and its subsequent impossibility. My sense, which reading your astonishing body of work only confirms, that you too are always in one disguise or another. And if I can't know you, my dearest brother, flesh of my flesh, heart of my heart, spirit of my spirit, then what in the universe can I ever hope to know? For you see, from the very beginning my attempts at knowledge were fully, repeatedly, devastatingly thwarted—"

Volodya looked at his watch. "Fascinating as this is, Seryosha, I fear my departure looms. I've got to get out to Nika's, retrieve my luggage, and make my way to the Gare du Nord. The human mind's a thicket where a bird sits camouflaged. Sometimes 'reality' loses its quotation marks. I've very much enjoyed our conversation. When I return to Paris, which I hope shall be very soon, and with Véra, whom you will meet at last, I trust we'll continue our friendly banter."

He laid his crumpled napkin on the table and made to rise from the table. "You'll pay the receipt?"

"Wait," I told him. "Of course, but..." A jumble of half-completed, passionate thoughts filled me, an acute consciousness of all we had not yet touched on, thirty years of silence and neglect and misunderstanding. "There's something else. Spare me five more minutes of your time. I said earlier my fondest wish is that you know me as you'd know anyone—"

"I'm not particularly famous for my friendships," he said.

"Still, if I could introduce you to my—my—my husband." (In humiliating haste, for lack of a better word.)

I saw I had thoroughly taken him off guard. "Who? Where?" It was his turn to sputter as I turned and gestured toward the man who had taken a seat at the next table.

"What? He's been eavesdropping all this time?" Volodya asked irritably.

"Not at all. He only just arrived. And he doesn't speak a word of Russian."

"*A u vas na sheike pauk,*" Volodya said to Hermann. *There is a spider on your neck.* Of course, understanding nothing, Hermann had no reaction at all other than to thrust his hand forward in friendly greeting. Volodya did not respond in kind, though he seemed satisfied. I wondered where he'd learned *that* spyworthy trick.

"All right. What does he speak, then? French?"

"French," I said, "and German. His name's Hermann Thieme."

Hermann's hand remained outstretched, and an awkward smile had fixed itself on his face.

"Really," Volodya said, still in Russian. "A German. First you become a Roman Catholic. Now a hausfrau. You're full of surprises, aren't you?" He turned his attention to Hermann, who was by now rather deflated looking. In his badly accented French, he said, "How are you, then?"

"I'm very pleased to meet you, *cher maître,*" Hermann said, rather resembling our canine Volsungs in his eagerness.

"Likewise," Volodya told him.

"You see, I've long admired your work. What little of it I've been able to find in German."

"I'm told they're wretched translations."

"Perhaps. They read impressively enough."

"Soon you'll have the opportunity to see them mangled in French as well. If you have a genuine interest in my work, though, I suggest you learn Russian. I'm sure my brother would be quite pleased to teach you. But what brings you to Paris, Herr Thieme?"

My brother had retreated to his remotest manner. I felt sheepish about having ambushed him not only with the fact but with the presence of Hermann.

Hermann seemed undeterred by Volodya's icy politeness. "Business brings me here quite often," he explained.

"And business is good at the moment? You seem rather well off. Much better off than the run-of-the-mill German I encounter these days in Berlin."

"I'm Austrian, actually. Not that it makes that much difference."

"No, I suppose it doesn't. Still, am I to gather that you're the one to whom I'm indebted for this excellent meal? If so, I thank you. It's..." He seemed to search for the word; his French was not particularly good. "It's reassuring to find my younger brother so well looked after. One worries. See that his talents don't drift too far into indolence." He looked once more at his watch. "Now, if you'll excuse me, I really must be getting along."

He shook Hermann's hand, then turned to me for what I fondly imagined might be an old-fashioned Russian kiss-and-embrace, but a shrill voice arrested him mid-gesture.

"*Mon cher!* At last I've tracked you down. Is this the new lair where you've been hiding? Is Le Sélect no longer select enough?"

Cocteau clung to the arm of muscular Desbordes, who

despite his poetic inclinations was really little more than an amiable teenaged thug. Beside them stood Bébé Bérard, merry, tousle-haired, paint-spattered. They shared a sleepy, gauzy look.

"It's the German's doing." Cocteau extended his walking stick in Hermann's direction. "I wish formally to accuse you of leading our darling astray. We'll meet at dawn in the Tuileries. Choose your second. Perhaps this elegant fellow... Wait! The angels vouchsafe me a revelation. You must be none other than the famous brother. Rumor had it you were in Paris wowing the émigrés. Word spreads quickly. Paris is a very small town."

I could see Volodya squirm under the assault of Cocteau's charm; how well I knew that look of discomfort.

"You surmise correctly," said Volodya. "I regret I cannot spare the time to make your acquaintance, but I have a train to catch. Good-bye, Seryosha. I leave you now to your friends."

Much like a respectable family man who finds he has mistakenly ventured into a brothel, he fled. No embrace, no kiss, not so much as a friendly touch.

"Is he always that skittish?" Cocteau asked.

"Our kind make him nervous," I explained. "Sometimes I wonder whether some experience in his past made him this way. If anything, he may have mellowed a bit over the years."

"I retract my challenge, by the way," Cocteau told Hermann. "A bit of Gallic wit. Do you Germans have a sense of humor? I didn't wish to leave you waiting for me in the cold fog at dawn, alone with a brace of well-oiled pistols and a heart of lead."

"Trust me," said Hermann, smiling pacifically, his lilac eyes aglow. "I would not have been there."

45

AND THUS HERMANN AND I LIVED HAPPILY EVER after—or at least for a few happy years. I will not bore my reader with a honeyed account of that time. As Tolstoy knew well, there was no story to tell in Eden—only afterward, once it had all come to ruin, once history had begun. For the most part, we remained contentedly ensconced in our aerie at Castle Weissenstein during those years. I grew accustomed to the fairy-tale village nestled beneath the uncanny looming peaks; no longer did it seem a place of vaguely sinister magic, but rather a cozy haven immune to the world's heartbreak.

Hermann's parents must have had some inkling of the nature of our relationship, though they gave no outward sign of it. Hermann insisted that I had charmed them thoroughly.

As I would have suspected, my prolonged removal from the Parisian scene caused little stir—except from Cocteau, who wrote me a note deploring my decision in terms which, far from giving umbrage, renewed my belief in his wisdom: "I fear your love for this Hermann is an abstract principle that will only lead you to the false haven of the settled, the bourgeois, the safe. There's no refuge, *mon cher.* Art, the church, opium, the love of boys: it's all temporary sanity that masks the madness beneath. Forget that at your peril."

Eventually a letter arrived from Volodya in response to several missives I had sent his way—perfectly friendly though not particularly forthcoming. Undeterred, I answered expansively, and gradually a somewhat regular correspondence ensued, each of my heartfelt and candid missives matched by a reply of reserved but undeniable affection. When I suggested that I might visit him and Véra in Berlin, he wrote back that I would be welcome, as long as my stay was brief.

It was not until January 1934 that I was finally able to arrange that visit.

Volodya was late to meet me at the station. I distracted myself by watching an old crone conjure a storm of pigeons out of thin air by dispersing breadcrumbs on the pavement before her, while several brutally disfigured war veterans looked on hungrily from their begging station on the sidewalk. I had just begun to rue having come all this way when at last I saw my brother walking briskly toward me. He was properly apologetic, claiming he had completely lost track of time.

"I'm surprised you'd want to come back here," he said. "Everyone else is trying to get out. There are virtually no Russians left anymore, except a few anti-Semites who seem to enjoy the current atmosphere."

I had not set foot in Berlin in a decade. The city seemed poorer and grimier than when I left, and at the same time more colorful, owing to the ubiquitous Nazi banners and posters which seemed more an instance of inspired graphic design than ominous symbol. By the end of my brief visit they would no longer appear to me in quite the same festive light.

It was late afternoon. Gloom was already settling in. He took me to a sparsely populated Russian café. Four stolid matrons occupied one table, and in a corner, two old men hunkered over a chess game. "Véra won't be home until late. She works far too much. Her hours are cruel, and leave her very little time to type for me. She had quite a good job before, but the firm was Jewish and was forced to dissolve. She now makes half what she once did. She doesn't complain, but she's very low these days, and her health is fragile. My own health has not been particularly good either. Even now I've got a cold which I can't manage to shake off. Everything here is much worse than it used to be. One tries not to notice, one tries to treat the place as a wretched rented room in which one resides for a short spell, but increasingly it's just impossible. See what I mean?"

Three youths in SA uniforms had entered the café. One held a tin box. They went first to the matrons' table, where the four women unhappily fished in their handbags for bills they stuffed in the proffered collection tin. The employees of the café were next, and they too surrendered their contributions. Then the trio—two brutish, one barely handsome, his looks sabotaged by an eruption of acne about his mouth—approached our table. "Even the weather around here stinks," Volodya said—with needless provocation, it seemed to me, though I knew the chances of our visitors understanding a word of Russian were nil.

"The air's increasingly foul," he went on. "Often smells like a pigsty, in fact. Don't even think of giving them money." As he spoke, he ignored the youths completely, even when the one with the tin box rattled it ominously beside his ear. The room had become completely quiet; all eyes were on us. I dared not look at the youths hovering over us; I dared look only at my brother's neutral expression as he continued to talk in a perfectly normal, and therefore perfectly eerie, tone of voice.

"It's a dreadful bore only to go on about the weather, don't you think? I once heard of a man who recorded thrice daily in his notebook the temperature and barometric pressure. He left behind no other record of his life save that meticulous accounting of the weather. Particular highs or lows he notated with an exclamation mark. His marriage, the births of his children, the death of his wife, his own eventual illness—nothing intruded on that seamless journal of his real life, his life in weather, so to speak."

Sweat crawled down my rib cage. With a harrumph, the lout abruptly lowered his collection tin and turned aside. "There're plenty of patriots elsewhere," he said. "Who needs to wait around this dump?" Casting a last baleful look in our direction, the disappointed threesome stumbled out the door. As soon as they were gone, the room erupted in nervous applause.

Volodya took a cigarette from his pocket, lit it, and blew out a long satisfied plume of smoke.

"Was that advisable?" I sputtered.

"Not at all. Entirely reckless, in fact. But I know their type. They're cowards, and easily cowed."

"Bring enough cowards together," I told him, "and you've got a mob, and we know what mobs can do. I'd be more careful if I were you."

Without a word he pulled from his pocket the set of brass knuckles that had somehow managed to accompany him through all his years of wandering.

"I'm just not sure how much good they'll do against a whole gang. You're going to get hurt one day, Volodya."

"Véra says the same. That's why *she* carries a pistol in her handbag."

"Really?" Parisian gossip, which I had always thought highly improbable, held that Véra had finally nabbed her future husband by pointing a gun at his chest and demanding, "Marry me or I'll kill you!" Now I was no longer quite so sure.

"A very handsome Browning 1900. 'My chum,' she calls it. Most efficient little device."

"This is madness," I said. "You must leave Berlin."

"I tell you, she won't leave. She's fearless that way. And I'm lethargic. So what can I do?"

I had never seen my brother in thrall before. Granted, I had not known most of his many girlfriends, with the notable exception of Svetlana Siewert, but I had always had the distinct impression that they were adoring followers and that he blithely accepted their adoration. But here seemed the hint of something quite different.

Many rumors circulated about Véra Nabokov, née Slonim. Was she the reason behind the distinctly "un-Russian" character of Sirin's work? Did she purposely isolate him from his fellow exiles? Was she a Bolshevik spy? Knowing my brother better than most of the rumormongers, I had privately figured Véra to be a version of the well-intentioned young wife in *Luzhin's Defense* who inadvertently sabotages the chess player's queer genius by insisting on bringing him out of the penumbra of his precious inner solitude and into the sunlit "normal" world. I imagined Volodya's portrait of such a wife was his means of pushing back at Véra's attempts to socialize him. But perhaps that was not the case. In any event, I was eager—if also somewhat anxious—to meet her.

"She won't be home till quite late," he told me as we walked toward their lodgings. "And she must leave in the mornings at an ungodly hour. She's not a morning person. She's practically blind till noon. Fortunately, tomorrow is her day off. So the three of us should manage to have some fun."

In the meantime, Volodya was having his own peculiar fun. To the evident consternation of passersby, he made a point of entering each shop that had been marked with a yellow Star of David. He bought nothing, but he browsed, he made himself visible, a Gentile publicly flaunting the boycott. I understood why he did what he did, but for the second time in the space of a half hour he made me very nervous indeed.

He and Véra lived in two large rooms they rented in an apartment on Nestorstrasse, not far from where our parents had lived in Berlin. Their landlady was an amiable Russian Jew named Anna Feigen, who immediately brought out the samovar for us.

As Volodya had predicted, it was late when Véra returned. My brother having retreated to the other room several hours before with the excuse that a recalcitrant sentence urgently claimed his attention, I was left to my own devices. Perusing the contents of his bookshelf I discovered, among the usual suspects, a distinct oddity given my brother's tastes: the complete works of Nicolay Chernyshevsky. With nothing better to do, I dipped into the old reformer's once popular novel *What Is to Be Done?* but was soon bored by its well-intentioned sermonizing. I was beginning to wonder whether I should check myself into a pension for the night when the door opened and in walked a petite, strikingly beautiful woman. Removing her beret to shake out a mass of wavy, prematurely graying hair, she seemed unfazed by my presence.

"He's neglecting you, of course."

"Of course," I told her. "He's my brother. What should I expect?"

"Perhaps rather too much of him, given the constraints on his time. He warned me you might be demanding."

"Oh, I'm hardly demanding at all," I said, a little nonplussed. "I've just been sitting here reading. Quite contentedly, as a matter of fact."

"Nonsense," she said. "You're reading Chernyshevsky. That can't be very pleasurable."

I had to laugh. "Well, actually..."

"See? No need to stand on niceties. I'm Véra, as I'm sure you've guessed." She shook my hand briskly. "Welcome to Berlin. May you never have to spend a moment longer in this wretched city than absolutely necessary."

"I wasn't contemplating moving back, if that's what you're suggesting."

"I'm glad to hear that."

Volodya poked his head through the door. "Ah, my Happiness, they've deigned to set you free at last. One never knows," he said to me. "I send her out in the morning, little knowing whether they'll allow her to return in the evening. But every night, somehow, she convinces them to release her. Despite everything"—he now addressed his wife—"I've managed to have a fairly productive day. I've left the pages out for you. Whenever you're ready."

That their manner with each other should be at once so arch and businesslike struck me as odd, and perhaps depressing. I suggested we might go to a restaurant for dinner. "I'll pay, of course. And I need to check into a pension."

"My goodness," said Véra. "You'll do no such thing. Did he suggest you should?"

"Not at all," Volodya and I both said at once.

"We haven't discussed..." said he.

"I just assumed..." said I.

"There's a perfectly adequate sofa. We insist you stay with us. We wouldn't think of you spending money on a hotel. Ridiculous."

"You won't win an argument with Véra; don't even try," said Volodya.

"As for dinner, Anieta has made some soup. There are sausages. Restaurants in Berlin are dreadful anymore. And we don't like to go out at night."

"Unless one's well armed," I said.

She shot Volodya a reproachful look. "You talk too much for all our sakes," she told him.

He made a humorous, self-deprecating shrug. "My Love hopes that eventually I will confine my utterances exclusively to paper. Perhaps she has a point."

"Talking, sometimes, can be a waste of time," she said.

Over soup and execrable sausage ("Only the finest sawdust!" Volodya claimed), I ribbed my brother: "So. Chernyshevsky. Your tastes have certainly changed."

"Research."

"A new novel?"

"Yes," he said, chewing stolidly. "But that's all you'll get out of me."

I told him I could see he was beginning to take Véra's advice.

The remainder of the evening was spent in polite conversation. Financial worries were foremost, to the extent that I decided I would leave them the balance of my reichsmarks when I departed. Volodya expressed his usual exasperation with Olga and her husband, the unhelpful ways they meddled in Mother's affairs. He was concerned about our brother Kirill's lack of direction with his studies. He worried that Elena was not as happy as she should be in her recent marriage.

Wishing to move our talk into richer realms, I ventured that I was curious to know how Volodya and Véra had met. "Suddenly, out of the blue, you were married. No one knew."

The two looked at each other.

"Surely there must be a story," I prompted.

"There's no story," Véra asserted.

Volodya had other ideas. "But my Rose Blossom, there's a marvelous story. When I first met my wife-to-be, she was wearing a black satin mask. Our meeting was by prior arrangement, on a bridge over a canal. She recited my poems to me. She had copied them from various journals into an album and learnt them all by heart. She never once removed her mask. She said she didn't want her beauty to distract me from her recitation, but I was already quite distracted! All I could see were her bright blue eyes. Afterward I wrote a poem. 'And night flowed,'" he began to declaim, more to Véra than to me, "'and silent there floated / Into its satin stream / That black mask's wolf-like profile / And those tender lips of yours.'"

Véra seemed put off by this display of sentiment.

"That's enough," she said. "It wasn't like that at all."

"Then let me hear your version," I teased.

But she only held up both her hands, palms out to me, shut her eyes, and shook her head.

"My wife's a great romantic," Volodya explained. "Not an exhibitionist: a great romantic. Most people fail to understand the difference."

That evening I fell asleep to the muffled clatter of Véra's typewriter in the adjoining room.

We occupied the next morning with a long walk around Wilmersdorf and Charlottenburg. The clouds had opened up, and Berlin showed a rare sunny aspect, and there, in the middle of a block of shops hunkered down behind their metal grates, was one storefront exposed to the world, its front windows shattered, its façade daubed with yellow Stars of David and JUDEN RAUS! It had been a pleasingly polyglot bookshop, I recalled—French, Russian, Italian, and Yiddish commingled with the smell of old paper and pipe smoke and a friendly tabby napping on the counter.

"Our latest bit of ugliness," Volodya said. "The hooligans made a pile of books in the middle of the street, set them on fire, and sang patriotic anthems and presumably felt better about themselves as Germans afterward."

I took the opportunity to bring up again—this time in Véra's presence—my conviction that the two of them might wish to follow the example of most other Russians and leave Berlin to its ugliness.

"We've nothing to fear," Volodya assured me once more. "True, I've been called a 'half-kike' by certain members of the émigré community who have been driven insane by my talents. Those of our countrymen who are still left in Berlin are the worst sort; they've practically embraced Hitler and his ilk in their desire to get back at the Jews who, they believe, stole Russia from them. They're a farcical bunch, hardly worth taking seriously. As for the homegrown German idiots, they're little more than comic bullies better suited to one of Mister Chaplin's movies than to real life."

His assessment of the situation struck me as somewhat delusional. "But surely, Véra," I implored, "it can't be very comfortable for you."

"Fortunately I pass easily for non-Jewish," she said. "I'm mistaken for a Gentile all the time. No, I have to agree with Volodya. We're perfectly safe for the time being."

"For the time being," I echoed dubiously.

"Come," Volodya said, "let's not trouble ourselves with shadows. Look!" He gestured toward a circus poster affixed to a kiosk, a forlorn enticement to enchantment nearly crowded out by the surrounding cacophony of National Socialist exhortations. "Isn't it marvelous?" He pointed to the variously colored letters spelling out ZIRKUS BELLI that arched above a roiling scene of elephants and camels, clowns and showgirls. "They've got it practically dead on. How extraordinary. Some poor, anonymous artist after my own sensibility. Look, my Peach. The drama of 'ZIRKUS,' beginning so stormily, with those lurid flashes of *I* and *U* separated by the sooty hues of *R* and *K*, and then clearing into the pale blue of that final *S*. Followed by such a lovely 'BELLI,' with its buttercups and creams and burnt siennas, a word of very pleasing chromatic integrity." Delicately he kissed the tips of his fingers in appreciation.

I had always known of my brother's strange ability to "see" the colors of the alphabet, though I confess I had more or less considered it an affectation. Thus I was unprepared for Véra's response.

"I agree with you entirely about 'ZIRKUS,'" she said, "but to my eye 'BELLI' is more a jumble. That double *L* is a livid green, velvety in texture, quite at odds with the marble-smooth tones that cradle it."

"Livid green? Extraordinary. *F, P, T*—now those are my shades of green."

"No, no, *T* is dark blue, almost inky."

And so they went on, merry as schoolchildren. If it was not a poster on a kiosk, it was the blue imp sparking above the streetcar, the shadows on a building, the speckled winter plumage of talkative starlings, a jowly old crone selling turnips who resembled—did she not?—a female version of Van Eyck's Canon van der Paele...

If I confess that I felt excluded from their banter, it is without any bitterness—for the exclusion, I saw, was not intentional, but instead the outward sign of a degree of harmony I had never in my life observed between two people, not even between my parents, whose marriage had always seemed formidably seamless.

My brother delighted in everything Véra said or did. If I could not get used to his playful terms of endearment—my Happiness, my Peach, my Fairy Tale—I could nonetheless see that, despite their poverty, their uncertain prospects, the ugliness closing in, he was divinely happy.

The following day, he accompanied me to the Hauptbahnhof to see me off. Though our visit had not afforded us the kind of thoughtful, prolonged conversation I had looked forward to, I was nonetheless grateful for the glimpses into his life. As we quaffed a last-minute Pilsener in the stale-smelling station saloon, I asked him whether, for the sake of my sanity, we might return to the old question of Davide Gornotsvetov.

He looked at me blankly.

"Davide Gornotsvetov," I prompted, "and the ballet dancer in *Mary*—and other things in your fiction as well. Only recently, for instance, I read your beautiful story 'The Admiralty Spire,' and once again noticed, well, that there were things there you couldn't possibly have known, little details, insignificant really, only they touched quite closely certain... How do I put it? Private experiences of mine. I really don't quite know what I'm trying to ask you."

He smiled patiently. Over his shoulder I noticed the minute hand on the wall clock lurch forward; it was one of those timepieces that suggests the medium it purports to measure is not flowing but rather a series of discrete moments, each isolated from what comes before or after.

"Nor do I," said my brother. "Listen, Seryosha. I'm a writer. A writer is always noticing; half the time he doesn't even notice what he's noticing. I understand that's not a very satisfactory answer. But I'm afraid it's the straightest response you're going to get from me."

"I understand," I said. The minute hand jerked forward. "I always keep hoping for more, even when I know there *is* no more."

"Without doubt an admirable quality. But one can only give what one has to give."

I reminded myself that I had not thought I would get much from him in the first place, but he surprised me.

"I suppose I've neglected to ask after Hermann," he said. "That *is* his name, isn't it? Hermann?" He pronounced it with a markedly German flourish.

"Yes, Hermann. He's wonderful. Quite simply, he saved my life. Were it not for him..."

"I do understand, Seryosha. We've more in common, you and I, than anyone might have thought. Without Véra I wouldn't have written a single novel."

The minute hand stuttered forward. "I presume that's not an attempt at a joke," I told him.

"Why should it be? I'm perfectly serious. I honor my own salvation, and yours as well."

"Then I hope we'll continue to exchange letters. I very much cherish this contact."

His hazel-green eyes met mine. His expression turned sheepish.

"What is it?" I asked him.

"Well, if you absolutely must know." He paused; I waited for the minute hand. There! "Véra's the one who handles the correspondence."

It took a moment to register.

"What?" I said. "I've been writing to *Véra* all this time?

"And she's been writing to you. She finds you a most charming correspondent. She's told me so many times. And rest assured, I do read your letters. It's just that I find answering them difficult. I'd explain, but I think you'd best board your train now. I can see you've been keeping your eye on the clock. We certainly don't want you stranded in Berlin."

46

I DID NOT ALTOGETHER BECOME A RECLUSE IN those happy years. From our Valkyrie perch in the mountains Hermann and I would descend at regular intervals to Munich, Salzburg, and Paris. When in Paris I saw my old friends less and less as time and circumstance dispersed them. Most of the Americans had gone home; even Tchelitchew and Tanner were now in America (though no longer together). The Ballets Russes had split into several quarreling entities, and Cocteau had thrown himself into playwriting.

Only once did I see Oleg—and only from afar, across the great width of the Champs-Elysées. His taxi had broken down—from its radiator rose a fume of angry steam—and as traffic flowed around him one could imagine the fume of angry steam rising from him as well. He did not see me, and I did not go to his assistance. Whatever help he needed was no longer mine to give. Mercilessly he flogged with his jacket the flank of his hapless vehicle, as a peasant might a long-suffering beast that had finally collapsed from its burden, a sight that must surely have seemed comic to most passersby but that spoke to me of a melancholy as deep as the memory of Russia herself.

Every August Hermann and I made a pilgrimage to Bayreuth, and if, as the decade wore on, one had to put up with swastikas and the paraphernalia of the National Socialists, it seemed a small price to pay for the privilege of hearing Richard Strauss conduct the 1933 *Parsifal*, or in that sweltering summer of 1937 the inimitable Furtwängler illuminating, as only his brooding genius could, the complete *Ring*. How I wished Father could have been there. These performances would have changed his mind about Wagner—but then I remembered the full-page photograph of Hitler in the printed program and was no longer so sure.

From Volodya—or was it from Véra?—I received the occasional cordial missive.

From V. Sirin, on the other hand, I received regular communiqués from that incomparably rich inner world he inhabited. In 1935 *Invitation to a Beheading* appeared, a wild dream of a book, harrowing and hilarious and tender and transcendent. I did not know at the time how closely my own situation would one day resemble that of the condemned man who wonders how he can begin writing without knowing how much time remains.

It was not until 1937 that I saw Volodya again. Halfway through a visit to Paris, I dropped by Le Sélect one afternoon, and was astonished to discover my brother seated in the rear of the café, absorbed in a chess game with his friend Mark Aldanov. My first shameful impulse was to turn and flee, so full was I of tumult—joy at seeing him, confusion that he should be in Paris, hurt that he had not informed me of his plans—but why should he have? I approached the table, touched him on the shoulder, and in as casual a tone as I could manage expressed my pleasure and surprise at having run into him.

He flinched at my touch (I should have known better), looked around for a very long second without any glimmer of recognition in his eyes, and then exclaimed, "Ah, Seryosha, what a delight to see you. What brings you down from the Alps?"

I told him, all a-stutter, that I could very well ask what brought him down from Berlin. Had he come to Paris for a reading? Had I missed the event? I'd seen no notices.

"No, no," he said. "I've been here for two months now. I'm done with Berlin."

"That's marvelous news, I'm so relieved for you and Véra."

"Véra, alas, remains in Berlin. As does our son."

"But how can that be?"

"She refuses to leave her job. She fears there's no work to be had in Paris."

"She's right," said Aldanov gloomily, without looking up from the chess board. "There's no work to be had anywhere. And even if there were work, she wouldn't be able to get working papers."

Volodya paid his companion no mind. "I don't understand her reluctance. As for myself, I've been desperate to get out. I don't know if you've heard the news—there's no reason you should, since what happens in Germany doesn't concern you in the least—but that hyena Biskupsky's been appointed head of the Department for Émigré Affairs. But that's not the worst of it. Prepare yourself. He's arranged for Taboritsky, of all people, to be his deputy. Taboritsky! That clockwork assassin, that miserable excuse for a man. Mother is beside herself, and rightly so. He should have been left to rot in prison for the rest of his days. Instead, he's been put in charge of all our fates. Already an order has gone out that all Russians in the Reich must be registered immediately. And word is that Taboritsky has been given leave to gather a team who can serve as translators and interrogators in the event of war with the Soviet Union. It's grotesque. It's absurd. It's unbearable."

For a man who prided himself on never reading the newspaper, my brother seemed monstrously well informed—better than I, in fact, who had not previously heard this news about one of Father's murderers.

"There'll be no war with the Soviet Union," said Aldanov. "Mark my word. Hitler's not that foolish." He gestured toward the chessboard. "I'm afraid I've no choice but to concede. I shall leave you two brothers to your reunion. I'm sure you've much to talk about."

I had always thought Aldanov a remarkably kind man; though Volodya had once penned a devastating review of his friend's latest novel, Aldanov appeared to have forgiven the treachery.

"You're looking well," Volodya informed me with uncharacteristic solicitude. "I believe you've put on a bit of weight. Life must be agreeing with you these days."

"As a matter of fact it is. I'm quite settled and content."

Volodya, on the other hand, looked dreadful. His jacket was threadbare, his cuffs worn, his shoes in abominable condition. He too seemed aware of the contrast. "And quite spiffily turned out these days, I see."

"I'm not going to apologize for my choices," I told him.

"You misunderstand me. I'm not asking you to do so. You're still quite sensitive, aren't you? But I don't wish to provoke a quarrel. For one thing, I need to ask your help. Véra can't get a work permit for France unless someone sponsors her. It's maddening to be treated as criminals by these loathsome bureaucrats, but there it is. I seem to remember meeting some French friends of yours. Is there any possibility one of them might have connections in the bureaucratic labyrinth? Véra won't come unless she feels she has a firm guarantee of a job, but under the circumstances that's completely impossible. I only know Russians, and Russians are useless in these matters, since in the eyes of the state we barely exist."

Gone was that Olympian confidence he used to exude. As he rolled himself a cigarette, his hands shook.

"Cocteau and Desbordes," I said, remembering that afternoon at Michaud's. "The latter is probably not much help, but the former may be. It's one of his hobbies to know everyone who's anyone. I'd be very happy to see what I can do."

Volodya looked at me full on. I had not noticed till then the circles under his eyes that made him resemble Uncle Ruka. "I'd be terribly grateful, Seryosha, for anything you can do. Terribly, terribly grateful."

It was as if Fate had decided, on some unfathomable lark, to let us trade places for a bit, to see what happened when the prince switched roles with the pauper—or was it the other way around?

I cabled Hermann that I was extending my stay in Paris indefinitely, as I felt my brother needed me. Then I set out to find Cocteau.

The sad truth was, after years of intimacy—or at least the enchanting appearance of intimacy—we no longer knew each other. He and Desbordes had affably drifted apart. These days he was said to consort with an American Negro boxer named "Panama" Al Brown, whose European career he was trying to manage with somewhat less success than he had once managed his nightclub.

It took me some days to track my old friend down; he was avoiding his usual cafés. His friends said he had become paranoid—all agreed the time for another opium cure drew nigh. My note to him at his new address went unanswered for nearly a fortnight.

In the meantime, Volodya's situation grew even more desperate; he had come down with a severe case of psoriasis—brought on by nerves, declared his doctor.

"It's driving me mad," he confided to me. "In the middle of the night I think, if I had Véra's pistol I'd put it against my temple and pull the trigger."

"It's best, then, you don't have it," I replied. "Perhaps she'd better not come after all, at least not till you're better."

"No, she must come at once. Besides, I miss Mitouchka. You've never been a father, you wouldn't know the insane tenderness, the hellish anxiety one feels at the thought of that helpless, miraculous life, that mingling of one's long blood shadow with another's. There's nothing like that feeling on this earth. But then there must be many things to rue about your predicament. How absurd it must feel to be so ill-fitted to the world one finds oneself in."

"I assure you I don't dwell on my predicament, as you call it. Really I don't. Finding the right shade of lip gloss is a far more troubling annoyance."

"Must your wit always be so obvious?" he asked.

When Cocteau finally rang me, it was Volodya who answered the telephone. He held the receiver out to me as if it were a distasteful object he wanted no part of.

"There's a man on the other end who keeps insisting that I am actually you, and I cannot seem to convince him otherwise. He also demands to know whether the line is bugged."

Cocteau's voice buzzed in my ear. "*Mon cher*, I thought your charming stutter had abandoned you. Your brother sounds so very much like you, though his voice is less musical and, shall we say, more muscular. I prefer your own sweet tones. Unfortunately, I wish I were calling with sweet notes of my own, but I've simply run up against a brick wall—make that a paper wall, but no less formidable for being built of innumerable bureaucratic forms. Are you certain there's not some other way? And must she absolutely find work immediately? It seems to me that many Russians over the years have simply wandered into our fair city. One sees them everywhere—not necessarily thriving, as none of us do that anymore, but bearing up perfectly well without showing any evidence at all of having been officially 'cleared.'

"So I'm afraid, *mon cher,* this means I've no help to offer. In the old days I would have called the Hugos, who are so efficient at everything worldly, but they've abandoned me, as has practically everyone else—even my own genius, I sometimes fear. But I cherish this opportunity to have gotten back in touch with *you.* I've missed you terribly, you know. You must grace me with your limpid presence soon." He paused; then, like a naughty child who cannot help himself, he murmured, "Perhaps you'd like to smoke a pipe or two for old times' sake."

By day Volodya worked on his novel *The Gift*, about which he would tell me only, "There's nothing like it in all of Russian literature." At night he frequented those émigré circles I had long avoided. However, Paris is a small city, especially for exiles, and one could not avoid hearing gossip. Sirin was charming the women who fluttered mothlike around his flame. His literary judgments were provoking outrage. He had offended Sorokin. He had insulted Adamovich to his face. The very mention of his name made Nobel laureate Bunin livid. He was having an affair.

At first I dismissed this last rumor as both ridiculous and malicious, but I soon began to hear it from many sources, though two different women tended to be identified, Nina Berberova and Irina Guadanini.

Resolving to acquaint my brother with the various speculations being bandied about, I proposed that we see each other on March 28, the fifteenth anniversary of Father's death. He demurred, saying he had other obligations, but suggested we might meet the following afternoon. He showed up thoroughly out of sorts, and when I asked why, he said that he had waited all the previous day for a letter from Véra which had never arrived.

When I suggested her letter must have been delayed, and surely would arrive today, he reminded me that today's post had already come. "She's not herself," he told me. "For some reason she refuses to move to Paris. One week she suggests we try living in Belgium, the next she's fixated on Italy. She's even mentioned Austria. And now this new wrinkle—she insists she must first travel to Czechoslovakia, so that Mother can see Mitouchka, and so that she can take a rheumatism cure. As if there aren't rheumatism cures available in France! I understand her desire to show Mother her grandchild, because he's certainly a very splendid grandchild, but why now, of all times? Surely it can wait a few more months until we're settled."

As he spoke, the troubling thought occurred to me: what if Véra had heard the rumors as well? What if that was the cause of her aversion to Paris?

"This may be neither here nor there," I said. "But you should know that malicious gossip's afoot. I'm sure it's—"

"Nonsense," he bellowed. "Of course it's nonsense. Nina Berberova's a very dear friend, and it's a difficult time for her, having separated from Khodasevich after so many years. So we're seen together in cafés. Does anyone really think I would jeopardize my relations with the greatest poet of our generation by having an affair with his estranged wife? I can assure you, Seryosha, there's nothing between us save friendship and our love of literature."

Struck by the forthrightness of his denial, I told him that I was grateful for the clarification, and that I knew how trying this spring must have been for him.

"You needn't fuss over me so, you know. You start to suffocate me with the mothering touch."

"But I haven't," I said.

"Really. I appreciate your attentions, but I'm perfectly well taken care of these days."

If I was a little wounded by that last bit, I tried not to show it, telling him instead that I was very much looking forward to the luncheon we had planned to have when Hermann came to Paris the following week.

"Thank you for reminding me," he said. "It had very nearly slipped my mind. I too shall look forward to it."

Only some time later did I realize he had failed to say a word about Irina Guadanini.

47

THE LUNCHEON WAS NOT A SUCCESS. THE TWO men who meant the most in the world to me were polite and cautious with each other. And how very different they were: Hermann impeccably turned out, flirtatious and gay, Volodya brusque and even coarse in the presence of other men.

Volodya seemed amused by Hermann's vegetarianism—and my own recent conversion to it. He asked the kind of questions one might ask of a newly discovered tribe of heathens. Hermann answered patiently—yes, there was sufficient protein to be found in a variety of foods without recourse to meat; no, he did not believe vegetables felt pain—but that line of inquiry could only advance so far. Hermann had of course not read Sirin—or any other Russian writer—in the original, and Volodya quickly let it be known that he was not particularly interested in discussing Pushkin or any other writer in translation.

Volodya of course knew nothing about music, and was completely uninterested in politics, and ventured to opine that he found Roman Catholicism a baffling mythology. For the duration of the meal I kept thinking there must be *something* they had in common other than the slender fact of me; the closest we came was when Hermann told Volodya about his father's passion for collecting alpine plants, and the herbarium where he raised them. Volodya tried to engage him in a discussion of which plants served as food for which butterflies, but in Oskar's absence that potentially promising topic went nowhere as well.

We did all manage to agree that it had been a particularly raw and rainy spring so far.

"I'd say that went off quite well," Hermann pronounced after we had parted from Volodya.

"Well enough," I told him with the sinking feeling that he was incapable of understanding the nature of my longing for Volodya. How *could* he, when after so many years I could not fully articulate it to myself?

"Let's take a turn into Saint-Roch," I said. "Indulge me, will you? It's not far out of the way."

A christening had just finished. A few people lingered, lighting candles in the side chapels, wandering about to look at the paintings and monuments. It was here I had first understood, with absolute clarity, how we are in the hands of God.

"Sometimes," I told Hermann as we knelt midway among the ranks of wooden chairs, "I don't even know what I'm praying for."

"I don't think there's anything wrong with that," he said. "Especially not after lunching with your brother."

Whether Volodya had an affair with Irina Guadanini I do not know, nor do I particularly care. That May, after much miserable wrangling, he finally joined Véra and Mitouchka in Prague, and from there went on to Menton in the south of France, where they would spend the next year.

I was relieved to see all this resolved, for his tumultuous spring had taken a bit of a toll on me as well.

In the fall of 1937 Chapter Two of Sirin's *The Gift* was published in *Contemporary Annals*. I read with trepidation. By the end of the chapter, my cheeks were streaked with tears. Through what superhuman discipline had my brother managed to set aside all the turbulence of his life in order to create the meltingly beautiful description of his young poet Fyodor's father? For Konstantin Kirillovich Godunov-Cherdyntsev (what a distinguished patrimony in that name!) was our own father.

How on earth could that be? Fyodor's father was neither a jurist nor a politician—he was instead an explorer and lepidopterist, "the conquistador of Russian entomology." Away from his family for protracted periods of time, engaged in fabulous, dangerous exploits, he returned home carrying within him an unshakable solitude, whatever he had attempted to flee still within him.

How difficult this was to put into words, and yet how tenderly Volodya managed it. How lovingly detailed was Fyodor's recreation of Konstantin's final expedition, undertaken in 1917, just as everything began to fall apart. How painfully detailed was his litany of all the possible deaths his father might have suffered—from illness, from exposure, from accident, by the hand of man—ending with the mad possibility that he might not have died, that he might still somehow be alive somewhere, ill, wounded, imprisoned, struggling to contact us if we could only hold out hope for just a little while longer. That was the rub, of course, the heartbreaking rub, for we knew exactly how our own father had died. No need to speculate about his capture by the Reds, his execution by firing squad—in a garden, as Fyodor imagines, at night, where in his father's last instant of consciousness the moonlight reveals a whitish moth hovering in the shadows. No, we had seen Father's waxen face in the coffin. We had seen the coffin lowered into the ground. We had heard the stuttering thud as clods of earth were shoveled into the grave. And yet—despite the facts, the immutable, incontrovertible, all too well understood facts—here Father lived again, here he shone, as enduring as those butterflies in display cases that outlast by centuries their long-forgotten collectors.

I saw now why Volodya had discouraged as foolish my notion of composing Father's biography. I knew this novel, his most humane and ambitious, had been under way for several years.

I had known, but never before so fully, the depths of Volodya's longing for Father—for his approval, his tutelage, his companionship. I understood now that the elusiveness my brother sensed in Father, and that I sensed in them both, was not a fault in either, but rather an essential element of their identity. And further, I understood that far from being an impediment to my love, their elusiveness was precisely the quality that had made me want to love them in the first place.

I saw now that Volodya, apparently so indifferent to me, had in reality all along been patiently teaching me that the only way to know him was through his art. Everything else was incidental; it was only in his books that he lived, intimately revealed, fully and forever available.

And I believe I have found something else as well—that we only, any of us, live in art. No matter whether it is in books, painting, music, or dance, it is there we flourish, there we survive. It has taken me many years to come to this realization.

Without my brother's pages I would never have been able to begin my own.

48

WE WERE NEITHER BLIND NOR DEAF NOR STUPID in Castle Weissenstein. We knew what was happening down below—how could we not? We frequently heard Hitler on the radio, and Hermann and Oskar would sometimes get into long, passionate discussions about the status of Austrian national identity after 1918. "Who are we, exactly?" Hermann would ask. "Are we German-Austrians, or Austro-Germans? Are we Tyroleans first and Austrians second? Or are we simply Germans in a second German state as mandated by the treaties of Versailles and Saint Germain?"

For his part, Oskar mourned the demise of the Austro-Hungarian Empire—the unnecessary demolition, he said, of a complex, many-tongued, many-peopled civilization, the felicitous marriage of East and West. In his study, he kept a portrait of Emperor Franz Joseph I; he was fond of reminding me that the sumptuous finale of the greatest symphony ever composed, by which he meant Bruckner's Eighth, was inspired by the historic meeting between Emperor Franz Joseph and Tsar

Alexander III, a confluence of histories, cultures, and languages he pronounced himself gratified to host in miniature every day under his own roof—a remark that never failed to elicit a raised eyebrow from Hermann.

In the beginning, Oskar was quite partial to Hitler; anyone who promised to bring an end to the conditions of near civil war that had prevailed throughout Germany for the last decade was to be welcomed, and besides, Oskar sensed the National Socialists, especially once they began to emphasize "National" at the expense of "Socialist," would be good for both business and morale.

Hermann accurately predicted from the beginning that Hitler would be a disaster for Germany, yet at the same time maintained a complicated attitude toward Nazi rule. He was outraged by Germany's annexation of Austria in March 1938, but understood the logic of gathering the lost territories—the Rhineland, the Saar, the Sudetenland—into the Greater Reich. When war finally came, he did not support it, but neither did he wish to see Germany defeated. I think he very much wished that Castle Weissenstein might be fitted with the Tarnhelm and simply vanish for the duration of the troubles.

As for myself, I entertained a very short-lived fascination with Hitler and his movement. Yes, he was odious, he was dangerous, he was unbalanced, he was delusional, but there was about the whole National Socialist panoply, at least initially, something dreadfully stylish and beguiling—one need only look at those stunning black-and-white Hitler posters for the 1933 election to understand what I mean. And I must admit, sheepishly, that I was rather taken by the party's emphasis on youth, the placards of fresh-faced, strapping young men in their uniforms with their arms flung about each other's shoulders in comradely affection. If they were looking toward the future, it was a future I was at least curious to take a look at as well. All that changed, of course, and changed quickly. What had seemed an idle spectacle with pleasingly erotic undertones soon became a full-fledged nightmare.

By the autumn of 1938 my brother and his family were finally in Paris, living in squalid quarters on rue Boileau. I would visit them whenever I was in the city. Volodya was, as ever, hard at work, writing a new novel in Russian, and another, he told me, in English. In the meantime Mitouchka, though clearly quite clever, had become a little terror, and his doting parents did absolutely nothing to control his anarchic spirits.

Véra was hardly an easy case herself; I am afraid we never got past our initial suspicions of each other. Her head was full of the sort of prejudices that are all too common. She seemed to think that I secretly desired to be a woman, that at heart I was little more than a thwarted showgirl, that my mother had loved me too well and my father not enough. Perhaps most offensively, she seemed to think that all men of my kind were uncontrollably attracted to little boys. I do not forget—and certainly did not mishear—her fiercely whispered reproach to Volodya, one afternoon when he had inveigled me to watch Mitouchka for a hour while she was out and he needed to work: "What on earth were you thinking? He's not to be left alone with our son under any circumstances."

Volodya was increasingly desperate to leave Paris in those years. I remember a conversation from the spring of 1939 in which he laid out his predicament in the starkest of terms. "I'm the best writer of my generation," he told me, "but there's no future for the Russian novel. It's starving to death, while the Soviet novel is stillborn. I've dabbled in French, but it's English I pin my hopes on. It's been almost unimaginably difficult. And to give up my beautiful Russian..." He shook his head.

"Were I ever to write something," I said in a misguided attempt to be helpful, "I would most certainly write in English. But then I shed Russia so much more quickly and easily than you did. Perhaps we inverts must be above all adaptable; it's how we survive. I feel fairly certain I can adapt to anything."

He laughed. "There's no end to your foolish notions, is there? In any event, you'll be much amused by the subject of my latest novel—which, as you may have surmised, I've composed in my benighted and stuttering English. It's about two brothers. One is a writer, the other is not. And yet, through a diverting set of circumstances, the other becomes a writer as well. I'm calling it *The Real Life of Sebastian Knight.* That's all I've got to say about it. Don't ask to read the manuscript. We'll see if anyone wants to publish it."

Where, I wonder, is that novel now? That novel I shall never see. Has it found a publisher in dream-bright America?

"I'm thinking of writing my next novel," he told me during that same conversation, "based on the life of that peculiar double monster I dream about now and then: how it runs away from home, its misadventures in the world, its various hapless loves, how the tragic death of one twin eventually liberates the other from his Siamese bondage. I've got so many more notions than I shall ever get down on paper, and always the clock is ticking, precious time slipping away. Even during this very conversation I'm wondering, Should I not be at my desk? I've got inside me a novel about an old man in hopeless, helpless, forbidden love with a young girl. Another about a distant northern land that resembles, in its fantastical tint and texture, our own hazy homeland. I'm urgently attempting to extract both, slowly, patiently, the way a robin pulls an earthworm from the soil. But I don't suppose you know the torment of that sort of careful urgency. Most people, happily, do not."

I gazed across the crowded sidewalk to busy boulevard Montparnasse, the beckoning neon of Café du Dôme and La Coupole over the way, and said to Volodya, "I'm content with whatever time God wishes to allot me. I believe He created us in order that we might live our lives fully. Beyond that, it's all a mystery we can't begin to solve on our own. That's why He gave us His church. So that we could have a means of believing, despite whatever evidence to the contrary, that a life beyond this one awaits us, a life that's loving and beautiful and everlasting. You believe in it as well, I think. Or at least your books do. And I have learned that it is your books I should trust, your secret truest self. Who can forget, in your unforgettable *Invitation to a Beheading*, the prisoner walking calmly away from his own death, toward those entirely real beings waiting for him beyond this shabby, fraudulent world? Or the way he longingly imagines that place—'There … *tam* … *là-bas* …'—I quote your own words—where everything pleases the soul, and from which the occasional chance reflection comes our way, reminding us, like Vermeer's patch of yellow wall in Proust, that everything in this life is arranged as though we came into it bearing obligations from a former life—why else, against all odds in this depraved world, should we be good, be charitable to others, kind to animals, love each other?"

I fear I did not say it half so eloquently at the time, or perhaps not at all, but never mind. I say it here.

One particular advantage of Matrei was its proximity to Prague, and I was thus able to visit Mother in her years of declining health with much greater frequency (and less difficulty, as there was but one border to cross with my "Nansensical" passport) than I ever could have managed had I remained in Paris. Her financial situation remained dire but was no longer dangerous, and Hermann insisted on contributing funds now and again, despite recent troubles in the family business. Mother had always been a chronic worrier (and how much life had given her, after all, to worry about), but whether it was her age—she was now in her early sixties—or the comforts of Christian Science, she had achieved some degree of serenity.

The end came on May 2, 1939, after a brief illness. Upon

receipt of Evgenia's telegram, I left as soon as possible for the Protectorate, as Czechoslovakia had been lovingly renamed by its Nazi occupiers. To his great regret, Volodya was unable to attend the funeral; neither was Elena, who was still weak after a torturous labor. The telegram to Kirill in Brussels was returned. Thus I found myself on my own with Olga, who had only grown stranger and more obstreperous with the years. She announced immediately upon my arrival that I was not to fear, she had already burnt all of our letters to Mother—Father's included. Her husband, who had abetted her in that evil deed, deferred obsequiously to each of his wife's bizarre requests. Would he mail an envelope to her friend Natasha from a particular post office halfway across the city? Would he go home and fetch her black umbrella which she had decided she must carry to the cemetery, even though no rain threatened that day? They might, on stage, have been a comic pair; in real life they were unbearable. Throughout these unbecoming antics, Evgenia displayed her usual calm and dignity, reminding me why Mother had so cherished her companionship.

One guest at the sparsely attended funeral whom I had not expected to encounter, and whom I did not at first recognize, so ancient, frail and shrunken did he appear, was my hated adversary of old, Dr. Bekhetev. His eyes were rheumy, his hands trembled. He did not have any idea who I was, or if he did have an idea, it was that I was my brother Kirill.

Dr. Bekhetev did not wish to speak of the past. He talked instead of pigeons. There were too many pigeons in Prague. Had I noticed? The city government refused to do anything about them. Not only were they a threat to the health of the general population, their excrement was fouling the lovely monuments to be found everywhere in the city. For Prague was such a charming place; didn't I agree? It very much behooved the city fathers to care for its fabric. Would I be interested in penning a letter urging—nay, demanding—that such a course of protection be implemented immediately?

He was as light as a ghost; one could almost see straight through him. I could easily have accused him of the considerable damage he once did to a boy so much more vulnerable than stone monuments. I could very easily have picked him up and tossed him across the room. I could very, very easily have thrashed him to within an inch of his life. But I did none of those things. I too had no wish to dwell on the past. All I felt was a keen eagerness to return as soon as possible to my beloved Hermann, whose exquisite presence in my own life Dr. Bekhetev had once done everything in his power to prevent.

49

BERLIN,
DECEMBER 15, 1943

I HAVE NOT BEEN OUT HALF AN HOUR, AND IN THAT interval Felix has stopped by and left a note for me with Onya:

> *I have information you will find astonishing. I will call again at three this afternoon. I very much hope to find you at home. Until then, I am your friend, Felix.*

Like a child called to bed who must leave the house of cards he has patiently been building, and thus in a single impatient gesture collapses all his careful handiwork, so I must scatter these final years before me.

In the spring of 1940, those months of the so-called phony war, Volodya informed me that he had finally received very good news: an offer from an American university, Stanford, to teach a course in Russian literature. Like the elegant solution to a vexing chess problem, the once apparently insurmountable difficulty of obtaining a U.S. visa was suddenly overcome.

We sat for one last time in Le Sélect. "America!" he exclaimed. Did I remember, so many years ago, how he and I had attempted our escape? How we had fled that wretched hotel and boarded that lovely steamer, and how as it pulled away from the dock into the gray current of the Rhine, it seemed possible we were on our way to unimaginable adventures.

"I seem to remember you were a rather reluctant accomplice," he said with a laugh.

"Nor do I intend to accompany you now into one more exile," I told him. "I've thought things through, considered my options, and for better or worse I'm staying put."

"Pah!" he said. "You'll soon enough be staring a full-fledged war in the face. I seriously advise you, Seryosha: Get out while you can."

"And if everyone flees, who will remain to turn the tide? Didn't Father always tell us the only way to defeat the bullies was to stand up to them? It's taken me far too long to learn that lesson, but now that I've learned it, I've no intention of disregarding it. I trust God's love won't abandon me. This is a test, you see. Do I have the courage to stay with Hermann, or do I seek only to save myself?"

"You speak with great courage," said my brother. "Still, this is madness. Surely your Hermann has enough connections to devise some plan of escape for the both of you. No? Then so be it, at least for now. I wish you well, my Sergeyushka. I wish you the very best."

Then he did something extraordinary. He made over me the sign of the Greek cross, as Father once had done, in another city, in another dangerous time of departures.

I did not see my brother again. The next time I was in Paris I called at his flat, but the concierge informed me that the Nabokov family had gone—without, it seemed, paying the final installment of their rent.

Beginning as early as the summer of 1934, when in the aftermath of the SA purge homosexuals were first declared *Volksfeinde* by the Reich, Hermann and I had exercised caution. Over the next years many of Hermann's German friends fled abroad, went into hiding, or were arrested. We heard rumors of internment camps. After 1938 we seldom appeared together in public, and my intermittent stays at Castle Weissenstein, where I arrived and departed under cover of darkness, began to resemble an incarceration—albeit a comfortable one.

Once war broke out, even secret visits became dangerous. Weeks would go by without our seeing each other, and then usually in Paris, where eyes were less prying. Still, things that have been seen cannot be unseen, and over the years in Matrei there were enough awkward incidents lingering in the villagers' minds: the odd amorous embrace, the peck on the cheek, the too familiar bit of touching observed by three peasant women who clucked disapprovingly. There was the unpleasant clutch of schoolboys who, arm in arm, paraded down the street in a parody of our stroll, lisping and stammering, and the guileless young automotive mechanic with whom we became perhaps a bit too friendly. There were the servants who professed perplexity at finding an item of Herr Nabokov's clothing in Herr Thieme's room, or vice versa.

Any of these could have been the culprit. Or none. It does not matter. I forgive them all, for what else can I do? Hermann and I were arrested in flagrante delicto early one morning in October 1941, scarcely ten hours after my arrival from Paris. We had dined with his parents, romped with Sigmund and Sieglinde, and retired to his bedchamber for a somewhat difficult reunion. He was not pleased with the risk I had taken in returning. He even suggested that it might be best for me to refrain from any future visits to Austria "until this mess clears up." He would see me when in Paris. Though we had not quarreled, exactly, our conversation was vexed. Nonetheless, by small degrees, we warmed again to each other. Had I chosen to return to my own bed an hour earlier, I am sure it would not have made any difference. When the police came, they already knew what they were looking for.

How I hate to write what I now must write, for I cannot ever forget the sight of Oskar and Anne Marie, carrying across the courtyard—Anne Marie tearfully staggering under her burden, Oskar bearing his with stoic grief—the limp bodies of Sigmund and Sieglinde, whose exuberance had "threatened" the officers' safety when they broke down the door.

The last time I saw Hermann was in Matrei's little police station. The police had not given us time to dress properly: my love was still wearing his lavender silk pajamas and, incongruously, a pair of black oxfords without socks. His face was pale and expressionless, his eyes without their customary luster. He did not look at me as he was led away into a back room for interrogation. I am quite certain I shall never see him again.

As he was an Aryan, his crime was much more serious than mine. A Slavic beast, I was merely sent to an Austrian jail; he was dispatched to the 999th Afrika Brigade, commonly known as the Straight-to-Heaven Battalion.

Upon my release from jail, desperate for work of any sort and incapable of facing Hermann's parents, upon whom I had brought such catastrophe, I wrote to my friends abroad seeking help. I even went so far as to write Gertrude and Alice, from whom I received the following prompt reply: *Miss Stein knows she knew you but no longer knows how she knew nor when nor where nor why she knew you when she knew you. Nonetheless she wishes you the very best.*

Cocteau also answered my pleas, commiserating, *My dear, don't panic; all will be well. Be very still and very small and all this will undoubtedly pass you by. These are difficult and unlovely times for everyone, mon petit. Would you happen to know any sources of opium? Bébé, Boris, and I are quite desperate.*

For a short time I worked at a half-Russian office in Prague. When that office was closed, I made my way, in March 1942, to Berlin.

I have been writing all this in a room whose windows have not been shattered, whose roof is intact, luxuries for which I am grateful. The ravaged city is quiet this midafternoon, though even here the smell of oblivion hangs in the air. For some time now, I realize, someone has been knocking on the front door. Has Onya gone out? Is it Felix? It is not yet three. I peer down from my window to see several men clustered on the sidewalk beyond the front garden. They wear the unmistakable green and black uniforms of the Sicherheitsdienst. Felix is not among them. There will be no news of Hugh; perhaps there never was.

From what I can see, some of the soldiers below look quite handsome. Ever since that lift boy in Wiesbaden so many years ago, I have loved Germans. Perhaps he is one of them. Would that not be sublime? In any event, I look forward to making their acquaintance, however briefly. Perhaps we shall even strike up an improbable friendship on our way to headquarters. One never stops longing, after all, for beauty, love, belonging.

The knocking continues. The whole world seems very still. For some reason I find myself remembering a moth pupa stirring in the warmth of a train compartment somewhere between the unforgotten past and the unforeseeable future. Someone is calling my name. Since I appear to be alone in this pleasant and suddenly quite useless villa, I believe I must go see who it is.

AFTERWORD

SERGEY VLADIMIROVICH NABOKOV WAS ARRESTED on December 15, 1943. Charged with having uttered subversive statements ("*staatsfeindlichen Äußerungen*"), he was conveyed to Arbeitserziehungslager Wuhlheide, and on March 15, 1944, dispatched as prisoner number 28631 to Konzentrationslager Neuengamme, a labor camp outside Hamburg, where he died on January 9, 1945, of dysentery, starvation, exhaustion.

His brother thrived in America. As he no longer needed to distinguish himself from his famous father, of whom no one in this new world had ever heard, Vladimir Vladimirovich shed the pseudonym "Sirin" and began to publish under his own name. *The Real Life of Sebastian Knight*, with its curious but bravura English, was issued by New Directions in 1941, and proved to be but the first of many masterpieces the magician would pull out of the astonishingly capacious top hat of his adopted language. In the late 1940s he wrote a first chapter to a novel titled *Scenes from the Life of a Double Monster.* Upon reading those pages, Véra dissuaded him from continuing the project, though that orphaned chapter eventually appeared as a short story in the *New Yorker.*

Only in 1966, when he and Véra were living comfortably in their adopted Switzerland—*Lolita* having propelled him to wealth and worldwide fame—did Nabokov briefly address the subject of his dead brother. The third version of his celebrated autobiography *Speak, Memory* contains two pages absent from the earlier editions. "For various reasons," he writes, "I find it inordinately hard to speak about my other brother. He is a mere shadow in the background of my richest and most detailed recollections." After enumerating their many differences, his perplexities and discoveries regarding Sergey's character, his various instances of regrettable behavior toward him, Nabokov concludes, with eloquent abjection, "It is one of those lives that hopelessly claim a belated something—compassion, understanding, no matter what—which the mere recognition of such a want can neither replace nor redeem."

Hermann Thieme survived the war and afterward returned to Castle Weissenstein, where he lived as a recluse until his death in 1972.

ACKNOWLEDGMENTS

THE FIRST THROB OF THIS NOVEL WAS PROVOKED by Lev Grossman's essay "The Gay Nabokov," published by Salon.com in 2000. I am indebted to Lev not only for his superb detective work but also for his encouragement and for providing me with translations of the four letters from Sergey which reside in the Berg Collection at the New York Public Library. One day, no doubt, a larger trove of letters will surface—from Paris, from Castle Weissenstein, who knows?—that will prove any number of my speculations dead wrong. Nonetheless, I hope some shadow of truth will continue to haunt these pages even if certain bare facts turn out to have been otherwise.

Vladimir Nabokov's *Speak, Memory* as well as Brian Boyd's *Vladimir Nabokov: The Russian Years* and Stacy Schiff's *Véra (Mrs. Vladimir Nabokov)* provided essential background information. Other helpful biographies included Francis Steegmuller's *Cocteau*, Parker Tyler's *The Divine Comedy of Pavel Tchelitchew*, Serge Lifar's *Serge Diaghilev: His Life, His Work, His Legend*, Richard Buckle's *Diaghilev*, John Malcolm Brinnin's *The Third*

Rose: Gertrude Stein and Her World, and Amanda Vaill's *Everybody Was So Young.* Diaries and memoirs were particularly useful in conveying precious ephemera, and I would point interested readers to the following: Tamara Karsavina's *Theatre Street,* Maurice Paléologue's *An Ambassador's Memoirs,* Prince Felix Youssoupoff's *Lost Splendour,* Konstantin Nabokov's *The Ordeal of a Diplomat,* Nadine (née Nadezhda Nabokov) Wonlar-Larsky's *The Russia That I Loved,* Nicholas Nabokov's *Bagazh,* Bravig Imbs's *Confessions of Another Young Man,* Jean Cocteau's *Opium,* Nina Berberova's *The Italics Are Mine,* Marie Vassiltchikov's *Berlin Diaries, 1940–45,* Christabel Bielenberg's *Ride Out the Dark: The Experiences of an Englishwoman in Wartime Germany,* and *While Berlin Burns: The Diary of Hans-Georg von Studnitz, 1943–1945.* Among useful other histories, too numerous to list in full, were Dan Healey's *Homosexual Desire in Revolutionary Russia,* Graham Robb's *Strangers: Homosexual Love in the Nineteenth Century,* Simon Volkov's *Saint Petersburg,* W. Bruce Lincoln's *Sunlight at Midnight: St. Petersburg and the Rise of Modern Russia,* Robert Leach's *Vsevolod Meyerhold,* and William Wiser's *The Crazy Years: Paris in the Twenties.* The text is suffused with borrowings from these sources, including interlarded and unattributed direct quotes or paraphrases from Cocteau, Lifar, Stein, and the various Nabokovs.

A lovely succession of research assistants aided me along the way: Alyssa Barrett, Craig Libman, Joseph Langdon, Matthew Hunter, Jieun Paik. I am solely responsible for any misuse or misinterpretation of the recondite information they heroically obtained for me. I would also like to thank David Young and David Walker, who first abetted my love of Nabokov's work while I was an undergraduate at Oberlin, and Daniel R. Schwarz, Edgar Rosenberg, and Harry Shaw, the very supportive members of my dissertation committee when I wrote on Nabokov at Cornell. Many Vassar students in the several Nabokov seminars I have taught over the years have also added immeasurably to my thinking on the subject.

Many, many thanks to my indefatigable agent Harvey Klinger, and to my brilliant editor at Cleis Press, Frédérique Delacoste. The advice of several trusted readers was invaluable in the long process of composition and recomposition, and I gratefully acknowledge the help given me by Chris Bram, Mary Beth Caschetta, Johnny Schmidt, Jieun Paik, and, most of all, the incomparable Raye Young (1916–2010), who not only read the manuscript multiple times but even encouraged me to deliver the whole intricate contraption aloud to her one crystalline Christmas week at Westbrook House in Frome, Somerset.

On a June evening in 2004, when I was first beginning to dabble in this dream, I went with my friend Karen Robertson to see the New York City Ballet dance three immortal Stravinsky/Balanchine creations, including *Apollo*, at whose 1928 première I have imagined Sergey. Afterward, we shared a late dinner at a restaurant near Lincoln Center, and at Karen's urging I talked about the novel, which was still inchoate though I had begun to do some research. I told her what I knew so far, and together, quite casually, as one does in conversation, we began to conjure him—the unhappy, rejected boy he had been, the young man finding his brave way amid the pleasures and perils of Paris, the adult rewarded all too briefly with love before the darkness swallowed up everything—and gradually, the way a moth will begin to haunt the window screen of a lit room on a summer night, there he was: this lovely, benign, ghostly, and not uncomplicated companion.

This book is dedicated to that ghost.

ABOUT THE AUTHOR

PAUL RUSSELL grew up in Memphis, Tennessee. He attended Oberlin College and later studied at Cornell University, where he earned an MFA in Creative Writing in 1982 and a PhD in English in 1983. He has taught at Vassar College and the University of Exeter. The recipient of a National Endowment for the Arts Creative Writing Fellowship, he is the author of six novels. Read more about him at paul-russell.org.